W.H van der Smissen

Kinder-Und Hausmarchen der Gebruder Grimm selected and edited together with Schiller's Ballad

W.H van der Smissen

Kinder-Und Hausmarchen der Gebruder Grimm selected and edited together with Schiller's Ballad

ISBN/EAN: 9783741109508

Manufactured in Europe, USA, Canada, Australia, Japa

Cover: Foto ©Andreas Hilbeck / pixelio.de

Manufactured and distributed by brebook publishing software (www.brebook.com)

W.H van der Smissen

Kinder-Und Hausmarchen der Gebruder Grimm selected and edited together with Schiller's Ballad

KINDER- UND HAUSMÄRCHEN

DER

GEBRÜDER GRIMM

SELECTED AND EDITED

TOGETHER WITH

SCHILLER'S BALLAD

"DER TAUCHER"

WITH

ENGLISH NOTES, GLOSSARIES AND GRAMMATICAL APPENDICES

BY

W. H. VAN DER SMISSEN, M.A.

Lecturer on German in University College, Toronto;
Délégué Régional de l'Institution Ethnographique.

TORONTO
WILLIAMSON & CO.
1885

PREFACE.

The Tales contained in the present selection form, together with Schiller's Ballad, " **Der Taucher**," the work prescribed for Junior Matriculation at the University of Toronto for the years 1886-88-90.

The charming simplicity of diction and thought in these Tales renders them so peculiarly fit for beginners in the German language to read, that it is difficult to imagine why no such selection has ever before (as far as the present editor is aware) been made and edited for junior pupils, either in England or the United States. The frequent occurrence of colloquial and idiomatic expressions may perhaps be in part the cause of this ; yet these colloquialisms and idioms are most indispensable to the student of the language ; and the sooner they are acquired the better.

In arranging this selection, the Tales of Cinderella, Little Red Riding-Hood, and the Sleeping Beauty, are placed first, as every child (it is to be hoped) is already familiar with the matter of these Tales, and thus the pupil's comprehension of the story as a connected whole is much facilitated.

The Notes and Glossary have both been made very full, and in the former more attention has been paid than usual to the very important subject of *the construction of sentences* in German, a subject frequently neglected or postponed until the pupil is supposed to be ripe enough to begin translating from English into German. This is, in the editor's opinion, a great mistake. The pupil should, in this branch of discipline, be drilled early and drilled often, and should be made to dissect and analyze each sentence, as he reads, until he is thoroughly *au fait* on this point. The value of the mental training afforded by careful dissection and analysis of this sort cannot easily be overrated ; for, next to the classical languages, no language affords so favourable an exercise-ground for this purpose as the German.

No pains have been spared to impress this and other points of grammar on the young student ; nor is any apology required for the frequent repetition of grammatical rules and axioms contained in the Notes, since repetition is one of the most effectual modes of impressing them on the mind of the beginner.

The Glossaries have also been made as full as possible, and grammatical remarks, as well as synonyms, are frequently given, in addition to the meanings ; the object being, as in the Notes, to save the pupil the time which would otherwise be taken up with frequent reference to the grammar.

The Appendices contain full sets of rules in the concisest possible form for the construction of German sentences, illustrated by examples, and for the declension of adjectives.

The Tales have been printed in the Roman character (following the example of the Clarendon Press edition of Schiller's " **Belagerung von Antwerpen** "), partly in order to accustom the pupil to the appearance of German words in this character (the use of which is rapidly gaining ground in Germany, in spite of Prince Bismarck's refusal to accord it official recognition), and partly for the sake of the pupils' eyes.

A word or two may be necessary as to the orthography. The letter **h** has in every case been rejected after the letter **t**, in accordance with the now almost universal custom in Germany. The latest (smaller) edition of the *Märchen*, though adopting this mode of spelling in most words (as **Tor**, **Not**, etc.), shrinks from doing so in certain words of common occurrence, such as **thun**, **Thüre** ; in the present edition the new orthography has been adhered to consistently throughout, since there is no more reason for the **h** in **thun** than in **Thor**. With regard to the **ss** and **sz** as replacing the German ß, the latter has only been retained when preceded by a single long vowel, *i.e.*, where it is really a guide to the proper pronunciation.

It was at first intended to drop the h wherever there was no etymological justification for its presence ; but the German practice is not yet sufficiently established on this point to allow of any such innovation in a school text-book.

On the other hand, a return has been made in one

respect to the older orthography, viz., in the spelling of
the imperfect of **gehen, hangen,** etc., with **ie (gierg,**
etc.) instead of **i** ; and this for the reason that the older
spelling is etymologically more correct.

The Ballad of Schiller (**Der Taucher**) is, however,
presented in the German type, so that the student may
not lose all recollection of this character. This fine
specimen of ballad literature will afford the pupil the
needed opportunity of becoming more or less familiar
with poetical and higher forms of diction and construction, as the Tales familiarize him with colloquial and
common forms, and will thus extend his knowledge of
the uses of words, and of the language in general.

The second Glossary contains only such words as,
occurring in the Ballad, are not contained in the first,
and is printed, like the other, in Roman type only.

The editor trusts that the minuteness of the Notes
and Glossary, and the copiousness of the grammatical
explanations, may tend to increase the number of
students of the noble German language in the schools
of this Province, by making it easier for both teacher
and pupil ; and if this aim should happily be attained,
he will consider himself amply repaid for all the
trouble and labour expended on this little book.

UNIVERSITY COLLEGE, TORONTO,
March, 1885.

EXPLANATION OF ABBREVIATIONS, ETC.

Letters or syllables in ( ) may be omitted; words in [ ] do not occur in the text; grammatical and other remarks in [ ] contain information for the teacher or more advanced pupil (such as derivations, synonymes, etc.).

A dash indicates that the word in question is to be supplied, as: **Blume, pl.-n,** means that the pl. of this word is **Blumen; Diener,** pl. ——, means that the pl. is the same as the sing.

The principal accent in a word is indicated by the acute accent (´); the secondary by the grave (`).

When the word is repeated, the first letter only is given; thus, under **anhaben, etwas a.** = etwas anhaben.

In the case of strong verbs, the principal parts are given in the following order: impf. indic., past part., second sing. imper., second sing. pres. ind.; the last two being given only when the radical vowel is changed. When other parts are given, they are named; for special reasons, the third sing. pres. ind. is sometimes also added.

A., Aschenputtel.
a., active.
acc., accusative.
adj., adjective, adjectives, adjectival.
adv., adverb, adverbial, adverbially.
affirm., affirmative.
antec., antecedent.
App., Appendix.
appos., apposition.

art., article.
attrib., attributive.
aux., auxil., auxiliary.
B., Brüderchen und Schwesterchen.
cap., capital (letter).
card., cardinal.
caus., causative.
coll., collective.
comm., common.
comp., compound, compounded, composition; compare.

compd., compound.
compar., comparative, comparison.
compos., composition.
conj., conjunction, conjugated.
conn., connected, connection.
cons., consonant.
constr., construction.
contr., contracted, contraction.
coörd., coördinate, coördinative.
D., Dornröschen.
dat., dative.
decl., declined, declinable, declension.
def., definite.
demonstr., demonstrative.
dep., dependent.
der., derived, derivative.
deriv., derivative.
dim., dimin., diminutive.
dir., direct.
dist., distinguish, distinguished, distinct.
Eng., Engl., English.
e.g., for example.
esp., especially.
exc., except, exception.
f., fem., feminine.
foll., following, followed.
fr., from.
Fr., French.
fract., fractional.
freq., frequentative, frequently.
fut., future.
gen., genitive.
Gloss., Glossary.
gov., governs, governing, governed.
H., Hans im Glück.
i.e., that is.
imp., impf., imperfect.
imper., imperative.
impers., impersonal.
incompar., incomparable (not compared).
ind., indic., indicative.
indecl., indeclinable.
indef., indefinite.
indep., independent.
indir., indirect.

inf., infinitive.
insep., inseparable.
int., interj., interjection.
interr., interrog., interrogative.
introd., introducing, introduced, introduction.
irreg., irregular.
J., der treue Johannes.
K., König Drosselbart.
l., line.
Lat., Latin.
lit., literal, literally.
m., masc., masculine.
metaphor., metaphorically, figuratively.
n., neut., neuter.
neg., negative.
num., numeral, number.
obj., object.
obs., observe.
oppos., opposition.
ord., ordinal.
orig., originally.
p., page.
part., particle, participle.
partic., participial.
pass., passive.
perf., perfect.
pers., person, personal.
pl., plur., plural.
plup., plupf., pluperfect.
poss., possessive.
prec., preceding.
pred., predicate, predicative.
pref., prefix.
prep., preposition.
pres., present.
princ., principal.
pron., pronoun, pronominal ; pronounce, pronunciation.
pronom., pronominal.
prop., proper, properly.
R., Rotkäppchen.
recipr., reciprocal.
refl., reflexive.
rel., relative, relates, relating.
S., Sneewittchen.
sent., sentence.

sep., separable.
sing., singular.
str., strong (of verbs, etc.).
subj., subject, subjunctive.
subord., subordinate, subordinative.
subst., substantive, substantives.
sup., supine.
superl., superlative.
syll., syllable.
syn., synonyme, synonymes.
term., termination, terminations.

trans., transitive.
transl., translate, translated, translation.
undecl., undeclined.
untransl., untranslated.
v., verb.
var., variative.
viz., namely.
vow., vowel.
vulg., vulgar, vulgarly.
w., weak.
=, equal, equivalent to.

CONTENTS.

I.

ASCHENPUTTEL.

(No. 14.)

———————

Einem reichen Manne dem ward seine Frau krank,
und als sie fühlte, dass ihr Ende herankam, rief sie
ihr einziges Töchterlein zu sich ans Bett und sprach :
" Liebes Kind, bleib' fromm und gut, so wird dir der
liebe Gott immer beistehen, und ich will vom Him- 5
mel auf dich herabblicken und will um dich sein."
Darauf tat sie die Augen zu und verschied. Das Mädchen gieng jeden Tag hinaus zu dem Grabe der Mutter und weinte und blieb fromm und gut. Als der
Winter kam, deckte der Schnee ein weisses Tüchlein 10
auf das Grab, und als die Sonne im Frühjahr es
wieder herabgezogen hatte, nahm sich der Mann
eine andere Frau.

Die Frau hatte zwei Töchter mit ins Haus gebracht, die schön und weiss von Angesicht waren, 15
aber garstig und schwarz von Herzen. Da gieng eine
schlimme Zeit für das arme Stiefkind an. "Soll die
dumme Gans bei uns in der Stube sitzen ?" sprachen
sie, "Wer Brot essen will, muss es verdienen ; hinaus
mit der Küchenmagd." Sie nahmen ihm seine schönen 20
Kleider weg, zogen ihm einen alten grauen Kittel an
und gaben ihm hölzerne Schuhe. Dann lachten sie

es aus und führten es in die Küche. Da musste es
so schwere Arbeit tun, früh vor Tag aufstehen, Wasser tragen, Feuer anmachen, kochen und waschen.
Obendrein taten ihm die Schwestern alles ersinn-
5 liche Herzeleid an, verspotteten es und schütteten
ihm die Erbsen und Linsen in die Asche, so dass es
sitzen und sie wieder auslesen musste. Abends, wenn
es sich müde gearbeitet hatte, kam es in kein Bett,
sondern musste sich neben den Herd in die Asche
10 legen. Und weil es darum immer staubig und
schmutzig aussah, nannten sie es *Aschenputtel.*
  Es trug sich zu, dass der Vater einmal in die Messe
ziehen wollte, da fragte er die beiden Stieftöchter,
was er ihnen mitbringen sollte? "Schöne Kleider,"
15 sagte die eine, "Perlen und Edelsteine," die zweite.
"Aber du, Aschenputtel," sprach er, "was willst du
haben?" "Vater, das erste Reis, das euch auf eurem
Heimweg an den Hut stöszt, das brecht für mich ab."
Er kaufte nun für die beiden Stiefschwestern schöne
20 Kleider, Perlen und Edelsteine, und auf dem Rückweg, als er durch einen grünen Busch ritt, streifte
ihn ein Haselreis und stiess ihm den Hut ab. Da
brach er das Reis ab und nahm es mit. Als er nach
Hause kam, gab er den Stieftöchtern, was sie sich
25 gewünscht hatten, und dem Aschenputtel gab er
das Reis von dem Haselbusch. Aschenputtel dankte
ihm, gieng zu seiner Mutter Grab und pflanzte das
Reis darauf und weinte so sehr, dass die Tränen
niederfielen und es begossen. Es wuchs aber und
30 ward ein schöner Baum. Aschenputtel gieng alle
Tage dreimal darunter, weinte und betete, und allemal kam ein weisses Vöglein auf den Baum, und das
Vöglein warf ihm herab, was es sich nur wünschte.

Es begab sich aber, dass der König ein Fest anstellte, das drei Tage dauern sollte, und wozu alle schönen Jungfrauen im Lande eingeladen wurden, damit sich sein Sohn eine Braut aussuchen möchte. Die zwei Stiefschwestern, als sie hörten, dass sie auch 5 dabei erscheinen sollten, waren guter Dinge, riefen Aschenputtel und sprachen : "Kämm' uns die Hare, bürste uns die Schuh' und mache uns die Schnallen fest, wir gehen zur Hochzeit auf des Königs Schloss." Aschenputtel gehorchte, weinte aber, weil es auch 10 gern zum Tanz mitgegangen wär', und bat die Stiefmutter, sie möchte es ihm erlauben. "Du Aschenputtel voll Staub und Schmutz," sprach sie, "du willst zur Hochzeit und hast keine Kleider! willst tanzen und hast keine Schuhe!" Als es aber mit 15 Bitten anhielt, sprach sie endlich : "Da habe ich dir eine Schüssel Linsen in die Asche geschüttet, und wenn du die Linsen in zwei Stunden wiede ausgelesen hast, so sollst du mitgehen." Das Mädchen gieng durch die Hintertür nach dem 20 Garten und rief : "Ihr zahmen Täubchen, ihr Turteltäubchen, all ihr Vöglein unter dem Himmel, kommt und helft mir lesen :

> Die guten ins Töpfchen,
> Die schlechten ins Kröpfchen." 25

Da kamen zum Küchenfenster zwei weisse Täubchen herein, und danach die Turteltäubchen, und endlich schwirrten und schwärmten alle Vöglein unter dem Himmel herein und liessen sich um die Asche nieder. Und die Täubchen nickten mit dem Köpfchen und 30 fiengen an pik, pik, pik, pik, und da fiengen die übrigen auch an pik, pik, pik, pik, und lasen alle guten

Körnlein in die Schüssel. Kaum war eine Stunde
herum, so waren sie fertig und flogen alle wieder hinaus. Da trug das Mädchen die Schüssel zu der Stiefmutter, freute sich und glaubte, es dürfte nun mit
5 auf die Hochzeit gehen. Aber sie sprach : "Nein,
Aschenputtel, du wirst nur ausgelacht, du hast keine
Kleider und kannst nicht tanzen." Als es nun weinte,
sprach sie : "Wenn du mir zwei Schüsseln voll Linsen in einer Stunde aus der Asche reinlesen kannst,
10 so sollst du mitgehen," und dachte : "Das kann es ja
nimmermehr." Sie schüttete die zwei Schüsseln Linsen in die Asche, aber das Mädchen gieng durch die
Hintertüre nach dem Garten und rief : "Ihr zahmen
Täubchen, ihr Turteltäubchen, all ihr Vöglein unter
15 dem Himmel, kommt und helft mir lesen :

Die guten ins Töpfchen,
Die schlechten ins Kröpfchen."

Da kamen zum Küchenfenster zwei weisse Täubchen
herein, und danach die Turteltäubchen, und endlich
20 schwirrten und schwärmten alle Vöglein unter dem
Himmel herein und liessen sich um die Asche nieder.
Und die Täubchen nickten mit ihrem Köpfchen und
fiengen an pik, pik, pik, pik, und da fiengen die übrigen auch an pik, pik, pik, pik, und lasen alle guten
25 Körner in die Schüsseln. Und eh' eine halbe Stunde
herum war, waren sie schon fertig und flogen alle
wieder hinaus. Da trug das Mädchen die Schüsseln
zu der Stiefmutter, freute sich und glaubte, nun dürfte es mit auf die Hochzeit gehen. Aber sie sprach :
30 "Es hilft dir alles nichts : du kommst nicht mit, denn
du hast keine Kleider und kannst nicht tanzen ; wir
müssten uns deiner schämen." Darauf kehrte sie

ihm den Rücken zu und gieng mit ihren zwei stolzen Töchtern fort. Als nun niemand mehr daheim war, gieng Aschenputtel zu seiner Mutter Grab unter den Haselbaum und rief : 5

" Bäumchen, rüttel' dich und schüttel' dich,
Wirf Gold und Silber über mich."

Da warf ihm der Vogel ein golden und silbern Kleid herunter und ein Par mit Seide und Silber ausgestickte Pantoffeln. Alsbald zog es Kleid und Pan- 10 toffeln an und gieng zur Hochzeit. Seine Schwestern aber und die Stiefmutter erkannten es nicht und meinten, es müsste eine fremde Königstochter sein, so schön sah es in dem goldenen Kleide aus. An Aschenputtel dachten sie gar nicht und glaubten, 15 es läge daheim im Schmutz. Der Königssohn kam ihm entgegen, nahm es bei der Hand und tanzte mit ihm. Er wollte auch mit sonst niemand tanzen, also dass er ihm die Hand nicht los liess, und wenn ein anderer kam, es aufzufordern, sprach er : " Das ist 20 meine Tänzerin."

Es tanzte bis es Abend war, da wollte es nach Hause gehen. Der Königssohn aber sprach : " Ich gehe mit und begleite dich," denn er wollte sehen, wem das schöne Mädchen angehörte. Sie ent- 25 wischte ihm aber und sprang in das Taubenhaus. Nun wartete der Königssohn, bis der Vater kam, und sagte ihm, das fremde Mädchen wär' in das Taubenhaus gesprungen. Da dachte er : " Sollte es Aschenputtel sein ?" and sie mussten ihm Axt und Hacken 30 bringen, damit er das Taubenhaus entzweischlagen konnte : aber es war niemand darin. Und als sie ins

Haus kamen, lag Aschenputtel in seinen schmutzigen
Kleidern in der Asche, und ein trübes Öllämpchen
brannte im Schornstein ; denn Aschenputtel war
geschwind aus dem Taubenhaus hinten herabge-
5 sprungen und war zu dem Haselbäumchen gelaufen :
da hatte es die schönen Kleider ausgetan und aufs
Grab gelegt, und der Vogel hatte sie wieder wegge-
nommen, und dann hatte es sich in seinem grauen
Kittelchen in die Küche zur Asche gesetzt.

10   Am andern Tag, als das Fest von neuem anhub
und die Eltern und Stiefschwestern wieder fort
waren, gieng Aschenputtel zu dem Haselbaum und
sprach :

        " Bäumchen, rüttel' dich und schüttel' dich,
15   Wirf Gold und Silber über mich."

Da warf der Vogel ein noch viel stolzeres Kleid
herab, als am vorigen Tag. Und als es mit diesem
Kleide auf der Hochzeit erschien, erstaunte jedermann über seine Schönheit. Der Königssohn aber
20 hatte gewartet, bis es kam, nahm es gleich bei der
Hand und tanzte nur allein mit ihm. Wenn die
andern kamen und es aufforderten, sprach er : " Das
ist meine Tänzerin." Als es nun Abend war, wollte
es fort, und der Königssohn gieng ihm nach und
25 wollte sehen, in welches Haus es gieng : aber es entsprang ihm und lief in den Garten hinter dem Haus.
Darin stand ein schöner groszer Baum mit den herrlichsten Birnen, auf den kletterte es behend wie ein
Eichhörnchen, und der Königssohn wusste nicht, wo
30 es hingekommen war. Er wartete aber, bis der
Vater kam, und sprach zu ihm : " Das fremde Mädchen ist mir entwischt, und ich glaube, es ist auf den

Birnbaum gesprungen." Der Vater dachte: "Sollte es Aschenputtel sein?" und liess sich die Axt holen und hieb den Baum um, aber es war niemand darauf. Und als sie in die Küche kamen, lag Aschenputtel da in der Asche, wie sonst auch, denn es war auf der 5 andern Seite vom Baum herabgesprungen, hatte dem Vogel auf dem Haselbäumchen die schönen Kleider wiedergebracht und sein graues Kittelchen angezogen.

Am dritten Tag, als die Eltern und Schwestern 10 fort waren, gieng Aschenputtel wieder zu seiner Mutter Grab und sprach zu dem Bäumchen:

"Bäumchen, rüttel' dich und schüttel' dich,
Wirf Gold und Silber über mich."

Nun warf ihm der Vogel ein Kleid herab, das war so 15 prächtig und glänzend, wie es noch keins gehabt hatte, und die Pantoffeln waren ganz golden. Als es in dem Kleid zu der Hochzeit kam, wussten sie alle nicht, was sie vor Verwunderung sagen sollten. Der Königssohn tanzte ganz allein mit ihm, und 20 wenn es einer aufforderte, sprach er: "Das ist meine Tänzerin."

Als es nun Abend war, wollte Aschenputtel fort, und der Königssohn wollte es begleiten, aber es entsprang ihm so geschwind, dass er nicht folgen 25 konnte. Der Königssohn hatte aber eine List gebraucht und hatte die ganze Treppe mit Pech bestreichen lassen: da war, als es hinabsprang, der linke Pantoffel des Mädchens hängen geblieben. Der Königssohn hob ihn auf, er war klein und zier- 30 lich und ganz golden. Am nächsten Morgen gieng er damit zu dem Manne und sagte zu ihm: "Keine

andere soll meine Gemahlin werden als die, an deren
Fusz dieser goldene Schuh passt." Da freuten sich
die beiden Schwestern, denn sie hatten schöne Füsze.
Die Älteste gieng mit dem Schuh in die Kammer
5 und wollte ihn anprobiren, und die Mutter stand dabei. Aber sie konnte mit der groszen Zehe nicht
hineinkommen, und der Schuh war ihr zu klein ; da
reichte ihr die Mutter ein Messer und sprach :
"Hau' die Zehe ab : wann du Königin bist, so
10 brauchst du nicht mehr zu Fusz zu gehen." Das
Mädchen hieb die Zehe ab, zwängte den Fusz in den
Schuh, verbiss den Schmerz und gieng heraus zum
Königssohn. Da nahm er sie als seine Braut aufs
Pferd und ritt mit ihr fort. Sie mussten aber an
15 dem Grabe vorbei, da saszen die zwei Täubchen auf
dem Haselbäumchen und riefen :

     " Rucke di guck, rucke di guck,
     Blut ist im Schuck (Schuh) :
     Der Schuck ist zu klein,
20   Die rechte Braut sitzt noch daheim."

Da blickte er auf ihren Fusz und sah, wie das
Blut herausquoll. Er wendete sein Pferd um,
brachte die falsche Braut wieder nach Hause und
sagte, das wäre nicht die rechte, die andere Schwes-
25 ter sollte den Schuh anziehen. Da gieng diese in
die Kammer und kam mit den Zehen glücklich in
den Schuh, aber die Ferse war zu grosz. Da reichte
ihr die Mutter ein Messer und sprach : "Hau' ein
Stück von der Ferse ab : wann du Königin bist,
30 brauchst du nicht mehr zu Fusz zu gehen." Das
Mädchen hieb ein Stück von der Ferse ab, zwängte
den Fusz in den Schuh, verbiss den Schmerz und

gieng heraus zum Königssohn. Da nahm er sie als
seine Braut aufs Pferd und ritt mit ihr fort. Als sie
an dem Haselbäumchen vorbei kamen, saszen die
zwei Täubchen darauf und riefen :

> " Rucke di guck, rucke di guck,   . 5
> Blut ist im Schuck :
> Der Schuck ist zu klein,
> Die rechte Braut sitzt noch daheim."

Er blickte nieder auf ihren Fusz und sah, wie das
Blut aus dem Schuh quoll und an den weissen 10
Strümpfen ganz rot heraufgestiegen war. Da
wendete er sein Pferd und brachte die falsche Braut
wieder nach Hause. " Das ist auch nicht die rechte,"
sprach er, "habt ihr keine andere Tochter?"
"Nein," sagte der Mann, "nur von meiner ver- 15
storbenen Frau ist noch ein kleines verbuttetes
Aschenputtel da, das kann unmöglich die Braut
sein." Der Königssohn sprach, er sollt' es herauf
schicken, die Mutter aber antwortete : "Ach nein,
das ist viel zu schmutzig, das darf sich nicht sehen 20
lassen." Er wollte es aber durchaus sehen, und
Aschenputtel musste gerufen werden. Da wusch es
sich erst Hände und Angesicht rein, gieng dann hin
und neigte sich vor dem Königssohn, der ihm den
goldenen Schuh reichte. Es setzte sich auf einen 25
Schemel, zog den linken Fusz aus dem schweren
Holzschuh, setzte ihn auf den goldenen Pantoffel,
und nur ein wenig brauchte es zu drücken, so stand
es darin, als wär' er ihm angegossen. Als es aber
das Gesicht erhob, da sah er, dass es die war, die mit 30
ihm getanzt hatte, und sprach : " Das ist die rechte
Braut!" Die Stiefmutter und die beiden Schwes-

tern erschraken und wurden bleich vor Ärger : er
aber nahm Aschenputtel aufs Pferd und ritt mit ihm
fort.   Als sie an dem Haselbäumchen vorbeikamen,
riefen die zwei weissen Täubchen :

5   " Rucke di guck, rucke di guck,
              Kein Blut ist im Schuck :
              Der Schuck ist nicht zu klein,
              Die rechte Braut die führt er heim."

Und als sie das gerufen hatten, kamen sie beide
10 herabgeflogen und setzten sich dem Aschenputtel
auf die Schultern, eine rechts, die andere links, und
blieben da sitzen.

   Als die Hochzeit mit dem Königssohn sollte gehalten werden, kamen die falschen Schwestern,
15 wollten sich einschmeicheln und Teil an seinem
Glück nehmen.   Als die Brautleute nun zur Kirche
giengen, war die älteste zur rechten, die jüngste zur
linken Seite : da pickten die Tauben einer jeden das
Eine Auge aus ; hernach als sie herausgiengen, war
20 die älteste zur linken, und die jüngste zur rechten,
da pickten die Tauben einer jeden das andere Auge
aus.   Und waren sie also für ihre Bosheit und
Falschheit auf ihr Lebtag gestraft.

II.

ROTKÄPPCHEN.

(No. 17.)

Es war einmal eine kleine süsze Dirne, die hatte jedermann lieb, der sie nur ansah, am allerliebsten aber die Groszmutter, die wusste gar nicht, was sie alles dem Kinde geben sollte. Einmal schenkte sie ihm ein Käppchen von rotem Sammet, und weil ihm das so wohl stand und es nichts anders mehr tragen wollte, hiess es nur das *Rotkäppchen*. Da sagte einmal seine Mutter zu ihm: "Komm', Rotkäppchen, da hast du ein Stück Kuchen und eine Flasche Wein, bring's der Groszmutter hinaus: sie ist krank und schwach und wird sich daran laben. Sei aber hübsch artig, guck' nicht gleich in alle Ecken herum, wenn du in die Stube kommst, und vergiss nicht 'guten Morgen' zu sagen. Geh' auch ordentlich und lauf' nicht vom Weg ab, sonst fällst du und zerbrichst das Glas: dann hat die kranke Groszmutter nichts."

Rotkäppchen sagte: "Ich will schon alles gut ausrichten," und gab der Mutter die Hand darauf. Die Groszmutter aber wohnte draussen im Wald, eine halbe Stunde vom Dorf. Wie nun Rotkäppchen in den Wald kam, begegnete ihm der Wolf. Rotkäppchen aber wusste nicht, was das für ein böses Tier

war, und fürchtete sich nicht vor ihm. "Guten Tag,
Rotkäppchen," sprach er. "Schönen Dank, Wolf."
"Wo hinaus so früh, Rotkäppchen?" "Zur Groszmutter." "Was trägst du unter der Schürze?" "Ku-
5 chen und Wein, gestern haben wir gebacken, da soll
sich die kranke schwache Groszmutter etwas zu gut
tun und sich damit stärken." "Rotkäppchen, wo
wohnt deine Groszmutter?" "Noch eine gute Vier-
telstunde weiter im Wald, unter den drei groszen
10 Eichbäumen, da steht ihr Haus, unten sind die Nuss-
hecken, das wirst du ja wissen," sagte Rotkäppchen.
Der Wolf dachte bei sich: "Das junge zarte Mädchen, das ist ein fetter Bissen, der wird noch besser
schmecken als die Alte: du musst es listig anfangen,
15 damit du beide erschnappst." Da gieng er ein Weilchen neben Rotkäppchen her, dann sprach er: "Rotkäppchen, sieh einmal die schönen Blumen, die rings
umher stehen, warum guckst du dich nicht um? Ich
glaube, du hörst gar nicht, wie die Vöglein so lieblich
20 singen? Du gehst ja für dich hin, als wenn du zur
Schule giengst, und ist so lustig haussen in dem Wald."
Rotkäppchen schlug die Augen auf, und als es sah,
wie die Sonnenstrahlen durch die Bäume hin und
her hüpften und alles voll schöner Blumen stand,
25 dachte es: "Wenn ich der Groszmutter einen frischen
Strauss mitbringe, der wird ihr auch Freude machen;
es ist so früh am Tag, dass ich doch zu rechter Zeit
ankomme," sprang in den Wald und suchte Blumen.
Und wenn es Eine gebrochen hatte, meinte es, weiter
30 hinaus stände eine noch schönere, und lief danach
und lief immer weiter in den Wald hinein. Der Wolf
aber gieng geradeswegs nach dem Hause der Groszmutter und klopfte an die Türe. "Wer ist draussen?"

"Rotkäppchen, das bringt Kuchen und Wein, mach'
auf." "Drück' nur auf die Klinke," rief die Groszmutter, "ich bin zu schwach und kann nicht aufstehen." Der Wolf drückte auf die Klinke, trat hinein
und gieng, ohne ein Wort zu sprechen, geradezu an 5
das Bett der Groszmutter und verschluckte sie. Da
nahm er ihre Kleider, tat sie an, setzte ihre Haube
auf, legte sich in ihr Bett und zog die Vorhänge vor.
Rotkäppchen aber war derweil nach den Blumen
gelaufen, und als es so viel hatte, dass es keine mehr 10
tragen konnte, fiel ihm die Groszmutter wieder ein,
und es machte sich auf den Weg zu ihr. Es wun-
derte sich, dass die Türe aufstand, und wie es in die
Stube trat, so kam es ihm so seltsam darin vor, dass
es dachte: "Ei, wie ängstlich wird mir's heut zu Mut, 15
und ich bin sonst so gerne bei der Groszmutter!" Es
sprach: "Guten Morgen," bekam aber keine Antwort. Darauf gieng es zum Bett und zog die Vorhänge zurück: da lag die Groszmutter und hatte die
Haube tief ins Gesicht gezogen und sah so wunder- 20
lich aus. "Ei, Groszmutter, was hast du für grosze
Ohren!" "Dass ich dich besser hören kann." "Ei,
Groszmutter, was hast du für grosze Augen!" "Dass
ich dich besser sehen kann." "Ei, Groszmutter,
was hast du für grosze Hände!" "Dass ich dich 25
besser packen kann." "Aber, Groszmutter, was hast
du für ein entsetzlich groszes Maul!" "Dass ich dich
besser fressen kann." Und wie der Wolf das gesagt
hatte, tat er einen Satz aus dem Bett auf das arme
Rotkäppchen und verschlang es. 30
Wie der Wolf sein Gelüsten gestillt hatte, legte er
sich wieder ins Bett, schlief ein und fieng an überlaut zu schnarchen. Der Jäger gieng eben vorbei

und dachte bei sich: "Wie kann die alte Frau so
schnarchen, du musst einmal nachsehen, ob ihr etwas fehlt." Da trat er in die Stube, und wie er vor
das Bett kam, so lag der Wolf darin. "Finde ich dich
5 endlich, alter Graukopf," sagte er, "ich habe dich
lange gesucht." Nun wollte er seine Büchse anlegen, da fiel ihm ein, der Wolf könnte die Groszmutter gefressen haben, und sie wäre noch zu retten,
schoss nicht, sondern nahm eine Schere und fieng
10 an dem schlafenden Wolf den Bauch aufzuschneiden.
Wie er ein par Schnitte getan hatte, da sah er das
rote Käppchen leuchten, und noch ein par Schnitte,
da sprang das Mädchen heraus und rief: "Ach, wie
war ich erschrocken, was war's so dunkel in dem
15 Wolf seinem Leib!" Und dann kam die alte Groszmutter auch noch lebendig heraus und konnte kaum
atmen. Rotkäppchen aber holte geschwind grosze
Steine, damit füllten sie dem Wolf den Leib, und wie
er aufwachte, wollte er fortspringen, aber die Steine
20 waren so schwer, dass er gleich niedersank und sich
tot fiel.

Da waren alle drei vergnügt; der Jäger nahm den
Pelz vom Wolf: die Groszmutter asz den Kuchen
und trank den Wein, den Rotkäppchen gebracht
25 hatte, und erholte sich wieder: Rotkäppchen aber
dachte: "Du willst dein Lebtag nicht wieder allein
vom Wege ab in den Wald laufen, wenn dir's die
Mutter verboten hat."

Es wird auch erzählt, dass einmal, als Rotkäpp-
30 chen der alten Groszmutter wieder Gebackenes
brachte, ein anderer Wolf ihm zugesprochen und es

vom Wege habe ableiten wollen, Rotkäppchen aber
hütete sich und gieng gerade fort seines Wegs und
sagte der Groszmutter, dass es dem Wolf begegnet
wäre, der ihm guten Tag gewünscht, aber so bös aus
den Augen geguckt hätte: "Wenn's nicht auf offener 5
Strasze gewesen wäre, er hätte mich gefressen."
"Komm'," sagte die Groszmutter, "wir wollen die
Türe verschliessen, dass er nicht herein kann." Bald
danach klopfte der Wolf an und rief: "Mach' auf,
Groszmutter, ich bin das Rotkäppchen, ich bring' 10
dir Gebackenes." Sie schwiegen aber still und mach-
ten die Türe nicht auf: da schlich der Böse etlichemal um das Haus und sprang endlich auf das Dach
und wollte warten, bis Rotkäppchen abends nach
Hause gienge, dann wollte er ihm nachschleichen und 15
wollt's in der Dunkelheit fressen. Aber die Groszmutter merkte, was er im Sinn hatte. Nun stand vor
dem Haus ein groszer Steintrog: da sprach sie zu
dem Kind: "Nimm den Eimer, Rotkäppchen, gestern
hab' ich Würste gekocht, da trag' das Wasser, worin 20
sie gekocht sind, in den Trog." Rotkäppchen trug
so lange, bis der grosze Trog ganz voll war. Da
stieg der Geruch von den Würsten dem Wolf in die
Nase, er schnupperte und guckte hinab, endlich
machte er den Hals so lang, dass er sich nicht mehr 25
halten konnte und anfieng zu rutschen: so rutschte
er vom Dach herab und gerade in den groszen Trog
hinein und ertrank. Rotkäppchen aber gieng fröhlich nach Hause und tat ihm niemand etwas zu Leid.

III.

DORNRÖSCHEN.

(No. 24.)

Vor Zeiten war ein König und eine Königin, die
sprachen jeden Tag : "Ach, wenn wir doch ein
Kind hätten!" und kriegten immer keins. Da trug
sich zu, als die Königin einmal im Bade sasz, dass
5 ein Frosch aus dem Wasser ans Land kroch und zu
ihr sprach : "Dein Wunsch soll erfüllt werden, ehe
ein Jahr vergeht, wirst du eine Tochter zur Welt
bringen." Was der Frosch gesagt hatte, das geschah,
und die Königin gebar ein Mädchen, das war so
10 schön, dass der König vor Freude sich nicht zu
lassen wusste und ein groszes Fest anstellte. Er
ladete nicht blos seine Verwandte, Freunde und Bekannte, sondern auch die weisen Frauen dazu ein,
damit sie dem Kind hold und gewogen wären. Es
15 waren ihrer dreizehn in seinem Reiche, weil er aber
nur zwölf goldene Teller hatte, von welchen sie essen
sollten, so musste Eine von ihnen daheimbleiben.
Das Fest ward mit aller Pracht gefeiert, und als es
zu Ende war, beschenkten die weisen Frauen das
20 Kind mit ihren Wundergaben : die Eine mit Tugend,
die andere mit Schönheit, die dritte mit Reichtum,
und so mit allem, was auf der Welt nur zu wünschen

ist. Als elfe ihre Sprüche eben getan hatten, trat
plötzlich die dreizehnte herein. Sie wollte sich dafür rächen, dass sie nicht eingeladen war, und ohne
jemand zu grüssen oder nur anzusehen, rief sie mit
lauter Stimme : "Die Königstochter soll sich in 5
ihrem fünfzehnten Jahr an einer Spindel stechen
und tot hinfallen." Und ohne ein Wort weiter zu
sprechen, kehrte sie sich um und verliess den Saal.
Alle waren erschrocken, da trat die zwölfte hervor,
die ihren Wunsch noch übrig hatte, und weil sie den 10
bösen Spruch nicht aufheben sondern nur ihn mildern konnte, so sagte sie : "Es soll aber kein Tod
sein, sondern ein hundertjähriger tiefer Schlaf, in
welchen die Königstochter fällt."

Der König, der sein liebes Kind vor so grossem 15
Unglück gern bewahren wollte, liess den Befehl ausgehen, dass die Spindeln im ganzen Königreiche
sollten verbrannt werden. An dem Mädchen aber
wurden die Gaben der weisen Frauen sämtlich erfüllt, denn es war so schön, sittsam, freundlich und 20
verständig, dass es jedermann, der es ansah, lieb
haben musste. Es geschah, dass an dem Tage, wo
es gerade fünfzehn Jahr' alt ward, der König und die
Königin nicht zu Hause waren, und das Mädchen
ganz allein im Schloss zurückblieb. Da gieng es 25
allerorten herum, besah Stuben und Kammern, wie
es Lust hatte, und kam endlich auch an einen alten
Turm. Es stieg die enge Wendeltreppe hinauf und
gelangte zu einer kleinen Türe. In dem Schloss
steckte ein verrosteter Schlüssel, und als es um- 30
drehte, sprang die Tür' auf, und sasz da in einem
kleinen Stübchen eine alte Frau mit einer Spindel
und spann emsig ihren Flachs. "Guten Tag, du

altes Mütterchen," sprach die Königstochter, "was
machst du da?" "Ich spinne," sagte die Alte und
nickte mit dem Kopf. "Was ist das für ein Ding,
das so lustig herumspringt?" sprach das Mädchen,
5 nahm die Spindel und wollte auch spinnen. Kaum
hatte sie aber die Spindel angerührt, so gieng der
Zauberspruch in Erfüllung, und sie stach sich damit
in den Finger.

In dem Augenblick aber, wo sie den Stich emp-
10 fand, fiel sie auf das Bett nieder, das da stand, und
lag in einem tiefen Schlaf. Und dieser Schlaf verbreitete sich über das ganze Schloss, der König und
die Königin, die eben heimgekommen und in den
Sal getreten waren, sanken nieder und schliefen ein
15 und der ganze Hofstat mit ihnen. Da schliefen
auch die Pferde im Stall, die Hunde im Hofe, die
Tauben auf dem Dache, die Fliegen an der Wand,
ja, das Feuer, das auf dem Herde flackerte, ward
still und schlief ein, und der Braten hörte auf zu
20 brutzeln, und der Koch, der den Küchenjungen, weil
er etwas versehen hatte, in den Haren ziehen wollte,
liess ihn los und schlief. Und der Wind legte sich,
und auf den Bäumen vor dem Schloss regte sich
kein Blättchen mehr.

25   Rings um das Schloss aber begann eine Dornenhecke zu wachsen, die jedes Jahr höher ward und
endlich das ganze Schloss umzog und darüber hinaus wuchs, dass gar nichts mehr davon zu sehen war,
selbst nicht die Fahne auf dem Dach. Es gieng
30 aber die Sage in dem Land von dem schönen schlafenden Dornröschen, denn so ward die Königstochter
genannt, also dass von Zeit zu Zeit Königssöhne
kamen und durch die Hecke in das Schloss dringen

wollten. Es war aber alle Mühe vergeblich, denn die
Dornen, als hätten sie Hände, hielten fest zusammen, und die Jünglinge blieben darin hängen,
konnten sich nicht wieder losmachen und starben
eines jämmerlichen Todes. Nach langen langen 5
Jahren kam wieder einmal ein Königssohn in das
Land und hörte, wie ein alter Mann von der Dornenhecke erzählte, es sollte ein Schloss dahinter stehen,
in welchem eine wunderschöne Königstochter, Dornröschen genannt, schon seit hundert Jahren schliefe, 10
und mit ihr schliefe der König und die Königin und
der ganze Hofstat. Er wusste auch von seinem
Groszvater, dass schon viele Königssöhne gekommen
wären und versucht hätten, durch die Dornenhecke
zu dringen, aber sie wären darin hängen geblieben 15
und eines traurigen Todes gestorben. Da sprach der
Jüngling : " Ich fürchte mich nicht, ich will hinaus
und das schöne Dornröschen sehen." Der gute Alte
riet ihm ab, aber er hörte nicht auf seine Worte.

Nun waren gerade die hundert Jahre verflossen, 20
und der Tag war gekommen, wo Dornröschen wieder
erwachen sollte. Als der Königssohn sich der Hecke
näherte, waren es lauter grosze schöne Blumen, die
taten sich von selbst auseinander und liessen ihn un-
beschädigt hindurch : und hinter ihm taten sie sich 25
wieder als eine Hecke zusammen. Im Schlosshof
sah er die Pferde und scheckigen Jagdhunde liegen
und schlafen : auf dem Dache saszen die Tauben
und hatten das Köpfchen unter den Flügel gesteckt.
Und als er ins Haus kam, schliefen die Fliegen an 30
der Wand, der Koch in der Küche hielt noch die
Hand, als wollte er den Jungen anpacken, und die
Magd sasz vor dem schwarzen Huhn, das sollte ge-

rupft werden. Da gieng er weiter und sah im Sale
den ganzen Hofstat liegen und schlafen, und oben
bei dem Throne lag der König und die Königin.
Da gieng er noch weiter, und alles war so still, dass
5 einer seinen Atem hören konnte, und endlich kam
er zu dem Turm und öffnete die Türe zu der kleinen
Stube, in welcher Dornröschen schlief. Da lag es
und war so schön, dass er die Augen nicht abwenden
konnte, und er konnte es auch nicht lassen, bückte
10 sich und gab ihm einen Kuss. Kaum hatte er es mit
dem Kuss berührt, so schlug Dornröschen die Augen auf, erwachte und blickte ihn ganz freundlich
an. Da giengen sie zusammen herab, und der König
erwachte und die Königin und der ganze Hofstat,
15 und sahen einander mit groszen Augen an. Und
die Pferde im Hof standen auf und rüttelten sich :
die Jagdhunde sprangen und wedelten : die Tauben
auf dem Dach zogen das Köpfchen unterm Flügel
hervor, sahen umher und flogen ins Feld : die Flie-
20 gen an den Wänden krochen weiter : das Feuer in
der Küche erhob sich, flackerte und kochte das
Essen : der Braten fieng wieder an zu brutzeln, und
der Koch gab dem Jungen eine Ohrfeige, dass er
schrie : und die Magd rupfte das Huhn fertig. Und
25 da ward die Hochzeit des Königssohnes mit dem
Dornröschen in aller Pracht gefeiert, und sie lebten
vergnügt bis an ihr Ende.

IV

DER TREUE JOHANNES.

(No. 5.)

Es war einmal ein alter König, der war krank und dachte : "Das wird wohl das Totenbett sein, auf dem ich liege." Da sprach er : "Lasst mir den getreuen Johannes kommen." Der getreue Johannes war aber sein liebster Diener, und hiess so, weil er 5 ihm sein Lebelang so treu gewesen war. Als er nun vor das Bett gekommen war, sprach der König : " Getreuester Johannes, ich fühle, dass mein Ende herannaht, und da hab' ich keine andere Sorge als um meinen Sohn : er ist noch in jungen Jahren, wo 10 er sich nicht immer zu raten weiss, und wenn du mir nicht versprichst, ihn zu unterrichten in allem, was er wissen muss, und sein Pflegevater zu sein, so kann ich meine Augen nicht in Ruhe zutun." Da antwortete der getreue Johannes : "Ich will ihn 15 nicht verlassen, und will ihm mit Treue dienen, wenn's auch mein Leben kostet." Da sagte der alte König : "So sterb' ich getrost und in Frieden." Und sprach dann weiter : "Nach meinem Tode sollst du ihm das ganze Schloss zeigen, alle Kammern, Säle 20 und Gewölbe, und alle Schätze, die darin liegen ; aber die letzte Kammer in dem langen Gange sollst

du ihm nicht zeigen, worin das Bild der Königstochter vom goldenen Dache verborgen steht. Wenn er
sie erblickt, wird er eine heftige Liebe zu ihr em-
pfinden, und wird in Ohnmacht niederfallen, und
5 wird ihretwillen in grosze Gefahren geraten ; davor
sollst du ihn hüten." Und als der treue Johannes
nochmals dem alten König die Hand darauf gegeben
hatte, ward dieser still, legte sein Haupt auf das Kissen und starb.

10 Als der alte König nun zu Grabe getragen war,
da erzählte der treue Johannes dem jungen König,
was er seinem Vater auf dem Sterbelager versprochen
hatte, und sagte : "Das will ich gewisslich halten,
und will dir treu sein, wie ich ihm gewesen bin, und
15 sollte es mein Leben kosten." Die Trauer gieng vorüber, da sprach der treue Johannes zu ihm : " Es ist
nun Zeit, dass du dein Erbe siehst : ich will dir dein
väterliches Schloss zeigen." Da führte er ihn über-
all herum, auf und ab, und liess ihn alle die Reich-
20 tümer und prächtigen Kammern sehen ; nur die eine
Kammer öffnete er nicht, worin das gefährliche Bild
stand. Das Bild war aber so gestellt, dass, wenn die
Tür aufgieng, man gerade darauf sah, und war so
herrlich gemacht, dass man meinte es leibte und
25 lebte, und es gäbe nichts Lieblicheres und Schöneres
auf der ganzen Welt. Der junge König merkte aber
wohl, dass der getreue Johannes immer an der Türe
vorübergieng, und sprach : "Warum schliessest du
mir diese niemals auf ?" "Es ist etwas darin," ant-
30 wortete er, "vor dem du erschrickst." Aber der
König antwortete : " Ich habe das ganze Schloss gesehen, so will ich auch wissen, was darin ist," und
gieng und wollte die Türe mit Gewalt öffnen. Da

hielt ihn der treue Johannes zurück und sagte : " Ich
habe es deinem Vater vor seinem Tode versprochen,
dass du nicht sehen sollst, was in der Kammer
steht : es könnte dir und mir zu groszem Unglück
ausschlagen." "Ach," antwortete der junge König, 5
"wenn ich nicht hinein komme, so ist's mein sich-
eres Verderben ; ich würde Tag und Nacht keine
Ruhe haben, bis ich's mit meinen Augen gesehen
hätte. Nun gehe ich nicht von der Stelle, bis du
aufgeschlossen hast." 10
Da sah der getreue Johannes, dass es nicht mehr
zu ändern war, und suchte mit schwerem Herzen und
vielem Seufzen aus dem groszen Bund den Schlüssel
heraus. Als er die Tür der Kammer geöffnet hatte,
trat er zuerst hinein und dachte, der König sollte 15
das Bildnis vor ihm nicht sehen : aber was half das?
Der König stellte sich auf die Fuszspitzen und sah
ihm über die Schulter. Und als er das Bildnis der
Jungfrau erblickte, das so herrlich war und von Gold
und Edelsteinen glänzte, da fiel er ohnmächtig zur 20
Erde nieder. Der getreue Johannes hob ihn auf,
trug ihn in sein Bett und dachte voll Sorgen : "Das
Unglück ist geschehen, was will daraus werden!"
Dann stärkte er ihn mit Wein, bis er wieder zu sich
selbst kam. Das erste Wort, das er sprach, war : 25
"Ach wer ist das schöne Bild?" "Das ist die Königstochter vom goldenen Dache," antwortete der
treue Johannes. Da sprach der König weiter :
"Meine Liebe zu ihr ist so grosz, wenn alle Blätter
an den Bäumen Zungen wären, sie könnten's nicht 30
aussagen ; mein Leben setze ich daran, dass ich sie
erlange. Du bist mein getreuester Johannes, du
musst mir beistehen."

Der treue Diener besann sich lange, wie es anzu-
fangen wäre, denn es hielt schwer, nur vor das Angesicht der Königstochter zu kommen. Endlich hatte
er ein Mittel ausgedacht, und sprach zu dem König:
5 "Alles, was sie um sich hat, ist von Gold: Tische,
Stühle, Schüsseln, Becher, Näpfe und alles Hausge-
rät: in deinem Schatze liegen fünf Tonnen Goldes,
lass' Eine von den Goldschmieden des Reichs verarbeiten zu allerhand Gefäszen und Gerätschaften, zu
10 allerhand Vögeln, Gewild und wunderbaren Tieren,
das wird ihr gefallen. Wir wollen hinfahren und
unser Glück versuchen." Der König liess alle Gold-
schmiede zusammenkommen: sie arbeiteten Tag und
Nacht, bis endlich die herrlichsten Dinge fertig
15 waren. Nun liess der getreue Johannes alles auf
ein Schiff laden, und zog Kaufmannskleider an, und
der König musste ein gleiches tun, um sich unkennt-
lich zu machen. Dann fuhren sie über das Meer
und fuhren so lange bis sie zur Stadt kamen, worin
20 die Königstochter vom goldenen Dache wohnte.

Der treue Johannes hiess den König auf dem
Schiffe zurückbleiben und auf ihn warten. "Vielleicht," sprach er, "bring' ich die Königstochter mit,
darum sorget, dass alles in Ordnung ist, lasst die
25 Goldgefäsze aufstellen und das ganze Schiff ausschmücken." Darauf suchte er sich in sein Schürzchen allerlei von den Goldsachen zusammen, stieg
aus Land und gieng gerade nach dem königlichen
Schloss. Als er in den Schlosshof kam, stand da beim
30 Brunnen ein schönes Mädchen, das hatte zwei goldene Eimer in der Hand und schöpfte damit. Und als
es das goldblinkende Wasser forttragen wollte und
sich umdrehte, sah es den fremden Mann und fragte

ihn, wer er wäre? Da antwortete er: "Ich bin ein Kaufmann," und öffnete sein Schürzchen und liess sie hinein schauen. Da rief sie: "Ei, was für schönes Goldzeug!" setzte die Eimer nieder und betrachtete Eins nach dem andern. Da sprach das Mädchen: 5 "Das muss die Königstochter sehen, die hat so grosze Freude an den Goldsachen, dass sie euch alles abkauft." Es nahm ihn bei der Hand und führte ihn hinauf, denn es war die Kammerjungfer. Als die Königstochter die Ware sah, war sie ganz vergnügt 10 und sprach: "Es ist so schön gearbeitet, dass ich dir alles abkaufen will." Aber der getreue Johannes sprach: "Ich bin nur der Diener von einem reichen Kaufmann: was ich hier habe, ist nichts gegen das, was mein Herr auf seinem Schiffe stehen hat und das 15 ist das künstlichste und köstlichste, was je in Gold ist gearbeitet worden." Sie wollte alles herauf gebracht haben, aber er sprach: "Dazu gehören viele Tage, so grosz ist die Menge, und so viele Säle, um es aufzustellen, dass euer Haus nicht Raum dafür 20 hat." Da ward ihre Neugierde und Lust immer mehr angeregt, so dass sie endlich sagte: "Führe mich hin zu dem Schiff, ich will selbst hingehen und deines Herrn Schätze betrachten."

Da führte sie der getreue Johannes zu dem Schiffe 25 hin und war ganz freudig, und der König, als er sie erblickte, sah, dass sie noch schöner war als das Bild und meinte nicht anders, als das Herz wollte ihm zerspringen. Nun stieg sie in das Schiff, und der König führte sie hinein; der getreue Johannes aber 30 blieb zurück bei dem Steuermann und hiess das Schiff abstoszen: "Spannt alle Segel auf, dass es fliegt wie ein Vogel in der Luft." Der König aber

zeigte ihr drinnen das goldene Geschirr, jedes einzeln, die Schüsseln, Becher, Näpfe, die Vögel, das
Gewild und die wunderbaren Tiere. Viele stunden
giengen herum, während sie alles besah, und in ihrer
5 Freude merkte sie nicht, dass das Schiff dahinfuhr.
Nachdem sie das letzte betrachtet hatte, dankte sie
dem Kaufmann und wollte heim ; als sie aber an des
Schiffes Rand kam, sah sie, dass es fern vom Land
auf hohem Meere gieng und mit vollen Segeln fort-
10 eilte. "Ach," rief sie erschrocken, "ich bin betrogen, ich bin entführt und in die Gewalt eines
Kaufmanns geraten ; lieber wollt' ich sterben !"
Der König aber fasste sie bei der Hand und sprach :
" Ein Kaufmann bin ich nicht, ich bin ein König
15 und nicht geringer an Geburt als du bist : aber dass
ich dich mit List entführt habe, das ist aus über-
groszer Liebe geschehen. Das erste mal, als ich
dein Bildnis gesehen habe, bin ich ohnmächtig zur
Erde gefallen." Als die Königstochter vom golde-
20 nen Dache das hörte, ward sie getröstet, und ihr
Herz ward ihm geneigt, so dass sie gerne einwilligte
seine Gemahlin zu werden.
    Es trug sich aber zu, während sie auf dem hohen
Meere dahinfuhren, dass der getreue Johannes, als
25 er vornen auf dem Schiffe sasz und Musik machte,
in der Luft drei Raben erblickte, die dahergeflogen
kamen. Da hörte er auf zu spielen und horchte was
sie mit einander sprachen, denn er verstand das wohl.
Die eine rief : "Ei, da führt er die Königstochter
30 vom goldenen Dache heim." "Ja," antwortete die
zweite, "er hat sie noch nicht." Sprach die dritte :
" Er hat sie doch, sie sitzt bei ihm im Schiffe." Da
fieng die erste wieder an und rief : "Was hilft ihm

das? wenn sie ans Land kommen, wird ihm ein
fuchsrotes Pferd entgegenspringen : da wird er sich
aufschwingen wollen, und tut er das, so sprengt es
mit ihm fort und in die Luft hinein, dass er nimmermehr seine Jungfrau wieder sieht." Sprach die 5
zweite : " Ist gar keine Rettung?" "O ja, wenn
ein anderer schnell aufsitzt, das Feuergewehr, das in
den Halftern stecken muss, herausnimmt und das
Pferd damit totschiesst, so ist der junge König gerettet. Aber wer weiss das? und wer's weiss und 10
sagt's ihm, der wird zu Stein von den Fuszzehen bis
zum Knie." Da sprach die zweite : " Ich weiss noch
mehr, wenn das Pferd auch getötet wird, so behält
der junge König doch nicht seine Braut : wenn sie
zusammen ins Schloss kommen, so liegt dort ein ge- 15
machtes Brautkleid in einer Schüssel, und sieht aus,
als wär's von Gold und Silber gewebt, ist aber nichts
als Schwefel und Pech : wenn er's antut, verbrennt
es ihn bis auf Mark und Knochen." Sprach die
dritte : "Ist da gar keine Rettung?" " O ja," ant- 20
wortete die zweite, "wenn einer mit Handschuhen
das Hemd packt und wirft es ins Feuer, dass es verbrennt, so ist der junge König gerettet. Aber was
hilft's ! wer's weiss und es ihm sagt, der wird halbes
Leibes Stein vom Knie bis zum Herzen!" Da sprach 25
die dritte : "Ich weiss noch mehr, wird das Brautkleid auch verbrannt, so hat der junge König seine
Braut doch noch nicht ; wenn nach der Hochzeit der
Tanz anhebt, und die junge Königin tanzt, wird sie
plötzlich erbleichen und wie tot hinfallen ; und hebt 30
sie nicht einer auf und zieht aus ihrer rechten Brust
drei Tropfen Blut und speit sie wieder aus, so stirbt
sie. Aber verrät das einer, der es weiss, so wird er

ganzes Leibes zu Stein vom Wirbel bis zur Fusz-
zehe." Als die Raben das mit einander gesprochen
hatten, flogen sie weiter, und der getreue Johannes
hatte alles wohl verstanden, aber von der Zeit an
5 war er still und traurig ; denn verschwieg er seinem
Herrn, was er gehört hatte, so war dieser unglück- .
lich : entdeckte er es ihm, so musste er selbst sein
Leben hingeben. Endlich aber sprach er bei sich :
"Meinen Herrn will ich retten, und sollt' ich selbst
10 darüber zu Grunde gehen."

Als sie nun ans Land kamen, da geschah es, wie
die Raben vorhergesagt hatten, und es sprengte ein
prächtiger fuchsroter Gaul daher. "Wohlan," sprach
der König, "der soll mich in mein Schloss tragen,"
15 und wollte sich aufsetzen, doch der getreue Johannes
kam ihm zuvor, schwang sich schnell darauf, zog das
Gewehr aus den Halftern und schoss ihn nieder.
Da riefen die anderen Diener des Königs, die dem
treuen Johannes doch nicht gut waren : "Wie schänd-
20 lich, das schöne Tier zu töten, das den König in
sein Schloss tragen sollte." Aber der König sprach :
"Schweigt und lasst ihn gehen, es ist mein getreuester Johannes, wer weiss, wozu das gut ist!" Nun
giengen sie ins Schloss, und da stand im Sal eine
25 Schüssel, und das gemachte Brautkleid lag darin und
sah aus nicht anders, als wäre es von Gold und Silber. Der junge König gieng darauf zu und wollte
es ergreifen, aber der treue Johannes schob ihn weg,
packte es mit Handschuhen an, trug es schnell ins
30 Feuer und liess es verbrennen. Die anderen Diener
fiengen wieder an zu murren und sagten : "Seht,
nun verbrennt er gar des Königs Brautkleid." Aber
der junge König sprach : "Wer weiss, wozu es gut

ist, lasst ihn gehen, es ist mein getreuester Johannes." Nun ward die Hochzeit gefeiert: der Tanz hub an, und die Braut trat auch hinein, da hatte der treue Johannes Acht und schaute ihr ins Antlitz : auf einmal erbleichte sie und fiel wie tot zur Erde. Da 5 sprang er eilends hinzu, hob sie auf und trug sie in eine Kammer, da legte er sie nieder, kniete und sog die drei Blutstropfen aus ihrer rechten Brust und speite sie aus. Alsbald atmete sie wieder und erholte sich, aber der junge König hatte es mit ange- 10 sehen, und wusste nicht, warum es der treue Johannes getan hatte, ward zornig darüber, und rief: "Werft ihn ins Gefängnis." Am anderen Morgen ward der treue Johannes verurteilt und zum Galgen geführt, und als er oben stand und gerichtet werden 15 sollte, sprach er : "Jeder der sterben soll, darf vor seinem Ende noch einmal reden, soll ich das Recht auch haben ?" "Ja," antwortete der König, "es soll dir vergönnt sein." Da sprach der treue Johannes : "Ich bin mit Unrecht verurteilt und bin dir immer 20 treu gewesen," und erzählte, wie er auf dem Meere das Gespräch der Raben gehört, und wie er, um seinen Herrn zu retten, das alles hätte tun müssen. Da rief der König : "O, mein getreuester Johannes, Gnade! Gnade ! Führt ihn herunter." Aber der 25 treue Johannes war bei dem letzten Wort, das er geredet hatte, leblos herabgefallen, und war ein Stein.

Darüber trug nun der König und die Königin groszes Leid, und der König sprach : "Ach, was hab' ich grosze Treue so übel belohnt!" und liess 30 das steinerne Bild aufheben und in seine Schlafkammer neben sein Bett stellen. So oft er es ansah, weinte er und sprach : "Ach, könnt' ich dich

wieder lebendig machen, mein getreuester Johannes." Es gieng eine Zeit herum, da gebar die
Königin Zwillinge, zwei Söhnlein, die wuchsen heran und waren ihre Freude. Einmal, als die Königin
5 in der Kirche war und die zwei Kinder bei dem
Vater saszen und spielten, sah dieser wieder das
steinerne Bildnis voll Trauer an, seufzte und rief :
" Ach, könnt' ich dich wieder lebendig machen,
mein getreuester Johannes." Da fieng der Stein an
10 zu reden und sprach : " Ja, du kannst mich wieder
lebendig machen, wenn du dein Liebstes daran-
wenden willst." Da rief der König : "Alles, was
ich auf der Welt habe, will ich für dich hingeben."
Sprach der Stein weiter : " Wenn du mit deiner
15 eigenen Hand deinen beiden Kindern den Kopf ab-
haust und mich mit ihrem Blute bestreichst, so er-
halte ich das Leben wieder." Der König erschrak,
als er hörte, dass er seine liebsten Kinder selbst
töten sollte, doch dachte er an die grosze Treue, und
20 dass der getreue Johannes für ihn gestorben war,
zog sein Schwert und hieb mit eigener Hand den
Kindern den Kopf ab. Und als er mit ihrem Blute
den Stein bestrichen hatte, kehrte das Leben zurück,
und der getreue Johannes stand wieder frisch und
25 gesund vor ihm. Er aber sprach zum König :
" Deine Treue soll nicht unbelohnt bleiben," und
nahm die Häupter der Kinder, setzte sie wieder auf
und bestrich die Wunde mit ihrem Blut : davon
wurden sie im Augenblick wieder heil, und sprangen
30 herum und spielten fort, als wäre ihnen nichts geschehen. Nun war der König voll Freude, und als
er die Königin kommen sah, versteckte er den
treuen Johannes und die beiden Kinder in einen

groszen Schrank. Wie sie hereintrat, sprach er zu
ihr : " Hast du gebetet in der Kirche ?" " Ja," antwortete sie, "aber ich habe beständig an den treu-
en Johannes gedacht, dass er so unglücklich durch
uns geworden ist." Da sprach er : " Liebe Frau, 5
wir können ihm das Leben wiedergeben, aber es
kostet uns unsre beiden Söhnlein, die müssen wir
opfern." Die Königin ward bleich und erschrak im
Herzen, doch sprach sie : " Wir sind's ihm schuldig
wegen seiner groszen Treue." Da freute er sich, 10
dass sie dachte, wie er gedacht hatte, gieng hin und
schloss den Schrank auf, und holte die Kinder und
den treuen Johannes heraus und sprach : " Gott sei
gelobt, er ist erlöst, und unsere Söhnlein haben wir
auch wieder," und erzählte ihr, wie es sich alles zu- 15
getragen hatte. Da lebten sie zusammen in Glückseligkeit bis an ihr Ende.

V.

BRÜDERCHEN UND SCHWESTERCHEN.
(No. 9.)

———

Brüderchen nahm sein Schwesterchen an der Hand und sprach : "Seit die Mutter tot ist, haben wir keine gute Stunde mehr : die Stiefmutter schlägt uns alle Tage, und wenn wir zu ihr kommen, stöszt
5 sie uns mit den Füszen fort. Die harten Brodkrusten, die übrig bleiben, sind unsere Speise, und dem Hündlein unter dem Tisch geht's besser : dem wirft sie doch manchmal einen guten Bissen zu. Dass Gott erbarm', wenn das unsere Mutter wüsste !
10 Komm', wir wollen mit einander in die weite Welt gehen." Sie giengen den ganzen Tag über Wiesen, Felder und Steine, und wenn es regnete, sprach das Schwesterchen : "Gott und unsere Herzen, die weinen zusammen !" Abends kamen sie in einen
15 groszen Wald und waren so müde von Jammer, Hunger und dem langen Weg, dass sie sich in einen hohlen Baum setzten und einschliefen.

Am andern Morgen, als sie aufwachten, stand die Sonne schon hoch am Himmel und schien heiss in
20 den Baum hinein. Da sprach das Brüderchen : "Schwesterchen, mich dürstet, wenn ich ein Brünnlein wüsste, ich gieng' und tränk' einmal ; ich mein',

Ich hört' eins rauschen." Brüderchen stand auf, nahm Schwesterchen an der Hand, und sie wollten das Brünnlein suchen. Die böse Stiefmutter aber war eine Hexe, und hatte wohl gesehen, wie die beiden Kinder fortgegangen waren, war ihnen nachge- 5 schlichen, heimlich, wie die Hexen schleichen, und hatte alle Brunnen im Walde verwünscht. Als sie nun ein Brünnlein fanden, das so glitzerig über die Steine sprang, wollte das Brüderchen daraus trinken : aber das Schwesterchen hörte, wie es im 10 Rauschen sprach : "Wer aus mir trinkt, wird ein Tiger ; wer aus mir trinkt, wird ein Tiger." Da rief das Schwesterchen : "Ich bitte dich, Brüderchen, trink' nicht, sonst wirst du ein wildes Tier und zerreissest mich." Das Brüderchen trank nicht, ob es 15 gleich so groszen Durst hatte, und sprach : "Ich will warten, bis zur nächsten Quelle." Als sie zum zweiten Brünnlein kamen, hörte das Schwesterchen, wie auch dieses sprach : "Wer aus mir trinkt, wird ein Wolf ; wer aus mir trinkt, wird ein Wolf." Da 20 rief das Schwesterchen : "Brüderchen, ich bitte dich, trink' nicht, sonst wirst du ein Wolf und frissest mich." Das Brüderchen trank nicht und sprach : "Ich will warten, bis wir zur nächsten Quelle kommen, aber dann muss ich trinken, du 25 magst sagen, was du willst ; mein Durst ist gar zu grosz." Und als sie zum dritten Brünnlein kamen, hörte das Schwesterlein, wie es im Rauschen sprach : "Wer aus mir trinkt, wird ein Reh ; wer aus mir trinkt, wird ein Reh." Das Schwesterchen sprach : 30 "Ach, Brüderchen, ich bitte dich, trink' nicht, sonst wirst du ein Reh und läufst mir fort." Aber das Brüderchen hatte sich gleich beim Brünnlein nieder-

gekniect, hinabgebeugt und von dem Wasser getrunken, und wie die ersten Tropfen auf seine Lip-
pen gekommen waren, lag es da als ein Rehkälbchen.
Nun weinte das Schwesterchen über das arme ver-
5 wünschte Brüderchen, und das Rehchen weinte auch
und sasz so traurig neben ihm. Da sprach das Mädchen endlich: "Sei still, liebes Rehchen, ich will
dich ja nimmermehr verlassen." Dann band es sein
goldenes Strumpfband ab und tat es dem Rehchen
10 um den Hals, und rupfte Binsen und flocht ein wei-
ches Seil daraus. Daran band es das Tierchen und
führte es weiter und gieng immer tiefer in den Wald
hinein. Und als sie lange lange gegangen waren,
kamen sie endlich an ein kleines Haus, und das Mäd-
15 chen schaute hinein, und weil es leer war, dachte es:
"Hier können wir bleiben und wohnen." Da suchte
es dem Rehchen Laub und Moos zu einem weichen
Lager, und jeden Morgen gieng es aus und sammelte
sich Wurzeln, Beeren und Nüsse, und für das Reh-
20 chen brachte es zartes Gras mit, das frasz es ihm
aus der Hand, war vergnügt und spielte vor ihm
herum. Abends, wenn Schwesterchen müde war
und sein Gebet gesagt hatte, legte es seinen Kopf
auf den Rücken des Rehkälbchens, das war sein Kis-
25 sen, darauf es sanft einschlief. Und hätte das Brüderchen nur seine menschliche Gestalt gehabt, es
wäre ein herrliches Leben gewesen.
Das dauerte nun eine Zeitlang, dass sie so allein
in der Wildnis waren. Da trug es sich zu, dass der
30 König des Landes eine grosze Jagd in den Wald
hielt. Da schallte das Hörnerblasen, Hundegebell
und das lustige Geschrei der Jäger durch die Bäume
und das Rehlein hörte es und wäre gar zu gerne da-

bei gewesen. "Ach," sprach es zum Schwesterlein,
"lass' mich hinaus in die Jagd, ich kann's nicht
länger mehr aushalten," und bat so lange, bis es einwilligte. "Aber," sprach es zu ihm, "komm' mir ja
abends wieder, vor den wilden Jägern schliess' ich 5
mein Türlein ; und damit ich dich kenne, so klopf'
und sprich : 'Mein Schwesterlein, lass' mich herein,'
und wenn du nicht so sprichst, so schliess' ich mein
Türlein nicht auf." Nun sprang das Rehchen hinaus,
und war ihm so wohl, und war so lustig in freier 10
Luft. Der König und seine Jäger sahen das schöne
Tier und setzten ihm nach, aber sie konnten es nicht
einholen, und wenn sie meinten, sie hätten es gewiss, da sprang es über das Gebüsch weg und war
verschwunden. Als es dunkel ward, lief es zu dem 15
Häuschen, klopfte und sprach : "Mein Schwesterlein,
lass' mich herein." Da ward ihm die kleine Tür auf-
getan, es sprang hinein und ruhte sich die ganze
Nacht auf seinem weichen Lager aus. Am andern
Morgen gieng die Jagd von neuem an, und als das 20
Rehlein wieder das Hifthorn hörte und das ho, ho !
der Jäger, da hatte es keine Ruhe und sprach :
"Schwesterchen, mach' mir auf, ich muss hinaus."
Das Schwesterchen öffnete ihm die Türe und sprach :
"Aber zu Abend musst du wieder da sein und dein 25
Sprüchlein sagen." Als der König und seine Jäger das Rehlein mit dem goldenen Halsband wieder
sahen, jagten sie ihm alle nach, aber es war ihnen zu
schnell und behend. Das währte den ganzen Tag,
endlich aber hatten es die Jäger abends umzingelt, 30
und Einer verwundete es ein wenig am Fusz, so
dass es hinken musste, und langsam fortlief. Da
schlich ihm ein Jäger nach bis zu dem Häuschen und

hörte, wie es rief : "Mein Schwesterlein, lass' mich
herein," und sah, dass die Tür ihm aufgetan und
alsbald wieder zugeschlossen ward. Der Jäger behielt das alles wohl im Sinn, gieng zum König und
5 erzählte ihm, was er gesehen und gehört hatte. Da
sprach der König : "Morgen soll noch einmal ge-
jagt werden."

Das Schwesterchen aber erschrak gewaltig, als es
sah, dass das Rehkälbchen verwundet war. Es wusch
10 ihm das Blut ab, legte Kräuter auf und sprach :
"Geh' auf dein Lager, lieb Rehchen, dass du wieder
heil wirst." Die Wunde aber war so gering, dass das
Rehchen am Morgen nichts mehr davon spürte. Und
als es die Jagdlust wieder draussen hörte, sprach es :
15 "Ich kann's nicht aushalten, ich muss dabei sein ; so
bald soll mich auch keiner kriegen." Das Schwesterchen weinte und sprach : "Nun werden sie dich
töten, und ich bin hier allein im Wald und verlassen
von aller Welt ; ich lass' dich nicht hinaus." "So
20 sterb' ich dir hier vor Betrübnis," antwortete das
Rehchen, "wenn ich das Hifthorn höre, so mein' ich,
ich müsst' aus den Schuhen springen !" Da konnte
das Schwesterchen nicht anders und schloss ihm mit
schwerem Herzen die Tür' auf und das Rehchen
25 sprang gesund und fröhlich in den Wald. Als es der
König erblickte, sprach er zu seinen Jägern : "Nun
jagt ihm nach den ganzen Tag bis in die Nacht, aber
dass ihm keiner etwas zu Leide tut." Wie die Sonne
untergegangen war, da sprach der König zum Jäger :
30 "Nun komm' und zeige mir das Waldhäuschen."
Und als er vor dem Türlein war, klopfte er an und
rief : "Lieb Schwesterlein, lass' mich herein." Da
gieng die Tür' auf, und der König trat hinein, und

da stand ein Mädchen, das war so schön, wie er noch keins erblickt hatte. Das Mädchen erschrak, als es sah, dass nicht sein Rehlein, sondern ein Mann herein kam, der eine goldene Krone auf dem Haupt hatte. Aber der König sah es freundlich an, reichte ihm die 5 Hand und sprach : "Willst du mit mir gehen auf mein Schloss und meine liebe Frau sein?" "Ach ja," antwortete das Mädchen, "aber das Rehchen muss auch mit, das verlass' ich nicht." Sprach der König : "Es soll bei dir bleiben, so lange du lebst, 10 und soll ihm an nichts fehlen." Indem kam es hereingesprungen, da band es das Schwesterchen wieder an das Binsenseil, nahm es selbst in die Hand und gieng mit ihm aus dem Waldhäuschen fort.

Der König nahm das schöne Mädchen auf sein 15 Pferd und führte es in sein Schloss, wo die Hochzeit mit groszer Pracht gefeiert wurde, und war es nun die Frau Königin und lebten sie lange Zeit vergnügt zusammen ; das Rehlein ward gehegt und gepflegt und sprang in dem Schlossgarten herum. Die böse 20 Stiefmutter aber, um derentwillen die Kinder in die Welt hineingegangen waren, die meinte nicht anders als Schwesterchen wäre von den wilden Tieren im Walde zerrissen worden und Brüderchen als ein Reh-kalb von den Jägern totgeschossen. Als sie nun 25 hörte, dass sie so glücklich waren, und es ihnen so wohl gieng, da wurden Neid und Missgunst in ihrem Herzen rege, und liessen ihr keine Ruhe, und sie hatte keinen anderen Gedanken, als wie sie die beiden doch noch ins Unglück bringen könnte. Ihre 30 rechte Tochter, die hässlich war wie die Nacht und nur Ein Auge hatte, die machte ihr Vorwürfe und sprach : "Eine Königin zu werden, das Glück hätte

mir gebührt." "Sei nur still," sagte die Alte und
sprach sie zufrieden, "wenn's Zeit ist, will ich schon
bei der Hand sein." Als nun die Zeit herangerückt
war, und die Königin ein schönes Knäblein zur Welt
5 gebracht hatte und der König gerade auf der Jagd
war, nahm die alte Hexe die Gestalt der Kammerfrau an, trat in die Stube, wo die Königin lag, und
sprach zu der Kranken : " Kommt, das Bad ist fertig,
das wird euch wohltun und frische Kräfte geben, ge-
10 schwind, ehe es kalt wird." Ihre Tochter war auch
bei der Hand, sie trugen die schwache Königin in
die Badstube und legten sie in die Wanne : dann
schlossen sie die Türe ab und liefen davon. In der
Badstube aber hatten sie ein rechtes Höllenfeuer an-
15 gemacht, dass die schöne junge Königin bald ersticken musste.

Als das geschehen war, nahm die Alte ihre Tochter, setzte ihr eine Haube auf und legte sie ins Bett
an der Königin Stelle. Sie gab ihr auch die Gestalt
20 und das Ansehen der Königin, nur das verlorne Auge
konnte sie ihr nicht wieder geben. Damit aber der
König es nicht merkte, musste sie sich auf die Seite
legen, wo sie kein Auge hatte. Am Abend, als der
König heimkam und hörte, dass ihm ein Söhnlein
25 geboren war, freute er sich herzlich und wollte ans
Bett zu seiner lieben Frau gehen, und wollte sehen,
was sie machte. Da rief die Alte geschwind : " Bei
Leibe lasst die Vorhänge zu, die Königin darf noch
nicht ins Licht sehen und muss Ruhe haben." Der
30 König gieng zurück und wusste nicht, dass eine
falsche Königin im Bette lag.

Als es aber Mitternacht war und alles schlief, da
sah die Kinderfrau, die in der Kinderstube neben der

Wiege sasz und allein noch wachte, wie die Türe aufgieng und die rechte Königin hereintrat. Sie nahm das Kind aus der Wiege, legte es in ihren Arm und gab ihm zu trinken. Dann schüttelte sie ihm sein Kisschen, legte es wieder hinein und deckte es 5 mit dem Deckbettchen zu. Sie vergasz aber auch das Rehchen nicht, gieng in die Ecke, wo es lag, und streichelte ihm über den Rücken. Darauf gieng sie ganz stillschweigend wieder zur Tür' hinaus, und die Kinderfrau fragte am andern Morgen die Wächter, 10 ob jemand während der Nacht ins Schloss gegangen wäre, aber sie antworteten : "Nein, wir haben niemand gesehen." So kam sie viele Nächte und sprach niemals ein Wort dabei ; die Kinderfrau sah sie immer, aber sie getraute sich nicht jemand etwas da- 15 von zu sagen.

Als nun so eine Zeit verflossen war, da hub die Königin in der Nacht an zu reden und sprach :

"Was macht mein Kind ? Was macht mein Reh ?
  Nun komm' ich noch zweimal und dann nim- 20
  mermehr."

Die Kinderfrau antwortete ihr nicht, aber als sie wieder verschwunden war, gieng sie zum König und erzählte ihm alles. Sprach der König : "Ach, was ist das? Ich will in der nächsten Nacht bei dem Kinde 25 wachen." Abends gieng er auch in die Kinderstube, aber um Mitternacht erschien die Königin wieder und sprach :

"Was macht mein Kind ? Was macht mein Reh ?
  Nun komm' ich noch einmal und dann nim- 30
  mermehr."

Und pflegte dann des Kindes, wie sie gewöhnlich tat, ehe sie verschwand. Der König getraute sich nicht sie anzureden, aber er wachte auch in der folgenden Nacht. Sie sprach abermals:

5   "Was macht mein Kind? Was macht mein Reh? Nun komm' ich noch diesmal und dann nimmermehr."

Da konnte sich der König nicht zurückhalten, sprang zu ihr und sprach : "Du kannst niemand anders sein
10 als meine liebe Frau." Da antwortete sie : "Ja, ich bin deine liebe Frau," und hatte in dem Augenblick durch Gottes Gnade das Leben wieder erhalten, war frisch, rot und gesund. Darauf erzählte sie dem König den Frevel den die böse Hexe und ihre Tochter
15 an ihr verübt hatten. Der König liess beide vor Gericht führen, und es ward ihnen das Urteil gesprochen. Die Tochter ward in den Wald geführt, wo sie die wilden Tiere zerrissen, die Hexe aber ward ins Feuer gelegt und musste jammervoll ver-
20 brennen. Und wie sie zu Asche verbrannt war, verwandelte sich auch das Rehkälbchen und erhielt seine menschliche Gestalt wieder ; Schwesterchen und Brüderchen aber lebten glücklich zusammen bis an ihr Ende.

VI.

KÖNIG DROSSELBART.

(No. 26.)

Ein König hatte eine Tochter, die war über
alle Maszen schön, dabei aber so stolz und übermütig, dass ihr kein Freier gut genug war. Sie wies
einen nach dem andern ab und trieb noch dazu Spott
mit ihnen. Einmal liess der König ein groszes Fest 5
anstellen und ladete dazu aus der Nähe und Ferne
die heiratslustigen Männer ein. Sie wurden alle in
eine Reihe nach Rang und Stand geordnet: erst
kamen die Könige, dann die Herzöge, die Fürsten,
Grafen und Freiherrn, zuletzt die Edelleute. Nun 10
ward die Königstochter durch die Reihen geführt,
aber an jedem hatte sie etwas auszusetzen. Der eine
war ihr zu dick: "Das Weinfass!" sprach sie. Der
andere zu lang: "Lang und schwank hat keinen
Gang." Der dritte zu kurz: "Kurz und dick hat 15
kein Geschick." Der vierte zu blass: "Der bleiche
Tod!" Der fünfte zu rot: "Der Zinshahn!" Der
sechste war nicht gerad genug: "Grünes Holz,
hinterm Ofen getrocknet." Und so hatte sie an
einem jeden etwas auszusetzen, besonders aber 20
machte sie sich über einen guten König lustig, der
ganz oben stand, und dem das Kinn ein wenig
krumm gewachsen war. "Ei," rief sie und lachte,

"der hat ein Kinn, wie die Drossel einen Schnabel," und seit der Zeit bekam er den Namen *Drosselbart*. Der alte König aber, als er sah, dass seine Tochter nichts tat als über die Leute spotten und alle Freier,
5 die da versammelt waren, verschmähte, ward er zornig und schwur sie sollte den ersten besten Bettler zum Mann nehmen, der vor seine Türe käme.

Ein par Tage darauf hub ein Spielmann an unter dem Fenster zu singen, um damit ein geringes Al-
10 mosen zu verdienen. Als es der König hörte, sprach er : "Lasst ihn heraufkommen." Da trat der Spielmann in seinen schmutzigen Kleidern herein, sang vor dem König und seiner Tochter und bat, als er fertig war, um eine milde Gabe. Der König sprach :
15 "Dein Gesang hat mir so wohl gefallen, dass ich dir meine Tochter da zur Frau geben will." Die Königstochter erschrak, aber der König sagte : "Ich habe den Eid getan, dich dem ersten besten Bettelmann zu geben, den will ich auch halten." Es half keine
20 Einrede, der Pfarrer ward geholt, und sie musste sich gleich mit dem Spielmann trauen lassen. Als das geschehen war, sprach der König : "Nun schickt sich nicht, dass du als ein Bettelweib noch länger in meinem Schloss bleibst, du kannst nun mit deinem
25 Manne weiterziehen."

Der Bettelmann führte sie an der Hand hinaus, und sie musste mit ihm zu Fusz fortgehen. Als sie da in einen groszen Wald kamen, fragte sie :

"Ach, wem gehört der schöne Wald ?"
30 "Der gehört dem König Drosselbart ;
Hättst du'n genommen, so wär' er dein."
"Ich arme Jungfer zart,
Ach, hätt' ich genommen den König Drosselbart !"

Darauf kamen sie über eine Wiese, da fragte sie
wieder :

"Wem gehört die schöne grüne Wiese ?"
"Sie gehört dem König Drosselbart ;
    Hättst du'n genommen, so wär' sie dein."   5
" Ich arme Jungfer zart,
    Ach, hätt' ich genommen den König Drosselbart !"

Dann kamen sie durch eine grosze Stadt, da fragte
sie wieder :

"Wem gehört diese schöne grosze Stadt ?"   10
" Sie gehört dem König Drosselbart ;
    Hättst du'n genommen, so wär' sie dein."
" Ich arme Jungfer zart,
    Ach, hätt' ich genommen den König Drosselbart !"

" Es gefällt mir gar nicht," sprach der Spielmann, 15
dass du dir immer einen andern zum Mann wünschest, bin ich dir nicht gut genug ?" Endlich kamen
sie an ein ganz kleines Häuschen, da sprach sie :

" Ach, was ist das Haus so klein !
    Wem mag das elende winzige Häuschen sein ?" 20

Der Spielmann antwortete : " Das ist mein und dein
Haus, wo wir zusammen wohnen." Sie musste sich
bücken, damit sie zu der niedrigen Tür hineinkam.
"Wo sind die Diener ?" sprach die Königstochter.
" Was Diener !" antwortete der Bettelmann, " du 25
musst selber tun, was du willst getan haben. Mach'
nur gleich Feuer an und stell' Wasser auf, dass du
mir ein Essen kochst ; ich bin ganz müde." Die
Königstochter verstand aber nichts vom Feueranmachen und Kochen, und der Bettelmann musste 30
selber mit Hand anlegen, dass es noch so leidlich

gieng. Als sie die schmale Kost verzehrt hatten,
legten sie sich zu Bett, aber am Morgen trieb er sie
schon ganz früh heraus, weil sie das Haus besorgen
sollte. Ein par Tage lebten sie auf diese Art
5 schlecht und recht, und zehrten ihren Vorrat auf.
Da sprach der Mann : "Frau, so geht's nicht länger,
dass wir hier zehren und nichts verdienen. Du sollst
Körbe flechten." Er gieng aus, schnitt Weiden und
brachte sie heim : da fieng sie an zu flechten, aber
10 die harten Weiden stachen ihr die zarten Hände
wund. "Ich sehe, das geht nicht," sprach der Mann,
"spinn' lieber, vielleicht kannst du das besser." Sie
setzte sich hin und versuchte zu spinnen, aber der
harte Faden schnitt ihr bald in die weichen Finger,
15 dass das Blut daran herunterlief. "Siehst du,"
sprach der Mann, "du taugst zu keiner Arbeit, mit
dir bin ich schlimm angekommen. Nun will ich's
versuchen und einen Handel mit Töpfen und irdenem
Geschirr anfangen : du sollst dich auf den Markt
20 setzen und die Ware feilhalten." "Ach," dachte sie,
"wenn auf den Markt Leute aus meines Vaters
Reich kommen und sehen mich da sitzen und feilhalten, wie werden sie mich verspotten!" Aber es
half nichts, sie musste sich fügen, wenn sie nicht
25 Hungers sterben wollten. Das erste Mal gieng's gut,
denn die Leute kauften der Frau, weil sie schön war,
gern ihre Ware ab und bezahlten, was sie forderte :
ja, viele gaben ihr das Geld und liessen ihr die Töpfe
noch dazu. Nun lebten sie von dem Erworbenen,
30 so lang es dauerte, da handelte der Mann wieder eine
Menge neues Geschirr ein. Sie setzte sich an eine
Ecke des Marktes und stellte es um sich her und
hielt feil. Da kam plötzlich ein trunkener Husar

dahergejagt und ritt gerade in die Töpfe hinein, dass
alles in tausend Scherben zersprang. Sie fieng an zu
weinen und wusste vor Angst nicht, was sie anfangen
sollte. "Ach, wie wird mir's ergehen!" rief sie, "was
wird mein Mann dazu sagen?" Sie lief heim und er- 5
zählte ihm das Unglück. "Wer setzt sich auch an die
Ecke des Marktes mit irdenem Geschirr!" sprach der
Mann, "lass' nur das Weinen, ich sehe wohl, du bist
zu keiner ordentlichen Arbeit zu gebrauchen. Da bin
ich in unsers Königs Schloss gewesen und habe ge- 10
fragt, ob sie nicht eine Küchenmagd brauchen könnten, und sie haben mir versprochen, sie wollten dich
dazu nehmen: dafür bekommst du freies Essen."

Nun ward die Königstochter Küchenmagd, musste
dem Koch zur Hand gehen und die sauerste Arbeit 15
tun. Sie machte sich in beiden Seitentaschen ein
Töpfchen fest, darin trug sie nach Hause, was ihr
von dem übriggebliebenen zu Teil ward, und davon
nährten sie sich. Einstmals sollte die Hochzeit des
ältesten Königssohnes gefeiert werden, da gieng die 20
arme Frau hinauf, stellte sich vor die Saltüre und
wollte zusehen. Als nun die Lichter angezündet
waren, und immer Einer schöner als der andere hereintrat, und alles voll Pracht und Herrlichkeit war,
da dachte sie mit betrübtem Herzen an ihr Schick- 25
sal und verwünschte ihren Stolz und Übermut, der
sie erniedrigt und in so grosze Armut gestürzt hatte.
Von den köstlichen Speisen, die da ein- und ausgetragen wurden, warfen ihr die Diener manchmal ein
par Brocken zu, die tat sie in ihr Töpfchen und 30
wollte sie heimtragen. Auf einmal trat der Königssohn heran, war in Samt und Seide gekleidet und
hatte goldene Ketten um den Hals, und als er die

schöne Frau in der Türe stehen sah, ergriff er sie
schnell bei der Hand und wollte mit ihr tanzen : aber
sie weigerte sich und erschrak, denn sie sah, dass es
der König Drosselbart war, der um sie gefreit und
5 den sie mit Spott abgewiesen hatte. Ihr Sträuben
half nichts, er zog sie in den Sal : da zerriss das
Band, an welchem die Taschen hiengen, und die
Töpfe fielen heraus, dass die Suppe floss und die
Brocken umhersprangen. Und wie das die Leute
10 sahen, entstand ein allgemeines Gelächter und
Spotten, und sie war so beschämt, dass sie sich
lieber tausend Klafter unter die Erde gewünscht
hätte. Sie sprang zur Türe hinaus und wollte ent-
fliehen, aber auf der Treppe holte sie ein Mann ein
15 und brachte sie zurück : und wie sie ihn ansah, war
es wieder der König Drosselbart. Er sprach ihr
freundlich zu : "Fürchte dich nicht, ich und der
Spielmann, der mit dir in dem elenden Häuschen ge-
wohnt hat, sind Eins : dir zu Liebe habe ich mich so
20 verstellt, und der Husar, der dir die Töpfe entzwei-
geritten hat, bin ich auch gewesen. Das alles ist geschehen, um deinen stolzen Sinn zu beugen und dich
für den Hochmut zu strafen, womit du mich verspottet hast." Da weinte sie bitterlich und sagte : "Ich
25 habe groszes Unrecht getan und bin nicht wert
deine Frau zu sein." Er aber sprach : "Tröste dich,
die bösen Tage sind vorüber : jetzt wollen wir unsere
Hochzeit feiern." Da kamen die Kammerfrauen
und taten ihr die prächtigsten Kleider an, und ihr
30 Vater kam und der ganze Hof, und wünschten ihr
Glück zu ihrer Vermählung mit dem König Drosselbart, und die rechte Freude fieng jetzt erst an. Ich
wollte du und ich, wir wären auch dabei gewesen.

VII.

SNEEWITTCHEN.

(No. 27.)

Es war einmal mitten im Winter, und die Schnee-
flocken fielen wie Federn vom Himmel herab, da
sasz eine Königin an einem Fenster, das einen Rahmen von schwarzem Ebenholz hatte, und nähte. Und
wie sie so nähte und nach dem Schnee aufblickte, 5
stach sie sich mit der Nadel in den Finger, und es
fielen drei Tropfen Blut in den Schnee. Und weil
das Rote im weissen Schnee so schön aussah, dachte
sie bei sich : " Hätt' ich ein Kind so weiss wie Schnee,
so rot wie Blut und so schwarz wie das Holz an dem 10
Rahmen." Bald darauf bekam sie ein Töchterlein,
das war so weiss wie Schnee, so rot wie Blut und so
schwarzharig wie Ebenholz, und ward darum das
Sneewittchen (Schneeweisschen) genannt. Und wie
das Kind geboren war, starb die Königin. 15
Über ein Jahr nahm sich der König eine andere
Gemahlin. Es war eine schöne Frau, aber sie war
stolz und übermütig und konnte nicht leiden, dass
sie an Schönheit von jemand sollte übertroffen werden. Sie hatte einen wunderlichen Spiegel, wenn 20
sie vor den trat und sich darin beschaute, sprach sie :

"Spieglein, Spieglein an der Wand,
Wer ist die schönste im ganzen Land ?"

und da antwortete der Spiegel :

"Frau Königin, ihr seid die schönste im Land."

Nun war sie zufrieden, denn sie wusste, dass der
Spiegel die Wahrheit sagte.

5 Sneewittchen aber wuchs heran und ward immer
schöner, und als es sieben Jahre alt war, war es so
schön, wie der klare Tag, und schöner als die Königin selbst.   Als diese einmal ihren Spiegel fragte :

"Spieglein, Spieglein an der Wand,
10   Wer ist die schönste im ganzen Land?"

so antwortete er :

"Frau Königin, ihr seid die schönste hier,
Aber Sneewittchen ist tausendmal schöner als ihr."

Da erschrak die Königin und ward gelb und grün
15 vor Neid.   Von Stund' an, wenn sie Sneewittchen erblickte, kehrte sich ihr das Herz im Leibe herum, so
hasste sie das Mädchen.   Und der Neid und Hochmut wuchsen wie ein Unkraut in ihrem Herzen,
immer höher, so dass sie Tag und Nacht keine Ruhe
20 hatte.   Da rief sie einen Jäger und sprach : "Bring'
das Kind hinaus in den Wald, ich will's nicht mehr
vor meinen Augen sehen.   Du sollst es töten und
mir Lunge und Leber zum Wahrzeichen mitbringen."
Der Jäger gehorchte und führte es hinaus, und als
25 er den Hirschfänger gezogen hatte und Sneewittchens unschuldiges Herz durchbohren wollte, fieng
es an zu weinen und sprach : "Ach, lieber Jäger, lass'
mir mein Leben, ich will in den Wald laufen und
nimmermehr wieder heimkommen."   Und weil es so
30 schön war, hatte der Jäger Mitleiden und sprach :

"So lauf' hin, du armes Kind." "Die wilden Tiere
werden dich bald gefressen haben," dachte er, und
doch war's ihm, als wäre ein Stein von seinem Herzen
gewälzt, weil er es nicht zu töten brauchte. Und als
gerade ein junger Frischling daher gesprungen kam, 5
stach er ihn ab, nahm Lunge und Leber heraus und
brachte sie als Wahrzeichen der Königin mit. Der
Koch musste sie in Salz kochen, und das boshafte
Weib asz sie auf und meinte, sie hätte Sneewittchens
Lunge und Leber gegessen. 10

Nun war das arme Kind in dem groszen Wald mutterseligallein, und ward ihm so angst, dass es alle
Blätter an den Bäumen ansah und nicht wusste, wie
es sich helfen sollte. Da fieng es an zu laufen und
lief über die spitzen Steine und durch die Dornen, 15
und die wilden Tiere sprangen an ihm vorbei, aber
sie taten ihm nichts. Es lief so lange nur die Füsze
noch fort konnten, bis es bald Abend werden wollte,
da sah es ein kleines Häuschen und gieng hinein, sich
zu ruhen. In dem Häuschen war alles klein, aber 20
so zierlich und reinlich, dass es nicht zu sagen ist.
Da stand ein weissgedecktes Tischlein mit sieben
kleinen Tellern, jedes Tellerlein mit seinem Löffelein,
ferner sieben Messerlein und Gäblein und sieben
Becherlein. An der Wand waren sieben Bettlein 25
neben einander aufgestellt und schneeweisse Laken
darüber gedeckt. Sneewittchen, weil es so hungrig
und durstig war, asz von jedem Tellerlein ein wenig
Gemüs und Brot, und trank aus jedem Becherlein
einen Tropfen Wein; denn es wollte nicht Einem 30
allein alles wegnehmen. Hernach, weil es so müde
war, legte es sich in ein Bettchen, aber keins passte:
das eine war zu lang, das andere zu kurz, bis endlich

das siebente recht war, und darin blieb es liegen, befahl sich Gott und schlief ein.

Als es ganz dunkel geworden war, kamen die Herren von dem Häuslein, das waren sieben Zwerge, 5 die in den Bergen nach Erz hackten und gruben. Sie zündeten ihre sieben Lichtlein an, und wie es nun hell im Häuslein ward, sahen sie, dass jemand darin gewesen war, denn es stand nicht alles so in der Ordnung, wie sie es verlassen hatten. Der erste 10 sprach : "Wer hat auf meinem Stühlchen gesessen?" Der zweite : "Wer hat von meinem Tellerchen gegessen?" Der dritte : "Wer hat von meinem Brötchen genommen?" Der vierte : "Wer hat von meinem Gemüschen gegessen?" Der fünfte: "Wer 15 hat mit meinem Gäbelchen gestochen?" Der sechste : "Wer hat mit meinem Messerchen geschnitten?" Der siebente : "Wer hat aus meinem Becherlein getrunken?" Dann sah sich der erste um und sah, dass auf seinem Bett eine kleine Dälle war, da sprach 20 er : "Wer hat in mein Bettchen getreten?" Die andern kamen gelaufen und riefen : "In meinem hat auch jemand gelegen." Der siebente aber, als er in sein Bett sah, erblickte Sneewittchen, das lag darin und schlief. Nun rief er die andern, die kamen her-25 beigelaufen und schrien vor Verwunderung, holten ihre sieben Lichtlein und beleuchteten Sneewittchen. "Ei, ei," riefen sie, "was ist das Kind schön!" und hatten so grosze Freude, dass sie es nicht aufweckten, sondern im Bettlein fortschlafen liessen. Der 30 siebente Zwerg aber schlief bei seinen Gesellen, bei jedem Eine Stunde, da war Eine Nacht herum.

Als es Morgen war, erwachte Sneewittchen, und wie es die sieben Zwerge sah, erschrak es. Sie waren

aber freundlich und fragten : "wie heisst du?" "Ich
heisse Sneewittchen," antwortete es. "Wie bist du
in unser Haus gekommen?" sprachen weiter die
Zwerge. Da erzählte es ihnen, dass seine Stiefmutter es hätte wollen umbringen lassen, der Jäger hätte 5
ihm aber das Leben geschenkt, und da wäre es gelaufen den ganzen Tag, bis es endlich ihr Häuslein
gefunden hätte. Die Zwerge sprachen : "Willst du
unsern Haushalt versehen, kochen, betten, waschen,
nähen und stricken, und willst du alles ordentlich 10
und reinlich halten, so kannst .du bei uns bleiben,
und es soll dir an nichts fehlen." "Ja," sagte Sneewittchen, "von Herzen gern," und blieb bei ihnen.
Es hielt ihnen das Haus in Ordnung : morgens
giengen sie in die Berge und suchten Erz und Gold, 15
abends kamen sie wieder, und da musste das Essen
bereit sein. Den Tag über war das Mädchen allein,
da warnten es die guten Zwerglein und sprachen :
"Hüte dich vor deiner Stiefmutter, die wird bald
wissen, dass du hier bist ; lass' ja niemand herein." 20
Die Königin aber, nachdem sie Sneewittchens
Lunge und Leber glaubte gegessen zu haben, dachte
nicht anders als sie wäre wieder die erste und allerschönste, trat vor ihren Spiegel und sprach :

> "Spieglein, Spieglein an der Wand,   25
> Wer ist die schönste im ganzen Land?"

Da antwortete der Spiegel :

> "Frau Königin, ihr seid die schönste hier,
> Aber Sneewittchen über den Bergen
> Bei den sieben Zwergen   30
> Ist noch tausendmal schöner als ihr."

Da erschrak sie, denn sie wusste, dass der Spiegel
keine Unwahrheit sprach, und merkte, dass der Jäger
sie betrogen hatte und Sneewittchen noch am Leben
war. Und da sann und sann sie aufs neue, wie sie
5 es umbringen wollte ; denn so lange sie nicht die
schönste war im ganzen Land, liess ihr der Neid
keine Ruhe. Und als sie sich endlich etwas ausgedacht hatte, färbte sie sich das Gesicht und kleidete
sich wie eine alte Krämerin und war ganz unkennt-
10 lich. In dieser Gestalt gieng sie über die sieben
Berge zu den sieben Zwergen, klopfte an die Türe
und rief : "Schöne Ware feil ! feil !" Sneewittchen
guckte zum Fenster heraus und rief : "Guten Tag,
liebe Frau, was habt ihr zu verkaufen ?" "Gute
15 Ware, schöne Ware," antwortete sie, "Schnürriemen
von allen Farben," und holte einen hervor, der aus
bunter Seide geflochten war. "Die ehrliche Frau
kann ich hereinlassen," dachte Sneewittchen, riegelte
die Tür' auf und kaufte sich den hübschen Schnür-
20 riemen. "Kind," sprach die Alte, "wie du aussiehst ! komm', ich will dich einmal ordentlich
schnüren !" Sneewittchen hatte kein Arg, stellte
sich vor sie und liess sich mit dem neuen Schnürriemen schnüren : aber die Alte schnürte geschwind
25 und schnürte so fest, dass dem Sneewittchen der
Atem vergieng, und es für tot hinfiel. "Nun bist
du die schönste gewesen !" sprach sie und eilte
hinaus.

Nicht lange darauf, zur Abendzeit, kamen die
30 sieben Zwerge nach Hause, aber wie erschraken sie,
als sie ihr liebes Sneewittchen auf der Erde liegen
sahen ; und es regte und bewegte sich nicht, als wäre
es tot. Sie hoben es in die Höhe, und weil sie sahen,

dass es zu fest geschnürt war, schnitten sie den
Schnürriemen entzwei : da fieng es an ein wenig zu
atmen und ward nach und nach wieder lebendig.
Als die Zwerge hörten, was geschehen war, sprachen
sie : " Die alte Krämerfrau war niemand als die gott· 5
lose Königin : hüte dich und lass' keinen Menschen
herein, wenn wir nicht bei dir sind."
Das böse Weib aber, als es nach Hause gekommen
war, gieng vor den Spiegel und fragte :

"Spieglein, Spieglein an der Wand,   10
   Wer ist die schönste im ganzen Land ?"

Da antwortete er wie sonst :

"Frau Königin, ihr seid die schönste hier,
   Aber Sneewittchen über den Bergen
   Bei den sieben Zwergen   15
   Ist noch tausendmal schöner als ihr."

Als sie das hörte, lief ihr alles Blut zum Herzen, so
erschrak sie, denn sie sah wohl, dass Sneewitchen
wieder lebendig geworden war. "Jetzt," sprach sie,
"will ich etwas aussinnen, das dich zu Grunde richten 20
soll," und mit Hexenkünsten, die sie verstand, machte
sie einen giftigen Kamm. Dann verkleidete sie sich
und nahm die Gestalt eines andern alten Weibes an.
So gieng sie hin über die sieben Berge zu den sieben
Zwergen, klopfte an die Türe und rief : "Gute Ware 25
feil! feil!" Sneewittchen schaute heraus und
sprach : "Geh' nur weiter, ich darf niemand hereinlassen." "Das Ansehen wird dir doch erlaubt sein,"
sprach die Alte, zog den giftigen Kamm heraus
und hielt ihn in die Höhe. Da gefiel er dem Kinde 30
so gut, dass es sich betören liess und die Türe

öffnete. Als sie des Kaufs einig waren, sprach die
Alte : "Nun will ich. dich einmal ordentlich kämmen." Das arme Sneewittchen dachte an nichts und
liess die alte gewähren, aber kaum hatte sie den
5 Kamm in die Hare gesteckt, als das Gift darin
wirkte und das Mädchen ohne Besinnung niederfiel.
" Du Ausbund von Schönheit," sprach das boshafte
Weib, "jetzt ist's um dich geschehen," und gieng fort.
Zum Glück aber war es bald Abend, wo die sieben
10 Zwerglein nach Hause kamen. Als sie Sneewittchen
wie tot auf der Erde liegen sahen, hatten sie gleich
die Stiefmutter in Verdacht, suchten nach und fanden
den giftigen Kamm, und kaum hatten sie ihn heraus-
gezogen, so kam Sneewitchen wieder zu sich und
15 erzählte, was vorgegangen war. Da warnten sie es
noch einmal, auf seiner Hut zu sein und niemand
die Türe zu öffnen.

Die Königin stellte sich daheim vor den Spiegel
und sprach :

20   "Spieglein, Spieglein an der Wand,
          Wer ist die schönste im ganzen Land ? "

Da antwortete er wie vorher :

          " Frau Königin, ihr seid die schönste hier,
          Aber Sneewittchen über den Bergen
25   Bei den sieben Zwergen
          Ist noch tausendmal schöner als ihr."

Als sie den Spiegel so reden hörte, zitterte und bebte
sie vor Zorn. "Sneewittchen soll sterben," rief sie,
"und wenn es mein eigenes Leben kostet." Darauf
30 gieng sie in eine ganz verborgene einsame Kammer,
wo niemand hinkam, und machte da einen giftigen
giftigen Apfel. Äusserlich sah er schön aus, weiss

mit roten Backen, dass jeder, der ihn erblickte, Lust
danach bekam, aber wer ein Stückchen davon asz,
der musste sterben. Als der Apfel fertig war, färbte
sie sich das Gesicht und verkleidete sich in eine
Bauersfrau, und so gieng sie über die sieben Berge 5
zu den sieben Zwergen. Sie klopfte an, Sneewittchen streckte den Kopf zum Fenster heraus und
sprach : " Ich darf keinen Menschen einlassen, die
sieben Zwerge haben mir's verboten." " Mir auch
recht," antwortete die Bäuerin, " meine Äpfel will 10
ich schon loswerden. Da, einen will ich dir
schenken." "Nein," sprach Sneewittchen, "ich
darf's nicht annehmen." "Fürchtest du dich vor
Gift?" sprach die Alte, "siehst du, da schneide ich
den Apfel in zwei Teile ; den roten Backen iss du, 15
den weissen will ich essen." Der Apfel war aber so
künstlich gemacht, dass der rote Backen allein vergiftet war. Sneewittchen lusterte den schönen
Apfel an, und als es sah, dass die Bäuerin davon
asz, so konnte es nicht länger widerstehen, streckte 20
die Hand hinaus und nahm die giftige Hälfte.
Kaum aber hatte es einen Bissen davon im Mund,
so fiel es tot zur Erde nieder. Da betrachtete es die
Königin mit grausigen Blicken und lachte überlaut
und sprach : "Weiss wie Schnee, rot wie Blut, 25
schwarz wie Ebenholz ! Diesmal können dich die
Zwerge nicht wieder erwecken." Und als sie daheim den Spiegel fragte :

"Spieglein, Spieglein an der Wand,
 Wer ist die schönste im ganzen Land?" 30

so antwortete er endlich :

"Frau Königin, ihr seid die schönste im Land."

Da hatte ihr neidisches Herz Ruhe, so gut ein böses und neidisches Herz Ruhe haben kann.

Die Zwerglein, wie sie abends nach Hause kamen, fanden Sneewittchen auf der Erde liegen, und gieng 5 kein Atem mehr aus seinem Mund, und es war tot. Sie hoben es auf, suchten, ob sie was Giftiges fänden, schnürten es auf, kämmten ihm die Hare, wuschen es mit Wasser und Wein, aber es half alles nichts: das liebe Kind war tot und blieb tot. Sie legten es 10 auf eine Bahre und setzten sich alle siebene daran und beweinten es, und weinten drei Tage lang. Da wollten sie es begraben, aber es sah noch zu frisch aus, wie ein lebender Mensch, und hatte noch seine schönen roten Backen. Sie sprachen: "Das können 15 wir nicht in die schwarze Erde versenken," und liessen einen Sarg von Glas machen, dass man von allen Seiten hindurchsehen konnte, legten Sneewittchen hinein und schrieben mit goldenen Buchstaben seinen Namen darauf, und dass es eine Königstochter 20 wäre. Dann setzten sie den Sarg hinaus auf den Berg, und einer von ihnen blieb immer dabei und bewachte ihn. Und die Tiere kamen auch und beweinten Sneewittchen, erst eine Eule, dann ein Rabe, zuletzt ein Täubchen.

25 Nun lag Sneewittchen lange lange Zeit in dem Sarg und verweste nicht, sondern sah aus als wenn es schliefe, denn es war noch so weiss als Schnee, so rot als Blut und so schwarzharig wie Ebenholz. Es geschah aber, dass ein Königssohn in den Wald ge- 30 riet und zu dem Zwergenhaus kam, da zu übernachten. Er sah auf dem Berg den Sarg und das schöne Sneewittchen darin, und las, was mit goldenen Buchstaben darauf geschrieben war. Da sprach er zu den

Zwergen : "Lasst mir den Sarg, ich will euch geben,
was ihr dafür haben wollt." Aber die Zwerge antworteten : "Wir geben ihn nicht um alles Gold in
der Welt." Da sprach er: "So schenkt mir ihn, denn
ich kann nicht leben ohne Sneewittchen zu sehen, 5
ich will es in Ehren halten wie mein Liebstes." Wie
er so sprach, empfanden die guten Zwerglein Mitleiden mit ihm und gaben ihm den Sarg. Der Königssohn liess ihn nun von seinen Dienern auf den
Schultern forttragen. Da geschah es, dass sie über 10
einen Strauch stolperten, und von dem Schüttern fuhr
der giftige Apfelgrütz, den Sneewittchen abgebissen
hatte, aus dem Hals. Und nicht lange, so öffnete es
die Augen, hob den Deckel vom Sarg in die Höhe,
richtete sich auf und war wieder lebendig. "Ach, wo 15
bin ich?" rief es. Der Königssohn sagte voll Freude :
"Du bist bei mir," und erzählte, was sich zugetragen
hatte, und sprach : "Ich habe dich lieber, als alles auf
der Welt : komm' mit mir in meines Vaters Schloss, du
sollst meine Gemahlin werden." Da war ihm Snee- 20
wittchen gut und gieng mit ihm, und ihre Hochzeit
ward mit groszer Pracht und Herrlichkeit angeordnet.

Zu dem Feste ward aber auch Sneewittchens gott-
lose Stiefmutter eingeladen. Wie sie sich nun mit
schönen Kleidern angetan hatte, trat sie vor den 25
Spiegel und sprach :

"Spieglein, Spieglein an der Wand,
  Wer ist die schönste im ganzen Land?"

Der Spiegel antwortete :

"Frau Königin, ihr seid die schönste hier, 30
  Aber die junge Königin ist tausendmal schöner
  als ihr."

Da stiess das böse Weib einen Fluch aus, und ward
ihr so angst, so angst, dass sie sich nicht zu lassen
wusste. Sie wollte zuerst gar nicht auf die Hochzeit
kommen: doch liess es ihr keine Ruhe, sie musste
5 fort und die junge Königin sehen. Und wie sie in
den königlichen Sal trat, erkannte sie Sneewittchen,
und vor Angst und Schrecken stand sie da und
konnte sich nicht regen. Aber es waren schon eiser-
ne Pantoffeln über Kohlenfeuer gestellt, die wurden
10 mit eisernen Zangen hereingetragen und vor sie hin-
gestellt. Da musste sie in die rotglühenden Schuhe
treten und musste darin tanzen, bis sie tot zur Erde
fiel.

VIII.

HANS IM GLÜCK.
(No. 33.)

Hans hatte sieben Jahre bei seinem Herrn gedient, da sprach er zu ihm: "Herr, meine Zeit ist
herum, nun wollte ich gerne wieder heim zu meiner
Mutter, gebt mir meinen Lohn." Der Herr antwortete: "Du hast mir treu und ehrlich gedient, wie der 5
Dienst war, so soll der Lohn sein," und gab ihm ein
Stück Gold, das so grosz als Hansens Kopf war.
Hans zog sein Tüchlein aus der Tasche, wickelte den
Klumpen hinein, setzte ihn auf die Schulter und
machte sich auf den Weg nach Hause. Wie er so 10
dahingieng und immer ein Bein vor das andere setzte,
kam ihm ein Reiter in die Augen, der frisch und
fröhlich auf einem muntern Pferde vorbeitrabte,
"Ach," sprach Hans ganz laut, "was ist das Reiten
ein schönes Ding! da sitzt einer wie auf einem Stuhl, 15
stöszt sich an keinen Stein, spart die Schuh' und
kommt fort, er weiss nicht wie." Der Reiter, der das
gehört hatte, hielt an und rief: "Ei Hans, warum
läufst du auch zu Fusz?" "Ich musz ja wohl, da
habe ich einen Klumpen heimzutragen, es ist zwar 20
Gold, aber ich kann den Kopf dabei nicht gerad'
halten: auch drückt mir's auf die Schulter." "Weisst
du was," sagte der Reiter, "wir wollen tauschen: ich

gebe dir mein Pferd, und du gibst mir deinen Klumpen." "Von Herzen gern," sprach Hans, "aber ich
sage euch, ihr müsst euch damit schleppen." Der
Reiter stieg ab, nahm das Gold und half dem Hans
5 hinauf, gab ihm die Zügel fest in die Hände und
sprach : "Wenn's nun recht geschwind soll gehen,
so musst du mit der Zunge schnalzen und 'hopp
hopp' rufen."

Hans war seelenfroh, als er auf dem Pferde sasz
10 und so frank und frei dahinritt. .Über ein Weilchen
fiel's ihm ein, es sollte noch schneller gehen, und
fieng an mit der Zunge zu schnalzen und "hopp
hopp" zu rufen. Das Pferd setzte sich in starken
Trab, und ehe sich's Hans versah, war er abgewor-
15 fen, und lag in einem Graben, der die Äcker von der
Landstrasze trennte. Das Pferd wäre auch durch-
gegangen, wenn es nicht ein Bauer aufgehalten hätte,
der des Weges kam und eine Kuh vor sich her trieb.
Hans suchte seine Glieder zusammen und machte
20 sich wieder auf die Beine. Er war aber verdriesslich
und sprach zu dem Bauer : "Es ist ein schlechter
Spasz, das Reiten, zumal wenn man auf so eine
Mähre gerät wie diese, die stöszt und einen herab
wirft, dass man den Hals brechen kann, ich setze
25 mich nun und nimmermehr wieder auf. Da lob' ich
mir eure Kuh, da kann einer mit Gemächlichkeit
hinterhergehen und hat obendrein seine Milch, Butter und Käse jeden Tag gewiss. Was gäb' ich darum,
wenn ich so eine Kuh hätte!" "Nun," sprach der
30 Bauer, "geschieht euch so ein groszer Gefallen, so
will ich euch wohl die Kuh für das Pferd vertau
schen." Hans willigte mit tausend Freuden ein : der
Bauer schwang sich aufs Pferd und ritt eilig davon.

Hans trieb seine Kuh ruhig vor sich her und bedachte den glücklichen Handel. "Hab' ich nur ein
Stück Brot, und daran wird mir's doch nicht fehlen, so
kann ich, so oft mir's beliebt, Butter und Käse dazu
essen: hab' ich Durst, so melk' ich meine Kuh und 5
trinke Milch. Herz, was verlangst du mehr?" Als er
zu einem Wirtshaus kam, machte er Halt, asz in der
groszen Freude alles, was er bei sich hatte, sein Mit-
tag- und Abendbrot, rein auf und liess sich für seine
letzten par Heller ein halbes Glas Bier einschenken. 10
Dann trieb er seine Kuh weiter, immer nach dem
Dorfe seiner Mutter zu. Die Hitze war drückender,
je näher der Mittag kam, und Hans befand sich in
einer Heide, die wohl noch eine Stunde dauerte. Da
ward es ihm ganz heiss, so dass ihm vor Durst die 15
Zunge am Gaumen klebte. "Dem Ding ist zu helfen," dachte Hans, "jetzt will ich meine Kuh melken
und mich an der Milch laben." Er band sie an einen
dürren Baum und stellte, da er keinen Eimer hatte,
seine Ledermütze unter: aber so sehr er sich auch 20
bemühte, es kam kein Tropfen Milch zum Vorschein.
Und weil er sich ungeschickt dabei anstellte, so gab
ihm das ungeduldige Tier endlich mit Einem der
Hinterfüsze einen solchen Schlag vor den Kopf, dass
er zu Boden taumelte und eine Zeitlang sich gar 25
nicht besinnen konnte, wo er war. Glücklicherweise kam gerade ein Metzger des Weges, der auf
einem Schubkarren ein junges Schwein liegen hatte.
"Was sind das für Streiche!" rief er und half dem
guten Hans auf. Hans erzählte, was vorgefallen 30
war. Der Metzger reichte ihm seine Flasche und
sprach: "Da, trinkt einmal, und erholt euch. Die
Kuh will wohl keine Milch geben, das ist ein altes

Tier, das höchstens noch zum Ziehen taugt oder zum
Schlachten." " Ei, ei," sprach Hans, und strich sich
die Haare über den Kopf, "wer hätte das gedacht!
Es ist freilich gut, wenn man so ein Tier ins Haus
5 abschlachten kann, was gibt's für Fleisch! Aber ich
mache mir aus dem Kuhfleisch nicht viel, es ist mir
nicht saftig genug. Ja, wer so ein junges Schwein
hätte! Das schmeckt anders, dabei noch die Würste."
" Hört, Hans," sprach der Metzger, " euch zu Liebe
10 will ich tauschen und will euch das Schwein für die
Kuh lassen." " Gott lohn' euch eure Freundschaft,"
sprach Hans, und übergab ihm die Kuh und liess sich
das Schweinchen vom Karren losmachen und den
Strick, woran es gebunden war, in die Hand geben.
15 Hans zog weiter und überdachte, wie ihm doch
alles nach Wunsch gienge; begegnete ihm ja eine
Verdriesslichkeit, so würde sie doch gleich wieder
gut gemacht. Es gesellte sich danach ein Bursch zu
ihm, der trug eine schöne weisse Gans unter dem
20 Arm. Sie boten einander die Zeit, und Hans fieng
an von seinem Glück zu erzählen und wie er immer
so vorteilhaft getauscht hätte. Der Bursch sagte
ihm, dass er die Gans zu einem Kindertaufschmaus
brächte. "Hebt einmal," fuhr er fort und packte
25 sie bei den Flügeln, " wie schwer sie ist, die ist aber
auch acht Wochen lang genudelt worden. Wer in
den Braten beisst, muss sich das Fett von beiden
Seiten abwischen." " Ja," sprach Hans und wog sie
mit der einen Hand, " die hat ihr Gewicht, aber
30 mein Schwein ist auch keine Sau." Indessen sah
sich der Bursch nach allen Seiten ganz bedenklich
um, schüttelte auch wohl mit dem Kopf. " Hört,"
fieng er darauf an, " mit eurem Schweine mag's nicht

so ganz richtig sein. In dem Dorfe, durch das ich
gekommen bin, ist eben dem Schulzen Eins aus
dem Stall gestohlen worden ; ich fürchte, ich fürchte,
ihr habt's da in der Hand. Sie haben Leute ausge-
schickt, und es wäre ein schlimmer Handel, wenn sie 5
euch mit dem Schweine erwischten : das geringste
ist, dass ihr ins finstre Loch gesteckt werdet." Dem
guten Hans ward bang, "Ach," sprach er, "helft mir
aus der Not, ihr wisst hier herum bessern Bescheid,
nehmt mein Schwein da und lasst mir eure Gans." 10
"Ich muss schon etwas aufs Spiel setzen." antwortete
der Bursche, "aber ich will doch nicht schuld sein,
dass ihr ins Unglück geratet." Er nahm also das
Seil in die Hand und trieb das Schwein schnell auf
einem Seitenweg fort : der gute Hans aber gieng, 15
seiner Sorgen entledigt, mit der Gans unter dem
Arme der Heimat zu. "Wenn ich's recht überlege,"
sprach er mit sich selbst, "habe ich noch Vorteil bei
dem Tausch : erstlich den guten Braten, hernach die
Menge von Fett, die heaustränfeln wird, das gibt 20
Gänsefettbrot auf ein Vierteljahr : und endlich die
schönen weissen Federn, die 'lass' ich mir in mein
Kopfkissen stopfen und darauf will ich wohl unge-
wiegt einschlafen. Was wird meine Mutter eine
Freude haben !" 25
Als er durch das letzte Dorf gekommen war, stand
da ein Scherenschleifer mit seinem Karren : das Rad
schnurrte und er sang dazu :

"Ich schleife die Schere und drehe geschwind,
Und hänge mein Mäntelchen nach dem Wind." 30

Hans blieb stehen und sah ihm zu : endlich redete
er ihn an und sprach : "Euch geht's wohl, weil ihr

so lustig bei eurem Schleifen seid." "Ja," antwortete der Scherenschleifer, "das Handwerk hat
einen güldenen Boden. Ein rechter Schleifer ist ein
Mann, der, so oft er in die Tasche greift, auch Geld
5 darin findet. Aber wo habt ihr die schöne Gans gekauft?" "Die hab' ich nicht gekauft, sondern für
mein Schwein eingetauscht." "Und das Schwein?"
"Das hab' ich für eine Kuh gekriegt." "Und die
Kuh?" "Die hab' ich für ein Pferd bekommen."
10 "Und das Pferd?" "Dafür hab' ich einen Klumpen
Gold, so grosz als mein Kopf, gegeben." "Und das
Gold?" "Ei, das war mein Lohn für sieben Jahre
Dienst." "Ihr habt euch jederzeit zu helfen ge-
wusst," sprach der Schleifer, "könnt ihr's nun dahin
15 bringen, dass ihr das Geld in der Tasche springen
hört, wenn ihr aufsteht, so habt ihr euer Glück gemacht." "Wie soll ich das anfangen?" sprach
Hans. "Ihr müsst ein Schleifer werden, wie ich;
dazu gehört eigentlich nichts, als ein Wetzstein, das
20 andere findet sich schon von selbst. Da hab' ich
einen, der ist zwar ein wenig schadhaft, dafür sollt
ihr mir aber auch weiter nichts als eure Gans geben;
wollt ihr das?" "Wie könnt ihr noch fragen?"
antwortete Hans, "ich werde ja zum glücklichsten
25 Menschen auf Erden: habe ich Geld, so oft ich in
die Tasche greife, was brauche ich da länger zu
sorgen?" reichte ihm die Gans hin und nahm den
Wetzstein in Empfang. "Nun," sprach der Schleifer
und hob einen gewöhnlichen schweren Feldstein,
30 der neben ihm lag, auf, "da habt ihr noch einen
tüchtigen Stein dazu, auf dem sich's gut schlagen
lässt und ihr eure alten Nägel gerade klopfen könnt.
Nehmt hin und hebt ihn ordentlich auf."

Hans lud den Stein auf und gieng mit vergnügtem Herzen weiter : seine Augen leuchteten vor Freude : "Ich muss in einer Glückshaut geboren sein," rief er aus, "alles was ich wünsche, trifft mir ein, wie einem Sonntagskind." Indessen, weil er seit Tages- 5 anbruch auf den Beinen gewesen war, begann er müde zu werden : auch plagte ihn der Hunger, da er allen Vorrat auf einmal in der Freude über die erhandelte Kuh aufgezehrt hatte. Er konnte endlich nur mit Mühe weiter gehen und musste jeden 10 Augenblick Halt machen ; dabei drückten ihn die Steine ganz erbärmlich. Da konnte er sich des Gedankens nicht erwehren, wie gut es wäre, wenn er sie gerade jetzt nicht zu tragen brauchte. Wie eine Schnecke kam er zu einem Feldbrunnen ge- 15 schlichen, wollte da ruhen und sich mit einem frischen Trunk laben ; damit er aber die Steine im Niedersitzen nicht beschädigte, legte er sie bedächtig neben sich auf den Rand des Brunnens. Darauf setzte er sich nieder und wollte sich zum Trinken 20 bücken, da versah er's, stiess ein klein wenig an, und beide Steine plumpten hinab. Hans, als er sie mit seinen Augen in die Tiefe hatte versinken sehen, sprang vor Freuden auf, kniete dann nieder und dankte Gott mit Tränen in den Augen, dass er ihm 25 auch diese Gnade noch erwiesen und ihn auf eine so gute Art und ohne dass er sich einen Vorwurf zu machen brauchte, von den schweren Steinen befreit hätte : das einzige wäre ihm nur noch hinderlich gewesen. "So glücklich wie ich," rief er aus, "gibt 30 es keinen Menschen unter der Sonne." Mit leichtem Herzen und frei von aller Last sprang er nun fort, bis er daheim bei seiner Mutter war.

NOTES.

ASCHENPUTTEL.

P. 1, l. 1. Einem reichen Manne, etc., 'A rich man's wife fell ill;' the dat. has the force of the gen.—**dem** is here demonstr., not rel., as shown by the verb being in the second place, not at the end. (See App. I., § 5.) This use is very frequent in the colloquial style of these **Märchen.**

l. 2. **herankam.** Verb last, because **dass** is a subord. conj., introducing a dep. sent. Obs. the use of the prefix **her** to indicate *motion towards* the subj. of the verb (so in **herabblicken** below).

l. 3. **einziges,** the only one she had. See Gloss. under **einzig** and **einzeln.—zu sich ans Bett,** 'to her bedside.'—**zu** indicates the motion to the *pers.*, **an** to the *thing.*

l. 4. **so wird dir,** etc., 'and God will, etc.;' **so** here indicates consequence, but it is coörd., not subord. conj., as shown by the position of the verb in the *second* place. (See App. I., § 5.) It very often introduces a princ. sent., when a conditional or other subord. sent. precedes, and must then generally remain untranslated. (App. I., § 10 (a), note.)—**der liebe Gott,** the dear God, God who is good. A favorite way of speaking of the deity in German.

l. 6. **auf dich,** acc., motion to (so **auf das Grab,** below).—**um dich,** 'about you,' 'near you.'

l. 8. **jeden Tag,** acc. of time.—**der Mutter,** 'of her mother.' The def. art. often replaces the poss. adj. when there can be no doubt as to the possessor.

l. 12. **nahm sich,** 'took to himself.'—**sich,** dat.

l. 14. **mit,** 'along with her.'

l. 15. **die schön,** etc. Here, of course, **die** is rel. pron., the verb being last, as the sent. is subord. (App. I., § 12.)

P. 1, l. 16. gieng . . . an, 'began, commenced.'

l. 18. bei uns, 'with us,' in our presence or company.

l. 19. wer Brot essen will, 'she who would eat bread ;' **wer** is here compound rel., including both rel. and antec. ; it throws the verb to the end, like a simple rel. ; the subj. of **muss** at the beginning of the next sent. is the antec. **der** (or rather, in this case, **die**) contained in **wer.—hinaus mit,** 'out with,' elliptical use of the adv., as in Eng., similar to an imperative.

l. 20. Sie nahmen ihm, etc. ; **ihm** is neut., referring to **Stiefkind** ; transl. 'her,' as throughout the Tale, where it relates to the neut. proper name.

P. 2, l. 4. taten ihm—an, 'inflicted every imaginable annoyance on her.'

l. 5. schütteten ihm, etc., 'for her, to spite her ;' **ihm** is here dat. of *disadvantage.*

l. 8. kam es in kein Bett, 'she never got to bed, had no bed to go to ;' in with acc., motion *to.*

l. 9. sondern musste ; sondern corrects the statement in a previous neg. sent. (See Gloss.)—**neben den Herd in die Asche.** Both preps. with acc. after **legen,** implying direction *towards.*

l. 12. in die Messe ziehen, 'go to the fair ;' **ziehen** is here neut. verb of motion, and as such conjugated with **sein.**

l. 15, sagte die eine. The verb here precedes the subj., because the first part of the quotation forms the *first idea* in the clause, the verb thus forming the *second idea,* as is the rule in a princ. sent. (See App. I., § 10 (b).)

l. 17. euch . . . an den Hut, 'against your hat ;' the dat. of the pers. pron., used in conjunction with the def. art., replaces the poss. adj. with parts of the person, dress, etc. Cinderella adresses her father in the second pers. pl., instead of by the more familiar **du,** used by children to their parents. See Gloss., **du.**

l. 18. das brecht. The imper. generally stands at the beginning of the sent., if in the second pers. (App. I., § 9.) Omit **das** in transl.

l. 19. Er kaufte nun, 'so he bought.'

l. 21. streifte ihn, 'brushed against him.' The verb begins the princ. sent., because the subord. sent. (**als—ritt**) precedes. (App. I., § 10 (a).)

l. 27. pflanzte . . . darauf, 'on it, thereon :' **da** in **darauf** relates to **Grab ;** so **darunter,** below (l. 31), refers to **Baum.**

P. 2, l. 30. gieng, etc. The impf. here indicates *repeated* action ; **alle Tage=jeden .Tag.** (Comp. Fr. *tous les jours.*)

l. 33. **was es sich nur wünschte,** 'whatever she wished (for herself).'

P. 3, l. 2. dauern sollte, 'was to last ;' **sollen** is often to be rendered in this way ; so : **erscheinen sollten** (l. 6), 'were to be present.'

l. 6. **dabei,** 'at it' (the feast), 'there ;' **erscheinen,** 'make their appearance,' 'be present.'—**waren guter Dinge,** 'were in a good humour, were rejoiced ;' adv. gen. of manner.

l. 9. **auf des Königs Schloss. auf** is the proper prep. with **Schloss,** as a castle or palace is generally in an elevated situation.

l. 10. **weil es auch gern . . . mitgegangen wäre,** 'because she too would like to have gone.' See Gloss., **gern.**

l. 12. **sie möchte—erlauben,** 'to allow her to (do so).' **es** re-refers to **zum Tanz gehen,** in previous sent.

l. 15. **Als es—anhielt,** 'but when she kept on begging (to go).' See Gloss., **anhalten.**

l. 17. **eine Schüssel Linsen. Linsen,** the thing measured, is, according to rule, in *apposition with* **Schüssel,** the word expressing the measure ; not in the gen., or with **von.**

l. 18. **wenn du, etc.; wenn** here='if ;' the sent. containing the consequence begins with **so,** as often. See App. I., § 10 (a), note. **So** is not to be trans. here.

l. 21. **ihr zahmen,** the adj. has the weak term. after pers. prons. in the pl.

l. 23. **helft mir lesen,** 'help me to pick' (not *read*).

l. 26. **zum Küchenfenster,** '*at* the kitchen-window.'

l. 28. **schwirrten und schwärmten . . . herein,** 'came fluttering and swarming in ;' **schwirren** is an imitative word, descriptive of the 'whirr' of their wings.

l. 30. **nickten mit dem Köpfchen,** 'nodded their dear little heads.' So we say : **mit dem Schwanze wedeln,** 'to wag the tail.'

P. 4, l. 1. kaum—herum, 'hardly had an hour passed. Almost before the hour was over.' Here again the second sent. opens with **so,** which may in this case be rendered by 'when.'

l. 4. **es dürfte, etc.** The conj. **dass** being omitted, the verb has the same position as in a princ. sent. (*i.e., second*), but is in the subj. mood, to indicate the subord. character of the sent. (App. I., § 17.)

P. 4, l. **6. du wirst nur,** etc., 'you will only be laughed at,' pres. for fut., a frequent usage.

l. **10. Das kann es ja,** etc., 'she can surely (ja) never do that.'

l. **11. zwei Schüsseln Linsen;** the noun of measure takes the noun whose measure is expressed in *apposition ;* but being fem., takes the sign of the pl.

l. **26. waren sie schon fertig ;** schon is redundant, the idea of priority being already expressed by eh', and may be left untranslated.

l. **30. es hilft dir alles nichts,** 'all this will do you no good.'

l. **31. wir—schämen,** 'we should be forced (have) to be ashamed of you,' 'you would put us to shame.'

P. 5, l. **3. niemand mehr,** etc., 'no body was left at home.'

l. **4. unter den;** the *motion* to implied in **zu** is continued in **unter;** hence acc.

l. **6. rüttel' dich,** etc., 'shake and quake.'

l. **8. ein golden und silbern Kleid,** 'a dress of gold and silver,' not 'a gold and a silver dress,' which would require the repetition of the art. Obs. also the omission of the term. of the adj. The strong term.—**es** may always be omitted in the nom. and acc. neut.

l. **9. mit—Pantoffeln,** 'slippers embroidered with silk and silver ;' the participle, which in Eng., when accompanied by enlargements, generally follows the subst., must precede it in German, as : 'the house standing on the hill,' **das auf dem Hügel stehende Haus.**

l. **10. Kleid und Pantoffeln;** obs. the omission of the art.

l. **15. dachten sie ;** the obj. (an A.) coming first, the subj. is thrown after the verb, which is thus in the *second* place. (App. I., § 5.)

l. **16. es läge;** here again, that being omitted, the constr. is that of a princ. sent. (verb second), but with the *subj.* mood. (App. I., § 17.)

l. **17. es bei der Hand,** 'her by the hand ;' **ihm die Hand.**—(l. 19.) 'her hand,' dat. of pers. pron. and def. art. for poss. adj.   See above, note to p. 2, l. 17.

l. **18. Er wollte auch mit—Niemand,** 'nor would he dance with any one else,' or, 'he would not dance with anybody else either ;' 'nor' or 'not—either' is frequently replaced in Germ. by **auch** and a neg., lit. : 'also not,' etc.

l. **20. es aufzufordern,** 'to ask her to dance.'—**sprach er;** the subord. sent. **(wenn—kam)** preceding, throws the subj. after the verb.

(See App. I., § 10 (a).)—**das ist,** 'this is;' the neut. demonstr. pron. used as indef. subj. before the verb, like **es.**

P. 5, l. 22. bis es Abend war; bis is here conj.; as such frequently has **dass** after it.—**es** is impers.—**nach Hause**='home' (motion to; **zu Hause**='at home'); **Haus** takes the same preps. as prop. names of places.

l. 23. **ich gehe mit,** etc., 'I shall go,' etc.; pres. for fut., frequent use.

l. 24. **er wollte sehen ;** 'he desired to see' (different from 'would see').

l. 25. **wem—angehörte.** A *dep.* question, hence with constr. of a dep. sent. (verb last).

l. 28. **wäre . . . gesprungen.** Obs. the constr. with **dass** omitted. Also the use of **sein** with **springen,** as neut. verb of motion.

l. 29. **sollte es . . . sein?** 'could it be?'

l. 31. **damit ;** here subord. conj.

P. 6, l. 1. lag ; verb before subj. on account of dep. sent. (**als—kamen**) preceding.

l. 3. **im Schornstein,** 'in the chimney-place, on the hearth.'—**denn ;** cöord., not subord., conj. ; hence the verb (**war**) is second.

l. 9. **in die Küche ;** the *motion to* extends to the kitchen as well as the ashes, though we would say in Eng.: 'by the ashes in the kitchen.'

l. 10. **am andern Tag,** 'the next day.' 'The other day' = **neulich.**—**von neuem anhub,** 'began anew, afresh.'

l. 11. **wieder fort waren,** 'were gone again' (supply **gegangen**).

l. 16. **ein noch—Kleid,** 'a dress, much more magnificent still than,' etc.

l. 20. **gleich,** 'at once.'

l. 21. **nur allein,** 'only,' 'exclusively ;' = **ganz allein,** below.

l. 23. **wollte es fort (gehen) ; wollen** here='wish, want,' as below : **wollte sehen.**

l. 29. **wo es hingekommen war,** 'where she had gone to,' 'what had become of her ;' dep. question, hence verb last.

l. 32. **ist mir entwischt,** 'has escaped me.' Verbs comp. with **ent**—gov. dat.—**ich glaube, es ist,** etc. Omission of **dass,** as in previous examples ; the principal verb, however, being in the present tense, the verb is indic., not subj.

P. 7, l. 2. liess . . . holen, 'sent for,' obj. of **lassen** understood, those who were to fetch, etc. ; **sich** is here what is called the ethical dat., and is not to be trans. 'The dat. of the pers. pron. . . . is sometimes used, to denote in a familiar manner an interest or participation of feeling on the part of the person speaking or spoken to.' (AUE, Larger Grammar, § 358.) This is also a common use of the dat. in Greek and Latin.

l. 5. **wie sonst auch,** 'just as usual,' lit. 'as on other occasions also.'

l. 15. **so prächtig—hatte,** 'more splendid and brilliant than any,' etc., lit. 'so splendid as she had yet had none.'

l. 19. **vor Verwunderung,** 'for astonishment '—**vor** here indicates *cause.*

l. 21. **einer,** 'anybody' (= **jemand**), here used as subst. (pron.), hence with strong term. —**er.**

l. 27. **hatte . . . bestreichen lassen,** 'had ordered to be besmeared (or painted), etc. ;' the inf. **lassen** here takes the place of the past part., as with all aux. verbs of mood in the comp. tenses, when a governed inf. precedes.

l. 28. **als es hinabsprang,** 'as she was running down.'—**war . . . hängen geblieben,** 'had stuck fast' (lit. 'remained hanging').

l. 30. **hob ihn auf,** i.e., the slipper, **Pantoffel** being masc.

P. 8, l. 6. konnte—hinein kommen, 'couldn't get her great toe in ' (lit. 'couldn't get in with,' etc.).

l. 9. **wann = wenn ; wann** is generally interrog. adv. — **so brauchst,** etc., **so** is simply redundant conj., not to be trans.

l. 14. **mussten vorbei (gehen).**

l. 15. **da saszen ; da** is redundant, not to be trans.

l. 18. **Schuck,** Low-Germ. for **Schuh.**   ᾽

l. 24. **das wäre,** etc., 'that was not the right one ;' conj. **dass** omitted ; the neut. pron. **das** before the verb, referring to a fem. subj. See Gloss., **das** and **es.**

l. 25. **sollte . . . anziehen,** 'was to put on ' (command).—**diese,** 'the latter.' (**die andere Schwester**).

l. 26. **kam—Schuh,** 'succeeded in getting her toes into the shoe ' (lit. 'got successfully into, etc., with her toes ').

P. 9, l. 10. und an den weissen—heraufgestiegen war, 'had risen up on her white stockings, making quite a red stain,' lit. 'risen up red on her,' etc.

P. 9, l. 13. das ist auch nicht die rechte, 'that's not the right one either.'

l. 16. **ein kleines verbuttetes A.,** 'a little dwarf of a Cinderella.'

l. 20. **darf—lassen,** 'dare not show herself,' lit. 'let herself be seen,' or 'let (anyone) see her.'

l. 21. **Er wollte—sehen,** 'he however insisted on seeing her,' lit. 'would see her by all means.'

l. 23. **sich . . . Hände, etc.,** '*her* hands, etc.' See note to p. 2, l. 17, above.—**erst,** i.e., before making her appearance.

l. 28. **und nur ein wenig—angegossen.** 'And only a slight pressure was needed, when she stood up in it (the slipper), as though it had been moulded (or cast) on her (foot).'—**so stand, etc.,** again the redundant **so** ; render as above, p. 8, l. 9, note.

l. 29. **als wär, etc.** The conj. **ob** being omitted, the verb comes immediately after **als.**

l. 30. **da sah er,** 'then he saw'—**da** is redundant, and may be left untransl.—**dass es die war, die, etc.** ; the first **die** is demonstr. ('the same'), the second rel.

P. 10, l. 1. erschraken, 'were thunderstruck ;' neut. verb.

l. 8. **die rechte Braut die, etc.** The second **die** is demonstr. and redundant ; omit in transl.

l. 9. **kamen sie . . . herabgeflogen,** 'they came flying down' ; **kommen** takes the verb specifying the motion in the past part., not in the pres. part., as in Eng.

l. 12. **blieben da sitzen ; bleiben** is followed by the inf., instead of the pres. part. as in Eng.

l. 13. **sollte gehalten werden.** This being a subord. sent. (introd. by **als**), we should expect the verb (**sollte**) last ; with aux. verbs of mood, however, the verb may precede the part. and inf. ; and *must* precede both infinitives in the past compound tenses ; as : **er sagte mir, dass er es habe tun müssen** (not : **tun müssen habe**), 'he told me that he had been obliged to do it.' (See App. I., § 15.)

l. 15. **wollten sich einschmeicheln,** 'tried to curry favor,' lit. 'to insinuate themselves into favor by flattery' ; **wollen** here expresses the desire or attempt.

l. 16. **die Brautleute,** 'the bridal pair,' 'bride and groom' (no sing.).

l. 17. **zur rechten, zur linken,** supply **Seite** or **Hand.**

P. 10, l. 18. einer jeden, etc., 'picked out one of the eyes of each ;' **einer jeden** is dat. with **das Auge,** instead of gen. (Comp. the use of the dat. pers. pron. and def. art. for the poss. adj., above, p. 2, l. 17, and note.)

l. 22. **Und waren sie,** etc.; **und** seldom comes after a period, except in colloquial usage, in which it may, as in the present instance, throw the subj. after the verb ; usually, a copulative conj. does not count as a member of a sent.

l. 23. **auf ihr Lebtag,** 'for life ;' **auf** with acc. in reference to a future period of time.

—　　　—

ROTKÄPPCHEN.

P. 11, l. 1. einmál, 'once upon a time ;' l. 4. below, **eínmal,** 'on one occasion.'—**Dirne,** 'maid ;' generally used of a servant-maid, or disrespectfully, but not so here.—**die hatte,** etc., 'of whom every-one was fond, whom everybody loved ;' **die** is demonstr., hence the verb precedes its subj. **jedermann.**

l. 2. **am allerliebsten,** etc., 'but her grandmother was fonder of her than anyone else' (lit. 'fondest of all') ; supply **hatte sie.**—**lieb haben**='to love.' See Gloss.

l. 3. **was alles,** 'what ever,' 'what to give her at all ;' i.e., she could never give her enough.

l. 5. **Käppchen von,** etc., **von** here indicates the *material.*

l. 6. **so wohl stand,** 'was so becoming.'

l. 7. **hiess es nur,** etc., 'she was always called, people never called her anything but Little Red Ridinghood (Little Redcap).'

l. 9. **Stück Kuchen,** etc.; these words of measure have the word measured usually in apposition, and do not change in the pl., exc. fems. in —e, as : **zwei Stück Kuchen,** but **drei Flaschen Wein.**

l. 10. **der Groszmutter,** dat. of advantage.

l. 11. **sei—artig,** 'but behave nicely and properly.'

l. 12. **guck'—herum,** 'don't begin peeping around into all the cor-ners at once when (as soon as) you get into the room.'

l. 13. **guten Morgen,** acc., gov. by **ich wünsche** understood.

P. 11, l. 15. sonst fällst du, 'or else you will fall;' pres. for fut.

l. 17. Ich will schon, etc., '1 shall be sure to, will not fail to.'—
gut, adv., 'well.'

l. 18. gab—darauf, 'gave her mother her hand on it,' as a pledge.

l. 19. draussen in Wald, 'out in the forest.'—**eine halbe
Stunde,** 'half an hour's walk.—**Stunde** is the commonest measure of
distance in Germany, and means as far as one can walk on foot in an
hour.

l. 20. Wie nun, 'now when;' **wie=als** here, and indicates a *point*
of time (like Eng. 'as ').

l. 22. was das für, etc., 'what a wicked beast he was;' **was für**
often has other words dividing it; **das** is indef. pron. neut., though
referring to the masc. **Wolf.**

P. 12, l. 2. schönen Dank, 'thank you kindly. '

l. 3. Wo hinaus, 'whither away.'

l. 5. gestern haben wir gebacken, 'we had a baking yesterday ;'
the perf. in Germ. indicates an action that has taken place in a def.
period of time which is wholly past and but just elapsed (as yesterday,
etc.) ; in Eng. we do not so use it.—**da soll, etc.** ; da here indicates
consequence, 'and so.' **soll—tun,** ' is to have a treat.'

l. 8. noch eine, etc., 'a good quarter of an hour's walk further into the forest.'

l. 10. unten, 'below it (lower down).'

l. 11. das wirst du ja, etc., ja='no doubt, of course.'

l. 13. das ist, redundant pron.

l. 14. du musst—anfangen, 'you must go about it craftily.'

l. 15. damit, conj., 'so that ;' **erschnappst,** 'may snap up, swallow.' The prefix **er—**gives the force of 'succeed in snapping up.'

l. 17. sieh einmál, etc., 'just look at.'

l. 19. wie . . . so lieblich ; so is redundant.

l. 20. du gehst—hin, 'why, you just go straight ahead ;' **für dich
hin=vor dich hin.**

l. 21. und ist, etc. The subj. **es** is to be supplied as preceding
the verb **ist.—haussen,** dialectic, **=hier aussen,** ' out here.'

l. 22. schlug . . . auf, 'raised.'

l. 23. hin und her, etc., 'were skipping hither and thither (up and
down).'

l. 24. alles—stand, 'all was full of, etc.'

l. 25. wenn, 'what if.'

P. 12, l. 26. auch, 'too,' i.e., as well as the cake, etc.

l. 27. doch, 'still, anyway.'

l. 30. stände, subjunctive, after **meinen,** a verb expressing *opinion,* not certainty.

l. 32. geradeswegs, adv. gen. of manner, 'straightway.' [N. B., 'right away,' 'right off,' are bad English.]

P. 13, l. 1. das bringt, 'bringing,' or simply 'with.'—**mach' auf,** 'open (the door).'

l. 2. Drück' nur, 'just press.'

l. 5. geradezu an, 'straight up to.'

l. 12. Machte—Weg, 'set out on her way.'

l. 13. aufstand, 'was open,' or 'ajar.'—**wie es, etc.,** 'as soon as, etc.'

l. 15. wie ängstlich—Mut, 'how timid I feel to-day.'

l. 16. bin sonst, etc., 'I am usually (on other occasions) so fond of being at grandmamma's.'

l. 20. tief ins Gesicht, 'far down over her face.'—**wunderlich,** 'queer, strange' (**wunderbar** = 'wonderful').

l. 22. Dass ich dich, etc., 'the better to hear you with.'

l. 27. Maul, fressen; both used of beasts.

l. 29. tat einen Satz, 'took a leap, made a spring.'

l. 33. gieng eben vorbei, 'was just going past.' The impf. here denotes an action going on *at the same time* (concurrently) with another.

P. 14, l. 1. bei sich, 'to himself.'

l. 2. ob—fehlt, 'whether anything ails her.'

l. 3. wie er, etc., 'when he, etc.' See above, p. 13, l. 13, note.

l. 4. Finde ich, etc., 'have I found you.'

l. 6. wollte er—anlegen, 'he was going to take aim with his rifle,' lit. 'lay it against (his cheek).'

l. 7. könnte . . . gefressen haben, 'might have eaten.' **hätte fressen können** = 'could have eaten, would have been able to eat.' **können** here expresses *probability.*

l. 8. sie wäre, etc., 'she might still be saved.'

l. 11. wie er—hatte, 'when he had made a few cuts.' **par** is here spelt with a small letter as meaning 'a few,' not 'a pair.' See Gloss. —**da sah er; da** is redundant.

l. 14. was war's, etc., 'how dark it was;' **was** = **wie;** so is redundant.—**in dem Wolf seinem Leib,** 'in the wolf's stomach'; this use of the dat. with poss. adj., instead of the gen. without, is very common in colloquial usage. The dat. with def. art. (as below, l. 18) is different.

P. 14, l. 19. **wollte er fortspringen,** 'he tried to run away.'

l. 20. **sich tot fiel,** 'fell down dead,' lit. 'fell himself dead (killed himself by falling).'

l. 25. **erholte sich wieder,** 'recovered again.'—**aber dachte;** when **aber** is not at the beginning of a sent., it is usually after the verb.

l. 27. **vom Wege ab,** 'off from the road.'

l. 30. **Gebackenes,** 'cakes,' lit. 'something baked.'

l. 31. **ihm zugesprochen (habe),** 'had addressed her, spoken to her.' The aux. of tense is in the next sent. The aux. **sein** or **haben** may however always be omitted in a subord. sent. **zusprechen** sometimes = 'speak words of comfort to, console.' (See p. 46, l. 16.)

P. 15, l. 1. **habe ableiten wollen,** 'had *tried* to lead astray.' Obs. the aux. of tense preceding the two infinitives in a subord. sent., which is always the rule in the comp. tenses of aux. verbs of mood. (See App. I., § 15.) **wollen** here stands for **gewollt,** as, in these verbs, the inf. takes the place of the part., when accompanied by a governed verb in the infin.

l. 2. **hütete sich,** 'was careful, mindful, took good care (not to listen to him).'—**gieng—Wegs,** 'went straight on her way.' **fort** indicates continuance ; **seines Wegs,** adv. gen. of manner ; comp. **geradeswegs,** above, p. 12, l. 32. (Eng., 'straightways.')

l. 4. **aber—hätte,** 'but had looked so wicked about the eyes.'

l. 6. **er hätte—gefressen.** The verb is here not at the beginning, though the general rule requires this when the dep. sent. precedes the princ. ; the two sentences are here considered as separate, instead of being taken (as is usually the case) as one complex clause.

l. 8. **dass er nicht,** etc.; **dass** here expresses *consequence.* **herein kann,** supply **kommen.**

l. 10. **das Rotkäppchen.** The def. art. is often used colloquially with proper names (particularly Christian or 'given' names).

l. 12. **der Böse,** 'the wicked beast' (often used like the Eng. 'the Evil One'). **etlichemal,** 'several times, two or three times.'

l. 14. **wollte warten,** etc., 'meant to wait ;' so also below.

l. 17. **was—hatte,** 'what his intentions were,' lit. 'what he had in his mind ;' dep. question, with verb last.

P. **15**, l. **19**. **gestern hab' ich**, etc.; for this use of the perf. see note to p. **12**, l. **55**, above.

l. **20**. **trag'** . . . **in den Trog,** 'carry . . . to (and empty into) the trough.'

l. **21**. **trug,** supply **Wasser**.

l. **22**. **so lange bis,** 'until.'

l. **23**. **Geruch von,** 'smell from' or 'of.'—**dem Wolf in die Nase,** 'into the wolf's nose.' See note to p. **2**, l. **17**, above.

l. **25**. **machte—lang,** 'he stretched out his neck so far.'

l. **29**. **und tat,** etc. The cöord. conj. **und** usually has the subj. or some other member of the sent. between it and the verb. Supply **es**.

DORNRÖSCHEN.

(THE SLEEPING BEAUTY.)

P. **16**, l. **1**. **Vor Zeiten,** 'in days of yore.'—**war ein König,** etc. The verb is frequently in the sing. in Germ. with several subjects *following*. See note to p. **19**, l. **11**, below.

l. **2**. **wenn wir doch,** etc., 'if we only had a child;' **doch** is often used with the subj. to express a wish.

l. **3**. **kriegten—keins,** 'never got one.'

l. **8**. **das geschah,** 'came to pass,' redundant pron.

l. **10**. **vor Freude—wusste,** 'didn't know what to do (how to contain himself) for joy.'

l. **12**. **ladete,** usually **lud**.—**Verwandte, Bekannte,** as adjs. preceded by **seine** should properly end in **—en**.

l. **14**. **hold und gewogen wären,** 'might be kindly and well-disposed;' **gewogen** is adj. here, not part.

l. **16**. **essen sollten,** 'were to eat,' 'could eat;' not a common use of **sollen**.

l. **19**. **zu Ende,** 'at an end.'

l. **21**. **die andere,** 'the second.'

l. **22**. **und so,** 'and so (on)'—**was—ist,** 'that one can ever wish for in this world.' The sup. **zu wünschen** is used, as often, in a passive sense.

P. **17**, l. **1**. **ihre Sprüche eben getan hatten,** 'had just said their say.'

P. 17, l. 2. **Sie wollte—war,** 'she wanted to take her revenge for not having been invited,' lit. 'for this (**dafür**), that she had not been invited.' Observe this mode of rendering the Eng. participial subst. gov. by a prep.

l. 3. **ohne . . . zu grüszen,** 'without greeting ;' **ohne** gov. the supine or **dass** with the indic.; the latter always when a different person is spoken of in the second sent.

l. 4. **oder nur,** 'or even.'

l. 10. **die—hatte,** 'who still had her wish left (unpronounced).'

l. 11. **aufheben,** 'do away with, annul, reverse.'

l. 14. **fällt,** 'will fall,' pres. for fut.

l. 16. **gern . . . wollte,** 'was anxious to.'—**liess . . . ausgehen,** 'issued,' lit. 'caused to go forth.'

l. 18. **sollten—werden.** Aux. of mood preceding part. and inf. in dep. sent. (See App. I., § 15.)—**An dem Mädchen,** 'in the person of the maiden.'

l. 19. **sämtlich,** 'every one, all,' lit. 'collectively' (adv.).

l. 21. **dass es jedermann ; es** of course is obj., **jedermann** subj. —**lieb haben musste,** 'was constrained to love her, couldn't help loving her.'

l. 22. **an dem Tage, wo,** 'on the day when (on which).'

l. 25. **zurückblieb,** 'was left at home.'

l. 26. **allerorten (= aller Orten),** 'everywhere,' adv. gen. pl. of place—**wie es Lust hatte,** 'just as she had a mind to.'

l. 30. **úmdrehte,** 'turned (the key),' accent on sep. part.

l. 31. **sprang . . . auf,** 'flew open.'—**sasz da ;** the verb immediately following **und ;** see note to p. 15, l. 29, above ; or supply **es** before the verb.

l. 33. **du altes Mütterchen,** 'you funny (or dear) old woman ;' observe the force of the dimin.

P. 18, l. 1. **was machst du da ?** 'what are you doing there ?'

l. 3. **Was—Ding ?** 'what kind of a thing?'

l. 4. **herumspringt,** 'runs around.'

l. 5. **wollte spinnen,** 'tried to spin.' **Kaum,** 'no sooner.'

l. 6. **so gieng,** etc., 'when the magic spell was fulfilled.'

l. 7. **stach—Finger,** 'pricked her finger with it ;' **sich in den Finger = in ihren Finger.** See note to p. 2, l. 17, above.

l. 17. **auf dem Dache, an der Wand.** Observe the different preps. See Gloss. **auf, an.**

P. 18, l. 18. ja, das **Feuer**, 'even the fire,' 'the very fire.'

l. 20. weil—hatte, 'because he had made some blunder.'—in—wollte, 'was going to pull (the scullion's) hair,' lit. 'the scullion by the hair.'

l. 27. darüber hinaus, 'out beyond, above it.'

l. 29. Es gieng, 'was current;' es is redundant, representing the real subj. (Sage); so es war below, p. 19, l. 1.

P. 19, l. 2. als hätten sie, 'as though they had;' ob is omitted; hielten zusammen, 'stuck together.'

l. 3. blieben hängen, 'stuck fast (remained, were left, hanging).'

l. 5. eines—Todes, adv. gen. of manner.—Nach langen Jahren, 'many years afterwards.'

l. 7. hörte, wie, etc., 'heard an old man telling.'

l. 10. schon—Jahren, 'for the last hundred years.'

l. 11. schliefe, 'was (said to be) sleeping;' indirect narration, hence subj.; the verb is often sing. with several subjects, when they all follow, but pl. if they *precede.*

l. 13. schon viele, etc., 'many before him,' lit. 'already.'

l. 17. ich will hinaus (gehen).

l. 19. hörte—Worte, 'wouldn't listen to his words;' seine is used here, though not referring to the subj. of the sent., instead of dessen, as there can be no doubt as to the person meant. See Gloss. under sein.

l. 22. der Hecke, dat.

l. 23. waren es, 'there were,' or 'they were,' *i.e.,* the thorns; lauter (adv. of quantity), 'nothing but.'

l. 24. taten—auseinander, 'opened up of their own accord.'

l. 25. taten—zusammen, 'closed again as a hedge.'

l. 27. liegen, 'lying;' inf. gov. by sehen, which has the construction of an aux. of mood.

P. 20, l. 3. lag der König, etc. Verb sing.; see note to p. 19, l. 11, above.

l. 5. einer = man, indef. pron., with strong term.

l. 9. und—lassen, 'and he couldn't help himself either.'

l. 15. und sahen—an, 'and stared at each other with great eyes (of wonderment).' Observe that the verb sahen, which follows the subjects, is pl., while erwachte, which precedes, is sing.

l. 17. sprangen (herum), 'jumped about.'—wedelten, 'wagged (their tails).'

P. 20, l. 18. unterm Flügel hervor, 'from under their wings.'

l. 19. ins Feld, 'into the fields.'

l. 23. eine—schrie, 'such a box on the ear, that he roared out.'

l. 24. rupfte . . . fertig, 'finished plucking.'

l. 25. mit dem Dornröschen; as to the use of the art., see note to p. 15, l. 10, above.

DER TREUE JOHANNES.

P. 21, l. 1. Es war, etc. Es is here the redundant pron. before the verb, representing the subj. after; a very frequently recurring construction.

l. 2. wohl, 'no doubt.'

l. 3. lasst . . . kommen, 'send for.' **mir** ethical dat., or dat. of advantage, which is generally left untranslated. See note to p. 7, l. 2.

l. 5. liebster, 'dearest, favorite.'—**hiess so,** 'was so called,' 'had this name.'

l. 6. sein Lebelang, acc. of time. See Gloss.—**gewesen war;** **weil** being a subord. conj., throws the verb to the end of the sent.—**Als—war. Als** is here used (not **wenn**), because the impf. is employed, denoting a particular action (not an habitual one, which would require **wenn**); and being a subord. conj., throws the verb to the end.

l. 7. vor das Bett, acc., because of the *motion towards* the bed.

l. 9. da hab' ich, 'so I have;' **da** here indicates cause (as adv., not conj., as you may see by the verb coming *second*); or it may be rendered 'now.' See Gloss.—**als um,** etc., **als** here = 'but' or 'then,' relating to **keine**; akin to its use with the comp. degree.

l. 10. in jungen Jahren, 'young in years.'

l. 11. wo—weiss, 'at which (age) he can't always know how to shape his conduct,' lit. 'to advise himself;' **sich** is dat., indir. obj. of **raten.**

l. 12. in allem was; was is used after neut. adjs. and prons.

l. 18. So sterb' ich, 'then I can die.'—**und sprach;** the subj. is to be supplied (as preceding the verb) from the previous sent.

P. 22, l. 2. vom goldenen Dache, 'of the golden roof;' **vom** here indicates *attribute;* **wenn er,** etc., 'if he,' etc.

l. 10. getragen (worden) war, 'had been carried,' plupf. pass.

P. 22, l. 14. **und sollte es,** 'though it should.' When the conj. **wenn** (or **ob**) is omitted, the verb begins the conditional sent.

l. 15. **Trauer,** 'period of mourning.'

l. 17. **Erbe,** n., 'inheritance ;' m., 'heir.'

l. 19. **alle die ; alle** is not usually followed by the art.

l. 20. **die eine,** 'the one.' See Gloss.

l. 24. **es leibte und lebte,** 'it breathed and lived' ('had body and life').

l. 25. **es gäbe,** 'there was (or could be) ;' subj. after meinen, expressing uncertainty.—**Es gibt** is less def. and more general than **es ist.** See Gloss., **geben.**

l. 30. **du erschrickst,** 'you would be startled ;' pres. for fut.

l. 32. **dárin,** 'in there,' the emphasis on the first syll.

P. 23, l. 4. **es könnte—ausschlagen,** 'it might result in great misfortune to you and me ;' **zu** here expresses *consequence.*

l. 8. **mit meinen Augen,** 'with my own eyes.'

l. 9. **Nun—Stelle,** 'now I won't budge from this spot.'

l. 11. **dass es—war,** 'that there was no help for it now,' lit. 'was no longer (possible) to change it,' or 'no longer to be changed,' with supine in passive sense.

l. 15. **zuerst,** 'first,' *i.e.,* before the king.—**dachte—sehen,** *i.e.,* he thought to prevent the king from seeing, etc.

l. 16. **vor ihm,** 'before he (John) did ;' **vor** referring to time.— **was half das ?** 'of what use was that ?'

l. 17. **stellte—Fuszspitzen,** 'stood on tip-toe.'

l. 22. **voll Sorgen ; voll** generally takes the acc., sometimes the gen.; it sometimes has the form **voller.** See Gloss.

l. 23. **ist geschehen ;** perf. to indicate an action wholly completed. —**was—werden,** 'what will come of this !'

l. 29. **wenn,** etc.; the conj. **(dass)** expressing the consequence is omitted, thus expressing the speaker's agitation.

l. 31. **mein—erlange,** 'I will risk my life to win her,' **dass** expressing *consequence ;* or 'I'll wager my life, that I shall win her,' **dass** expressing merely *the fact that ;* in both cases, pres. for fut.

P. 24, l. 1. **wie—wäre,** 'how to go about it ; how it was to be accomplished ;' note the (apparently passive) use of the supine, and compare note to p. 23, l. 11.

l. 2. **es hielt schwer,** 'it was a difficult matter.'—**nur—kommen,** 'even to get into the presence of the princess.'

P. 24, l. 7. **fünf Tonnen Goldes;** the substance measured is here in the gen., instead of being in apposition to the word of measure, as is usually the case. See note to p. 3, l. 17.

l. 8. **lass' Eine . . . verarbeiten,** 'cause one of them (the tons) to be worked by,' etc.

l. 9. **zu,** 'into, to make,' **zu** expressing *result.*

l. 10. **Gewild,** 'wild animals (of the chase),' large game (such as stags, boars, etc.).

l. 12. **liess . . . zusammenkommen,** 'assembled.'

l. 15. **liess . . . laden,** 'had it laden.'

l. 17. **musste—tun,** 'was required to do the same.'

l. 19. **fuhren,** etc., 'they sailed (journeyed).'

l. 21. **hiess,** 'bade.'

l. 24. **sorget;** he here addresses the king in the second pers. pl.; usually in the second sing.

l. 27. **allerlei,** here subst.—**stieg ans Land,** 'went ashore.'

l. 31. **schöpfte,** 'was drawing (water);' supply **Wasser.**

l. 32. **das goldblinkende Wasser,** 'the water that gleamed with gold (with a golden sheen),' from the reflection of the golden pails.

P. 25, l. 5. **Eins,** 'one piece;' with strong term., as standing alone (without subst.), and num. adj., hence spelt with capital letter.

l. 6. **hat—an,** 'takes such great delight in,' etc.

l. 7. **abkauft,** pres. for fut.

l. 15. **stehen hat,** 'has standing,' inf. for pres. part.

l. 17. **ist . . . worden,** the aux. preceding the inf. and part. in a subord. sent. See note, p. 10, l. 13, above.

l. 18. **dazu gehören,** 'are (would be) necessary to do this (for this purpose).'

l. 21. **Lust,** 'desire, longing.'

l. 28. **meinte—zerspringen,** 'thought surely his heart was going to burst,' lit. 'thought not otherwise, than that,' etc.; supply **dass** after **als.**

l. 29. **stieg—Schiff,** 'she went on board of the vessel.'

l. 31. **hiess—abstoszen,** 'ordered the ship to set sail,' lit. 'bade (them) push off the ship.'

P. 26, l. 1. **jedes einzeln,** 'each piece separately, by itself.'

l. 5. **dahinfuhr,** 'was sailing off.'

l. 6. **nachdem,** subord. conj., as shown by the position of the verb at the end.

P. 26, l. 7. wollte heim (gehen).

l. 8. Rand, 'side.'

l. 9. auf—gieng, 'was sailing on the high (or open) sea.'

l. 10. bin betrogen, '*have been* deceived,' perf. ind. pass., supply worden. The Eng. verb 'to be' with the pass. voice is rendered by sein (*i.e.*, perf. and plupf.) in Germ. when it = 'have been,' etc., *i.e.*, when the action is completed ; otherwise (when = 'am being,' etc.) by werden (*i.e.*, pres. and impf.).

l. 11. und—geraten, 'and have got into the power of a trader ;' geraten is part. of geraten, not of raten.

l. 15. aber—geschehen, 'but as to my having carried you off by stratagem, that I have done (has been done) from (through) excessive love ;' the subj. of ist is the clause dass—habe, represented by das following ; aus indicates *cause.*

l. 18. gesehen habe, bin ich . . . gefallen ; the perf. here indicates a single, isolated, completed action, in contradistinction to the impf., which indicates *continuous* action.

l. 21. geneigt, 'well disposed to, fond of him.'

l. 25. vornen, 'in the front part (the bow) of the vessel.'—Musik machte, 'was playing and singing.'

l. 26. dahergeflogen kamen, past part. with kommen ; see note, p. 10, l. 9, above.

l. 29. die eine ; Rabe is here fem. ; so also in the title to one of the Tales in Grimm's large collection : 'Die Rabe' (No. 93), and nowhere else, as far as I have been able to discover.

l. 30. heim, 'to his own home,' as a bride.

l. 32. er hat sie doch, 'he has her after all,' 'yes, but he *has* got her ;' doch is often used for ja in giving an affirmative reply to a negative statement or question.—bei ihm, 'with him.'

P. 27, l. 2. da belongs to aufschwingen, 'to vault upon it ;' or it may be rendered 'then.'

l. 4. hinein, redundant.—dass er, etc., dass = so dass (consequence).—nimmer mehr, 'never again' (two words).

l. 5. wiedersieht, pres. for fut.—sprach die zweite ; supply da before the verb.

l. 7. ein anderer, 'some other person.'—aufsitzt, 'mounts.'—Feuergewehr, 'fire-arms, pistol.'

l. 9. ist . . . gerettet, perf. for fut. perf.

l. 11. wird zu Stein, 'will turn to stone.'

P. 27, l. 13. wenn . . . auch, 'even if.'—**doch,** 'after all.'

l. 16. **Schüssel,** 'salver, tray.'—**und sieht aus,** 'looking, that will look ;' pres. for fut.

l. 19. **bis—Knochen,** 'to the very (marrow and) bone.'

l. 21. **wenn einer,** 'if somebody ;' **einer = jemand.**

l. 22. **und wirft,** etc. ; the verb (**wirft**) should properly be last, as **und** connects it with a subord. sent. (**wenn—packt).—verbrennt,** 'is consumed' (neut. verb).

l. 24. **halbes Leibes,** 'half way up his body ;' adv. gen. of manner.

l. 26. **wird—auch verbrannt,** 'even though the bridal robe be burnt ;' **wenn** is omitted, hence the verb (**wird**) is first.

l. 32. **Blut,** in apposition to **Tropfen,** as noun of quantity.

P. 28, l. 1. vom Wirbel, etc., 'from the crown of the head to the toe of his foot.'

l. 2. **das—hatten,** 'had finished this conversation,' lit. 'had spoken this with one another.'

l. 4. **von der Zeit an,** 'from that time forward (on).'

l. 5. **verschwieg—Herrn,** 'if he concealed from his master ;' **wenn** omitted, hence verb first.

l. 6. **dieser,** 'the latter' (**sein Herr**).

l. 18. **die—waren,** 'who did not wish well to Faithful John as it was (**doch**),' or (anyway).

l. 22. **lasst ihn gehen,** 'leave him alone.'

l. 23. **wozu—ist,** 'what may be the good of it.'

l. 26. **nicht anders als,** 'just as if.'

l. 27. **gieng darauf zu,** 'walked up to it.'—**mit Handschuhen,** 'with gloved hands.'

l. 32. **nun—gar,** 'now he even (dares to) burn,' not content with shooting the horse.

P. 29, l. 3. trat . . . hinein, 'joined in.'

l. 4. **hatte—Acht,** 'paid attention, watched closely.'—**auf einmal,** 'all at once.'

l. 6. **sprang . . . hinzu,** 'ran to (her aid).'

l. 10. **hatte angesehen,** 'had seen it also.'

l. 20. **bin . . . verurteilt (worden),** perf. See note to p. 26, l. 10, above.—**mit Unrecht,** 'wrongfully, unjustly.'

l. 23. **hätte tun müssen,** 'had been obliged to do ;' aux. of mood preceding the inf. in subord. sent. (See App., § 15.)

P. 29, l. 28. trug . . . groszes Leid, 'felt great sorrow.'

l. 29. was . . . so übel, 'how ill;' **was = wie.**

l. 30. liess . . . aufheben, 'had it preserved,' or 'raised up;' either meaning is admissible.

l. 33. könnt' ich, etc., 'if I only could.' The verb is first in an elliptical sent. expressing a wish.

P. 30, l. 2. eine Zeit, 'some time, a considerable period.'—**da,** 'after which' (when).

l. 11. wenn—willst, 'if you are willing to sacrifice what is dearest to you.'

l. 19. die grosze Treue, 'the great devotion (shown to him).'

l. 21. den Kindern den Kopf, 'the children's heads;' **Kopf** is sing., though there are two heads.

l. 24. frisch und gesund, 'sound and whole.'

l. 28. davon wurden sie, etc., 'by this they were made whole again.'

l. 30. als—geschehen, 'as if nothing had happened to them.'

P. 31, l. 2. hast du gebetet, the part. should be last, according to the general rule.

l. 11. gieng hin, 'went;' **hin** is redundant.

BRÜDERCHEN UND SCHWESTERCHEN.

P. 32, l. 1. Brüderchen, 'Little Brother,' used like a prop. name. —**an der Hand = bei der Hand.**

l. 2. seit, conj., **= seitdem.**—**haben—mehr,** 'we never have a moment's peace,' lit. 'a good hour.'—**die Stiefmutter,** 'our stepmother;' def. art. for poss. adj.

l. 4. alle Tage = jeden Tag, 'every day.'—**stöszt—fort,** 'she spurns us with her feet.'

l. 7. geht's besser, 'fares better.'—**doch,** 'at least.'

l. 9. Dass Gott erbarm', 'God have mercy!' Elliptic sent., expressing a wish; supply **sich** before **erbarm',** which is properly a refl. verb.

l. 13. Gott—zusammen, 'Heaven and our hearts are weeping together' (in allusion to the rain); **die** is redundant.

l. 15. von Jammer, 'from misery;' **von** indicates cause.

l. 21. mich dürstet, 'I am thirsty.' See Gloss.

P. 32, l. 22. wüsste, 'knew of.'—**gieng**', **tränk'**, impf. subj., 'I would go,' etc.—**einmál**, 'just.'—**ich mein'**, **ich hört'** ; the pres. is usually followed by the pres., not by the impf.

P. 33, l. 4. hatte—waren, 'had in truth **(wohl)** seen the children going off.'

l. 7. **verwünscht**, 'laid under a spell.'

l. 8. **glitzerig**, 'glittering, sparkling.'

l. 10. **im Rauschen**, 'as it rushed murmuring by.'

l. 11. **wer = derjenige, welcher,** 'any one who ;' includes both rel. and antec. ; the rel. part has its verb **(trinkt)** last ; the antec. part in the second place **(wird)**.—**wird,** 'will be turned into ;' pres. for fut.

l. 15. **ob es gleich,** etc., 'although it ;' **obgleich** is often thus divided ; **es** is to be rendered by 'he' when referring to **Brüderchen**, and by 'she' when relating to **Schwesterchen**.

l. 26. **gar zu grosz,** 'excessive' (too great for anything).

l. 32. **läufts mir fort,** 'will run away from me ;' **mir** is dat. of disadvantage, or ethical dat. See note to p. 7, l. 2.

P. 34, l. 2. wie—waren, 'as soon as the first drops had touched his lips.'

l. 3. **als**, etc., 'in the shape of a fawn.'

l. 7. **ich—verlassen**, 'I will never leave you, you know **(ja)**.'

l. 11. **Daran**, 'to this (rope).'

l. 13. **lange, lange,** 'for a long, long while.'

l. 17. **zu—Lager,** 'to make a soft couch ;' **zu** expresses *purpose.*

l. 20. **das—Hand,** 'which it **(das Rehchen)** ate out of her hand ;' **das** demonstr.

l. 26. **es wäre** ; the ordinary rules of constr. would require the verb first (or after **so**) in the princ. clause, when preceded by the subord. clause.

l. 28. **eine Zeitlang,** 'for some time ;' often written as two words.

l. 29. **Da—zu,** 'then (*i.e.*, at the end of this time) it happened.'

l. 33. **wäre—gewesen,** 'would have been only too glad to join in it,' lit. 'be present at it.'

P. 35, l. 2. ich kann's—aushalten, 'I can't stand it any longer ;' **mehr** is redundant.

l. 3. **bis es,** 'till she,' *i.e.*, Sister.

l. 4. **sprach es zu ihm,** 'said she to it.'—**komm' mir ja,** etc., 'be sure to return to me in the evening ;' **mir** is ethical dat.

P. 35, l. 5. **vor den wilden Jägern,** 'against the wild hunters.'

l. 10. **und war ihm—Luft,** 'and felt so well, and was so merry in the open air ;' **ihm** dat. gov. by **war,** supply **zu Mut,** and see p. 13, l. 15, above.

l. 13. **wenn—gewiss,** 'when they thought they had (caught) it beyond a doubt ;' **sie hätten, dass** being omitted, the constr. is that of a princ. sent.

l. 21. **das ho! ho!** 'the shouts,' 'the tally-ho.'

l. 23. **ich muss hinaus (springen).**

l. 25. **zu Abend,** 'by evening.'—**wieder da sein,** 'be here (back) again.'

l. 26. **Sprüchlein,** 'speech' (to obtain admission).

l. 31. **Einer,** 'one (of them).'

l. 32. **musste,** 'had to.'

P. 36, l. 2. **erschrak gewaltig,** 'was terribly frightened.'

l. 5. **Kräuter,** 'herbs,' to heal it.

l. 6. **lieb,** for **liebes.** See note to p. 5, l. 8.—**heil,** 'healed, cured.'

l. 10. **die Jagdlust,** 'the merry chase.'

l. 15. **so bald—kriegen,** 'and I won't let anybody catch me so easily either.'

l. 16. **ich bin,** 'I shall be,' pres. for fut.

l. 17. **So sterb',** etc., 'then I shall die here of grief ;' **dir** is ethical dat., not to be trans.; **vor** indicates *cause*.

l. 20. **so mein' ich—springen,** 'I feel like jumping out of my skin,' lit. 'shoes.'

l. 22. **konnte . . . nicht anders,** 'couldn't help herself.'

l. 25. **gesund,** 'unharmed.'

l. 27. **jagt ihm nach ;** according to rule, the sep. part. should be last in the princ. sent. with a simple tense.—**aber dass,** etc., 'but (see) that not one of you does it any harm ;' supply **seht zu.**

l. 29. **zum Jäger ;** *i.e.*, the one who had followed the fawn on the previous occasion.

l. 33. **gieng . . . auf,** 'was opened.'

P. 37, l. 1. **so schön—hatte,** 'fairer than any he had ever looked upon,' lit. 'as fair as none,' etc.

l. 3. **dass nicht,** etc., 'that it was not,' etc.

l. 6. **mit mir gehen ;** the rule requires the inf. last.

l. 9. **muss auch mit (gehen).—das verlass' ich nicht,** 'I won't forsake *it* ;' obj. first for the sake of emphasis.

P. 37. l. 11. und (es) soll—fehlen, 'and it shall want for nothing.'—**Indém** (adv.), 'in the meanwhile,' *i.e.*, while they were speaking. See Gloss.

l. 12. **band es,** etc.; **es** is obj., **Schwesterchen** subj.

l. 13. **nahm es,** 'took it into her own hand ;' **es** here relates to **Binsenseil.**

l. 17. **und war es,** for **und es war.** See note to p. 10, l. 22.

l. 18. **die Frau Königin,** 'my Lady the Queen.'

l. 19. **gehegt und gepflegt,** 'cherished and tended.'

l. 21. **um derentwillen,** 'on whose account, by reason of whom.'—**in die Welt—waren,** 'had gone forth into the world.'

l. 22. **die meinte—als,** 'supposed (not otherwise than) that ;' the pron. **die** is redundant ; the conj. **dass** being omitted after **als,** the sent. has the constr. of a princ. sent., but with the verb in the subj.

l. 26. **und—gieng,** 'and that they were so well off.'

l. 27. **wurden . . . rege,** 'were stirred up.'

l. 29. **die beiden,** 'these two.'

l. 30. **doch noch,** 'after all,' 'in spite of all.'—**Ihre rechte Tochter,** 'her own daughter.'—**nur Ein Auge,** 'only one eye.' **Ein** is here num., not art.

l. 32. **die machte—gebührt,** 'heaped reproaches on her, and said : "The good fortune to become a queen, should belong properly to me ;"' **die** redundant pron. ; **eine Königin zu werden,** sent. in apposition to **das Glück.**

P. 38, l. 1. Sei nur still, 'pray, be quiet.'—**die Alte,** 'the old woman.'

l. 2. **sprach sie zufrieden,** 'comforted her.'—**wenn's—Hand sein,** 'when the time comes, I shall be sure **(schon)** to be on hand.'

l. 5. **gerade—war,** 'just happened to be.'

l 6. **nahm . . . an,** 'assumed.'

l. 12. **Wanne,** 'bath.'

l. 14 **ein rechtes Höllenfeuer,** 'a most hellish fire.'

l. 16. **ersticken musste,** 'was smothered ;' **musste** is redundant, not to be trans.

l. 20. **das verlorne Auge,** 'the eye she had lost.'

l. 27. **was sie machte,** 'how she was.'—**bei Leibe,** 'on your life.'

P. 39, l. 1. allein noch wachte, 'was the only person still awake.'

l. 8. **streichelte—Rücken,** 'stroked its back.'

P. 39, l. 9. zur Tür hinaus, 'out at the door.'

l. 11. **ob,** 'whether, if' (not **wenn**).

l. 14. **dabei,** 'all the time (she was doing this).'

l. 24. **sprach der König,** supply **da** before **sprach.**

P. 40, l. 6. noch diesmal, 'only this once.'

l. 11. **in dém Augenblick,** 'at that moment;' **dem** is demonstr.,
and as such is to be emphasized ; the def. art. is never emphasized.

l. 16. **es ward—gesprochen,** 'judgment was pronounced upon
them.'

KÖNIG DROSSELBART.

P. 41, l. 1. über—schön, 'exceeding fair.'

l. 2. **dabei,** 'withal.'

l. 4. **trieb—ihnen,** 'and made sport of them into the bargain.'

l. 8. **Rang und Stand,** 'rank and condition.'

l. 10. **Edelleute,** pl. of **Edelmann.**

l. 12. **aber—auszusetzen,** 'but to each one she had some objection to make.'

l. 13. **das Weinfass,** 'what a wine-butt.'

l. 14. **lang—Gang ;** these rhyming saws cannot be reproduced
except by a paraphrase ; render 'lank and long's not worth a song ;'
Gang is used like **Geschick** in the following rhyme.

l. 15. **kurz—Geschick,** 'short and stout, count him out ;' **hat
kein Geschick,** lit. 'has no fitness' (or 'value').

l. 16. **der bleiche Tod,** 'as pale as death,' or 'pale death (himself).'

l. 17. **der Zinshahn,** 'the red-faced cock ;' a cock was one of the
commonest forms of payment for ground-rent, and hence **Zinshahn,**
lit. 'rent-cock, toll-cock,' means simply 'cock ;' the allusion of
course is to the red comb and wattles of the cock.

l. 18. **gerad,** 'straight.'—**grünes—getrocknet,** 'green wood, dried
behind the stove,' hence warped by the sudden heat.

l. 20. **besonders—war,** 'but she made particularly merry over a
good king, who stood at the very top, and whose chin had grown a
little crooked.'

P. 42, l. 1. wie—Schnabel, 'like a thrush (has) a bill,' *i.e.*, like a thrush's bill.

l. 5. die da, 'who ;' this use of the redundant **da** after the rel. pron. was formerly very common.—**ward er ;** the pron. is redundant, being inserted because the real subject **(der alte König)** is so far from its verb.

l. 6. den ersten nehmen, 'take for a husband the first beggar that turned up.'

l. 8. darauf, 'afterwards.'

l. 14. eine milde Gabe, 'a kind gift.'

l. 16. meine Tochter da, 'my daughter there.—**getan,** 'taken.'

l. 19. den—halten, 'and I'll keep it too ;' **den** is demonstr.— **Es half keine Einrede,** 'no resistance (objection) was of any use,' 'there was no use objecting.'

l. 22. nun schickt sich nicht, 'now it is not seemly ;' supply **es** after **schickt.**

l. 23. noch länger, 'any longer.'—**weiterziehen,** 'wander forth.'

l. 27. als . . . da, 'when now,' 'so when ;' **da** is redundant.

l. 31. du'n = du ihn, 'had you taken him ;' **er,** in the same line, 'it' (the forest).

l. 32. zart, adj. after the subst., though really attrib., not pred.

l. 33. hätt' ich genommen ; the part. would be last in prose.

P. 43, l. 15. Es gefällt—wünschest, "'I don't at all like,' said the minstrel, 'your continually wishing somebody else for a husband.'"

l. 19. was . . . so klein, 'how small ;' **wie = was; so** redundant.

l. 20. wem mag . . . sein, 'to whom can . . . belong ?'

l. 23. damit—kam, 'to get in at the low door ;' **damit** expresses purpose, and generally has the verb in the subj.

l. 25. Was Diener, 'Servants indeed!' Exclamation of surprise and dissent, 'What do you mean by talking of servants? What should I do with servants?'

l. 26. was du willst; willst, as in a rel. sent., should come last, but precedes the part. and inf.—**Mach'—müde,** 'just (go to work and) kindle a fire at once, and put water on, to cook me a meal ; I am very tired.'

l. 30. musste—gieng, 'was obliged to lend a hand himself, so that things might get on even tolerably.'

P. 44, l. 1. schmale Kost, 'scanty fare.'

P. 44, l. 3. schon ganz früh, 'while it was yet quite early,' 'at a very early hour.'

l. 5. **schlecht und recht,** 'plainly and honestly ;' **schlecht** here = **schlicht.**

l. 6. **so geht's,** etc., 'it won't do any longer, for us to spend (our substance) here, without earning anything.'

l. 10. **stachen . . . wund,** 'lacerated ;' the adj. **wund** is here used as sep. part.

l. 11. **das geht nicht,** 'that won't do.'

l. 12. **spinn' lieber,** 'you had better spin.'—**kannst—besser,** supply **tun** or **machen.**

l. 15. **daran herunter lief,** 'ran down (on) them.'

l. 16. **du taugst—angekommen,** 'you are not fit for any work ; I got a bad bargain with you,' _i.e._, when I took you.

l. 22. **feilhalten,** 'selling (my wares).'

l. 23. **es half nichts,** 'there was no help for it.'—**sich fügen,** 'submit' (adapt herself to circumstances).

l. 25. **Hungers,** adv. gen., 'of hunger' (= **vor Hunger**).—**gieng's gut,** she 'was successful.'

l. 26. **der Frau,** 'from the woman,' dat. after **abkaufen.**

l. 28. **ja, viele,** etc., 'many even,' etc.—**liessen—dazu,** 'and left her the pots into the bargain,' _i.e._, did not take them away.

l. 29. **von dem Erworbenen,** 'on their earnings (what they had made).'

P. 45, l. 1. dahergejagt, 'galloping along.'—**ritt—hinein,** 'rode straight into the pots.'

l. 3. **was—sollte,** 'what to do.'

l. 4. **Ach—ergehen,** 'alas ! how shall I fare !'

l. 6. **Wer—auch,** 'well, who ever would sit down.'

l. 8. **du bist—zu gebrauchen,** 'you are of no use for any respectable work ;' **zu gebrauchen,** supine with passive meaning.

l. 9. **Da bin ich . . . gewesen,** 'so I have been.'

l. 13. **dafür,** 'in return (for your services).'

l. 14. **musste—tun,** 'had to assist the cook (be at his beck and call), and do the hardest of work.'

l. 18. **von dem—zu Teil ward,** 'what fell to her share from the remnants (what was left over).'

l. 22. **angezündet (worden) wären,** 'were (had been) lit,' plupf. pass.

P. 45, l. 23. und immer—hereintrat, 'and each person that came in was handsomer than the last (the one before),' lit. 'one always entered handsomer than the other.'

l. 28. **die da ; da** redundant. See note to p. 42, l. 5.

P. 46, l. 8. floss, 'was spilt,' lit. 'flowed out.'—**umhersprangen,** 'were scattered (jumped) about.'

l. 11. **dass—hätte,** 'that she would rather have wished herself a thousand fathoms beneath the earth,' *i.e.*, that she wished herself, etc.

l. 16. **sprach—zu,** 'spoke kindly to her (and said).'

l. 19. **sind Eins,** 'are one (and the same person) ;' **Eins** is neut., as being indef., though here referring to animate objects.—**dir zu Liebe,** 'for love of you.'

l. 21. **Das—geschehen,** 'I have done all this.'

l. 33. **wir wären ; wir** includes **du** and **ich.**

SNEEWITTCHEN.

P. 47, l. 1. mitten im Winter, 'in the midst of winter, in mid-winter ;' **mitten** is adv. of place ; sometimes it has the prep. **in** preceding, written as part of the same word and is followed by a gen., as, **inmitten des Winters.**

l. 2. **da sasz,** 'when there sat,' or 'that a queen was sitting.'

l. 4. **und nähte,** 'sewing.'

l. 5. **wie—nähte,** 'as she was sewing away ;' obs. the force of **so.** —**aufblickte,** 'looked up.'

l. 6. **es fielen,** etc., 'then fell three drops of blood into the snow.' **Es** represents the actual subj. (**Tropfen**) before the verb. (See Gloss., **es.**) **Blut** is in apposition to **Tropfen,** the noun of quantity.

l. 8. **das Rote,** adj. used as subst., 'the red (spots).'—**so schön aussah,** 'looked so beautiful.'

l. 9. **Hätt' ich,** 'if I only had,' 'I wish I had ;' the verb first in a sent. expressing a wish.

l. 11. **Bald darauf,** 'soon afterwards.'

l. 12. **das war,** 'who was ;' redundant demonstr. pron.

l. 14. **Sneewittchen,** Low-German form of **Schneeweisschen,** 'Snow-white.'

P. 47, l. 15. **geboren war,** 'had been born,' plupf. pass.

l. 16. **über ein Jahr,** 'at the end of a year.'

l. 17. **Es war,** 'she was.'

l. 18. **konnte—werden,** 'could't bear (the idea) of being surpassed by any one in beauty,' lit. 'couldn't bear that she should be surpassed,' etc.

l. 20. **einen wunderlichen Spiegel,** 'a strange (wondrous) mirror ;' **wunderlich** here = **wunderbar.—wenn—beschaute,** 'whenever she stood before (stepped up to) it and regarded herself in it ;' **wenn** is here used before the impf. as indicating repeated action, not **als,** which is used of an instantaneous act ; see following note ; so **wenn . . . erblickte,** below.

P. 48, l. 8. **als diese—fragte ;** here **als** is used, as the act is instantaneous.

l. 15. **vor Neid,** 'for (with) envy ;' **vor** indicating cause. —**Von Stund' an,** 'from that hour forth ;' **an** is adv.

l. 16. **kehrte—Mädchen,** 'her heart turned round in her body, she hated the girl so much ;' the expression **kehrte—herum** is used to express the violence of her emotion ; **so** is here adv. (= 'so much ').

l. 19. **immer höher,** 'higher and higher ;' Ill weeds grow apace, says the Eng. proverb.—**Tag—Ruhe,** 'no peace day or night.'

l. 21. **ich will's—sehen,** 'I don't want to set eyes on her again ;' observe the force of **wollen** here.

l. 25. **gezogen,** 'drawn (forth).'

l. 26. **durchbóhren ;** insep. part., hence the accent is on the verb.

P. 49, l. 2. **werden—haben,** 'will soon have eaten you,' *i.e.,* it won't be long before they will have eaten you.

l. 3. **doch war's ihm,** 'yet he felt ;' supply **zu Mute ; doch,** adversative conj.

l. 4. **und als—kam,** 'and a young wild boar just happening to run past,' lit. 'when just . . . ran past.'

l. 7. **als Wahrzeichen,** 'as proofs' (of his having done the deed).

l. 8. **musste,** 'was required.'—**sie hätte ;** obs. the omission, and the constr. of the sent.

l. 11. **mutterseligallein,** 'forsaken and forlorn ;' the more usual form is **mutterseelenallein.**

l. 12. **ward—angst,** 'and was so terrified, felt such terror ;' impers. verb, supply **es.—dass es—ansah ;** *i.e.,* in her terror, she stared at every leaf (if it but moved).

P. 49, l. 13. **und nicht—sollte,** 'and didn't know what to do,' lit. 'how she should help herself.'

l. 16. **sprangen—vorbei,** 'ran past her.'—**taten ihm nichts,** 'did her no harm.'

l. 17. **Es—konnten,** 'she ran as long as ever her feet could carry her,' lit. 'could get on ;' supply **kommen** after **fort.**

l. 18. **bis—wollte,** 'till near night-fall,' lit. 'till it was nearly about to become evening.'

l. 19. **sich zu ruhen,** 'to rest ;' ruhen = ausruhen; the simple verb is seldom refl.

l. 21. **so zierlich—ist,** 'neat and cleanly beyond expression,' lit. ' so neat, etc., that it can't be expressed ;' **zu sagen,** supine with pass. force.

l. 22. **ein weissgedecktes Tischlein,** 'a dear little table covered with a white cloth,' lit. 'a white-covered table.'

l. 24. **ferner,** 'besides, also.'

l. 25. **An der Wand,** 'along the wall.'

l. 28. **ein wenig Gemüs,** 'a little of the vegetables ;' **wenig** is here undeclined, as is usual in the sing., and also, when expressing *quantity,* in the pl.

l. 30. **denn—wegnehmen,** 'for she did not wish to deprive any one person (only) of everything (he had).'

l. 32. **keins passte,** 'not one (of them) fitted (her).'

P. 50, l. 1. **befahl sich Gott,** 'commended herself (in prayer) to God.'

l. 4. **das waren,** 'who were,' demonstr. for rel.; neut. sing. pron. referring to **Herren.**

l. 5. **nach Erz,** 'for ore ;' **nach** expressing *purpose.*

l. 8. **denn—hatten,** 'for everything was not just in the (same) order, as (in which) they had left it.' The dwarfs or cobolds of German folk-lore are represented as living in the bowels of the earth, and digging for precious metals. They are sometimes kindly, as in this tale, but often mischievous and malicious.

l. 14. **wer hat—gestochen ?** 'Who's been using my little fork ?' lit. 'sticking with.'

l. 19. **Dälle,** 'a hollow,' a depression made by the figure of Snee-wittchen having lain in it.

l. 23. **das lag—schlief,** 'lying in it asleep.'

l. 24. **kamen herbeigelaufen,** 'came running up.'

/ **P. 50, l. 27. was—schön,** 'how beautiful the child is ;' **was** = **wie.**

l. 28. **hatten—Freude,** 'were so delighted.'

l. 31. **da—herum,** 'and then one night was over ;' supply **gegang-en.**

P. 51, l. 1. Wie heisst du? 'What is your name?' ; **heisst** contr. for **heissest.**

l. 2. **Wie bist—gekommen?** 'How did you get into our house?'

l. 5. **es hätte—lassen,** 'had meant to have her killed.' The constr. is that of a principal sent., **dass** being omitted ; and the verb in the subj. mood to indicate the indirect narration. (See App. I., § 18.) The aux. verb of mood **wollen** (which is the inf. for the part.) gov. the inf. **lassen,** which gov. **umbringen,** also in the inf.; **umbringen,** with the obj. of the prep. **um** not expressed, = 'to kill ;' the obj. to be supplied is **das leben** (= 'to deprive of life') ; **jemanden** (acc.) **um etwas** (acc.) **bringen,** meaning 'to deprive a person of a thing.'

l. 6. **und da,** 'and then (or so) ;' **gelaufen,** observe the irregular position of the part.

l. 8. **willst du,** etc., 'if you will,' etc.; the conj. **wenn** being omitted, the verb stands first.

l. 9. **unsern Haushalt versehen,** 'attend to, manage our house, be our housekeeper.' — **betten,** 'make the beds' (= **die Betten machen**).

l. 12. **es soll—fehlen,** 'you shall want for nothing.' See Gloss., **fehlen.**

l. 13. **von Herzen gern,** 'with all my heart.'

l. 16. **musste—sein,** 'had to be, was expected to be, ready.'

l. 17. **Den Tag über,** 'throughout the day, all day long ;' the prep. after its case.

l. 18. **da,** 'so.'

l. 19. **Hüte dich vor,** 'take care of, beware of.'

l. 20. **lass' ja—herein,** '*be sure* (ja) to let nobody in.'

l. 22. **glaubte** ; the verb here precedes the inf. phrase dependent on it, which is always admissible, and is even preferable, to avoid confusion, when the inf. clause is of any considerable length.

l. 23. **dachte nicht anders,** etc., 'was sure she was,' etc., lit. 'thought not otherwise than that she was ;' **dass** is omitted after **als.**

l. 29. **über den Bergen,** 'over, beyond, the mountains.'

P. 52, l. 1. dass—sprach, 'that the mirror never said what was not true,' lit. 'spoke no untruth.'

P. 52, l. 3. am Leben, 'alive.'

l. 4. Und da—wollte, '.\nd so she kept thinking and thinking over and over again, how she could manage to slay her.'—**aufs neue,** adv. phrase ; **von neuem =** 'afresh, beginning over again.'

l. 10. über die sieben Berge ; über here with acc., indicating motion *towards* as well as across.

l. 20. wie du aussiehst, 'what a fright (or figure) you are,' lit. 'what do you look like ;' an exclamation, in form of an interrogation.

l. 25. dass—vergieng, 'so that Sneewittchen couldn't breathe,' lit. 'that the breath passed away from,' etc.

l. 26. für tot, 'as though dead.'—**Nun—gewesen,** 'now you are no longer (have done with being) the fairest,' etc., lit. 'you have been the fairest ;' the perf. indicating an action that is *complete*, and therefore *over*, or done with, at an end.

l. 32. regte—nicht, 'neither moved nor stirred.' The German language abounds in similar duplicate rhyming or alliterative expressions, which are almost synonymous ; compare **hegen und pflegen,** above, p. 37, l. 19.

l. 33. hoben—Höhe, 'raised her up.'

P. 53, l. 3. nach und nach, etc., 'gradually came to life again.'

l. 6. keinen Menschen, 'not a soul.' See Gloss., **Mensch** and **Mann.**

l. 20. das dich—soil, 'that shall be your ruin.'

l. 28. Das Ansehen, etc., 'Surely (**doch**) you will be allowed to take a look at my wares ;' lit. 'looking at (my wares) will surely be allowed you.'

l. 30. Da gefiel, etc., 'then the child was so pleased with it, that she allowed herself to be deceived.'

P. 54, l. 1. Als—waren, 'When they had concluded their bargain :' **·des Kaufs,** gen. gov. by **einig.**

l. 2. einmál, 'for once, just once.'

l. 3. dachte an nichts, 'thought of, suspected, no harm.'

l. 4. liess—gewähren, 'let the old woman do her will.'

l. 7. Ausbund, 'paragon.' See Gloss.

l. 8. jetzt—geschehen, 'now it's all over with you.'

l. 9. Zum Glück, 'fortunately ;' **zu** expresses *result*—**wo,** 'when' (of time).

l. 11. hatten . . . in Verdacht, 'suspected.'

l. 12. suchten nach, 'made an investigation.'

P. 54, l. 18. daheim, 'at home, when she got home.'

l. 31. wo niemand hinkam, 'into which nobody (ever) came.'

P. 55, l. 1. Lust—bekam, 'would long for it.'

l. 2. wer—sterben, 'any one who ate a bit of it, would necessarily (would have to) die;' wer = derjenige welcher; der is redundant.

l. 4. in eine, etc., 'as a peasant-woman;' in with acc.

l. 9. Mir (ist das) auch recht, 'it's all the same to me,' or 'all right, I don't care.'

l. 10. meine—loswerden, 'I shall have no difficulty in disposing (getting rid) of my apples;' schon = 'easily enough, soon enough;' los (in loswerden) gov. acc.

l. 14. da schneide ich, 'now I will cut.'

l. 15. iss du, 'do *you* eat;' the subj. of the imper. expressed for emphasis or contrast between the two persons (du and ich); also obs. the deviation from the rule for the position of the imper. verb, for the same reason, viz.: contrast between the objects (den roten—den weissen).

l. 18. lusterte . . . an, 'gazed longingly at;' an unusual expression.—so gut, 'as well as;' supply wie; gut is adv.

P. 56, l. 3. wie sie . . . kamen, 'when they came;' wie = als.

l. 4. gieng, 'there came;' supply es.

l. 6. ob—fänden, 'whether they could find anything poisonous;' was = etwas; fänden is subj. after ob.

l. 7. schnürten es auf, 'unlaced her (corsets).'

l. 10. alle siebene, 'all seven of them;' the card. nums. frequently have the term. —e in the nom. when used without a subst.; zwei and drei also take —er in the gen., and all, up to ten at least, —en in the dat., under the same circumstances.

l. 12. frisch, 'life-like.'

l. 14. Das können wir, etc., 'we can't put her under, etc.;' das = es; observe the prominence given to the obj. by putting it in the first place.

l. 19. dass es, 'that she;' es refers to Sneewittchen (not indef.).

l. 26. und verweste nicht, 'without decaying.'

l. 31. auf dem Berg, etc.; exception to the rule. See App. I., § 18, (a).

P. 57, l. 1. lasst—Sarg, 'let me have the coffin,' lit. 'leave the coffin to me.'

l. 2. was—wollt, 'whatever you want (to have) for it.'

P. 57, l. 3. um alles Gold ; um here indicates *price.*

l. 4. **So schenkt,** etc., 'then make me a present of it.'

l. 6. **ich will—Liebstes,** 'I will do her honour, as the dearest thing I have ;' or, 'as (if she were) my true-love ;' **Ehren,** dat. sing. with the old weak term., which all weak fem. substs. formerly had ; so **auf Erden,** 'on earth.'

l. 9. **liess ihn . . . forttragen,** 'ordered it to be carried away ;' the inf. is here really pass. in meaning.

l. 11. **von dem—Hals,** 'with (from) the shock, the poisonous bit of apple, which S. had bitten off, was ejected (started) from her throat ;' **von** indicates *cause ;* **Schüttern,** inf. used as subst. See Gloss., **Hals.**

l. 13. **Und—Augen,** 'and it was not long before she opened her eyes.'

l. 18. **Ich habe—Welt,** 'I love you more than all the world besides,' lit. 'I am fonder of you, than of everything (all) in the world.'

l. 20. **war ihm . . . gut,** 'loved him,' lit. 'was good (kindly disposed) to him.'

l. 24. **Wie sie—hatte,** 'now when she had arrayed herself in fine attire.'

P. 58, l. 1. und ward—wusste, 'and began to feel so very, very terrified, that she didn't know what to do (how to contain herself)' ; comp. the repetition of **giftig** above, p. 54, l. 31.

l. 4. **doch liess—Ruhe,** 'yet she had no rest, couldn't rest,' lit. 'it left her no rest ;' **es** is indef.—**sie musste fort (gehen),** 'she was compelled to go.'

l. 6. **erkannte sie ; sie** is nom.

l. 7. **vor—regen,** 'and for fear and fright she stood still, and couldn't move ;' **vor** indicates *cause.*

l. 8. **Aber es waren,** etc., **es** represents the actual subj. (**Pantoffeln**) before the verb.

l. 9. **Kohlenfeuer,** pl., but trans. 'over a coal-fire,' as though it were sing.

l. 11. **musste sie—treten,** 'she was forced to put her feet in (step into) these red-hot shoes.'

HANS IM GLÜCK.

P. 59, l. 2. sprach er ; er, the latter, the master ; **dieser** would be clearer.

l. 3. **herum,** supply **gegangen,** 'is over, at an end.'—**wollte—Mutter,** 'now I should like to go home again to my mother ;' supply **gehen.**

l. 4. **Lohn,** m., 'wages ;' in this sense it is also neut.   See Gloss.

l. 9. **hinein,** 'up in it.'

l. 10. **machte—Hause,** 'set out on the way home.'—**so dahingieng,** 'was just walking along,' and thinking of nothing.

l. 11. **und immer—setzte,** 'and kept setting one foot (leg) before the other ;' *i.e.,* step by step.

l. 12. **kam—Augen,** 'he descried a rider,' lit. 'a rider came into his eyes (field of vision).'—**frisch und fröhlich,** 'gaily and merrily.'

l. 14. **was—Ding,** 'what a fine thing riding is ;' **was = was für.**

l. 15. **einer,** indef. pron., = **man.**

l. 16. **stöszt—Stein,** 'without knocking (kicking) against a stone.'

l. 17. **kommt—wie,** 'gets on, without knowing how.'

l. 18. **Ei—Fusz,** 'well, Jack, then (auch) why do you go on foot ?'

l. 19. **Ich muss ja wohl,** 'well, I suppose I must (can't help it).'

l. 20. **zwar,** 'to be sure.'—**dabei,** 'at the same time,' *i.e.,* while I am carrying it ; or 'for it,' by reason of it.

l. 22. **Weisst du was,** 'do you know what, I'll tell you what.'

P. 60, l. 3. ihr—schleppen, 'you'll have a load to carry, you'll find it heavy,' lit. 'you'll have to drag yourself with it.'

l. 4. **half—hinauf,** 'helped Jack up,' *i.e.,* to mount the horse.

l. 6. **Wenn's—gehen,** 'if you want to go very quickly ;' **soll** should be last, according to the rule ; **es** is impers., lit. 'when you mean it to go.'

l. 7. **mit—schnalzen,** 'to smack (click with) your tongue.'

l. 10. **frank und frei,** 'gaily.'—**über ein Weilchen,** 'after a little while.'

l. 11. **es sollte . . . gehen,** 'that he would like to go.'

l. 13. **setzte—Trab,** 'began to trot smartly,' lit. 'put itself into a sharp (strong) trot.'

l. 14. **ehe—versah,** 'before Jack knew what he was about, where he was,' lit. 'expected it.'—**war er abgeworfen** (worden), 'he had been (was) thrown;' plupf. pass.

P. 60, l. 16. wäre auch, 'would have run away, too.'

l. 18. **des Weges,** 'that way,' adv. gen.

l. 19. **suchte—zusammen,** 'picked himself (lit. his limbs) up (together).'—**machte—Beine,** 'got on his legs again.'

l. 21. **ein schlechter Spasz,** 'poor fun.'

l. 23. **stöszt,** 'bumps you, jolts you,' or 'kicks.'

l. 24. **dass man—kann,** 'so that a fellow might break his neck;' **können** expressing possibility.—**ich setze—auf,** 'never, never will I mount (a horse) again.'

l. 25. **da lob' ich—Kuh,** 'now, I much prefer, would rather have (lit. praise) your cow,' or 'your cow is worth having;' **mir** is ethical dat. (refl.). See note to p. 7, l. 2.

l. 28. **Was—hätte,** 'what would I (not) give, to have a cow like that.'

l. 30. **geschieht—Gefallen,** 'if it would be doing you so great a favour;' so **ein = ein so.**—**so will—wohl,** 'I'll manage, make shift to (wohl) exchange,' etc., 'I wouldn't mind exchanging.'

l. 32. **mit tausend Freuden,** 'with the greatest delight.'

P. 61, l. 1. vor sich her, 'along before him.'

l. 3. **daran—fehlen,** 'surely I shall not want for that.'

l. 4. **dazu,** 'with it.'

l. 7. **asz . . . rein auf,** 'devoured,' lit. 'eat clean up.'

l. 9. **Mittag-;** a hyphen after a word indicates that the latter component of a compound word (here **Brot**) is common to several nouns, and expressed only with the last. Compare '**ein- und ausgetragen,**' etc., p. 45, l. 28.—**liess sich . . . einschenken,** 'ordered,' lit. 'ordered to be poured out for himself;' **sich,** dat. of advantage.

l. 11. **immer—zu,** 'straight on towards his mother's village,' *i.e.*, where she lived.

l. 14. **wohl—dauerte,** which extended probably (wohl) an hour's walk further.'—**Da ward—klebte,** 'then he grew quite hot, so that his tongue clave to his palate for thirst,' *i.e.*, his mouth was parched with thirst.

l. 16. **Dem—helfen,** 'there's a remedy for this,' lit. 'this thing is to be (can be) remedied;' the supine expresses capability.

l. 19. **stellte . . . unter,** 'held under (the cow),' to serve as a pail.—**da er,** etc., 'as he, since he,' etc.; **da** is causative conj.

P. 61, l. 20. aber—bemühte, 'however much he exerted himself' (no matter how much, etc.).

l. 21. **kam . . . zum Vorschein,** 'would make its appearance.'

l. 22. **Und weil—anstellte,** 'and because he was (behaved himself) awkward in doing this **(dabei).**'

l. 24. **Schlag vor den Kopf,** 'kick on the head;' so: **er schoss sich vor den Kopf,** 'he shot himself through head.'

l. 25. **sich gar nicht—war,** 'couldn't recollect at all, where he was,' *i.e.,* he was unconscious.

l. 26. **Glücklicherweise,** 'fortunately,' lit. 'in fortunate manner (wise),' adv. gen. of manner.   This is a very common mode of forming adverbs of manner from adjectives.

l. 29. **Was—Streiche,** 'what's the matter here,' 'here's a pretty piece of work,' lit. 'what sort of tricks are these;' **das** (sing.) representing the subj. **Streiche** after the verb.—**half . . . auf,** 'helped him up (to rise).'

l. 31. **seine,** 'his own,' *i.e.,* the butcher's; **sein** relating to the subj. of the sent. **(Metzger).**

l. 32. **Da, trinkt einmal,** 'there, just take a drink.'

l. 33. **wohl,** 'no doubt, I suppose.'

P. 62, l. 1. das höchstens—Schlachten, 'which is fit at most for draught (purposes), or for slaughtering.'   Cows are sometimes used in Germany for draught purposes as well as oxen and horses; **Ziehen, Schlachten,** are subst. infs. ; **zu** expresses *purpose.*

l. 2. **Ei, ei,** 'ah! indeed ;' expression of astonishment.—**strich—Kopf,** 'smoothed his hair down over his head.'

l. 4. **es ist—gut,** 'to be sure it's a good thing.'—**ins Haus abschlachten,** 'slaughter for domestic use,' lit. 'into the house.'

l. 5. **was—Fleisch,** 'what quantities of meat you have (it gives) ;' **was für** here expresses quantity (= **wie viel**), not, as is generally the case, quality ('what kind of').—**Aber ich—viel,** 'but I don't care much for beef ;' **Rindfleisch** is the general word for beef.

l. 7. **Ja, wer—hätte,** 'yes, (happy the man) who has (should have) a pig like yours (such a pig) ;' supply **glücklich wäre** before **wer.**

l. 8. **Das schmeckt—Würste,** 'that has quite a different (*i.e.,* better) taste ; and then (there are) the sausages into the bargain.'

l. 9. **Hört,** 'hark ye,' 'look here.'—**euch zu Liebe,** 'to please, oblige you,' lit. 'for love to (of) you.'

l. 11. **Gott lohn',** etc., 'God reward you for your friendliness,' lit. 'reward your friendliness to you;' **euch** is dat., **Freundschaft** acc.

P. 62, l. 12. ihm, the butcher; **liess sich—geben,** 'had the pig untied from the barrow (for himself), and the rope to which it was tied put into his hand.'

l. 15. zog weiter, 'went on;' **ziehen** is here neut. verb of motion. **—wie ihm—gienge,** 'how everything actually turned out just as he wished,' lit. 'went according to his wish;' **doch** may be left untranslated.

l. 16. begegnete—gemacht, 'if he met with any annoyance whatever (ja) it was at least (**doch**) immediately made good (remedied) again.'

l. 18. danach, 'after this.'—der trug, 'carrying.'

l. 20. Sie boten—Zeit, 'they gave each other good day.'

l. 24. Hebt einmál, 'just lift it (and feel).'

l. 25. die ist—worden, 'but then (auch) it's been fattening for eight weeks.'

l. 29. die—Sau, 'it *is* a good weight (lit. 'has its weight'), but my pig is no hog either,' *i.e.*, is not a bad pig, not to be despised.

l. 30. sah sich . . . ganz bedenklich um, 'looked round with a most alarmed air.'

l. 32. schüttelte auch wohl, etc., 'and shook his head as well (**auch wohl**).'

l. 33. mag's—sein, 'I am afraid there's something wrong about your pig,' lit. 'it may not be all right with, etc.;' **mögen** expressing *probability*. See Gloss.

P. 63, l. 2. ist eben--worden, 'one has just been stolen out of the bailiff's sty.'

l. 4. ihr habt's--Hand, 'that's the one you have there in your hand.'—Sie haben; sie is indef.

l. 5. es—Handel, 'it would be a bad business.'

l. 6. das geringste—werdet, 'at the very least, you'll be put in the black-hole (lock-up),' lit. 'the least thing will be, etc.;' **dass** is omitted in the second sent.

l. 7. dem guten—bang, 'poor Jack got frightened;' **Hans,** dat. after bang werden.

l. 9. ihr wisst—Bescheid, 'you are better acquainted in this neighborhood (than I am).'

l. 11. Ich muss schon, etc., 'I shall have to risk something, to be sure (schon).'

P. 63, l. 12. schuld sein—geratet, 'be the cause of your coming to grief.'

l. 17. **Wenn—überlege**, 'when I (come to) consider the matter carefully.'

l. 18. **mit sich selbst**, 'to himself' (= **bei sich**).—**habe ich—Tausch**, 'I even have the best (the advantage) of the bargain.'

l. 19. **hernach**, 'and next.'

l. 20. **das gibt**, 'that will furnish ;' pres. for fut.

l. 21. **auf**, 'for,' in reference to future time with acc.

l. 23. **will ich wohl**, 'I shall be sure to.'

l. 24. **Was wird—haben**, 'how delighted my mother will be ;' **was = was für**.

l. 28. **dazu**, 'to it,' *i.e.*, to the humming of the wheel.

l. 30. **und hänge—Wind**, 'and hang my cloak to suit the wind,' *i.e.*, to keep it off me ; a proverb meaning that he can adapt himself to circumstances ; as we speak of 'trimming one's sails' in English one translator renders very well : 'For all that I meet with just serves my turn.'

l. 31. **sah ihm zu**, 'watched him.'

l. 32. **Euch geht's wohl**, etc., 'you must be getting on well, prospering, since,' etc., lit. 'it fares well with you,' etc.

P. 64, l. 1. bei eurem Schleifen, 'over your grinding.'

l. 2. **das Handwerk—Boden**, 'trade has a golden foundation (bottom) ;' a common German proverb.

l. 3. **Ein rechter Schleifer**, 'a good grinder.'

l. 4. **so oft—greift**, 'as often as he puts his hand **(greift)** into his pocket ;' supply **wie** after **oft**.

l. 12. **Ei, das war**, etc., 'Oh ! (or Why !) that was,' etc.—**sieben Jahre Dienst**, 'seven years' service ;' the two substs. are in apposition, as in the case of nouns of measure.

l. 14. **könnt ihr's—gemacht**, 'if you can only manage (lit. bring it to that) to hear (that you hear) the money rattle (jump) in your pocket whenever you stand up, you will have made your fortune.'

l. 19. **gehört**, 'is necessary.'—**eigentlich**, 'really.'—**das andere—selbst**, 'the rest will come of its own accord,' *i.e.*, easily enough, lit. 'will find itself.'

l. 21. **dafür—geben**, 'but then you shall not (I won't ask you to) give me anything else for it but your goose.'

l. 23. **wollt ihr das (tun).—noch fragen**, 'stop to ask,' lit. 'still ask.'

P. 64, l. 24. ich werde—Erden, 'why (ja), I shall become (come to be) the happiest mortal on earth ; **zu** expresses result, after **werden ; auf Erden,** dat. sing. with weak term., compare **in Ehren,** above, p. 57, l. 6, and note ; 'on the earth ' = **auf der Erde.**

l. 26. **was brauche ich,** etc., 'what need shall I then have for any more cares (anxiety).'

l. 27. **nahm . . . in Empfang,** 'received.'

l. 30. **noch—dazu,** 'another good stone into the bargain.'

l. 31. **auf dem—lässt,** 'on which it is good striking,' *i.e.*, on which you can strike a good blow, lit. 'on which it lets itself be struck well ;' **schlagen** is pass. in force, after **lässt ; es** is impers. and indef.

l. 33. **Nehmt hin—auf,** 'take it to you, and take proper care of it,' lit. 'preserve it properly,' *not* 'lift it up.'

P. 65, l. 1. lud—auf, 'loaded himself with the stone.'

l. 3. **Glückshaut,** 'a lucky skin,' *i.e.*, under lucky stars.

l. 4. **trifft mir ein,** etc., 'is fulfilled (realized), as if I were (a child) born on Sunday,' lit. 'is fulfilled for me, as for a Sunday-child ;' in allusion to the superstition, that children born on a Sunday were particularly lucky ; **mir,** dat. of advantage, or ethical dat. See note to p. 7, l. 2.

l. 8. **über die erhandelte Kuh,** 'at the cow he had obtained in barter,' or 'at getting the cow.'—**Er konnte—gehen,** 'at last it was only with difficulty that he could get on.'

l. 11. **dabei,** 'at the same time.'

l. 12. **Da konnte—erwehren,** 'then he couldn't get rid of the thought, help thinking.'

l. 14. **wie eine Schnecke,** 'at a snail's pace.'

l. 15. **kam . . . geschlichen,** 'came crawling along.'

l. 17. **damit er . . . nicht beschädigte,** 'in order not to injure.'

l. 20. **zum Trinken,** 'in order to drink,' lit. 'for (the purpose of) drinking ;' **Trinken,** inf. as subst.; **zu** expressing *purpose.*

l. 21. **stiess—hinab,** 'knocked (against them) a little, and both the stones fell down plump (into the water).'

l. 23. **mit seinen Augen,** 'with his own eyes.'—**hatte . . . sehen,** 'had seen ;' **sehen** is inf. for part., after the gov. inf. **versinken,** following the construction of aux. verbs of mood. See App. I., § 15.

l. 26. **auf eine so gute Art,** 'so nicely,' lit. 'in so good a fashion.'

P. 65, l. 27. ohne dass er . . . brauchte, 'without his having ;' **dass** is here used instead of the supine, since the subj. of the two clauses is different.

l. 29. das einzige—gewesen, 'this had been the only thing left to trouble him,' lit. 'only still troublesome to him.'

l. 30. So glücklich—Sonne, 'there is not a human being under the sun, cried he, as fortunate as I am.'

GLOSSARY

GRIMM'S KINDER- UND HAUSMÄRCHEN.

A

A, the first letter of the alphabet, is always pronounced like *a* in Engl. *father*, never as in *hat*, *hate*, *ball*, or in *any*. Ä or Ae, ä, is pronounced like *a* in *any* when short; like *a* in *hate* (or more strictly like the French *è ouvert*, or the Fr. diphthong *ai*) when long.

ab, adv. (principally used in comp. with verbs), off from ; **vom Wege ab**, off from the road ; down ; **auf und ab**, up and down stairs.

ábbeissen, v. a. sep., biss, ge- bissen, to bite off.

ábbinden, v. a. sep., band, ge- bunden, to untie.

ábbrechen, v. a. sep., brach, ge- brochen, brich, brichst, to break off.

Abend, subst. m., gen. -s, pl. -e, evening ; **am Abend, des Abends** or **ábends** (adv. gen.), in the evening.

Abendbrot, subst. comp. n., gen. (-e)s, evening-meal, supper.

Abendzeit, subst. comp. f., pl. -en, evening-tide, even-tide.

áber, coörd. conj., but ; however (when not beginning a sent.).

ábermàls, adv., time, a second time, again, once more.

ábhauen, v. a. sep., hieb, ge- hauen, to hew off, hack off, cut off.

ábkaufen, v. a. sep. w., to buy from, purchase from (dat. of pers. without prep.).

áblaufen, v. n. (sein) sep., lief, gelaufen, läufst, etc., to run out, expire (of time).

ábleiten, v. a. sep. w., leitete, geleitet, to lead off, lead aside or astray.

ábraten, v. a. sep., riet, geraten, rätst, rät, to dissuade (dat. of pers.).

abschlachten, v. a. sep. w., to butcher, slaughter.

abschlieszen, v. a. sep., schlosz, geschlossen, to lock, close.

ábstechen, v. a. sep., stach, ge- stochen, stich, stichst, to stick (a pig, etc.), to kill.

ábsteigen, v. n. (sein), sep., stieg, gestiegen, to descend, dis- mount (from a horse, etc., gov. von).

ábstoszen, v. a. sep., **stiess, ge-stoszen, stöszest,** to push off ;
v. n., to set sail (of a vessel).

ábwaschen, v. a. sep., **wusch, gewaschen,** to wash off.

ábweisen, v. a. sep., **wies, gewiesen,** to send away, dismiss, reject.

ábwenden, v. a. sep., **wendete** or **wandte, gewendet** or **gewandt,** to turn away, keep off ;
v. refl., to turn away.

ábwerfen, v. a. sep., **warf, geworfen, wirf, wirfst,** to throw off.

ábwischen, v. a. sep. w., to wipe off.

ach, int., ah ! oh ! alas !

Acht, subst. f., no pl., heed, guard;
Acht haben, geben, to take heed, pay attention (gov. **auf** with acc.) ; **in Acht nehmen,** to take care of ; **sich in Acht nehmen,** to be careful, take care.

acht, card. num., indecl., eight ;
ord., **der achte,** the eighth.

achten, v. a. w., to value, esteem ;
hoch achten, to respect or esteem highly.

Acker (Engl. "acre"), subst. m., gen. -s, pl. **Aecker,** field, ploughed field [acre, (measure of land) ; in this sense has pl. ——].

all (**aller, alle, alles,** pl. **alle**), indef. num. adj., all, every ; n. sing.

Alles (subst.), everything, everybody ; pl. **Alle,** everybody, all ;
was alles, whatever (see R., p. 11, l. 3, note).

allein, adj., alone (used as pred. only, with few exceptions).

allein, adv., only ; conj., but (if at beginning of sent., throws subj. after verb).

allemal, frequent. num. adv., on every occasion, always.

aller—, prefix before superl. adj. and adv., used to make them more emphatic, as; **allerschönste** (**der, die, das**), the fairest, most beautiful of all ; **am allerliebsten,** most willingly (of all).

allerhand, allerlei, var. indecl. num., of all kinds or sorts (really a compound gen. f., **aller-Lei** or -**Hand** ; **Lei** is obsolete).

allerorten, adv. gen. pl., everywhere (= **aller Orten,** (in) every place). D., p. 17, l. 26.

allgemein, adj., universal, general; adv., universally, generally.

Almosen, subst. n., gen. -s, pl. —, alms, charity [from same source as Eng. "alms"].

als, conj., than (in comparisons of inequality) ; as (of equality) ; when (of time past, but with impf. and plupf. only, and then of a single, isolated, past action, concurrent with some other action ; of habitual action **wenn** is used, even with these tenses ; **wann** is interrog. (see under **wenn** and **wann**); but (after a neg.); nichts als, nothing but. Syn., wie ; als is preferable to wie in comparisons of inequality, *i.e.,* after the compar. degree, though both are common ; in comparisons of equality (= Eng. "as"), als indicates *identity,* wie *similarity,* thus : er kommt ALS ein König, "he comes *as* a king" (*i.e.,* he is really a king) ; er kommt WIE ein König, he comes *like* a king (though he is not necessarily a king). See wie.

áls(o)bald, adv. of time, immediately, straightway.

also, adv., accordingly, thus [never = "also"].

alt, adj., comp. älter, old ; subst. m., der Alte, the old man ; ein Alter, an old man (follows decl.

of adj.) ; f., die **Alte**, the old woman.

am, contr. for **an dem**.

an, prep., gov. dat. and acc., on, upon, by, adjacent to (signifies position parallel to a non-horizontal surface); with acc., to, towards, against, on (motion *towards* such a surface ; as **an den Berg**, towards the mountain, to the foot of it ; **auf den Berg**, to the top of it) ; of time (dat. only), on, upon (used in giving dates with the day of the month, as : **am 18ten August**, on the 18th of August ; interchangeable with the simple acc. of time, without prep.).

ánblicken, v. a. sep. w., to look at, regard, glance at.

ánbrechen, v. a. sep., **brach, gebrochen, brich, brichst**, to break (begin breaking, of daylight).

Anbruch, subst. m., gen. -(e)s, no pl., breaking, break (of day, **Tagesanbruch**).

ánder, indef. num. adj., other ; next ; second (D. p. 16, l. 21).

ánders, adv., otherwise (from **ander**), other, else (for **anderes**, as : **niemand a.**, "no other person, nobody else ").

ändern, v. a. w., to alter, change (from **ander**).

ánfangen, v. a. and n. (with **haben**) sep., **fieng, gefangen, fängst**, to begin, commence ; to go about a thing.

ángegossen, part. adj. (from **angieszen**), moulded on—**wie angegossen**, as though moulded on, or made to order. A. p. 9, l. 29.

ángehen, v. n. (sein) sep., (**gieng, gegangen**), to go on ; begin, commence ; v. a., to concern ; **es geht dich nichts an**, "it

does not concern you, is none of your business ;" imp., **es geht nicht an** = it will not do.

ángehören, v. n. (**haben**), sep. w., to belong to.

ángiessen, v. a. sep., **goss, gegossen**, to mould or cast on to anything.

Angesicht, subst. n., gen. -(e)s, pl. **-er**, face, countenance ; presence.

Angst, subst. f., pl. **Aengste**, fear, terror, anxiety.

ángst, adj., indecl., incomp. (used only as pred.), anxious, timid, fearful ; **angst werden** (with dat.), to grow or become frightened ; [**einen** (or **einem**) **angst machen**, to frighten, terrify].

ängstlich, adj., timid, anxious, fearful ; adv., timidly ; **wie ä. wird mir's zu Mut**, how timid I feel to-day. R., p. 13, l. 15.

ánhaben, v. a. sep. irreg., (**hatte, gehabt, hast, hat**), to have on, wear ; **einem etwas a.**, to have some power against a person, to be able to do a person harm or injury ; (**antun** is used with the same meaning).

ánhalten, v. a. sep., **hielt, gehalten, hältst, hält**, to spur on to (gov. **zu**); v. n., to continue, go on ; (also in the directly opposite sense) to stop, halt (*i.e.*, "continue in the same place").

ánheben, v. a. and n. sep., **hob** or **hub, gehoben**, to begin, commence.

ánklopfen, v. a. sep. w., to knock (at a door, etc.; gov. **an** with acc.).

ánkommen, v. n. (sein) sep., **kam, gekommen, kommst** or **kömmst**, to arrive ; **schlimm a.**, to come off badly, make a bad bargain.

ánlegen, v. a. sep. w., to lay a

plan, a plot, etc., to lay alongside; to put on (clothes, etc.); **die Büchse a.**, to take aim with the rifle (lay it against the check). K., p. 14, l. 6; **Hand a.**, to lend a hand. K., p. 43, l. 30.

ánlustern, v. a. sep. w., to desire, long for. S., see note p. 55, l. 18.

ánmachen, v. a. sep. w., to kindle (a fire, etc.).

ánnehmen, v. a. sep., **nahm, genommen, nimm, nimmst,** to accept, to take on, assume.

ánordnen, v. a. sep. w., to order, arrange, ordain.

ánpacken, v. a. sep. w., to seize, take hold of.

ánprobiren, v. a. sep. w. (part. **probirt**), to try on.

ánreden, v. a. sep. w., **redete, geredet,** to speak to, address.

ánregen, v. a. sep. w., to stir up, incite.

ánrühren, v. a. sep. w., to touch. **ans**, contr. for **an das.**

ánsehen, v. a. sep., **sah, gesehen, sieh, siehst,** to regard, look at, esteem.

Ansehen, subst. n. (inf. of preceding), gen. -s, no pl., appearance; B., p. 38, l. 20; look, looking at; S., p. 53, l. 28.

ánstellen, v. a. sep. w., to appoint, arrange, institute; v. refl., to pretend.

ánstoszen, v. a. sep., **stiess, gestoszen, stöszest, stöszt,** to knock, strike against (gov. **an** with acc.).

ántun, v. a. sep., **tat, getan,** to put on, inflict (dat. of pers.); put on (clothing, etc.); **es jemanden** (dat.) **antun,** to charm, bewitch a person; v. refl., to attire, array, clothe one's self (gov. **mit**).

Antlitz, subst. n., gen. -es, pl. -e, face, countenance.

Antwort, subst. f., pl. -en, answer, reply; (the primitive **Wort,** "word," is n.).

ántworten, v. n. (haben) w., **antwortete, geantwortet,** to answer, reply (with dat. of pers.).

ánziehen, v. a. sep., **zog, gezogen,** to attract; to put on (of clothing); refl., to dress, clothe one's self.

ánzünden, v. a. sep. w., **zündete, gezündet,** to kindle, light (a candle, etc.).

Apfel, subst. m., gen. -s, pl. **Aepfel**, apple.

Apfelgrütz, subst. m., gen. -es, pl. -e, bit of an apple (of the core). S.

Arbeit, subst. f., pl. -en, labour, toil, work. (Syn., **Werk** = the work done).

árbeiten, v. n. (haben) w., **arbeitete, gearbeitet,** to labor, toil, work.

Arg, subst. m., indecl., suspicion; **Arg haben,** to be suspicious.

arg, adj., comp. **ärger,** bad.

Aerger, subst. m., gen. -s, vexation, anger.

Arm, subst. m., gen. -(e)s, pl. -e, arm.

arm, adj., comp. **ärmer,** poor.

Armut, subst. f., no pl., poverty.

Art, subst. f., pl. -en, manner, kind, species; **auf diese Art,** in this manner.

ártig, adj., good, well-behaved; [pretty].

Asche, subst. f., no pl., ashes.

Aschenputtel, subst. n., prop. gen. -s, Cinderella (from **Asche** and **putteln,** Hessian dial.; Engl. "puddle," to roll, wallow; Scotch "Ashiepattle").

Atem, subst. m., gen. -s, no pl., breath.

átmen, v. a. and n. (haben) w., atmete, geatmet, to breathe, draw breath.

auch, adv. and conj., too, also; besides.

auf, adv., up; **auf und ab,** up and down (stairs).

auf, prep., gov. dat. and acc., (Engl. "up"); with dat., on, upon (refers to anything resting upon or over, or moving towards, a horizontal surface, in reference to place; used also of places that are on an eminence, as castle, etc.); with acc., to, to the top of (see **an**); **auf diese Art, Weise,** "in this manner;" (of time) for (in reference to a future period of time), as: **auf ihr Lebtag,** "for life;" **auf zwei Tage,** "for two days (to come)."

auf einmal, adv. phrase, at once, all at once, suddenly.

aufblicken, v. n. (haben) sep. w., to look up, glance upwards.

aufessen, v. a. sep., **asz, gegessen, iss, issest, isst,** to eat up, consume, devour.

auffordern, v. a. sep. w., to summon, demand, challenge, require (a pers. to do a thing; gov. **zu**); invite, ask (a person to dance, etc.; claim (as a partner); A., p. 5, l. 20.

aufgehen, v. n. (sein) sep., **gieng, gegangen,** to rise (of the sun, moon, etc.); to open (of a door, etc.); [**aufstehen** = "to rise" of persons (out of bed)].

aufhalten, v. a. sep., **hielt, gehalten, hältst, hält,** to hold up; to detain.

aufheben, v. a. sep., **hob** or **hub, gehoben,** to lift up, raise; to preserve; to do away with, annul, make of no effect.

aufhelfen, v. n. sep., **half, ge-**

holfen, hilf, hilfst, to help up (with dat. of pers.).

aufhören, v. n. (haben) sep. w., to stop, cease, desist.

aufladen, v. a. sep., **lud, geladen,** to load on one's self, to take up.

auflegen, v. a. sep. w., to lay upon, impose (dat. of pers., acc. of thing).

aufmachen, v. a. sep. w., to open (a door, etc.); [**sich aufmachen** (or **auf den Weg machen**), to set out].

aufrichten, v. a. sep. w., **richtete, gerichtet,** to raise up, set up, set upright; v. refl., to raise one's self up, sit upright.

aufriegeln, v. a. sep. w., to unbolt, open (a door, etc.).

aufs, contr. for **auf das.**

aufschlagen, v. a. sep., **schlug, geschlagen, schlägst,** to cast up, raise (the eyes).

aufschliessen, v. a. sep., **schloss, geschlossen,** to unlock, open (a door, etc.).

aufschneiden, v. a. sep., **schnitt, geschnitten,** to cut up, cut open.

aufschnüren, v. a. sep. w., to unlace.

aufschwingen, v. refl. sep., **schwang, geschwungen,** to mount (a horse, etc.); vault (into a saddle, on horseback, etc.).

aufsetzen, v. a. sep. w., to set on, upon, put on; v. refl., to mount (a horse, etc.).

aufsitzen, v. n. (sein) sep., **sasz, gesessen,** to sit up; to mount (a horse, etc., = **sich aufsetzen;** J., p. 27, l. 7).

aufspannen, v. a. sep. w., to hoist (sail).

aufspringen, v. n. (sein) sep., **sprang, gesprungen,** to jump up, spring up; spring open, fly open (of a door).

aufstehen, v. n. (sein) sep.,
stand, gestanden, to stand up,
get up, rise (from bed); [of pers.;
aufgehen, of the sun, etc.] : to
stand open or ajar (of a door).

aufstellen, v. a. sep. w., to set
up, place upright ; set on, put on.

auftun, v. a. sep., tat, getan, to
open.

aufwachen, v. n. (sein) sep. w.,
to awake, wake up.

aufwecken, v. a. sep. w., to
awaken, arouse.

aufzehren, v. a. sep. w., to consume, devour.

Auge, subst. n., gen. -s, pl. -n,
eye.

Augenblick, subst. m. compd.
(Auge, "eye," Blick, "glance"),
gen. -(e) s, pl. -e, moment, min-
ute (lit. "glance or flash of the
eyes ").

aus, prep., gov. dat. only, out of,
from (motion), from, through
(cause).

Ausbund, subst. m., gen. -es,
pl. -bünde, or -bunde, pattern,
paragon (of excellence) [orig.
the piece of cloth turned out-
wards as a sample of the ware,
hence the best of the piece].

ausdenken, v. a. sep. irreg.,
dachte, gedacht, to think out,
devise, invent.

auseinander, part., asunder,
apart (compd. from aus, "out
of," einander, indecl. recipr.
pron., "one another, each
other ").

auseinandertun, v. refl. sep., tat,
getan, to open up.

ausgehen, v. n. (sein) sep., gieng,
gegangen, to go out ; to be
extinguished (of a light) ; a.
lassen, to issue, publish ; D.,
p. 17, l. 16.

ausgestickt, partic. adj. (from
aussticken), embroidered.

aushalten, v. a. sep., hielt, gehalten, hältst, hält, to hold
out, endure ; v. n. (haben) to
last ; to endure.

auslachen, v. a. sep. w., to laugh
at, ridicule, jeer at, deride.

auslesen, v. a. sep., las, gelesen, lies, liesest, liest, to
pick out, select.

auspicken, v. a. sep. w., to peck
out.

ausrichten, v. a. sep. w., richtete,
gerichtet, to attend to (a mes-
sage), perform (an errand).

ausruhen, v. n. (haben) and refl.,
sep. w., to rest, repose.

aussagen, v. a. sep. w., to express, J., p. 23, l. 31, to spread
(a report, etc.).

ausschicken, v. a. sep. w., to
send out.

ausschlagen, v. a. sep., schlug,
geschlagen, schlägst, to knock
or strike out ; to refuse ; v. n.
(sein) imp., to turn out, issue,
end, result.

ausschmücken, v. a. sep. w., to
bedeck, adorn.

aussehen, v. n. (haben) sep. sah,
gesehen, sieh, siehst, to look
out ; to look, seem (with nach
and dat., or wie) ; to look like ;
to resemble ; wie du aussiehst,
what a figure (or guy) you are.
S., p. 52, l. 20.

äusserlich, adj. (from aus), outward, external ; adv. outwardly,
etc.

aussetzen, v. a. sep. w., to set
out ; etwas an jemandem
(dat.) auszusetzen haben, to
find some objection to a person.

aussinnen, v. a. sep., sann, gesonnen, to think out, devise,
invent.

ausspeien, v. a. sep., spie, ge-
spie(e)n, to spit out, expecto-
rate.

áussticken, v. a. sep. w., to embroider.

áusstoszen, v. a. sep., **stiess, gestoszen, stöszest, stöszt,** to thrust out, eject ; utter (a cry, etc.).

áussuchen, v. a. sep. w., to seek out, choose, select.

áustragen, v. a. sep., **trug, getragen, trägst,** to carry out [spread (a report, etc.)].

áustun, v. a. sep., **tat, getan,** to put off, take off (clothes, etc.).

áusziehen, v. a. sep., **zog, gezogen,** to pull out, draw out ; v. n., to march out, walk out, go forth, move out.

Axt, subst. f., pl. **Aexte,** axe.

B

Backen, subst. m., gen.-s, pl.
——, cheek [also **Backe,** f.].

backen, v. a., **buk** (rare) or **backte, gebacken** or (rarely) **gebackt, bäckst,** or **backst,** to bake.

Bad, subst. n., gen.-es, pl. **Bäder,** bath.

Bád[e]stube, subst. f., pl.-n, bath-room.

Bahre, subst. f., pl.-n, bier. litter.

bald, adv. of time ; comp. **bälder,** soon ; almost, nearly.

Band, subst. n., gen.-es, pl. **Bänder,** ribbon. (When it signifies "bond, tie, connection," etc., it has pl.-e. **Band,** m., means "volume," and has pl. **Bände.—Bande,** f., pl.-n, is a "band, gang," etc.) [Conn. with **binden,** "bind."]

bang(e), adj., timid, anxious, fearful ; **b. werden,** to get frightened (dat. of pers., or with the pers. as subject).

bat, impf. of **bitten,** "beg."

Bauch, subst. m., gen.–(e)s, pl. **Bäuche,** stomach, belly.

Bauer, subst. m., gen.–n or s, pl.-n, peasant, farmer, countryman.

Bäu[e]rin(n), subst. f. (from prec., pl.-en), peasant-woman, country-woman.

Báuersfràu, subst. (also **Bauernfrau),** subst. f. comp. (**Bauer** and **Frau,** "woman"), pl.-en, peasant-woman, country-woman.

Baum, subst. n., gen.–(e)s, pl. **Bäume,** tree ; dim. **Bäumchen, -lein,** n. [Eng. "beam."]

bedächtig, adj. (from **bedenken),** cautious, careful ; adv. cautiously, etc.

bedénken, v. a. insep. irreg., **bedachte, bedacht,** to consider, reflect ; v. refl., to bethink one's self.

bedénklich, adj. (from prec.), serious (needing consideration) ; dangerous.

Beere, subst. f., pl.-n, berry.

Beféhl, subst. m., gen.–(e)s, pl. -e, command, order.

beféhlen, v. a. insep. (from prec.), **befahl, befohlen, befiehl, befiehlst,** to command, order (dat. of pers.) ; v. refl., to commend one's self.

befínden, v. refl. insep., **befand, befunden,** to find one's self, to be (of place, or of health).

befreíen, v. a. insep. w., to free, set free, liberate.

begében, v. a. imp. refl. insep., **begab, begeben, begib, begibst,** to take place, happen, come to pass. [v. a. pers., to betake one's self, go to (a place), gov. **an** with acc. ; or, with gen. of obj., to give up.]

begégnen, v. n. (**sein)** insep. w., **begegnete, begegnet,** to meet ; impers. to happen (dat. of pers.).

begíessen, v. a. insep., **begoss, begossen,** to water (flowers etc.).

begínnen, v. a. and n. (haben) insep., **begann, begonnen,** to begin, go about a thing ; impers. to begin, commence.

begleíten, v. a. insep. w., **begleilete, begleitet** (*not* **beglitt** ; has nothing to do with **gleiten,** "glide," but is deriv. of **geleiten**), to accompany.

begráben, v. a. insep., **begrub, begraben begräbst,** to bury (from **Grab,** "grave").

behálten, v. a. insep., **behielt, behalten, behältst, behält,** to keep, retain ; to remember.

behénd(e), adj., quick, agile ; adv. quickly.

bei, prep., gov. dat. only, by, at, near ; at the house of (Fr. *chez*) [Indicates nearness to the obj.; it is not used, in correct language, when motion to is expressed ; **neben** in that case replaces it] ; also used, like Eng. "by," of a part of the person touched, as : **bei der Hand nehmen,** "to take by the hand."

beide, indef. num. pl. m. and f., both ; with def. art. **die beiden,** both, both of them.

beides, indef. num. n. sing., both things.

beim, contr. for **bei dem.**

Bein (Eng. "bone"), subst. n., gen.-(e)s, pl.-e, leg [orig. = "bone," hence coll. **Gebein,** "bones"].

beístehen, v. n. (generally with **haben,** sometimes with **sein),** sep. **stand, gestanden,** to stand by, assist (dat. of pers.).

bekánnt, partic. adj. (from **bekennen),** known to (dat. of pers.).

Bekánnte (der, die, das, pl.-n),

Bekannter, -e, -es (ein, eine, ein), adj. subst., person or thing known, acquaintance (decl. as adj.).

bekénnen, v. a. insep. irreg., **bekannte, bekannt,** to confess, acknowledge.

bekómmen, v. a. insep., **bekam, bekommen, bekömmst,** or **bekommst,** to get, receive.

beleúchten (from **licht,** "light"), v. a. insep. w., **beleuchtete, beleuchtet,** to light up, illumine.

belíeben, v. n. (haben) impers. insep. w., to please, like (dat. of pers.).

bellen, v. n. (haben) w., to bark.

belóhnen, v. a. insep. w., to reward, requite, repay.

bemühen, v. a. insep. w., to trouble, give trouble ; refl., to take trouble, exert one's self.

bereít, adj. (pred. only, or rarely attrib.), ready, prepared (of persons) [Also of things, when it is contraction of **bereitet,** part. of **bereiten,** adv. **bereits,** "already"].

Berg, subst. m., gen.-es, pl.-e, mountain, hill.

berühren, v. a. insep. w., to touch ; touch upon ; come in contact with.

beschädigen, v. a. insep. w., to harm, injure (from **Schaden,** "harm").

beschämen, v. a. insep. w., to put to shame, make ashamed.

beschämt, adj. (part. of prec.), ashamed.

beschúuen, v. a. insep. w., to regard, examine ; v. refl., to examine, look at one's self (in a mirror).

Bescheíd, subst. m., gen.-(e's, no pl., information ; B. **wissen,** to know, be informed ; B.

geben, to give information, tell ; B. tun, to drink a person's health (dat. of pers.).

beschénken, v. a. insep. w. (with acc. of person, and mit), to make a present, presént ; endow.

beséhen, v. a. insep., besah, besehen, besieh, besiehst, to look at, examine, regard.

besínnen, v. a. refl. insep., besann, besonnen, to bethink one's self, consider, ponder, reflect ; remember (gov. gen. or auf with acc. of thing), sich eines andern b., to change one's mind.

Besínnung, subst. f., no pl., consciousness, reflection ; zur B. kommen, to regain consciousness.

besónders, adv., especially, particularly (from sonder, Eng. "asunder").

besórgen, v. a. insep. w., to take care of, attend to.

besser, adj. comp. of gut, better.

beste (superl. of gut), best ; der erste beste, the first that comes to hand.

beständig, adj., constant, continual ; adv., constantly, continually (from following).

bestéhen, v. a. insep., bestand, bestanden, to stand (trial, etc.).

bestreíchen, v. a. insep., bestrich, bestrichen, to besmear, paint.

béten, v. n. insep. w., betete, gebetet, to offer up prayer, to pray [to be distinguished from bitten, v. a. "beg," and bieten, "bid "].

betören, v. a. insep. w., to befool, cheat, deceive (from Tor, "fool").

betráchten, v. a. insep. w., be-

trachtete, betrachtet, to regard, consider, examine.

betríegen (or betrügen), v. a. insep., betrog, betrogen, to cheat, deceive.

betrüben, v. a. insep. w., to grieve, sadden (from trübe, "sad ").

Betrübniss, subst. f., pl.-e, sorrow, grief.

betrübt, part. adj., grieved, sorry, sad (from betrüben).

betrügen, see betriegen.

Bett, subst. n., gen.-es, pl.-en, bed ; dim. -chen, -lein, n.

Béttelmànn, subst. m., gen.-(e)s, pl.-leute, beggar, beggar-man.

Béttelwèib, subst. n., gen.-(e)s, pl.-er, beggar-woman.

betten, v. a., w., bettete, gebettet, to make a bed, or beds [refl., to lie down on a bed].

Bettler, subst. m., gen.-s, pl.-, beggar [from betteln, "beg, go a-begging," and that from bitten, "ask "].

beugen, v. a. and refl. w., to cause to bend or bow, to bend, bow down.

Beute, subst. f., no pl., booty.

bewáchen, v. a. insep. w., to watch over, guard.

bewähren, v. a. insep. w., to keep, preserve.

bewégen, v. a. insep., bewog, bewogen, to induce (a person to do a thing ; gov. zu).

bewégen, v. a. insep. w., to set in motion, move ; v. refl., to move.

beweínen, v. a. insep. w., to weep for, weep over.

bezáhlen, v. a., w., to pay (gov. acc. of thing, and acc. or dat. of pers.).

Bier, subst. n., gen.-es, pl.-e, beer.

bieten, v. a., bot, geboten, to

offer, bid ; **die Zeit b.**, to bid good-day (to be distinguished from **beten** and **bitten**).

Bild, subst. n., gen.-es, pl.-er, picture, image.

Bildniss, subst. n., gen.-es, pl.- e, picture, portrait.

binden, v. a., **band, gebunden,** to bind, tie.

Binse, subst. f., pl.-n, reed, rush.

Binsenseil, subst. n. comp., gen. -(e)s, pl.-e, rope of rushes, rush-rope.

Birne, subst. f., pl.-n, pear.

Birnbaum, subst. m., gen.-es, pl.-bäume, pear-tree.

bis, conj. and prep. (with acc.), till, until. [As prep. it frequently takes another prep., signifying motion toward, after it.]

Bissen, subst. m., gen.-s, pl.-, bit, morsel.

Bitte, subst. f., pl.-n, prayer, request.

bitten, v. a., **bat, gebeten,** to beg, ask, request (to be distinguished from **beten**, "offer prayer," and **bieten**). [bitte, (for **ich bitte**)="please, pray."]

Bitten, subst., inf. of prec. gen. -s, no pl., request, prayer. A., p. 3, l. 16.

bitter, adj., bitter.

bitterlich, adv., bitterly.

blasen, v. n. (haben), **blies, geblasen, bläsest, bläst,** to blow.

blass, adj., comp., **blässer,** pale.

Blatt, subst. n., gen.-es, pl. **Blätter**, leaf ; dim. **Blättchen.**

bleiben, v. n. (sein), **blieb, geblieben,** to stay, remain.

bleich, adj., pale (Eng. "bleach").

Blick, subst. m., gen.-(e)s, pl.-e, look, glance.

blicken, v. n. (haben) w., to glance, look.

blinken, v. n. (haben) w., to shine, glitter, flash (of metals).

blos, adj., bare, naked ; adv., barely, merely, only.

Blume, subst. f., pl.-n, flower, blossom.

Blut, subst. n., gen.-es, no pl., blood.

Blutstropfen, subst. m. comp., gen.-s, pl.——, drop of blood.

Boden, subst. m., gen.-s, pl. **Böden**, bottom ; ground, soil ; floor.

bohren, v. a. w., to bore.

bös(e), adj., evil, wicked, angry ; adv., wickedly, maliciously.

böshaft, adj., spiteful, malicious.

Bosheit, subst. f., pl.-en, wickedness, malice.

Braten, subst. m., gen.-s, pl. ——, roast (of meat).

braten, v. a. and n. (haben and sein), briet, gebraten, brätst, brät,** to roast.

brauchen, v. a. w., to use, make use of ; to need, require (gov. another verb in the supine, *i.e.*, with **zu**).

Braut, subst. f., pl. **Bräute,** bride, betrothed.

Brautkleid, subst. n. comp., gen. -es, pl.-er, bridal garment.

Brautleute, subst. pl. comp., betrothed couple, bride and groom.

brechen, v. a., **brach, gebrochen, brich, brichst,** to break ; to pick (flowers) ; v. n. (sein), to break.

brennen, v. n. (haben) irreg., **brannte, gebrannt,** to be on fire, be consumed, be burnt, burn.

bringen, v. a. irreg., **brachte, gebracht,** to bring, fetch.

Brocken, subst. m., gen.-s, pl. ——, crumb, bit, morsel.

Brot (or **Brod**), subst. n., gen.-es, pl. **Bröte,** bread ; loaf, dim. **Brötchen**, little loaf.

Brotkruste, subst. f. comp., pl.
-n, bread-crust.
Bruder, subst. m., gen.-s, pl.
Brüder, brother ; dim. Brüderchen.
Brunnen, subst. m., gen.-s, pl.
——, spring, well, fountain ;
dim. Brünnlein [Scotch,
"burn"].
Brust, subst. f., pl. Brüste,
breast, bosom.
brützeln, v. n. (haben) w., to
crackle, sputter (the noise made
by frying meat, etc.). [Imita-
tive word.]
Büchse, subst. f., pl.-n, rifle, gun.
Büchstab(e) (or Buchstaben),
subst. m., gen.-n, -ns, dat.
acc.-n, pl.-n, letter of the
alphabet [from Buch, "book,"
and Stab, "staff," since the
old Germanic letters (runes)
were in the shape of staves or
twigs. Compare decl. of
Friede, Glaube, etc.]
bücken, v. refl., w., to stoop,
bend down.
Bund, subst. m., gen.-es, pl.-e
(sometimes Bünde), bunch (of
keys) ; bond, band, union.
bunt, adj., motley, variegated, of
many colors, bright.
Bursch, gen.-n, pl.-e [or
Bursche, gen.-n, pl.-n], fellow, lad.
bürsten, v. a. w., bürstete, ge-
bürstet, to brush.
Busch, subst. m., gen-es, pl.
Büsche, bush.
Butter, subst. f., no pl., butter.

C

[This letter never, or rarely, appears at the beginning of German
words, or indeed at all, except in
the combinations ch, ck, the latter
standing for kk.]

D

D. This letter is pronounced as
in English, except at the end of
words, or of syllables before a
cons.
da, adv. of place, there ; used before preps. that gov. dat. or
acc., instead of the neut. pers.
pron. when referring to things
without life; may also in this case
replace the m. or f. pers. pron.,
as darauf, thereon, on it, etc.
da, rel. adv. of place, where ; used
also for rel. pron. referring to
things (see was).
da, adv. of time, then, thereupon ;
now ; so, therefore. J., p. 21,
l. 9, note.
da, rel. adv. of time, when, where-
on, whereupon.
da, caus. conj., whereas, since,
because ; so.
dabei, adv., near it, (close) by it
(of position) ; at it, thereat ; at
the same time ; withal.
dabeistehen, v. n. (haben) sep.,
stand, gestanden, to stand by,
stand close by, be near.
Dach, subst. n. (Eng. "thatch"),
gen.-(e)s, pl. Dächer, roof.
dachte, impf. ind. of denken,
"think."
dafür, adv., for it, in return for
it, in place of it.
daheim, adv. of place, at home.
daheimbleiben, v. n. (sein) sep.,
blieb, geblieben, to stay at
home.
daheimsitzen, v. n. (preferably
conj. with haben, sometimes
sein) sep., sasz, gesessen, to
sit at home.
daher, adv., up, along (toward
the speaker or spectator).
daherfliegen, v. n. (sein) sep.,
flog, geflogen, to fly up, to fly
along.

dahérjagen, v. n. (sein) sep. w., to come rushing or plunging along.

dahérspringen, v. n. (sein) sep., sprang, gesprungen, to come jumping, running along or up.

dahín, adv., along (away from or past speaker or spectator) [; gone (with **gegangen** understood)].

dahínbringen, v. a. sep. irreg., brachte, gebracht, to bring up to a certain point (remote from speaker or spectator) ; es d., to succeed in (obtaining a certain point or object) ; to manage.

dahínfahren, v. n. (sein) sep., fuhr, gefahren, fährst, to move along, away, pass away.

dahíngehen, v. n. (sein) sep., gieng, gegangen, to go along, away ; pass away.

dahínreiten, v. n. (sein) sep., ritt, geritten, to ride along, away.

dahínter, adv., behind it, after it, at the back of it.

dáliegen, v. n. (sein), lag, gelegen, liege, liegst, to lie there.

Dälle [also **Dalle**], subst. f., pl. -n, hollow, dent, depression (impression made by the figure of a person lying on a bed). S. [Conn. with **Tal**, "valley."]

damít, adv., therewith, with it ; conj., in order that.

danách, adv., thereafter, after that ; afterward ; according to that, accordingly.

Dank, subst. m., gen.-(e)s, no pl., thanks ; reward.

danken, v. n. w., to thank, return thanks for (gov. **für**) ; to owe (acc. of thing, dat. of pers.).

dann, adv. of time, then (dist. fr. **denn**, conj., "for").

darán, thereto, to it, up to it (contr. **dran**).

daránsetzen, v. a. refl. sep. w.,

to set to work at anything ; etwas d., to stake something on it.

daránwenden, v. a. sep. w., wendete or wandte, gewendet or gewandt, to spend time or trouble on a thing ; to sacrifice ; etwas d., to take some trouble about it.

daráuf, adv., thereon, thereupon, thereat, thereto ; on it, at it, to it (contr. **drauf**) ; adv. of time, thereupon, then.

daráufschwingen, v. refl. sep., schwang, geschwungen, to vault upon (a horse, into the saddle).

daráus, adv., out of it, therefrom, from it (contr. **draus**).

darf, pres. ind. of **dürfen** ; see below.

darín, adv., therein, in it (contr. **drin**).

darínstehen, v. n. (haben) sep., stand, gestanden, to stand therein, in it.

darüber, adv., above it, over it ; about or concerning it, at it (contr. **drüber**).

darúm, adv., for this or that reason, therefore, for it, about it (contr. **drum**).

darúnter, adv., under it, beneath it (contr. **drunter**) ; among it or them.

das, neut. of **der**, def. art., demonstr. and rel. pron.; used before the verb "to be" even when a m., f., or pl. subj. follows, the verb then agreeing with the subj. that *follows* in number, e.g., **das sind meine Schwestern**, "those are my sisters."

dass, subord. conj., that. [When **dass** is omitted, the sent. has the constr. of a principal sent., and is put in the subj. See App. I., § 18.]

dauern, v. n. (haben) w., to last, endure. [There is another verb **dauern**, a. impers., "to move to pity," *e.g.*, **es dauert mich**, I pity, am sorry.]

davón, adv., thereof, of it ; therefrom, from it, by reason of this ; away, off.

davónlaufen, v. n. (sein) sep., lief, gelaufen, läufst, to run away or off.

davónreiten, v. n. (sein) sep., ritt, geritten, to ride away or off.

davór, adv., before it, before that (time, order) ; at it, from it (cause).

dazú, adv., thereto, to it ; besides.

Deckbettchen, subst. n. dim., gen.-s, pl.——, coverlet.

Decke, subst. f., pl.-n, cover.

Deckel, subst. m., gen.-s, pl.——, lid, cover.

decken, v. a. w., to cover.

dein, pers. pron., gen. of **du**, "thou ;" hence :

dein, deine, dein, poss. adj., second pers. sing., thine, your.

denken, v. n. (haben) w., irreg., dachte, gedacht, to think (gov. gen. or **an** with acc.).

denn, cöord. conj., for (dist. from **dann, adv.** "then").

der, die, das, def. art., the.

der, die, das, demonstr. pron. (when used without subst. has gen. sing. **dessen, deren, dessen** ; gen. pl. **deren**, dat. pl. **denen**), this, that.

der, die, das, rel. pron. (interchangeable with **welcher**, which it always replaces in gen. sing. m. and n., and after a pers. pron.), who (of persons), which (of things), that (persons and things). [The rel. pron. is never omitted in Germ.]

dere(n)twillen (um), rel. pron. and prep., for the sake of, or on account of, whom or which.

derweil, rel. adv., in the meantime, meanwhile ; whilst (compounded of **der**, demonstr. or rel. pron. f. sing. gen., and **Weile**, "while," adv. gen. of time).

dick, adj. [thick, dense], stout.

dienen, v. n. (haben) w., to serve, do service (dat. of pers.).

Diener, subst. m., gen.-s, pl. ——, servant (from prec.).

Dienst, subst. m., gen.-es, pl.-e, service (from **dienen**).

dieser, -e, -es, demonstr. pron., this, that (more common than **jener**) ; denotes the nearer of two objects, hence the latter, last mentioned, in oppos. to **jener**.

diesmal, adv., this time.

Ding, subst. n., gen.-(e)s, pl.-e, thing [the pl. **Dinger** is used in speaking of children, etc., as "little things," or "creatures"]; **guter Dinge sein**, "to be of good cheer," "be in a good humour." A., p. 3, l. 6.

Dirne, subst. f., pl.-n, maidservant, girl, wench [from same root as **dienen**].

doch, cöord. conj. and adv., still, yet, however, nevertheless, indeed, at least. [When it begins the princ. sent., the verb comes after it ; sometimes it causes the verb even to stand first ; it generally, however, follows the verb. It is often very difficult to give the exact force of this particle in Eng.; see the notes. With the imper. it means "pray, please, do," conveying emphasis.]

Dorf, subst. n. (Eng. "thorp," in prop. names), gen.-(e)s, pl. **Dörfer**, village.

Dorn, subst. m., gen.-(e)s, pl.-e, and -en, thorn.

Dórnenhècke, subst. f. comp., pl.-n, thorn-hedge.

Dórnröschen, subst. n. dim. prop., gen.-s, Briar-rose, Rosamond (the name of the Sleeping Beauty).

dort, adv. of place, there, in that place (more definite than **da**).

dorthín, adv. of place, to that place, thither (motion from speaker toward the place).

draussen (for **da-r-aussen**), adv., outside, without.

drehen, v. a. w., to turn, twist.

drei(e), card. num., three; ord. **dritte**, third.

dreímal, freq. num. adv., three times.

dreízehn, comp. card. num., thirteen; ord. **dreizehnte**, thirteenth.

dringen, v. n. (sein), drang, ge-drungen, to penetrate (gov. **durch** and in with acc.); in jemanden (acc.) **d.** (haben), to urge a person strongly.

drinnen (contr. for **da-r-innen**), adv., within.

dritte (der, die, das; ein dritter), third (ord. of **drei**).

Drossel, subst. f., pl.-n, thrush.

Drósselbart, subst. m. prop., gen.-(e)s, Thrush-beard, nickname given to the hero of the Tale of that name.

drücken, v. a. w., to press, squeeze.

drückend, adj. (part. of prec.), pressing, oppressive.

du, pers. pron. second pers. (gen. **dein**, dat. **dir**, acc. **dich**, pl. **ihr**, gen. **euer**, dat. acc. **euch**), thou, you (used in addressing any pers. with whom we do not use ceremony, as the Deity, intimate friends, parents, children).

dumm, adj., compar. dümmer, stupid.

dunkel, adj. (compar. **dunkler**), dark [, obscure. Syn. **finster**, dark, gloomy, melancholy].

Dunkelheit, subst. f., no pl., darkness, obscurity.

durch, prep. (gov. acc. only), through, by means (agency or instr.).

durcháus, adv., by all means, in any case (emphatic. See A., p. 9, l. 21, note).

durchbóhren, v. a. insep. w., to pierce.

dúrchgehen, v. n. (sein) sep., gieng, gegangen, to run away (of a horse) [original meaning: "to go through" —durch-géhen, insep., means "to go over"].

dürfen, v. n. (haben) irreg. (pres. ind. **darf**, **darfst**, **darf**, pl. **dürfen**, etc.; pres. subj. **dürfe**; impf. ind. **durfte**; impf. subj. **dürfte**; part. **gedurft**), aux. v. of mood, to dare, be permitted, be allowed, may. [Indicates permission, possibility, probability (in subj.); like the other verbs of this class, takes inf. for part. after another inf. in comp. tenses, e.g., **er hat es tun dürfen**, he has been allowed to do it. In a subord. sent., the aux. of tense precedes the inf., as: **Er sagte, dass er es habe tun dürfen**, "he said he had been allowed to do it." See App. I., § 15]

dürr, adj., dry, dried up, barren; dead (of a tree, etc., H., p. 61, l. 19).

Durst, subst. m., gen.-es, no pl., thirst.

dürsten, v. n. (haben) impers. w., dürstete, gedürstet, to thirst, be thirsty (with acc. of the pers.

corresponding to subj. of Eng.
verb, *e.g.*, **mich dürstet**, "I
am thirsty").
durstig, adj., thirsty.

E

E, the fifth letter of the alphabet,
has five different pronunciations :
(1) when long, like *a* in *hate :*
(2) when short, like *e* in *hen ;*
(3) before *r*, almost like *ai* in
air, or rather like the French *è
ouvert :* (4) in terminal and
formative unaccented syllables
followed by a consonant, almost
mute, *e.g.*, **enden**, pron. as
though spelt **endn** ; (5) in final
unaccented syllables, not followed by a consonant, like a
short final *a*, as in *Louisa*, *e.g.*,
Ende, pron. *enddh*, not *enday*
or *endee*.
eben, adj., even; adv. just, just now.
Ebenholz, subst. comp. n. (from
Eben, "ebony," **holz**, "wood"),
gen.**-es**, no pl., ebony, ebony-
wood (a black, glossy substance).
Ecke, subst. f., pl.**-n**, corner.
edel, adj., noble [found in the
Saxon names *Athelstan*, etc.].
Edelman, subst. comp. m., gen.
-(e)s, pl.**-leute**, nobleman.
Edelstein, subst. comp. m., gen.
-(e)s, pl.**-e**, precious stone,
jewel.
Ehe, subst. f., pl.**-n**, marriage,
wedlock, matrimony.
ehe (or **eh'**), adv. (comp. **eher**)
and conj., before (often foll.
by the conj. **dass**).
Ehre, subst. f., pl.**-n**, honor.
ehrlich, adj., honourable, honest ;
adv., honourably, etc.
ei ! interj. of surprise or admiration, ah ! oh !
Eiche, subst. f., pl.**-n**, oak.

Eichbaum, subst. comp. m., gen.
-(e)s, pl.**-bäume**, oak-tree, oak.
Eichhorn, subst. n., gen.**-(e)s**,
pl.**-hörner**, squirrel ; dim.
-hörnchen [not conn. with
Horn].
Eid, subst. m., gen.**-(e)s**, pl.**-e**,
oath, sworn pledge [Syn. **Fluch**
= "curse"].
eigen, adj. (no compar.), belonging
to a person, own [, peculiar].
eigentlich, adj., real, actual ; adv.
really, actually, properly or
strictly speaking.
Eile, subst. f., no pl., haste, hurry.
eilen, v. n. (**haben**) w., to hasten,
make haste, hurry.
eilends, adv. (adv. form of pres.
part. of prec.), in haste, hur-
riedly.
eilig, adj., quick ; adv. quickly,
hastily.
Eimer, subst. m., gen.**-s**, pl.——,
bucket, pail.
ein, adv. and sep. prefix, in, into
(hence, as signifying motion,
usually with **her** or **hin** before
verb of motion).
ein, **-e**, **ein**, indef. art., a or an.
Ein, **Eine**, **Ein**, or, when not
foll. by a subst., **Einer**, **Eine**,
Eines, num. adj., one (often
spelt with capital to dist. it from
the art.), also used with def.
art. **der**, **die**, **das Eine**, etc.,
with weak decl., "the one," as
opposed **der andere**, "the
other;" **einer**, somebody (= jemand), one (= **man**).
einander, recipr. pron. indecl.
(dat. and acc.), one another,
each other. [Sometimes the two
parts are separated, when each
is decl., as : **einer schlug den
Andern**, for **sie schlugen einander**.]
einfallen, v. n. (**sein**) impers. sep.,
fiel, **gefallen**, **fällst**, to occur,

come into one's mind (dat. of pers.).

einhandeln, v. a. sep. w., to purchase, buy, make a purchase of.

-einholen, v. a. sep. w., to overtake.

einig, adj. (of several people), united, agreed upon anything (with gen. of thing) ; des Kaufs e. sein, to be agreed upon a purchase or bargain [; **einige,** num. adj. (usually pl.), some, a few, several].

einladen, v. a. sep., lud or ladete, geladen, lädst or ladest, lädt or ladet, to invite, bid.

einlassen, v. a. sep., liess, gelassen, lässest, lässt, to let in, admit (see also **herein-, hineinlassen**); sich auf etwas e., to enter into a thing, entertain a proposition or project.

einmal (often contr. 'mal in conversation), num. adv., once ; einmál, once upon a time, on one occasion (see also **einst, einstmals**); auf e., at once, suddenly [; nicht einmal = "not once ;" nicht einmál (contr. nicht 'mal) = "not even"].

Einrede, subst. f., pl.-n, objection ; E. tun, machen, to make objection (gov. **gegen**) [; lit. "in-speech," "interruption"].

einsam, adj., lonely, lonesome, solitary.

einschenken, v. a. and n., sep. w., to pour out, fill up (a glass, etc.).

einschlafen, v. n. (sein) sep., schlief, geschlafen, schläfst, to fall asleep, go to sleep.

einschmeicheln, v. a. refl. sep. w., to insinuate one's self (into a person's good graces) by flattery, ingratiate one's self, curry

favour (gov. **bei** with pers.). A., p. 10, l. 15.

einst, einstmals, once, once upon a time.

eintauschen, v. a. sep. w., to obtain in exchange for (gov. **für**).

eintragen, v. a. sep., **trug, getragen, trägst,** to bring in.

eintreffen, v. n. (sein) sep., **traf, getroffen, triff, triffst,** to happen in, arrive ; impers. to happen, arrive, come to pass.

einwilligen, v. n. sep. w., to agree, consent to anything (gov. in with acc.).

einzeln, adj. (no compar.), solitary, separate [standing alone, separate from others].

einzig, adj. (no compar.), sole ; only ; unique [only occurring once, as : ihr einziges Kind, "her only child," "the only child she had," A. ; this and the prec. word are not always strictly dist.].

Eisen, subst. n., gen.-s, no pl., iron.

eisern, adj., no compar., of iron, iron.

Elend, subst. n., gen.-(e)s, no pl., wretchedness, misery.

elend, adj., wretched, miserable ; adv. wretchedly, etc.

elf(e) [or eilf(e)], card. num., eleven ; ord. elfte, eleventh.

Eltern (or Aeltern), subst. pl. comm., parents (from älter, comp. of alt, lit. "elders").

emp-, insep. prefix, used before words beginning with f- for ent-.

Empfang, subst. m., gen.-(e)s, no pl., reception ; in E. nehmen, to receive.

empfangen, v. a. insep., empfieng, empfangen, empfängst, to receive [Syn. erhalten, "to receive ;" annehmen implies acceptance on the part of the recipient].

empfínden, v. a. sep., empfand, empfunden, to feel.

emsig, adj., busy, industrious, assiduous ; adv. busily, etc.

Ende, subst. n., gen.-s, pl.-n, end, termination ; zu E., at an end [to an end (after verb of motion)].

endlich, adv., at last, finally.

eng(e), adj., narrow.

ent-, insep. pref., signifying deprivation, loss, "away from," etc., = Eng. "un-" or "dis-," as : gehen, "to go," entgehen, "to go away from, escape :" decken, "to cover," entdecken, "to *discover*," etc.

entdécken, v. a. insep. w., to discover, find out.

entflíehen, v. n. (sein) insep., entfloh, entflohen, to escape (dat. of pers.).

entführen, v. a. insep. w., to carry off, abduct (dat. of pers.).

entgégen, adv. and prep. (always follows the noun, gov. dat.), toward [usually in comp. with verbs].

entgégenkòmmen, v. n. (sein) sep., kam, gekommen, kömmst or kommst, to come to meet, go to meet, advance toward.

entgégenspringen, v. n. (sein) sep., sprang. gesprungen, to run toward, run to meet (dat. of pers.).

entlédigen, v. a. insep. w., to dispose of ; refl. (with gen. of thing), to rid one's self of a thing, dispose of anything.

entledigt. partic. adj. (from prec.), relieved of or from (gen. of thing).

entsetzen, v. refl., insep. w., to be startled, terrified (gov. über).

entsetzlich, adj., terrible, dreadful, frightful ; adv. terribly, etc.

entspringen, v. n. (sein) insep., entsprang, entsprungen, to escape (gov. dat. of pers.).

entstehen, v. n. (sein) insep., entstand, entstanden, to arise, originate.

entwischen, v. n. (sein) insep. w., to escape, get off, slip away.

entzwei, adv., in two, in pieces, to pieces.

entzweíreiten, v. a. sep., ritt, geritten, to ride to pieces, break by riding into, ride into and break. K., p. 46, l. 20.

entzweíschlagen, v. a. sep., schlug, geschlagen, schlägst, to knock or break in two, or to pieces.

entzweíschneiden, v. a. sep., schnitt, geschnitten, to cut in two, cut asunder.

er, pers. pron. first sing. m. (f. sie, n. es, gen.-seiner, sein, dat. ihm, acc. ihn), he (of persons), it (of things when referring to a masc. subj.).

er-, insep. prefix. The force of this prefix is acquisitive, signifying the acquisition of a thing by the action implied in the verb, as jagen, "to chase," erjagen, "to acquire, get by chasing." Most verbs with this prefix are trans.

erbarmen, v. refl. insep. w., to have mercy on, take pity on (gen. of obj.).

Erbarmen, subst. n. (inf. of prec.), gen.-s, no pl., mercy, pity, compassion.

erbärmlich, adj., wretched, miserable, pitiable ; adv. wretchedly, unmercifully.

Erbe, subst. m., gen.-n, pl.-n, heir, inheritor.

Erbe, subst. n., gen.-s, no pl., inheritance, patrimony.

erbleíchen, v. n. (sein) insep.,

erblích or erbleichte, erblichen or erbleicht, to turn or grow pale ; to die, expire.
erblícken, v. a. insep. w., to catch sight of, see, perceive.
Erbse, subst. f., pl.-n, pea.
Erde, subst. f., pl.-n, earth [; in the phrase auf Erden, "on earth," the old weak dat. term. appears].
erfüllen, v. a. insep. w., to fulfil.
Erfüllung, subst. f., pl.-n, fulfilment ; in E. gehen, to be fulfilled.
ergéhen, v. n. (sein) insep. impers., ergieng, ergangen, to fare, prosper (dat. of pers. corresp. with subj. of Eng. verb).
ergreífen, v. a. insep., ergriff, ergriffen, to seize, take hold of.
erhálten, v. a. insep., erhielt, erhalten, erhältst, erhält, to keep, preserve ; to get, receive, obtain [Syn. empfangen, annehmen ; see empfangen].
erhándeln, v. a. insep. w., to gain by purchase or barter, purchase, buy.
erhándelt, partic. adj. (from prec.), bought, purchased.
erhében, v. a. insep., erhob or erhub, erhoben, to raise, lift up ; to exalt ; refl., to raise one's self, rise. [The old part. erhaben is now only used as adj., "exalted, lofty, sublime."]
erhólen, v. refl. insep. w., to recover, regain strength, health, etc.; to amuse one's self, take recreation.
erkénnen, v. a. insep. irreg., erkannte, erkannt, to recognize ; to acknowledge.
erlángen, v. a. insep. w., to receive, obtain, attain (by active exertion, as dist. from erhalten and empfangen).
erláuben, v. a. insep. w., to allow,

permit (acc. of thing, dat. of pers.).
erlösen, v. a. insep. w., to release, redeem.
erníedrigen, v. a. insep. w., to lower, debase, degrade ; refl., to lower one's self, stoop, condescend.
erscheínen, v. n. (sein) insep., erschien, erschienen, to appear, make one's appearance (not = "appear" in the sense of "seem," which is rendered by the simple v. scheinen).
erschnáppen, v. a. insep. w., to snap up, get hold of, swallow.
erschrécken, v. n. (sein) insep., erschrak, erschrocken (sein), to be frightened, startled, terrified.
erschrécken, v. a. insep. w., to frighten, startle, terrify.
ersínnen, v. a. insep., ersann, ersonnen, to think out, invent, imagine.
ersínnlich, adj., imaginable, possible.
erst (der, die, das erste), ord. num. adj., first (conn. with ehe, eher, before) ; der erste beste, the first that turns up, comes to hand. K., p. 42, l. 18.
erst, adv., only, not before, no sooner than (of time, as : erst morgen, not before tomorrow) ; sometimes used as = erstens or erstlich, first, at first, or in the first place ; only, no more than (of number).
erstáunen, v. n. (sein) insep. w., to wonder, to be astonished or surprised at (gov. über with acc.).
erstáunlich, adj., wonderful, astonishing, surprising ; adv., wonderfully, etc.
erstícken, v. a. insep. w., to

smother, suffocate ; v. n. (sein), to be smothered, suffocated.

ertrínken, v. n. (sein) insep., ertrank, ertrunken, to be drowned, to drown.

erwáchen, v. n. (sein) insep. w., to awake.

erwécken, v. a. insep. w. (caus. of prec.), to awaken, wake up, arouse ; to bring to life. S., p. 55. l. 27.

erwéhren, v. refl. insep. w., to defend one's self against, keep away, get rid of (gen. of obj. without prep.).

erweísen, v. a. insep., erwies, erwiesen, to prove ; to show (a pers. a favour, etc.; dat. of pers.).

erwerben, v. a. insep., erwarb, erworben, erwirb, erwirbst, to earn, gain, procure.

erwischen, v. a. insep. w., to get hold of, seize, obtain.

Erworbene (das), partic. subst. (from erwerben), what one has earned, earnings (decl. as weak adj.). K., p. 44, l. 29.

Erz, subst. n., gen.-es, pl.-e, ore, metal, brass, bronze. [Conn. with Lat. *æs, æris*, "brass."]

erzählen, v. a. insep. w., to tell, relate, narrate.

es, pers. pron. third neut. sing., gen. seiner, sein, dat. ihm, acc. es, it. [The gen. and dat., and the acc. gov. by a prep., are only used when referring to persons (as : Mädchen, Aschenputtel, Rotkäppchen, etc.). When referring to things, the gen. and dat. (without prep.) are replaced by the neut. demonstr. pron. das or dasselbe ; when gov. by a prep., both dat. and acc. are replaced by the adv. da (dar) before the prep., *e.g.*, darauf, "on it ;" dazu, "to

it," dafür, "for it," etc., etc. Es before the verb "to be" represents the actual subj., and may be followed by a pl. verb. as : es sind meine Brüder, they are my brothers. For es ist, es sind, "there is, are," see under geben, es gibt, etc.] It also represents a prec. adj., as : Ich bin krank, aber mein Bruder ist es nicht, "I am ill, but my brother is not (so)."

essen, v. a., asz, gegessen, iss, issest, isst, to eat (of men ; fressen is used of beasts, or of excessive bestial eating in men).

Essen, subst. n., gen.-s, no pl. (inf. of prec.), eating, meal, victuals.

etlicher, etliche, etliches, pl. etliche, some, several (used in sing. only before nouns of quantity) ; etlichemal, several times.

etwas, indef. num. subst. indecl., something, anything ["not anything" = nichts, not nicht etwas] ; sometimes written was.

euch, dat. and acc. of ihr, pers. pron. second pl. (also used as sing.), you.

euer, gen. of the same, your.

euer, eure, euer, poss. adj. from the same, your.

Eule, subst. f., pl.-n, owl.

F

F, the sixth letter of the alphabet, pronounced as in Eng. It occurs in combination with p, as in Pferd, etc. In many words, Eng. *f* is represented by German v, as Vater, Eng. "father."

Fahne, subst. f., pl.-n, flag.

fahren, v. n. (sein), **fuhr, gefahren, fährst,** to proceed, drive ; journey (in any sort of conveyance, as a waggon, ship, etc.) ; f. **aus,** etc., to start from, be shot out from. S., p. 57, l. 11.

fallen, v. n. (sein), **fiel, gefallen, fällst,** to fall.

falsch, adj., compar. **fälscher,** false (of character), untruthful ; spiteful, wicked.

Falschheit, subst. f., no pl., falseness, untruthfulness ; wickedness, malice, spite.

fangen, v. a., **fieng, gefangen, fängst,** to catch, capture.

Farbe, subst. f., pl.-n, colour.

färben, v. a. and refl. w., to colour, dye (one's skin, etc.).

Fass, subst. n. (Eng. "vat"), gen.-es, pl. **Fässer,** vat, puncheon, barrel (large vessel for containing liquids).

fassen, v. a. w., to grasp, seize ; to comprehend.

Feder, subst. f., pl.-n, feather, quill ; (hence like Fr. *plume*) pen.

fehlen, v. n. (haben) w., to be missing, wanting, absent, to lack ; impers. to be wanting ; to want, miss [in this sense the Eng. subj. (pers.) is dat. in Germ., the Eng. obj. is the obj. of the prep. **an,** as : es **fehlt mir an Geld,** "I want money, I have no money"] ; etwas **fehlt mir,** something ails me, is the matter with me.

Feier, subst. f., pl.-n, feast, festival ; celebration, ceremonial.

feiern, v. a. w., to celebrate, solemnize (a festival, wedding, etc.) [; v. n., to have holidays, be free from work].

feil, adj. (in this sense pred. only), for sale, salable (of things). [As attrib. adj. it means venial, corrupt, purchasable, of persons.]

feilhalten, v. a. sep., **hielt, gehalten, hältst, hält,** to keep for sale, expose for sale, sell.

Feld, subst. n., gen.-es, pl.-er, field.

Feldbrunnen, subst. m. comp., gen.-s, pl.——, spring (of water) in the open field, a country or wayside spring or well.

Feldstein, subst. m. comp., gen. -(e)s, pl.-e, boulder, common stone found in the fields, stone.

Fenster, subst. n. (from Lat. *fenestra*), gen.-s, pl.——, window.

fern(e), adv., distant, far off, in the distance ; comp. **ferner,** further, moreover, besides.

Ferne, subst. f., pl.-n (rare), distance.

Ferse, subst. f., pl.-n, heel [syn. **Hacken**].

fertig, adj., ready, finished, prepared.

fertigrupfen, v. a. sep. w., to finish plucking (a fowl, etc.). D., p. 20, l. 24.

Fest, subst. n., gen.-es, pl.-e, feast, festival.

fest, adj., fast (not = "quick" but) tight, firm ; adv., fast, tightly, firmly.

festhalten, v. a. sep., **hielt, gehalten, hältst, hält,** to hold fast or tight.

festmachen, v. a. sep. w., to fasten, make fast.

Fett, subst. n., gen.-es, pl.-e, fat.

fett, adj., fat, stout.

Feuer, subst. n., gen.-s, pl.——, fire.

Feueranmachen, subst. n. comp. (inf.), gen.-s, no pl., kindling a fire.

Feuergewehr, gen.-(e)s, pl.-e, fire-arm, gun ; pistol. J., p. 27, l. 7.

finden, v. a., fand, gefunden, to find ; impers. refl., to come about (of its own accord). II., p. 64, l. 20.

Finger, subst. m., gen.-s, pl. ———, finger [pron. Fing-er, as in "singer," not as in Eng. "fing-ger"].

finster, adj., dark, gloomy, sinister [; dunkel is used of physical gloom, finster also of character].

Flachs, subst. m., gen.-es, no pl., flax.

flackern, v. n. (haben), to flicker, dance (of fire, flame, etc.).

Flasche, subst. f., pl.-n, flask, bottle.

flechten, v. a., flocht, geflochten, flicht, flichtst, flicht, to weave, plait.

Fleisch, subst. n., gen.-es, no pl., flesh, meat.

Fliege, subst. f., pl.-n, fly, housefly.

fliegen, v. n. (sein), flog, geflogen, to fly [fliehen = "flee"].

Fluch, subst. m., gen.-(e)s, pl. Flüche, curse [Eid = oath, sworn pledge; Flug = "flight"].

Flügel, subst. m., gen.-s, pl. ———, from fliegen, wing, pinion.

folgen, v. n. (sein) w., to follow; to obey (with haben), gov. dat. of pers.

folgend, part. adj., no compar., following, subsequent, next.

fördern, v. a. w., to ask, demand, insist on [fördern = "help on, promote"].

fort, adv., away, off ; (of continuance) on.

fórteilen, v. n. (sein) sep. w., to hasten away, depart in haste.

fórtgehen, v. n. (sein) sep., gieng, gegangen, to go away, leave, depart.

fórtlaufen, v. n. (sein) sep., lief, gelaufen, läufst, to run away, run off.

fórtreiten, v. n. (sein) sep., ritt, geritten, to ride away, ride off.

fórtschlafen, v. n. (haben) sep., schlief, geschlafen, schläfst, to sleep on, continue sleeping.

fórtsprengen [v. a. sep. w. (caus. of foll.), to cause to run away, chase away, disperse] ; v. n. (sein), to gallop off (of a horse).

fórtspringen, v. n. (sein) sep., sprang, gesprungen, to run away, run off, escape.

fórtstoszen, v. a. sep., stiess, gestoszen, stöszest, to push away, spurn, reject ; mit den Füszen f., to spurn with the feet, kick away.

fórttragen, v. a. sep., trug, getragen, trägst, to carry off, bear away.

fórttreiben, v. a. sep., trieb, getrieben, to drive off, chase away.

fragen, v. a., fragte or frug, gefragt, frägst or fragest, frägt or fragt, to ask, inquire.

frank, adj., frank, open (used only as pred., as in the phrase frank und frei, frank and free, merrily).

Frau, subst. f., pl.-en, woman, lady, wife [more respectful than Weib. Dame, from Fr. *dame*, = "lady"].

frei, adj., free ; adv. freely, merrily.

freien, v. a. w., to woo, sue for the hand of, ask in marriage.

Freier, subst. m., gen.-s, pl. ———. wooer, suitor.

Freihèrr, subst. m., gen.-n, pl. -en, baron (lit. "free lord").

freílich, adv., to be sure ; of course.

fremd, adj., strange, foreign [Der

Fremde, "the stranger," ein Fremder, "a stranger" (m.)].

fressen, v. a., frasz, gefressen, friss, frissest, frisst, to eat (of animals ; essen of men).

Freude, subst. f., pl.-n, joy, delight, pleasure, gladness. [In the phrase : mit Freuden (in which the noun is sing., not pl.), the old weak term. of the dat. appears. See also Erde.]

freudig, adj., glad, joyful, delighted, pleased ; adv., gladly, etc.

freuen, v. a. refl., to be rejoiced, be glad, rejoice (gov. über with acc. of thing) ; v. a. impers., to rejoice, to be glad (acc. of pers. corresp. to Eng. subj., as : es freut mich, I rejoice, am glad).

Freund, subst. m., gen.-es, pl. -e, friend ; f. Freundin.

freúndlich, adj., friendly, kind ; adv., kindly.

Freúndschaft, subst. f., pl.-en, friendship, friendliness ; (coll.) one's friends and acquaintances.

Frével, subst. m., gen.-s, pl. ——, wrong, sin, crime.

Frieden, subst. m., nom. Friede, -n ; gen.-n, -ns ; dat. acc., -e, -n, no pl., peace. [Buchstabe, Fels, Glaube, Name, etc., have the same double forms of decl.]

frisch, adj., fresh, lively, cheerful, joyous ; frisch und gesund, sound and whole ; adv., freshly, briskly.

Fríschling, subst. m., dim., gen. -(e)s, pl.-e, a young wild boar (orig. the young of any animal).

froh, adj., glad, joyous, cheerful ; adv., gladly, etc.

fröhlich, adj. (from prec.), joyous, merry, cheerful.

fromm, adj., comp. frömmer, pious, good ; kindly, affectionate (of natural affection, comp. Lat. pius).

Frosch, subst. m., gen.-es, pl. Frösche, frog.

früh(e), adj., early.

Frühjahr, subst. n., gen.-(e)s, pl.-e, spring (season of the year).

Frühling, subst. m., gen.-(e)s, pl.-e, spring (season of the year).

Fuchs, subst. m., gen.-es, pl. Füchse, fox. [From the fem. Füchsin comes Eng. "vixen." It also means "a sorrel," bright bay, or chestnut horse (see foll.) ; also a freshman, or student of the first year at a German university.]

fúchsroth, adj., no compar., foxy-red ; sorrel (of a horse). J., p. 27, l. 2.

fügen, v. a. w., to join, fit in, accommodate ; v. refl., to accommodate one's self to, submit to, acquiesce in (gov. in with acc.).

fühlen, v. a. w., to feel, perceive.

führen, v. a. w., to lead, guide (caus. of fahren).

füllen, v. a. w., to fill, replenish.

fünf(e) (pron. fümf), card. num., five ; ord. fünfte, fifth.

funfzehn (or fünfzehn), card. num., fifteen ; ord. funfzehnte, fünfzehnte, fifteenth.

für, prep., gov. acc. only, for, instead of, in behalf of, in return for. [Never expresses purpose as "for" does in Eng. ; in this sense is to be rendered generally by zu, or by some other prep. Orig. identical with vor ; so we find für Angst = vor Angst, "for, by reason of terror."]

Furcht, subst. f., no pl., fear, dread, terror.

fürchten, v. a. w., fürchtete, gefürchtet, to fear, dread ; v.

refl., to be afraid of, fear (gov. vor with dat.).

Fürst, subst. m., gen.-en, pl. -en, prince, monarch, sovereign [superl. of vor or für = der Vorderste, Eng. "first." Means a *reigning* prince ; the foreign word Prinz is a titular prince only, thus : Fürst Bismarck, but : der Prinz von Wales].

Fusz, subst. m., gen.-es, pl. Füsze, foot [as noun of measure, pl. same as sing.] ; zu F., on foot, afoot.

Fászspitze, subst. f. comp., pl. -n, point or end of the foot.

Fászzehe, subst. f. comp., pl.-n, toe (of the foot).

G

G. the seventh letter of the alphabet, when at the beginning of a syll., is always pron. hard as in *get, give* (never like j, as in *ginger*). When final, after a vowel, the best pron. is identical with that of ch, though in many parts it is pron. like k, esp. after n. Tag, pron. Tach (or Tak), but gen. Ta-ges. When between i and another vow. (in the adj. term -ig), pron. very softly, almost like a slightly aspirated *y*.

Gabe, subst. f., pl.-n, gift, present, donation [conn. with geben].

Gabel, subst. f., pl.-n, fork. [Compare Eng. "gable"] ; dim. Gäbelchen, Gäbelein, n. [conn. with Eng. "gable"].

Galgen, subst. m., gen.-s, pl. ——— gallows.

Gang, subst. m., gen.-(e)s, pl. Gänge, gait, walk ; path ; passage, corridor [same root as gegangen, part. of gehen].

Gans, subst. f., pl. Gänse, goose.

Gänsefett, subst. n. comp., gen. -(e)s, no pl., goose-fat.

Gänsefettbrod, subst. n. comp., gen.-(e)s, no pl., bread dipped or soaked in goose-fat or gravy ; bread and dripping.

ganz, adj. of quant., whole, all [like halb, it is decl. in the sing. only when accompanied by an art., etc. (which always precedes it), as : ganz Deutschland, "all Germany," das ganze Deutschland, "the whole of Germany." In the pl. it is always decl.]; adv., wholly, altogether, quite, with foll., ganz und gar, wholly and entirely.

gar, adj., prepared, ready (of meat, etc.) ; cooked, done ; adv. (with verbs), even (= sogar) ; with adj. and adv., very, exceedingly (= sehr), (emphatic), *e.g.*, gar sehr, very much indeed ; gar zu gut, much too good, far too good, only too good ; gar nicht, not at all.

garstig, adj., nasty, disagreeable, unpleasant.

Garten, subst. m., gen.-s, pl. Gärten, garden [conn. with Eng. "garden" and "yard," Lat. *hortus*].

Gaul, subst. m., gen.-(e)s, pl. Gäule, horse, nag [the common word is Pferd ; of a noble, wellbred horse we generally use Ross ; Gaul is usually, though not always, used of a workhorse, or in depreciation].

Gaumen, subst. m., gen.-s, pl. ——, gum, roof of the mouth, palate.

ge-, insep. prefix ; with substs. it has originally a collective or frequentative force : with verbs it may indicate, besides this, perfect action ; hence its use as the regular prefix of the past part.

Gebáckenes (das Gebackene), partic. subst. (from **backen,** "bake"), baked things, cakes (decl. as adj.).

gebären, v. a. insep., **gebar, geboren,** no imper., **gebierst,** to give birth to, bear ; v. refl., to conduct one's self, bear one's self [the simple verb is not in use].

Gebéll, subst. n. freq., gen.-es, no pl., barking (of dogs, from **bellen).**

geben, v. a., **gab, gegeben, gib, gibst,** to give ; v. a. impers. es **gibt,** etc., there is, there are, taking the Eng. subj. in the acc. **Es gibt** is more indef. than es **ist,** which should always be used when a definite circumscribed space is specified, as : **es ist ein Vogel in diesem Käfig,** "there is a bird in this cage," but : **es gibt dieses Jar viel Obst,** "there will be much fruit this year."

Gebet, subst. n. freq., gen.-(e)s, pl.-e, prayer (from **beten).**

gebráuchen, v. a. insep. w., to use ; need, want.

gebühren, v. n. (haben) impers. insep. w., to belong to, befit, beseem.

Gebúrt, subst. f., pl.-en, birth (from **gebären).**

Gebüsch, subst. n. coll., gen.-es, pl.-e, bush, bushes (from **Busch).**

Gedanke(n), subst. m., gen.-n or -ns, dat. acc.-n, pl.-n, thought, idea [Comp. **Buchstabe,** etc.].

Gefáhr, subst. f., pl.-en, danger, peril.

gefährlich, adj. (from prec.), dangerous, perilous ; adv. dangerously.

gefállen, v. n. (haben) impers. insep., **gefiel, gefallen,** no imper., **gefällst,** to please, delight (dat. of person).

Gefállen, subst. m., inf. of prec., gen.-s, no pl., pleasure, delight. [G. **haben, finden,** to take pleasure or delight in a thing, be pleased with (gov. an with dat.).]

Gefängnis, subst. n., gen.-es, pl.-nisse, prison (from **fangen,** "to catch, capture ").

Gefäsz, subst. n., gen.-es, pl.-e, vessel (for holding anything, from **fassen,** "hold, contain ").

gégen, prep. (acc. only), against, toward [gegen does not necessarily imply opposition, as **wieder** does].

géhen, v. n. (sein), **gieng, gegangen,** to go, walk ; **zur Hand gehen,** to assist (dat. of pers.) ; v. impers., to fare (of health, etc.), as : **wie geht es Ihnen?** "how are you? how do you do?" ; **das geht nicht,** that won't do.

gehören, v. n. (haben) impers. insep. w., to belong, appertain to (dat. of pers.).

gehórchen, v. n. (haben) insep. w., to obey (dat. of pers.).

Gelächter, subst. n. freq., gen. -s, no pl., laughter (continuous or prolonged, hence) a peal of laughter.

gelangen, v. n. (sein, rarely haben) insep. w., to arrive at, reach (gov. zu) [dist. from **gelingen, gelang, gelingen,** strong impers., "to succeed"].

gelb, adj., yellow.

Geld, subst. n., gen.-(e)s, pl.-er, money [conn. with **gelten,** "to have value"].

gelüsten, v. n. (haben) impers. insep. w., **gelüstete, gelüstet,**

to lust for, desire, long for (acc.
of pers., obj. gov. by **nach**, as :
es gelüstet mich nach Geld,
I desire, feel a longing for
money.
Gelüsten, subst. n. (inf. of prec.),
gen.-**s**, no pl., lusting, longing,
desire, appetite.
gemacht, adj. (part. of **machen**),
ready-made ; J., p. **25**, l. **17**.
gemächlich, adj., comfortable,
easy ; adv. comfortably.
Gemächlichkeit, subst. f., no pl.,
comfort, ease, love of ease ;
mit G., with comfort or ease,
comfortably.
Gemahl, subst. m. [or n.], gen.
-**(e)s**, pl.-**e**, husband, spouse
[as n. subst. it may mean
either husband or wife, as in
Uhland, "*Das Schloss am
Meer*," den **König und sein
Gemahl** (wife, n.)].
Gemahlin, subst. f., (deriv. of
prec.), pl.-**innen**, wife.
Gemüs[e], subst. n., gen.-**es**, pl.
-**e**, dish of vegetables [conn.
with Eng. "mash," "mess."
"mush ; " something mashed :
it may also mean "porridge"] ;
dim. -**chen**. S.
geneigt, adj. (part. of **neigen**,
"incline"), inclined to, favor-
able.
genug, adv. of quant., enough,
sufficient, sufficiently (generally
follows the subst.)
g(e)rad(e), adj., straight, upright ;
adv. just, just now ; just, exactly.
geradeswegs, adv. gen. (from
prec. and **Weg**), straightway,
directly (of direction or time).
[Do not translate "right off,"
or "right away," which are
both bad English.]
geradezu, adv., straight onward,
straightway (direction) ; im-

mediately (of time) ; precisely,
exactly (manner).
geráten, v. n. (**sein**) insep., ge-
**riet, geraten, gerät, gerätst,
gerät**, to get, come (to get into a
particular position, situation, by
accident or involuntarily).
Gerät, subst. n., gen.-**(e)s**, pl.
-**e**, same as foll.
Gerätschaft, subst. f., pl.-**en**,
vessel, utensil, tool.
Gerícht, subst. n., gen.-**(e)s**, pl.
-**e**, judgment, sentence ; court
(from **richten**, "to judge") ;
dish (of food), mess (from
richten, "to prepare").
gering, adj., slight, small ; mean,
base.
gern(e), compar. **lieber**, superl.
am **liebsten**, willingly, gladly ;
gerne tun, to be fond of doing, like to do ; **g. essen,
trinken**, to be fond of (eating,
drinking).
Gerúch, subst. m., gen.-**(e)s**, pl.
-**e**, smell, odour ; sense of smell
(from **riechen**).
Gesáng, subst. m., gen.-**(e)s**, pl.
Gesänge, song (music, or words
for singing) [; in the latter sense
Lied is also used].
geschéhen, v. n. (**sein**) impers.
insep., **geschah, geschehen**, no
imper., **geschieht**, to happen,
come to pass (with dat. of pers.) ;
to serve (as : **es geschieht dir
recht**, "it serves you right") ;
take place, be done. **jetzt ist's
um dich g.**, now it's all over,
at an end, with you. S., p. **54**,
l. **8.**
Geschíck, subst. n., gen.-**(e)s**,
pl.-**e**, fate, lot, destiny ; clever-
ness (from **schicken**, = "what
is sent" by God) ; adaptability ;
fitness ; **kurz und dick hat
kein G.** K., see note to p. **41**,
l. **15**.

Geschírr, subst. n., gen.-(e)s, pl.
-e, vessel, tool, utensil [; harness
(of a horse, etc.)].

Geschreí, subst. n. freq., gen.
-(e)s, no pl., cry, cries, crying
out, screaming, shouting, calling.

geschwínd(e), adj., quick, fast,
rapid ; adv. quickly, etc.

Geséll(e), subst. m., gen.-en, pl.
-en, fellow, associate, companion [; apprentice].

geséllen, v. a. refl. insep. w., to
associate with, join (gov. zu).

Gesícht, subst. n., gen.-(e)s, no
pl., sense of sight, sight, vision
(pl.-e) ; thing seen, sight, vision
(in sleep or otherwise) ; (pl.-er)
face (from sehen).

Gespräch, subst. n. freq., gen.
-(e)s, pl.-e, talking, conversation (from sprechen).

Gestált, subst. f., pl.-en, shape,
form, figure (from stellen).

géstern, adv. of time, yesterday.

gesúnd, adj., comp. gesünder,
sound, healthy.

getán, part. of tun, "to do."

getráuen, v. refl. insep. w., to
venture, dare (from trauen,
"to trust, have confidence ;"
with refl. pron. in dat.).

getreu, adj., faithful ; adv. faithfully (freq. form of treu).

getrost, adv. confidently, with
confidence, without fear.

gewähren, v. a. insep. w., to
grant, allow (dat. of pers.) ; g.
lassen, to let a pers. do as he
pleases, leave him to himself,
to his own devices.

Gewalt, subst. f., pl.-en, power,
might ; violence.

gewaltig, adj., powerful, mighty ;
adv. powerfully ; mightily, very.

Gewehr, subst. n., gen.-(e)s,
pl.-e, weapon (properly of defence), arms (military ; from
wehren, "defend").

gewesen, part. of sein, "to be."

Gewicht, subst. n., gen.-(e)s, pl.
-e, weight.

Gewild, subst. n. coll., gen.-(e)s,
no pl., wild animals, (large)
animals of the chase, game
(from wild).

gewiss, adj., sure, certain (like
Eng. "certain," sometimes with
indef. meaning) ; adv., surely,
certainly, doubtlessly, no doubt.

gewisslich, adv. (from prec.),
assuredly, certainly.

gewogen, adj., well-inclined, favourable (dat. of pers.).

gewöhnlich, adj., usual, common, customary, general ; adv.
usually, generally, etc. [from
gewöhnen, "accustom ;" conn.
with wohnen, "dwell"].

Gewölbe, subst. n., gen.-s, pl.
——, vault, arched chamber.

gi(e)ng, impf. of gehen, "to
go."

Gift, subst. n. (sometimes m.),
gen.-(e)s, pl.-e, poison, venom
[f. = "gift," now hardly used
exc. in comp. Mitgift, "dowry ;"
both conn. with geben].

giftig, adj., poisonous, venomous ;
(metaphor.) spiteful, malicious,
venomous.

glänzen, v. n. (haben) w., to
shine, glitter.

glänzend, adj. (part. of prec.),
shining, glittering, brilliant,
bright.

Glas, subst. n., gen.-es, pl.
Gläser, glass (the substance, or
vessel of that substance).

Glaube(n), subst. m., gen.-n or
-ns, dat. acc.-n, pl.-n, faith,
belief.

glauben, v. a. and n. (haben), to
believe, credit, dat. of pers.

gleich, adj., no compar., equal,
like, similar, the same ; n. ein
gleiches, the same (thing), J.,

p. 24, 1. 17 ; adv. (of manner) equally ; (of time) at once (= so-gleich). [See also obgleich.]

Glied, subst. n., gen.-(e)s, pl. -er, limb, member (of body, etc.) [= Eng. "lid" in "eye-lid"].

glitzerig, adj., shining, bright ; adv. brightly ; B., p. 33, l. 8.

Glück, subst. n., gen.-(e)s, no pl., luck, fortune ; happiness ; zum G., luckily, fortunately.

glücklich, adj., happy ; fortunate ; adv. happily. [See foll.]

glücklicherweise, adv. gen. (of manner), fortunately (lit. "in fortunate wise, or manner").

[glückselig, adj., happy, blissful ; hence]

Glückseligkeit, subst. f., pl.-en, happiness, bliss.

Glückshaut, subst. f. comp., pl. -häute, lucky skin.

glühen, v. n. (haben) w., to glow, grow hot, get red hot.

glühend, adj. (part. of prec.), glowing, red-hot.

Gnade, subst. f., pl.-n, grace, mercy. [The pl. is used as a title of distinction, as : Euer or Ihro Gnaden, "Your Honour."]

Gold, subst. n., gen.-es, no pl., gold.

goldblinkend, comp. adj., no compar., glittering or gleaming with or like gold.

golden, gülden, adj., no compar., golden, of gold, gold.

Goldgefäsz, subst. n. comp., gen. -es, pl.-e, vessel, utensil of gold.

Goldsache, subst. f. comp., pl. -n, thing, object, article, etc., of gold.

Goldschmied, subst. m. comp., gen.-(e)s, pl.-e, goldsmith, worker in gold.

Goldzeug, subst. n. comp. coll., gen.-(e)s, no pl., articles of gold.

Gott, subst. m., gen.-es, pl. Götter, God, divinity, deity.

gottlos, adj., godless, wicked.

Grab, subst. n., gen.-(e)s, pl. Gräber, grave, pit.

Graben, subst. m., gen.-s, pl. Gräben, ditch.

graben, v. a. and n. (haben), grub, gegraben, gräbst, to dig, delve.

grad(e) ; see g(e)rad(e).

Graf, subst. m., gen.-en, pl.-en, count, earl (title of nobility).

Gras, subst. n., gen.-es, pl. Gräser, grass.

grau, adj., gray.

Graukopf, subst. m. comp., gen. -(e)s, pl.-köpfe, gray-head, gray-headed fellow (used of the Wolf in R.).

grausig, adj., horrible, fearful, terrible (conn. with grau).

greifen, v. a., griff, gegriffen, to grip, seize.

grosz, adj. (compar. gröszer, superl. gröszt), great, large, big ; grand.

Groszmutter, subst. f. comp., pl.-mütter, grandmother.

Groszvater, subst. m. comp., gen.-s, pl.-väter, grandfather.

grün, adj., green.

Grund, subst. m., gen.-(e)s, pl. Gründe, ground, bottom ; foundation ; soil ; zu Grunde richten, to ruin, destroy (lit. "run into the ground").

Grusz, subst. m., gen.-es, pl. Grüsze, greeting, salutation.

grüszen, v. a. w., to greet, salute, send greetings to.

[Grütz, subst. m., only occurs in S., in the comp. Apfelgrütz. The simple subst. is gen. f. ; conn. with Eng. "grit."]

gucken [or kucken], v. n. (haben) w., to look, peep.

gülden, golden, see golden.

gut, adj., compar. besser, sup. best, good ; kind ; adv. well (see wohl) ; Etwas zu gute tun, to confer a kindness, do a kindness, treat kindly (dat. of person) ; sich etwas zu gut tun, to give one's self a treat ; wieder gut machen, to make up for a thing ; gut sein (with dat. of pers.), to be fond of, to love.

H

H, the eighth letter of the alphabet, is never mute at the beginning of a word or syll.; it is mute between two vowels, or before a consonant. It occurs in combination with c, and in foreign (Greek) words, with p. The modern orthography rejects it entirely after t.

Haar, see Har.

haben, v. a. aux. of tense irreg., hatte, gehabt, hast, hat, to have, possess [used as aux. with perf. and plupf. of all trans. and refl., and many intrans. verbs] ; arg haben, to entertain a suspicion, suspect.

hacken, v. a. and n. (haben) w., to hack, hew ; pick (with a pick-axe).

Hacke, subst. f., pl. -n, hatchet ; heel.

Hacken, subst. m., gen.-s, pl. ——, hatchet ; heel [Haken = "hook"].

Haide, see Heide.

halb, adj., fract. num., half [like ganz, is not decl. before subst. not accompanied by an art.,

etc. (which always precedes it), as : halb Frankreich, das halbe Frankreich ; eine halbe Stunde, half an hour].

Hälfte, subst. f., pl. -n, half (one of two equal portions of a whole).

Halfter, subst. m. (gen.-s, pl. ——) and f. (pl.-n), holster (place in a saddle for pistols). [orig. = "halter."]

hallen, v. n. (haben) w., to sound, resound, echo, reecho.

Hals, subst. m., gen.-es, pl. Hälse, throat, neck (the front of the neck or throat ; Nacken is the back of the neck, nape).

Halsband, subst. n. comp., gen. -(e)s, pl.-bänder, necklace ; collar (of a dog, etc.) [; necktie].

Halt, subst. m. (not decl.), halt ; H. machen, to halt, stop.

halten, v. a., hielt, gehalten, hältst, hält, to hold ; v. n. (haben), to halt, stop) ; es hielt schwer, "it was a difficult matter."

Hand, subst. f., pl. Hände, hand ; zur H. gehen, to help, assist (dat. of pers.).

Handel, subst. m., gen.-s, no pl., trade, commerce ; bargain. [The pl. Händel means "a quarrel."]

handeln, v. n. (haben) w., to trade, make a bargain ; deal in (gov. mit).

Handschuh, subst. m. comp., gen.-es, pl.-e, glove (lit. handshoe).

Handwerk, subst. n. comp., gen. -(e)s, pl.-e, trade, mechanical occupation (lit. hand-work).

hangen, v. n. (haben), hieng, gehangen, hängst, to hang, be suspended.

hängen, v. a. w., to hang up, suspend. [This and the prec. are often interchanged.]

Hans, subst. m. prop., gen.-ens (nickname of **Johannes**), Hans, Jack.

Hār, subst. n., gen.-es, pl.-e, hair.

hart, adj., compar. **härter** hard ; harsh.

Hásel, subst. f., pl.-n hazel (tree).

Háselbaum, subst. m. comp., gen.-(e)s, pl.-bäume, hazel-tree ; dim.-bäumchen.

Háselbusch, subst. m. comp., gen.-es, pl.-büsche, hazel-bush.

Háselreis, subst. n. comp., gen. -es, pl.-er, hazel-twig or branch.

hässlich, adj., ugly [; hateful ; (from **hassen**, "to hate")].

Haube, subst. f., pl.-n, woman's-cap, mob-cap [conn. with **Haupt**].

hauen, v. a., **hieb**, **gehauen**, to hew, chop.

Haupt, subst. n., gen.-(e)s, pl. **Häupter**, head, chief. [Syn. **Kopf**. **Haupt** is used in choice or elevated language ; they are both of the same origin as Lat. *caput*, "head."]

Haus, subst. n., gen.-es, pl. **Häuser**, house, abode, dwelling ; dim. **Häuschen**, hut, cottage, hovel ; **nach H.**, home (motion to) ; **zu H.**, at home (rest in).

Háusgerät, subst. n. comp. coll., gen.-(e)s, pl.-e, household furniture, utensils.

Haushalt, subst. m. comp., gen. (e)s, no pl., housekeeping, household affairs.

haussen, adv., outside here (contr. for **hier-aussen** ; compare **draussen** for **dar-aussen**).

Haut, subst. f., pl. **Häute**, skin ; hide (of animals).

heben, v. a., **hob** or **hub**, **gehoben**, to heave, raise, lift ; **in die Höhe h.**, to raise up, lift up.

Hecke, subst. f., pl.-n, hedge.

heftig, adj., violent ; adv. violently.

hegen, v. a. w., to cherish, nourish ; entertain (a sentiment).

Heide (or **Haide**), subst. f., pl. -n, heath [**Heide**, m. (gen.-n, pl.-n), = "heathen"].

heil, adj., whole, sound ; healed. [Conn. with Eng. "whole" and "heal," "hale," Scotch "haill."]

heim, adv. of place, home (motion to), homeward [also used as subst. n. ; "at home" = da-heim].

Heímat, subst. f., pl.-en, home, abode ; native place.

heímbringen, v. a. sep. irreg., **brachte**, **gebracht**, to bring home, fetch home (as a bride).

heímlaufen, v. n. (sein) sep., **lief**, **gelaufen**, **läufst**, to run home walk home, go home.

heímlich, adj., secret ; adv. secretly [from **heim**, "done at home," hence "in secret"].

heímführen, v. a. sep. w., to lead home, bring home (as a bride. J., p. 26, l. 29).

heímkommen, v. n. (sein) sep., **kam**, **gekommen**, **kömmst** or **kommst**, to come home, return home.

heímtragen, v. a. sep., **trug**, **getragen**, **trägst**, to bear home, carry home.

Heímweg, subst. m. comp., gen. -(e)s, pl.-e, way home, road home.

Heírat, subst. f., pl.-en, marriage.

heíratslústig, adj. comp., desirous of marriage, willing or anxious to marry ; marriageable.

heiss, adj., hot ; adv., hotly.

heissen, v. n. (haben), hiess, geheissen, to be called, named (thus : er heisst Karl, "his name is Charles") ; v. a., to order, bid.

helfen, v. n. (haben), half, geholfen, hilf, hilfst, to help, assist (dat. of pers.).

hell, adj., bright, light, clear (of sight) ; clear (of sound).

Heller, subst. m., gen.-s, pl. ——, a small coin, farthing.

[Hemd(e), subst. n., gen.-es, pl. -en, shirt, under-garment.]

her, adv., hither. [Indicates motion or direction toward the speaker or spectator. Nearly all verbs of motion, compounded with preps. or particles indicating direction, further indicate also the direction to or from by prefixing either her or hin (the latter meaning "hence," motion or direction from speaker or spectator). Thus, ausgehen simply "to go out," hinausgehen, "to go out from" (the house, etc.) ; aufgehen, "to rise" (of the sun, etc.) ; hinaufgehen, "to go up" (to a particular place), etc.] ; hin und her, hither and thither, up and down.

heráb, adv., down upon.

herábblicken, v. n. (haben) sep. w., to look or gaze down upon, regard from above (gov. auf with acc.).

herábfallen, v. n. (sein) sep., fiel, gefallen, fällst, to fall down (on the ground, etc.).

herábfliegen, v. n. (sein) sep., flog, geflogen, to fly down (toward).

herábgehen, v. n. (sein) sep., gieng, gegangen, to go down (toward).

herábkommen, v. n. (sein), sep., kam, gekommen, kömmst or kommst, to come down (from above toward the speaker).

herábrutschen, v. n. (sein), sep. w., to slip or slide down (toward).

herábspringen, v. n. (sein), sep., sprang, gesprungen, to jump down, run down to.

herábwerfen, v. a. sep., warf, geworfen, wirf, wirfst, to throw down to (dat. of pers.).

herábziehen, v. a. sep., zog, gezogen, to pull down, draw down toward ; v. n. (sein), to march down, move down toward.

herán, adv., up to, toward [= herbei].

heránkommen, v. n. (sein) sep., kam, gekommen, kömmst or kommst; to come up, come near, approach.

heránnahen, v. n. (sein) sep. w., to draw near, approach.

heránrücken, v. n. (sein) sep. w., to come near, advance.

herántreten, v. n. (sein) sep., trat, getreten, tritt, trittst, tritt, to step up, approach.

heránwachsen, v. n. (sein) sep., wuchs, gewachsen, wächsest, wächst, to grow up.

heráuf, adv. up to, toward.

heráufkommen, v. n. (sein) sep., kam, gekommen, kömmst or kommst, to come up.

heráufschicken, v. a. sep. w., to send up.

heráufsteigen, v. n. (sein) sep., stieg, gestiegen, to rise up, ascend (toward).

heráus, adv., out to or toward.

heráusfallen, v. n. (sein) sep., fiel, gefallen, fällst, to fall out.

heráusgehen, v. n. (sein) sep., gieng. gegangen, to go out (toward), walk out, go forth.

heráusgucken, v. n. (haben) sep. w., to look out, peep out (at the window, zum Fenster).

heráusholen, v. a. sep. w., to fetch out, bring out or forth.

heráuskommen, v. n. (sein) sep., kam, gekommen, kömmst or kommst, to come out, issue, come forth.

heráusnehmen, v. a. sep., nahm, genommen, nimm, nimmst, to take [; sich etwas h., to take a liberty, presume].

heráusquillen, v. n. (sein) sep., quoll, gequollen, to gush forth, well forth.

heráusschauen, v. n. (haben) sep. w., to look out.

heráusspringen, v. n. (sein) sep., sprang, gesprungen, to jump out, run out or forth.

heráusstrecken, v. a. sep. w., to stretch out or forth (toward).

heráussuchen, v. a. sep. w., to seek out (from among), pick out.

heráusträufeln, v. n. (sein) sep. w., to come out drop by drop, drip forth.

heráustreiben, v. a. sep., trieb, getrieben, to drive out or forth.

heráusziehen, v. a. sep., zog, gezogen, to pull out, draw forth [; v. n. (sein), to march forth, pass out].

herbeí, adv., up to, close to. [= heran.]

herbeílaufen, v. n. (sein) sep., lief, gelaufen, läufst, to run up, come near, approach quickly.

He(e)rd, subst. m., gen.-es, pl. -e, hearth, chimney-place 'die Herde, f., = flock, herd].

hereín, adv., in toward.

hereínkommen, v. n. (sein) sep., kam, gekommen, kömmst or kommst, to come in (toward).

hereínlassen, v. a. sep., liess, gelassen, lässest, lässt, to let in, admit (when the speaker is within).

hereínspringen, v. n. (sein) sep., sprang, gesprungen, to jump in, bound in, run in (toward).

hereíntreten, v. n. (sein) sep., trat, getreten, tritt, trittst, tritt, to step in, enter.

hérgehen, v. n. (sein) sep., gieng, gegangen, to go along ; v. impers. to go on ; es gieng´ hoch her, "there were great goings on."

hernách, adv. of time, afterward, subsequently (= nachher).

Herr, subst. m., gen.-n, pl.-en, gentleman ; master ; lord ; [as title = Mr.].

hérrlich, adj., glorious, splendid, magnificent, grand.

Hérrlichkeit, subst. f., pl.-en, grandeur, splendour, magnificence.

herúm, adv., round, about ; (of time) over, past, ended, up (with gegangen understood).

herúmführen, v. a. sep. w., to lead or take round or about.

herúmgehen, v. n. (sein) sep., gieng, gegangen, to go round, walk round or about ; v. impers. (of time) to pass by, pass away ; return.

herúmkehren, v. a. refl. sep. w., to turn round or about.

herúmspielen, v. n. (haben) sep. w., to play or frolic round or about.

herúmspringen, v. n. (sein) sep., sprang, gesprungen, to jump or run round or about, frisk about, frolic about.

herúnter, adv., down to, toward [= herab].

herúnterführen, v. a. sep. w., to lead or guide down (toward), bring down.

herúnterláufen, v. n. (sein) sep., lief, gelaufen, läufst, to run down.

herúnterwèrfen, v. a. sep., warf, geworfen, wirf, wirfst, to throw or cast down to or upon (gov. dat. or auf with acc.).

hervór, adv., forth, forth from.

hervórhòlen, v. a. sep. w., to fetch forth, bring forth or out.

hervórtrèten, v. n. (sein) sep., . trat, getreten, tritt, trittst, tritt, to come forward or forth.

hervórziehen, v. a. sep., zog, gezogen, to draw forth, pull out.

Herz, subst. n., gen.–ens, dat. –en, pl.–en, heart.

Herzeleid, subst. n. comp., gen. –(e)s, no pl., injury, annoyance (lit. "heart-hurt").

herzen, v. a. w., to hug, caress.

herzlich, adj., hearty, cordial ; adv. heartily, cordially.

Herzog. subst. m., gen.–es, pl. Herzöge, duke.

Hexe, subst. f., pl.–n, witch. [Conn. with Eng. "hag."]

Hexenkunst, subst. f. comp., pl. –künste, witch's art, witchery, magic, magic art.

hieb, impf. of hauen.

hielt, impf. of halten.

hier, adv. of place, here, in this place ; hier herum, hereabouts, in this neighbourhood, in these parts.

Hífthorn, subst. n. comp., gen. –es, pl.–hörner, bugle, hunting-horn. [= horn on which the "Hift," or view-halloo, is blown ; not Hüfthorn, as it has nothing to do with Hüfte, "hip."]

Himmel, subst. m., gen.–s, pl. ——, heaven.

hin, adv., hence (motion from the speaker or spectator. See her, of which it is the opposite) ; hin und her, hither and thither, up and down, to and fro.

hináb, adv., down, downward.

hinábbeugen, v. a. refl. sep. w., to bow down, bend down, bend over.

hinábgucken, v. n. (haben) sep. w., to look down (from).

hinábplumpen, v. n. (sein) sep. w., to roll down, plump down (into the water, with a splash).

hináuf, adv., up, upward (from).

hináufführen, v. a. sep. w., to lead up, guide up ; take up, bring up.

hináufhelfen, v. n. (haben) sep., half, geholfen, hilf, hilfst, to help up (to a particular spot remote from the speaker as on a horse ; dat. of pers.) [aufhelfen = "to assist a pers. to rise"].

hináufsteigen, v. n. (sein) sep., stieg, gestiegen, to ascend.

hináus, adv., outward, out.

hináusbringen, v. a. sep. irreg., brachte, gebracht, to bring out or forth.

hináuseilen, v. n. (sein) sep. w., to hasten out.

hináusfliegen. v. n. (sein) sep., flog, geflogen, to fly out or forth (from).

hináusführen, v. a. sep. w., to lead out or forth (from a particular place).

hináusgehen, v. n. (sein) sep., gieng. gegangen, to go out or forth from a particular place ; ausgehen means simply to go out for a walk, etc.

hináuslassen, v. a. sep., liess, gelassen, lässest, lässt, to let out (from a particular place).

hináusspringen. v. n. (sein) sep., sprang, gesprungen, to jump out, run out or forth (from).

hináusstrecken, v. a. sep. w., to stretch out or forth.

hináuswachsen, v. n. (sein) sep., wuchs, gewachsen, wächsest, wächst, to grow out.

hinderlich, adj., hindering, obstructive (from foll.).

[hindern, v. a. w., to hinder; and that conn. with hinter, behind.]

hindúrch, adv., through, throughout; frequently used like a prep. after an acc., as : den ganzen Tag hindurch, "the whole day long."

hindúrchlassen, v. a. sep., liess, gelassen, lässest, to let through.

hindúrchsehen, v. a. sep., sah, gesehen, sieh, siehst, to see through.

hinein, adv., into, inwards (when the speaker is without).

hineínfallen. v. n. (sein) sep., fiel, gefallen, fällst, to fall into.

hineíngehen, v. n. (sein), sep., gieng, gegangen, to go in or into.

hineínkommen, v. n. (sein) sep., kam, gekommen, kömmst or kommst, to get in or into ["To come in" = hereinkommen].

hineínlegen, v. a. sep. w., to lay into, put into.

hineínschauen, v. n. (haben) sep. w., to look into, gaze into.

hineínscheinen, v. n. haben) sep., schien, geschienen, to shine into.

hineínspringen, v. n. (sein) sep., sprang, gesprungen, to jump into, run into.

hineíntreten, v. n. (sein) sep., trat, getreten, tritt, trittst, tritt, to step into, enter ; to join in (a dance, J., p. 29, l. 3).

hineínwickeln, v. a. sep. w., to wrap up in.

hínfahren, v. n. (sein) sep., fuhr, gefahren, fährst, to drive or go away (to a remote place) ; go on, proceed, move along.

hínfallen, v. n. (sein) sep., fiel, gefallen, fällst, to fall down, tumble over.

hínführen, v. a. sep. w., to guide, lead to a place.

híngeben, v. a. sep., gab, gegeben, gib, gibst, to give up.

híngehen, v. n. (sein) sep., gieng, gegangen, to go away to (a remote place).

hinken, v. n. (haben) w., to limp, go lame.

hínkommen, v. n. (sein) sep., kam, gekommen, kömmst or kommst, to come to, get to or at (a remote place).

hínlaufen, v. n. (sein) sep., lief, gelaufen, läufst, to run away, go off.

hínnehmen, v. a. sep., nahm, genommen, nimm, nimmst, to take to (a remote place). [It frequently = "to take to one's self," in violation of the usual meaning of hin.]

hínstellen, v. a. sep. w., to put in position, place, set down.

hínten, adv. of place, at the back, behind ; to be dist. from foll.

hinter, prep., behind, after.

hinterhér, adv. of place, behind, along behind (motion toward the thing preceding).

hinterhérgehen, v. n. (sein) sep., gieng, gegangen, to go or walk along behind.

Hínterfusz, subst. m. comp., gen.-es, pl.-füsze, hind-foot.

Hintertür(e), subst. f. comp., pl. -en, back-door.

hinzú, adv. of place, up to (a remote place).

hinzúspringen, v. n. (sein) sep.,
sprang, gesprungen, to jump
up to, run up to (the aid of).
[Hirsch, subst. m., gen.-es, pl.
-e, stag, deer.]
Hírschfänger, subst. m. comp.,
gen.-s, pl.——, hunting-knife.
ho! ho! double interj., ho! ho!
hob (or hub), impf. of heben,
"lift."
hoch, adj., compar. höher, superl.
höchst; when in declension a
vowel follows, h is dropped, as
hohe, hohes, etc., high, lofty;
adv. highly.
hóchachten, v. a. sep. w., acht-
ete geachtet, to esteem
highly.
Hóchmut, subst. m. comp., gen.
-(e)s, no pl., haughtiness, pride,
arrogance [an unpardonable
pride ; Stolz may be a pardon-
able pride].
höchstens, superl. adv. of compar., at most [höchst = exceedingly, most ; am höchsten,
most highly].
Hochzeit, subst. f. comp., pl.
-en, feast, festival ; wedding,
marriage [lit. "high time,"
orig. = a feast of any kind].
Hof, subst. m., gen.-(e)s, pl.
Höfe, yard ; court (of a palace :
hence of a king or prince).
Hofstaat, subst. m. comp. coll.,
gen.-(e)s, no pl., the courtiers,
court (persons in the court)
hence retinue.
Höhe, subst. f., pl.-n, height ;
in die H. heben, to raise up,
lift up.
hohl, adj., hollow.
hold, adj., fair, beautiful, charming ; kind, kindly.
holen, v. a. w., to fetch, bring.
Hölle, subst. f., no pl., hell (in-
fernal world).
Höllenfeuer, subst. n. comp.,

gen.-s, pl.——, hell-fire, hellish
fire, fire of intense heat (like that
of hell).
Holz, subst. n., gen.-es, pl.-e
and Hölzer, wood [; forest].
hölzern, adj., wooden, of wood.
Hólzschuh, subst. m. comp.,
gen.-(e)s, pl.-e, wooden shoe,
patten.
hopp! hopp! interj., used to
make a horse trot ; trot! trot!,
gee-up, get-up.
horchen, v. n. (haben) w., to
hearken, listen (gov. auf with
acc. of obj.).
hören, v. a. and n. (haben) w.,
to hear (gov. acc., or auf with
acc., in sense of "hearkening
to").
Horn, subst. n., gen.-(e)s, pl.
Hörner, horn.
Hörnerblasen, subst. n. comp.
inf., gen.-s, no pl., blowing of
horns, horn-blowing.
hub (or hob), impf. of heben,
"to lift."
hübsch, adj., pretty [orig. höfisch
(from Hof). courtly, polished,
elegant] ; adv. nicely, prettily
(see K., p. 11, l. 11, note).
Huhn, subst. n., gen.-(e)s, pl.
Hühner, fowl [the generic word;
the male bird is Hahn, the female Henne].
Hund, subst. m., gen.-(e)s, pl.
-e, dog [Eng. "hound," used
only for hunting dogs] ; dim.
Hündchen, -lein, n.
Hundegebell, subst. n. comp.
freq., gen.-(e)s, no pl., barking
of dogs, baying of hounds.
hundert, card. num., pl.-e, hundred.
hundertjährig, adj. comp., last-
ing for a hundred years.
Hunger, subst. m., gen.-s, no pl.,
hunger [pronounce hung-er,
not hung-ger].

hüpfen, v. n. (haben) w., to hop, skip, jump.

Husar, subst. m., gen.-en, or -s, pl.-en, hussar (light horse-soldier).

Hut, subst. m., gen.-(e)s, pl. Hüte, hat ; dist. from foll.

Hut, subst. f., no pl., heed, guard, protection, ward ; **auf der H. sein**, to be on one's guard.

hüten, v. a. w., hütete, gehütet (from prec.), to watch over, protect, guard ; v. refl., to be on one's guard (gov. **vor** with dat. of obj.).

I

I, the ninth letter of the alphabet and third vow., has the sound of *ee* in *heel* when long ; of *i* in *skin* when short.

ich, pers. pron., first pers. sing., gen. **meiner** or **mein**, dat. **mir**, acc. **mich**, pl. nom. **wir**, gen. **unser**, dat. acc. **uns**, I (not written with a capital letter, unless it begins a sent.).

ihn, acc. sing. of er, pers. pron. third sing., him (direct obj.) ; it (of masc. inanimate obj.).

ihnen, dat. pl., of all genders, third pers. (nom. sie), to them, them (indirect obj.).

ihr, pers. pron. second pl., gen. **euer**, dat. acc. **euch**, ye, you (the pl. of du, used in addressing several persons, each of whom may be addressed as du ; also used, in some parts of Germany, in addressing a single pers., either superiors or inferiors, like Eng. "you," but not in common use).

ihr, pers. pron. third sing. f., dat. of sie, "she," to her, her (as indir. obj.) ; to it, it (of fem. inanimate obj.).

ihr (or ihrer), gen. sing. of same, of her, her ; also gen. pl. third pers. all genders (nom. sie), of them, their ; hence :

ihr, ihre, ihr, poss. adj. of third sing. fem., her ; its (of inanimate objects) ; also of third pl. of all genders, their : **um ihretwillen**, for her sake, for their sake.

im, contr. for in dem.

immer, adv., always, on every occasion (neg. nimmer ; see je) [comp. of ie (= je) and mêr (mehr), "evermore"].

in, prep. (with dat.) in, within ; (with acc.) into (motion or direction to). [Not used as prefix with verbs ; ein takes its place.]

indém, indéssen, adv., in the meanwhile (takes verb in second place, throwing subj. after verb when it begins sent.) ; subord. conj., while, whilst (throws verb to end of sent. ; indem is generally conj.).

ins, contr. for in das.

írden, adj., no compar., earthen, of earthenware [from Erde ; irdisch = "earthly"].

iss, imper. second sing., from essen, "to eat."

isst, third sing. pres. ind. of same.

ist, third sing. pres. ind. of sein, "to be."

J

J, the tenth letter of the alphabet, is the cons. form of I, and is pron. like the Eng. cons. *y* in *yes*, etc.

ja, affirm. adv., yes ; by all means (to emphasize an imper., etc.) ; you know, I'm sure ; why (er

hat es ja, "he has it, you know;" **Sie wissen es ja,** "I'm sure you know it ;" **da ist er ja,** "why, there he is "); [**ja nicht,** by no means].

Jagd, subst. f., pl.-en, hunt, chase.

Jágdhund, subst. m. comp., gen. -(e)s, pl.-e, hunting-dog, hound.

Jágdlust, subst. f. comp., no pl., delight in the chase, in hunting, pleasure of hunting.

jagen, v. a. and n. (**haben** or **sein**), to hunt, chase ; pursue, drive.

Jäger, subst. m., gen.-s, pl.——, hunter, huntsman.

Jahr, subst. n., gen.-(e)s, pl.-e, year.

Jammer, subst. m., gen.-s, no pl., misery, wretchedness ; grief, sorrow.

jämmerlich, adj., miserable, wretched, pitiable ; adv. wretchedly, etc.

jámmern, v. n. (**haben**) w., to grieve, sorrow, be sorry. [The Scotch "yammer" means to make a noise expressive of grief, etc.]

jámmervoll, adj. comp., wretched, miserable, pitiable, piteous ; adv. wretchedly, etc.

je, indef. adv. of time, ever, on any occasion [= **jemals.** Eng. "ever" is sometimes used as = "always ;" **je** is never thus used].

jeder, -e, -es, indef. pronom. adj., every, each ; sometimes prec. by indef. art., **ein jeder, eines jeden,** etc.

jédermann, indef. pronom. subst., gen.-s, no pl., every one, every person, everybody.

jéderzeit, adv. gen. of time, at

every time, on each occasion, at all times.

[**jemals,** adv. gen. of time, at any time, ever.]

jemand, indef. pronom. subst., gen.-(e)s, dat.- or -en, acc.-, no pl., some or any one, some or any person, somebody, anybody ["not any one, etc." = **niemand,** not **nicht jemand**].

jetzt, adv. of time, now, at the present time [formerly **itzt, itzo** or **jetzo**].

Johannes, subst. m. prop., John [nickname, **Hans**].

jung, adj., compar. **jünger,** young, youthful.

Jungfer, subst. f., pl.-n, young (unmarried) woman, maid ; virgin.

Jungfrau, subst. f. comp., pl.-en, young (unmarried) woman, maid ; virgin.

Jüngling, subst. m. dim., gen. -(e)s, pl.-e, young man, youth.

K

K, the eleventh letter of the alphabet, is pron. as in English. When doubled, it is written **ck,** except when the two letters are divided between two different lines in printing, when they are written **k-k.**

[**Kalb,** subst. n., gen.-es, pl. **Kälber,** calf.]

kalt, adj., compar. **kälter,** cold.

Kamm, subst. m., gen.-(e)s, pl. **Kämme,** comb.

kämmen, v. a. w., to comb.

Kammer, subst. f., pl.-n, room, chamber ; apartment [from Lat. *camera*].

Kammerfrau, subst. f. comp., pl.

-en, chamber-woman, tire-woman, lady-in-waiting.

Kammerjungfer, subst. f. comp., pl.-n, chamber-woman (unmarried), lady's-maid, tire-woman. [It means the lady's maid : "chamber-maid," the Eng. etymological equivalent, having a different meaning.]

kann, pres. ind. of können.

Kappe, subst. f., pl.-n, cap: dim. Käppchen. [Syn. Mütze.]

Karren, subst. m., gen.-s, pl. ——, car, cart, barrow.

Käse, subst. m., gen.-s, pl,——, cheese.

Kauf, subst. m., gen.-(e)s, pl. Käufe, purchase, bargain ; des Kaufs einig sein, to agree upon a bargain, strike a bargain.

kaufen, v. a. w., to buy, purchase.

Kaufmann, subst. m. comp., gen.-(e)s, pl.-leute, merchant, trader.

Kaufmannskleid, subst. n. comp., gen.-es, pl.-er, costume or robe of a merchant or trader.

kaum, adv., scarcely, hardly ; (of time) scarcely, hardly, but now, no sooner.

kehren, v. a., to turn ; v. n., to return.

kein, -e, - (when before a subst.), indef. num. adj., no, not any.

keiner, -e, -es (when without a subst.), indef. num., none, not one, not any (person or thing).

kennen, v. a. irreg., kannte, gekannt, to know, be acquainted with. [kennen (conn. with Scotch "ken") = Fr. connaître, is generally used of a knowledge of or acquaintance with persons ; sometimes of an intimate knowledge of things, e.g. : wissen Sie den Weg = "do you know the road (sufficiently not to go astray), do you know which

road to take ;" kennen Sie den Weg, "are you familiar with the road."]

Kette, subst. f., pl.-n, chain, fetter.

Kind, subst. n., gen.-es, pl.-er, child. [Conn. with Eng. "kin" and "kind."]

Kinderfrau, subst. f. comp., pl. -en, nurse.

Kindermädchen, subst. n. comp. dim., gen.-s, pl.——, nursemaid, nurse.

Kinderstube, subst. f. comp., pl.-n, nursery [lit. "children's room "].

Kind(er)taufe, subst. f. comp., pl.-n, baptism of a child, christening.

Kind(er)taufschmaus, subst. m. comp., gen.-es, pl.-schmäuse, christening-feast.

Kinn, subst. n., gen.-(e)s, pl.-e, chin.

Kirche, subst. f., pl.-n, church.

Kissen, subst. n., gen.-s, pl. ——, cushion ; dim. Kisschen.

Kittel, subst. m., gen.-s, pl.——, kirtle (of a woman), blouse (of a man, loose outer garment of coarse stuff worn by workingmen) ; dim.-chen.

Klafter, subst. m. or n. (gen.-s, pl. ——), or f. (pl.-n), a measure of length, of the distance between the extremities of the outstretched arms, fathom (but not confined, as in Eng., to measuring at sea, as length of cables, depth of water, etc.) [also used as cubic measure of wood, like Eng. "cord"].

klar, adj., clear.

kleben, v. n. (haben) w., to cleave, stick, adhere.

Kleid, subst. n., gen.-es, pl.-er, dress, garment, robe, gown [conn. with Eng. "cloth"].

kleiden, v. a. w., **kleidete, ge-kleidet,** to clothe, dress ; v. refl. to clothe one's self, attire one's self, dress.

klein, adj., small, little (never used, like the latter word in Eng., of quantity, but only of size).

klettern, v. n. (haben and **sein**) w., to climb, clamber.

Klinke, subst. f., pl.-n, handle, latch (of a door, etc.).

klopfen, v. a. and n. w., to knock.

Klumpen, subst. m., gen.-s, pl. ——, lump, mass.

Knie, subst. n., gen.-(e)s, pl. -(e), knee.

knie(e)n, v. n. (haben) w., to kneel, lie on one's knees (when spelt with one **e,** pron. as two syll.).

Knochen, subst. m., gen.-s, pl. ——, bone [more usual in this sense than **Bein**].

kochen, v. a. and n. (sein) w., to boil, cook.

Kochen, subst. n., gen.-s, no pl. (inf. of prec.), cooking.

Kohle, subst. f., pl.-n, coal (live coal) ; cinder (dead coal, of wood or other material). [Coal, as a mineral product, = **Steinkohle.** Kohl, m., = "cabbage."]

Kohlenfeuer, subst. n. comp., gen.-s, pl.— -, coal-fire.

kommen, v. n. (sein), **kam, ge-kommen, kömmst** or **kommst,** to come ; **zu sich k.,** to come to one's self or senses, to return to consciousness ; **zum Vor-schein k.,** to make one's appearance, come forth. [When accompanied by another verb defining the motion, it gov. the past, not the pres. part., as : **er kam gelaufen,** "he came running," etc.]

König, subst. m., gen.-(e)s, pl. -e, king.

Königin, subst. f., pl.-innen, queen.

königlich, adj., kingly, royal.

Königreich, subst. n. comp., gen.-(e)s, pl.-e, kingdom, realm.

König(s)sohn, subst. m. comp., gen.-(e)s, pl.-söhne, king's son, prince.

Königstochter, subst. f. comp., pl.-töchter, king's daughter, princess.

können, v. a. irreg., pres. ind. **kann, kannst,** kann, **können,** etc.; pres. subj. könne, impf. ind., **konnte,** impf. subj. **könnte,** part. gekonnt ; can, to be able. [Indicates ability (generally physical) of persons, and possibility (of things) ; hence, by a loose and incorrect usage (as in Eng.) permission, for which **dürfen** is the proper word. When indicating possibility, it is rendered by "may," as : **es kann sein,** "it may be."]

Kopf, subst. m., gen.-(e)s, pl. **Köpfe,** head ; dim. **Köpfchen** [Syn. Haupt].

Kopfkissen, subst. n. comp., gen.-s, pl.——, pillow [lit. "head-cushion"].

Korb, subst. m., gen.-(e)s, pl. **Körbe,** basket.

Korn, subst. n., gen.-(e)s, pl. **Körner,** grain (single seed) ; grain (coll.), wheat, corn ; dim. **Körnlein** (in first sense).

Kost, subst. f. [pl.-en, cost, expense ;], fare (of eating), food (no pl. in the latter sense).

kosten, v. a. and n. (haben) w., **kostete, gekostet,** to cost [gov. acc. of price, and dat. or acc. of pers. ; also = to taste].

köstlich, adj., costly ; precious ; delicious, K., p. 45, l. 28.

Kraft, subst. f., pl. Kräfte, strength, power, might. [Used in the first place of *physical* strength, then of ability to do a thing ; Gewalt = "violence," Macht = "authority, power" (as an attribute of a ruler, etc.). Kraft is used also as a so-called prep. with gen. (really a subst. in instrumental case) = "by virtue of."]

Krämer, subst. m., gen.-s, pl. ——, pedlar, hawker.

Krämerfrau, subst. f. comp., pl. -en, pedlar-woman.

Krämerin, subst. f., pl.-innen, pedlar-woman.

krank, adj., compar. kränker, ill, sick ; der, die, das -e, ein, -er, subst. (decl. as adj.), a sick person, patient.

Kraut, subst. n., gen.-es, pl. Kräuter, herb.

kriechen, v. n. (generally with sein, esp. when indicating *change* of *place ;* also with haben, esp. when indicating the *mode* of motion), kroch, gekrochen, to creep, crawl.

kriegen, v. a. w., to get, obtain [not used in elevated language ; syn. erhalten, etc.; as v. n. = "to make war" (from Krieg)].

Krone, subst. f., pl.-n, crown.

Kropf, subst. m., gen.-(e)s, pl. Kröpfe, crop (throat of birds) ; dim. Kröpfchen.

krumm, adj., compar. krümmer, crooked, twisted.

Küche, subst. f., pl.-n, kitchen [conn. with kochen, "cook," etc.].

Kuchen, subst. m., gen.-s, pl. ——, cake [of same origin as prec.].

Küchenfenster, subst. n. comp., gen.-s, pl.——, kitchen-window.

Küchenjunge, subst. m. comp., gen.-n, pl.-n, kitchen-boy, scullion.

Küchenmagd, subst. f. comp., pl.-mägde, kitchen-maid, scullion.

Kuh, subst. f., pl. Kühe, cow.

Kuhfleisch, subst. n., gen.-es, no pl., beef [cow-flesh].

[Kunst, subst. f., pl. Künste, art, artifice ; hence :]

künstlich, adj., artificial, artistic, skilful ; adv. skilfully, etc.

kurz, adj., compar. kürzer, short, brief.

Kuss, subst. m., gen.-es, pl. Küsse, kiss.

L

L, the twelfth letter of the alphabet, pronounce as in Eng.

laben, v. a. w., to refresh.

lachen, v. n. (haben) w., to laugh. [dim. lächeln = "smile."]

laden, v. a., lud or ladete, geladen, ladest or lädst, ladet or lädt, to load ; to invite [= einladen. The weak impf. is rare, though occurring in this work. Both forms of the second and third sing. pres. ind. given are used without distinction. The two forms (weak and strong) were orig. from different roots, but are now fused into one].

Lager, subst. n., gen.-s, pl.——. couch (from legen, liegen) [also means a place where anything is deposited, a warehouse, magazine].

10

146 GLOSSARY.

Laken, subst. n., gen. -s, pl. —,
sheet.
Lampe, subst. f., pl.-n, lamp;
dim. Lämpchen, n.
Land, subst. n., gen.-es, pl.-e,
or Länder, land, country; [also
country as opposed to town, in
which sense the prep. auf is
used (with dat. = "in," and
acc. = "into") to indicate
locality, as opposed to in, used
in the other sense. The pl.
Lande is used in poetical language, or as indicating provinces,
or small divisions of a larger
country (e.g., die Niederlande,
"the Netherlands").]
Landstrasze, subst. f. comp.,
pl.-n, high-road, turnpike-road.
lang(e), adj., compar. länger,
long (of time or space); adv.
for a long time; schon l., for a
long time past; also used as a
sort of postposition, as: eine
Zeit lang (or Zeitlang, in one
word), "for some time," eine
Stunde lang, "for an hour."
lángsam, adj., slow; tedious (of
things); adv. slowly, etc.
lassen, v. a., liess, gelassen,
lässest, lässt, to let, permit,
allow; to have a thing done by
another; order a thing to be
done. [Shares the peculiarities
of auxil. verbs of mood as to construction and government, as:
ich habe es tun lassen (for
gelassen), "I have had it
done;" dass er es habe tun
lassen, "that he may have had it
done"]; sich nicht zu lassen
wissen, "not to know how to
contain one's self." D., p. 16,
l. 10.
Last, subst. f., pl.-en, load,
burden.
Laub, subst. n. coll., gen.-es, no
pl., foliage, leaves.

laufen, v. n. (sein), lief, gelaufen, läufst, läuft, to run;
(colloq.) to walk, go on foot;
zu Fusz l., to go on foot, walk.
[rennen = "to run at full
speed, race;" rinnen (rann,
geronnen), "to flow, run" (of
liquids only).]
laut, adj., loud.
[lauter, adj., pure, clear.]
lauter, adv., merely, nothing but.
[This and prec. to be dist. from
the comp. of laut.]
leben, v. n. (haben) w., to live;
pres. part. and adj., -d, living,
alive.
Leben, subst. n. (inf. of prec.),
gen.-s, pl. —, life.
lebéndig, adj., alive, living.
Léb(e)lang, subst. n. indecl., life-
time [used only as acc. of time;
really Leben with lang as postposition; see lang].
Leber, subst. f., pl.-n, liver
(digestive organ).
leblos, adj., lifeless, without life.
Lebtag, subst. n. comp. indecl.,
generally used as neut. acc. of
time, like Lebelang, life-long
[= Leben, Lebenszeit].
Leder, subst. n., gen.-s, no pl.,
leather.
Ledermütze, subst. f. comp., pl.
-n, leather-cap.
leer, adj., empty, void.
legen, v. a. w., to lay [caus. of
liegen]; v. refl., to lie down;
to subside (of the wind, D., p.
18, l. 22).
Leib, subst. n., gen.-es, pl.-er,
body, person; [orig. also =
"life," hence] bei Leibe, "on
your life, as you value your life,
for your life." D., p. 38, l. 27.
leiben, v. n. (haben) w., used in
the combination: leiben und
leben — to have body and life,
be actually alive. J., p. 22, l. 24.

leicht, adj., light (of weight) ;
easy ; adv. lightly ; easily.

Leid, subst. n., gen.-es, no pl.,
sorrow, harm, injury ; **Einem
etwas zu Leide tun**, to do a
pers. an injury.

leid, adj., painful, disagreeable, unpleasant (causing pain or sorrow);
es tut mir l., " I am sorry for
it " [also used in neut. as subst.
with strong term. : **Leid(e)s**,
"an injury," as : **Erlkönig hat
mir ein Leids getan**(GOETHE);
see also **leider** below].

leiden, v. a. and n., **litt, gelitten**,
to suffer, endure, bear, tolerate.

Leiden, subst. n. (inf. of prec.),
gen.-s, pl.——, suffering, sorrow.

leider, interj., unfortunately,
alas! [really compar. of **leid** ;
see above].

leidlich, adj., tolerable.

lesen, v. a., **las, gelesen, lies,
liesest**, to pick, choose ; (hence
the secondary meaning, to pick
out letters) to read ; [compare
Lat. *lego*.]

letzt, adj. superl., last ; **zuletzt**,
at last ; last ; finally ; at the
end. [Conn. with **lassen** (and
Eng. "let "), = "the one that is
left."]

leuchten, v. n. (haben) w.,
leuchtete, geleuchtet, to show
a light, shine ; sparkle, flash.

Leute, subst. pl. comm., people,
persons ; used to form pl. of
comp. nouns ending with
-mann, as **Kaufmann**, etc.

Licht, subst. n., gen.-es, pl.-er
(lights) and **-e** (candles), light ;
candle ; dim. **-lein**, n. [The
pl.-er is more common, and is
also used in the latter meaning.]

lieb, adj., beloved, dear (of persons) ; agreeable, pleasant (of
things) ; **es ist mir lieb**, " I

am glad of it ;" **lieb haben**, to
be fond of (with acc.).

lieb, adv., dearly ; the compar.
lieber and superl. **am liebsten**
are used as compar. and superl.
of **gern**.

Liebe, subst. f., no pl., love, affection.

lieben, v. a. w., to love, be fond
of.

lieblich, adj., lovely, beautiful ;
adv., beautifully.

Liebster, superl. of **lieb** (der,
die, das **Liebste**—adj. used as
subst.), lover, beloved.

liegen, v. n. (haben), **lag, gelegen, liege, liegst**, to lie (be
recumbent *or* situated). [**legen**
="to lay " (trans.); **lügen** (log,
gelogen), "to lie " (tell a falsehood ; with the prep. **an** (meaning "to take an interest in "), it
is conj. with **sein** ; also when it
indicates *situation*.]

link, adj., no compar., left (on the
left hand) [opposed to **recht**,
"right"] ; **die Linke (Hand)**,
subst. f., the left (hand) ; **zur
linken (Hand)**, on the left
(hand).

links, adv. of place, on the left
(hand).

Linse, subst. f., pl. -n, lentil.

Lippe, subst. f., pl.-n, lip.

List, subst. f., pl.-en, cunning,
fraud ; wile, deceit, stratagem.

listig, adj., cunning, artful, de-
ceitful, crafty, wily ; adv.
craftily, etc.

loben, v. a. w., to praise, extol.

Loch, subst. n., gen.-(e)s, pl.
Löcher, hole, pit ; dungeon ;
das schwarze L., "the black
hole, lock-up."

Löffel, subst. m., gen.-s, pl.——,
spoon ; dim. **Löffelein**, n.

Lohn, subst. m. and n., gen.-(e)s,
pl. **Löhne**, reward ; wages,

salary. [m. only in former sense ; m. or n. in latter.]

lohnen, v. n. (haben), to reward, repay (dat. of pers.).

los, adj., loose ; free (with acc. of obj.).

loslassen, v. a. sep., liess, gelassen, lässest, to let loose, set free, release.

losmachen, v. a. sep. w., to make loose, loosen, untie.

loswerden, v. n. sep. (sein), ward or wurde, geworden, wirst, wird, to get rid of (acc. of obj., gov. by adj. prefix los).

Luft, subst. f., pl. Lüfte, air ; breeze.

Lunge, subst. f., pl.-n, lung.

Lust, subst. f., pl. Lüste [lust] ; pleasure, delight ; desire, longing ; Lust haben etwas zu tun, "to have a mind to do anything."

lustig, adj., merry, joyful, jolly, jovial ; adv., merrily, etc.

[lustern, v. (see anlustern).]

M

M, the thirteenth letter of the alphabet, pron. as in Eng.

machen, v. a. w., to make, perform, manufacture, do ; refl., sich an etwas (acc.) machen, to set to work at anything ; sich auf den Weg machen, to set out on one's way ; etwas wieder gut machen, to make a thing all right, atone for ; was machen Sie ? How do you do ? [Syn. tun, which is never used in the sense of "manufacturing," like machen.]

Mädchen, subst. n. dim., gen. -s, pl.——, girl, maid, maiden [dim. of Magd, which is now generally used for "maid-servant"].

mag, pres. ind. of mögen.

Magd, subst. f., pl. Mägde, maid, maid-servant ; dim. Mädchen, girl.

Mähre, subst. f., pl.-n, mare, jade [generally and correctly spelt with h ; dist. from Märe, "news, story," also f., of which Mä[h]rchen (see below) is dim. form].

Mal, subst. n. [gen.-(e)s, pl.——, mole, mark (sometimes spelt Maal)] ; generally used as indecl. subst. with a card. or ord. num., as : einmal, "once, zweimal, "twice ;" das erste mal, "the first time," zum letzten mal, "for the last time," etc. Also in the adv. gen., as : mehrmals, "several times," einstmals (or -malen), "once upon a time ;" but never in this form with a card. num. [Eng. "mole."]

man, indef. indecl. pers. pron. (third pers., = Fr. *on*), one, they, people. [Einer is used to replace the oblique cases.]

manch or mancher, -e, -es. pl. -e, many a, many, several (used of a number of objects considered *singly* and *individually*).

manchmal, adv., many a time, often, repeatedly, occasionally.

Mann, subst. m., gen.-(e)s, pl. Männer, man, husband. [Comp. subst. with this word as the second component, change M. in the pl. into Leute, when a class is spoken of, as : Kaufmann, pl.-leute. The pl. Mannen = "vassals," "men-at-arms." It is unchanged in pl. when used as noun of number, as : Eine Armee von 50,000 Mann. Mensch = "human being" (male or female—Lat. *homo*); **Mann**, "the male human being" (Lat. *vir*); the latter is used when speaking respectfully; the former when speaking contemptuously, and is the less honourable title.]

Mantel, subst. m., gen.-s, pl. **Mäntel**, mantle, cloak; dim. **Mäntelchen**, n.

Mä[h]rchen, subst. n. dim., gen. -s, pl.——, tale, fairy-tale, story. [Dim. of **Mä[h]re**, a tale.]

Mark, subst. n., gen.-(e)s, no pl., marrow [die **Mark** = "the limit, boundary, mark"].

Markt, subst. m., gen.-es, pl. **Märkte**, market.

Masz, subst. n., gen.-es, pl.-e. and f., pl.-e, and **Masze**, subst. f., pl.-n, measure; [as a measure of capacity, also f.; when used as word of measure, not changed in pl.;] **über alle Maszen**, beyond measure, exceedingly. K., p. 41, l. 1.

Maul, subst. n., gen.-(e)s, pl. **Mäuler**, mouth (of beasts), muzzle.

Meer, subst. n., gen.-(e)s, pl.-e, sea, ocean. [Syn. die **See**.]

mehr, adj. and adv. of quant. (compar. of viel), more. [The pl. subst. form **mehre** or **mehrere** (also used in n. sing. **mehreres**), = several.]

mein, gen. of ich, first pers. pron., hence :

mein, -e, mein, poss. adj. (decl. like indef. art.), my [; poss. pron. **meiner**, -e, -es (without a noun following), or **der, die, das meinige** or **meine**, mine].

meinen, v. a. w., to mean, intend.

melken, v. a. strong (**molk, gemolken, milk, milkst**), and w., to milk.

Menge, subst. f. coll., pl.-n,

crowd; large quantity, mass (vulg. "lot").

Mensch, subst. m., gen.-en, pl. -en, human being [see **Mann**. When neut., it is used disrespectfully of a woman (= "wench")].

menschlich, adj., human [; humane] ; adv. humanly, etc. ["manly" = **männlich**.]

merken, v. a. w., to mark, notice, observe.

Messe, subst. f., pl.-n, fair (market-fair) [also = "mass" (religious ceremony) : the former meaning is deriv. from the latter, "feast," "fair"].

Messer, subst. n., gen.-s, pl. ——, knife ; dim. -**lein**, n.

Metzger, subst. m., gen.-s, pl. ——, butcher.

Milch, subst. f., no pl., milk.

mild(e), adj., mild, gentle, soft (of character).

mildern, v. a. w., to soften, alleviate, mitigate.

mis(s)-, prefix before subst., adj., and verbs, = Eng. "mis-," of negative or disparaging force, as :

Mis(s)gunst, subst. f., no. pl. [dislike], jealousy.

mit, prep., gov. dat. only, with, along with. [Indicates association, companionship ; also the means or instr., with things (not with persons) ; see **durch, von**, and a good grammar for full distinction.]

mitánsehen, v. a. sep., **sah, gesehen, sieh, siehst**, to view a thing in company with others.

mítbringen, v. a. sep. irreg., **brachte, gebracht**, to bring along, bring with one.

mítgehen, v. n. (**sein**) sep., **gieng, gegangen**, to go along with, accompany.

mitkommen, v. n. (sein) sep.;
kam, gekommen, kömmst or
kommst, to come along, go
with (any person), go along;
keep up with a person.
Mitleiden, subst n. comp., gen.
-s, no pl., pity, compassion.
[Inf. of mitleiden, "to suffer
with a person," compare the
formation of the Lat. word com-
passio.]
Mittag, subst. m. comp., gen.
-(e)s, pl.-e, mid-day, noon.
[from Mitte, "middle."]
Mittagsbrot, subst. n. comp.,
gen.-es, no pl., mid-day meal,
lunch, dinner.
Mittel, subst. n., gen.-s, pl.——,
means; remedy [from Mitte].
mitten, adv. of place, amidst, in
the middle (foll. by in with dat.,
as: mitten im Winter, or
prec. by in and foll. by gen.:
in mitten des Winters, in the
middle of winter.
Mitternacht, subst. f. comp., pl.
-nächte, midnight.
mögen, v. a. and n. (haben)
irreg., aux. of mood, pres. ind.
mag, magst, mag, pl. mögen,
etc.; pres. subj. möge, impf. ind.
mochte, impf. subj. möchte,
part. gemocht, no imper.; like,
may (in past tense "might"),
can. [The fundamental meaning is that of preference on the
part of the subj. of the verb; in
the second and third pers. it
may mean (like Eng. "may")
permission; and (of things) possibility. It shares the peculiarities of inflexion and constr. of
the other aux. of mood (see
under dürfen).]
Moos, subst. n., gen.-es, pl.-e,
moss.
Morgen, subst. m., gen.-s, pl.
——, morning, morn; des

Morgens or am M., "in the
morning."
morgen, adv. of time, to-morrow
(next day).
müde, adj., tired, weary, fatigued.
Mühe, subst. f., pl.-n, trouble, toil.
Mund, subst. m., gen.-es, pl. e
or Münde (both rare), mouth
(human). [Compounds indicating persons (as Vormund) have
pl.-münder.]
munter, adj. [wakeful, awake;],
lively, vivacious.
murren, v. n. (haben), to mutter,
grumble, murmur.
Musik, subst. f., no pl., music.
müssen, v. n. (haben), aux. of
mood, irreg., pres. ind. muss,
musst, muss, pl. müssen,
etc.; pres. subj. müsse; impf.
ind. musste; impf. subj.
müsste; part. gemusst; no
imper., must, to be obliged.
[Implies an obligation or necessity imposed by circumstances
rather than a moral obligation
(which is expressed by sollen);
shares the peculiarities of other
auxils. of mood (see dürfen).]
Mut(h), courage; disposition,
feeling, state of mind: schlecht,
wohl, etc., zu Mut(e) sein,
werden, "to feel ill, well," etc.
Mutter, subst. f., pl. Mütter,
mother; dim. Mütterchen, n.
[little mother, mother dear];
little or poor old woman. D.,
p. 18, l. 1.
mutterseligallein, adj. comp.,
no compar., alone and forsaken
[gen. mutterseelenallein].
[Mütze, subst. f., pl.-n, cap.]

N

N, the fourteenth letter of the
alphabet, is generally pron. as in

Eng.; but when occurring with g between two vowels, one g only is heard ; as : **Fing-er** (as in Eng. *sing–er*, not as in *Fing-ger*). The g in final –ng is often pron. like k, as **Ring**, pron. **Rink** or **Ring**, etc.

nach, prep., gov. dat. only, to, toward ; after (of time and order) ; for (purpose see note to p. 50, l. 5) ; according to (consequence). [The Eng. prep. "to" is rendered by **nach** before names of towns and countries, as : **ich gehe nach Paris**, **nach Frankreich**, "I am going *to* Paris, *to* France (not **zu**) ; so also with **Haus**, as **nach Hause**, "home."] It frequently takes **zu** after the noun, to indicate "in the direction of," as : **nach dem Hause zu**, "in the direction of the house ;" **nach und nach** (adv.), gradually, by degrees. (Compare Eng. "by and by.")

nachdém, adv. conj., after that, after. [Comp. of prep. **nach** and **dem**, pron. **da.**]

náchgehen, v. n. (sein) sep., gieng, gegangen, to follow after, pursue (dat. of obj.).

náchjagen, v. n. (haben) sep. w., to hunt after, chase, pursue (dat. of obj.).

náchschleichen, v. n. (sein) sep., schlich, geschlichen, to sneak after, slink after, follow secretly (dat. of obj.).

náchsehen, v. n. (haben) sep., sah, gesehen, sieh, siehst, to look after (a pers. who is disappearing, gov. dat. of obj.) ; to look after, attend to (a thing) ; inquire (R., p. 14, l. 2).

náchsetzen, v. n. (haben) sep. w., to pursue.

náchsuchen, v. a. and n. (haben) sep. w., to make a search.

Nacht, subst. f., pl. **Nächte**, night [adv. gen. **Nachts**, or **des Nachts**, by night].

Nagel, subst. m., gen.-s, pl. **Nägel**, nail.

nah(e), adj., comp. **näher**, superl. **nächst**, near, next (with dat. of obj.) [conn. with prep. **nach**].

Nähe, subst. f., no pl., nearness, presence, proximity.

nahen, v. a. and refl. w., to draw near, come near, approach (dat. of obj.).

nähen, v. a. and n. (haben) w., to sew.

nähern, v. a. refl., to draw nearer, approach (dat. of obj.).

nahm, impf. ind. of **nehmen**, "to take."

nähren, v. a. w., to nourish, foster, cherish ; v. refl., to be fed or nourished, to live.

Name(n), subst. m., gen.-ns (or rarely -n), dat. acc.-n, pl.-n, name [comp. decl. of **Buchstabe(n)**, **Friede(n)**, **Glaube(n)**, etc.].

Napf, subst. m., gen.-es, pl. **Näpfe**, pot, vessel, utensil.

Nase, subst. f., pl.-n, nose.

neben, prep., gov. dat. and acc., near, alongside of, adjacent to [coincides with **bei** in this sense].

nehmen, v. a., **nahm**, genommen, nimm, nimmst, to take ; in **Empfang n.**, to receive ; **Teil nehmen** [to take interest in], to share in (gov. **an** with dat.).

Neid, subst. m., gen.-es, no pl., envy, jealousy [the strict equivalent for the latter is **Eifersucht**].

neidisch, adj., envious, jealous.

neigen, v. a. n. and refl. w., to bow, bow down ; bend down, incline. [Hence the subst. **Neigung** = "inclination, affection."]

nein, neg. adv., no. ["No," as adj. = **kein.**]

nennen, v. a. irreg., **nannte, genannt,** to name, call.

neu, adj., new ; **von neuem** or **auf's neue,** anew, again.

Neugierde, subst. f., no pl., curiosity, inquisitiveness [lit. "greed of something new"].

nicht, neg. adv., not.

nichts, indef. neg. pron. indecl. n., nothing.

nicken, v. n. (haben) w., to nod ; **mit dem Kopfe n.,** to nod the head.

nie, neg. adv. of time (past or fut.), never [= **je** with neg. pref. **n-**].

nieder, adv., downward, down.

niederblicken, v. a. sep. w., to look down (gov. **auf** with acc. of obj.).

niederfallen, v. n. (sein) sep., **fiel, gefallen, fällst,** to fall down.

niederknie(e)n, v. n. (haben, sein) and refl. sep. w., to kneel down, fall on one's knees.

niederlassen [v. a., to let down, lower] ; v. refl. sep., **liess, gelassen, lässest, lässt,** to let one's self down, lower one's self ; settle down, sit down ; settle ; alight (of birds).

niederschiessen, v. a. sep., **schöss, geschossen,** to shoot down.

niedersetzen, v. a. sep. w., to set down, put down ; v. refl., to sit down, seat one's self.

niedersinken, v. n. (sein) sep., **sank, gesunken,** to sink down, fall down.

niedersitzen, v. n. (haben) sep., **sasz, gesessen,** to sit down ; **im N.** (inf. as subst.), in sitting down.

niedrig, adj., lowly, low ; base, mean (of character).

niemals, never, not on any occasion [= **nie,** but more explicit].

niemand, gen.-(e)s, dat.-em or -en, acc.-, or -en, indef. neg. pron., no one, nobody, no person, not any one, etc. ; n. **anders** [or **sonst**] (**als**), "no one else, no other person (than)."

[nimmer], nimmermehr, adv. (of future time), never, never again, nevermore.

noch, adv., still, yet (of time or comparison). [The Eng. "still, yet," when advers. conj. (— "nevertheless") are rendered by **doch** ; **noch heute** = "while it is yet to-day, before to-day is over ;" with num., **noch** = "more," "another," as : **noch zwei,** "two more," **noch eine Tasse,** "another cup."]

nochmals, once more, again [= **noch einmal**].

Not(h), subst. f., pl. **Nöte,** need, necessity ; trouble ; [**not tun,** "to be necessary ;" here **not** is adj. rather than subst. ; = **nötig sein**].

nüdeln, v. a. w., to fatten, cram, stuff (a goose for fattening).

nun, adv. of time and conj., now, at present ; well (; parenthetic) ; accordingly.

nur, adv., only, just ; even ; [used with imper. for emphasis or encouragement, as : **tun Sie es nur,** "do it by all means,

go on doing it"] (comp. Fr.
toujours). Also joined with
rel. **wer**, as : **wer nur** = "whoever."
Nuss, subst. f., pl. **Nüsse,**
nut.
Nússhecke, subst. f. comp., pl.
-n, hedge of nut-trees, nut-
hedge.

O

O, the fifteenth letter of the alphabet, pron. as in Eng.; when it
has the **Umlaut (ö, Oe)** it has
no equivalent in Eng., being
pron. much like the Fr. *eu* (as
in *jeu*), with rounded and pro-
truding lips.
O! interj., O! Oh!
ob, conj., whether, if, as : "ask
him *if, i.e.,* 'whether,' he will
come," **fragen Sie ihn ob** (not
wenn) er kommen wolle;
generally with subj. mood
[sometimes **ob = obgleich,** "although ;" still sometimes found
as prep. with dat. = "on account
of, over, about ;" **ob auch,**
although (= **obgleich**)].
óben, adv. of place (from prec.),
above, at the top [as prep.
"above"= **über**].
obendréin, adv., besides, into the
bargain, in addition.
obgléich, conj., although, though.
[The two parts are sometimes
separated ; see note to p. 33, l.
15.]
oder, disj. cöord. conj., or.
Ofen, subst. m., gen.-s, pl.
Oefen, stove ; oven.
offen, adj., open ; hence :
öffnen, v. a. w., **öffnete, geöffnet,** to open.
oft, adv., often, ofttimes, frequently.

ohne, prep., with acc. only,
without [not "outside," but
= "devoid of ;" conn. with
Ger. and Eng. pref. *un-*].
Óhnmacht, subst. f. comp., pl.
-en, faint, fainting-fit ; weak-
ness, feebleness, powerlessness
[= **Unmacht**].
óhnmächtig, adj. comp., faint-
ing, unconscious [; feeble, weak,
powerless].
Ohr, subst. n., gen.-(e)s, pl.
-en, ear (organ of hearing).
Óhrfeige, subst. f. comp., pl.
-n, box on the ear.
Öl, subst. n., gen.-(e)s, pl.-e,
oil.
[**Öllampe,** subst. f. comp.. pl.-n,
oil-lamp ;] dim.-**lämpchen,** n.
opfern, v. a. w., to offer up, sacrifice.
ordentlich, adj., orderly. regular,
proper, real, actual ; adv.,
actually ; properly.
ordnen, v. a. w., **ordnete, geordnet,** to order, arrange.
Órdnung, subst. f., no pl., ar-
rangement, order [not = "command," in which sense "order"
= **Befehl**].
Ort, subst. m., gen.-(e)s, pl.-e,
or **Oerter,** place ; village, ham-
let. [The latter form of the pl.
is more common ; that in -e is
used of places collectively, or as
localities ; so the adv. gen. pl.:
aller Orten, "everywhere,"
where a third pl. form occurs
(in -**en**).]

P

P, the sixteenth letter of the alphabet, pron. as in Eng. The
Germ. aspirate **pf** replaces *ph*,
which occurs only in foreign
(Greek) words.

packen, v. a. w., to seize, grasp.

Pantóffel, subst. m., gen.-s, pl. -, or -n, slipper.

Par, subst. n., gen.-(e)s, pl. -e, pair, couple (two belonging together). As noun of num. does not change in pl., as: **zwei P. Schuhe,** "two pair of shoes."

par, with small **p,** is really identical with prec., but is frequently thus written, as though it were an adv. of quant., and by an incorrect use means "a few" (like the Eng. "couple" by a similar incorrect usage).

passen, v. n. (**haben**) w., to fit, suit (gov. dat. of pers., or **an** with acc.).

Pech, subst. n., gen.-(e)s, no pl., pitch [used in slang as = "ill-luck." **Pech haben,** "to be unlucky"].

Pelz, subst. n., gen.-es, pl.-e, hide, skin, fur (generally of fur-bearing animals; compare Eng. "pelt, peltries").

Perle, subst. f., pl.-n, pearl.

Pfarrer, subst. m., gen.-s, pl. ——, pastor, minister, parson.

Pferd, subst. n., gen.-es, pl.-e, horse [the most general word, comp. **Gaul**].

pflanzen, v. a. w., to plant.

pflegen, v. a. w., to cherish, nourish, foster, care for, nurse (gov. gen. or acc.); v. n., to be wont, be accustomed or used; [the strong forms (**pflog** or **pflag, gepflogen**) are only used in the sense of attending to, practising (a business, trade, etc.)].

Pflegevàter, subst. comp. m., gen.-s, pl.-väter, foster-father.

picken, v. a. w., to peck, pick.

pik! pik! pick! pick! imitative word, used of birds pecking.

plagen, v. a. w., to plague, torment, tease, bother.

plötzlich, adj., sudden; adv. suddenly, all at once.

plumpen, v. n. (**sein**) w., to fall or roll awkwardly, with a splash.

Pracht, subst. f. [pl.-en, rare], splendour, magnificence, grandeur, pomp.

prächtig, adj., splendid, magnificent, gorgeous; adv. splendidly, etc.

[**probíren,** v. a. w. (part. **probirt**), to try, prove; attempt.]

Q

Q, the seventeenth letter of the alphabet, is rare in Germ. words. It is always followed by **u,** and is pron. like Eng. *qu* in *question.*

Quelle, subst. f., spring, (of water) fountain; source. [The form **Quell,** m., is also found, as in Schiller's "**Taucher;**" conn. with Eng. "well."]

[**quillen** or **quellen,** v. n. (**sein** or **haben**), **quoll, gequollen,** to gush, well (from prec.).]

R

R, the eighteenth letter of the alphabet, is rolled much more strongly than in Eng., being formed by closing the mouth-tube by a slight pressure of the back of the tongue, point *downward* (i.e., convexly) against the palate. The letter is therefore *guttural* in Germ. In pron. Eng. *r* the point of the tongue is turned *upward* (concavely), the tip touching the roots of the teeth; the position is reversed in Germ.

Rábe, subst. m., gen.-n, pl.-n, and f. (rare), pl.-n, raven. [The f. form occurs, as far as I know, only in J., pp. 26, 27. where the f. nums. **eine** refers to it ; and in the title to one of Grimm's other stories, **Die Rabe,** No. 93.]

rächen, v. a. w. (part. **gerächt** and **gerochen**), to avenge, take revenge for ; v. refl., to revenge one's self, take vengeance on (gov. **an** with dat. of pers.).

Rad, subst. n., gen.-es, pl. **Räder,** wheel.

Ráhmen, subst. m., gen.-s, pl. ——, frame (of a picture, etc.).

Rand, subst. m., gen.-es, pl. **Ränder,** edge, margin ; side (of a ship) ; rim ; brim (of a hat) ; brink (of a precipice).

Rang, subst. m., gen.-(e)s, pl. **Ränge** (rare), rank ; order ; condition (of life).

raten, v. a. and n. (haben), riet, geraten, to advise, counsel (dat. of pers.) [; to guess, conjecture].

Raum, subst. m., gen.-(e)s, pl. **Räume,** room, space.

rauschen, v. n. (haben) w., to rush ; to rustle (refers to noise rather than motion).

Rauschen, subst. n. (inf. of prec.), gen.-s, no pl., rushing, rustling.

recht, adj., no compar., right, correct (moral rectitude or truth) ; right, on the right hand (adv. **rechts**) of position ; **zur rechten (Hand), rechts,** on the right (hand) ; adv. [rightly, before verbs] very (before adj.).

Recht, subst. n., gen.-es, pl.-e, right, privilege, justice [; law] ; **Recht haben** = "to be right."

reden, v. n. (haben) w., redete, geredet, to speak, make a

speech [used of more formal speech than **sprechen**].

rege, adj., stirring, lively ; **rege werden,** to get astir, be aroused, be stirred up. B., p. 37, l. 27.

regen, v. refl. w., to stir, bestir one's self.

Regen, subst. m., gen.-s, no pl., rain.

regnen, v. n. (haben) impers. w., regnete, geregnet, to rain.

Reh, subst. n., gen.-(e)s, pl.-e, roe, roe-deer ; dim. -chen, -lein, n., fawn.

Réhkalb, subst. n. comp., gen. -(e)s, pl.-kälber, roe-fawn, fawn [lit. "roe-calf"] ; dim. -kälbchen, n.

reich, adj., rich, wealthy ["rich *in*" = **reich an**].

Reich, subst. n., gen.-(e)s, pl.-e, realm, empire, kingdom [conn. with the Eng. suffix -"ric," as in "bishopric," etc.].

reichen, v. a. and n., to reach ; stretch out ; attain.

Reichtum, subst. m., gen.-(e)s, pl.-tümer, wealth, riches. [The suffix -tum = Eng. suffix -"dom," as in "kingdom," etc. Nouns in -tum are n., exc. this one, and **Irrtum** ("error") ; **Wachstum** ("growth") is m. or n.]

Reihe, subst. f., pl.-n, row, order [series, succession].

[**Reihen,** m. (or **Reigen**), dance.]

rein, adj., clean, pure.

reínlesen, v. a. sep., las, gelesen, lies, liesest, to pick clean.

reínlich, adj. and adv., cleanly, clean.

reínwaschen, v. a. sep., wusch, gewaschen, wäschest, to wash clean.

Reis, subst. n., gen.-es, pl.-er

(rarely -e), twig, small branch.
[der **Reis**, m., = "rice."]

reiten, v. n. (sein, sometimes haben), **ritt, geritten**, to ride (on the back of an animal; **fahren** is used of driving, etc., in a vehicle). [Takes **haben** when **reiten** = "to take riding exercise," and when no destination is mentioned.]

Reiten, subst. n. (inf. of prec.), gen.-s, no pl., riding, horseback-exercise.

Reiter, subst. m., gen.-s, pl. ——, rider [**Ritter** = "knight"].

retten, v. a. w., **rettete, gerettet**, to save, rescue.

Réttung, subst. f., pl.-en, saving, rescue, deliverance.

richten, v. a. w., **richtete, gerichtet**, to direct, guide; **zu Grunde r.**, to ruin.

richtig, adj., right, correct; adv. correctly.

riechen, v. a., **roch, gerochen**, to smell; v. n. (haben), to smell, be fragrant.

riegeln, v. a. w., to bolt.

Riemen, subst. m., gen.-s, pl. ——, strap (generally of leather).

Ring, subst. m., gen.-(e)s, pl. -e, ring, circle; hence:

rings (umher), adv. gen., round about (in a ring or circle).

[**Rose**, subst. f., pl.-n, rose (flower); dim. **Röschen**, n.; both used as proper names; - see **Dornröschen**.]

rot, adj., compar. **röter**, red.

rótglühend, adj. (part.), glowing red, red-hot.

Rótkäppchen, subst. n. prop. dim., Little Redcap, Little Red Ridinghood.

Rücken, subst. m., gen.-s, pl. ——, back.

rücken, v. n. (sein) and a., to move; shove, push.

Rückweg, subst. m. comp., gen. -(e)s, pl.-e, way-back, return.

rúcke-di-gúck, sound imitative of the cooing of doves. A.

rufen, v. a. and n. (haben), **rief, gerufen**, to call; summon. [The w. form of impf. (**rufte**) also occurs, but is now no longer in use.]

Ruhe, subst. f., no pl., rest, repose; peace.

rühren, v. a. and refl. w., to move, stir.

ruhen, v. n. (haben) and refl. w., to rest, repose.

rupfen, v. a. w., to pluck (the feathers from fowls).

rutschen, v. n. (sein) w., to slide, slip.

rütteln, v. a. w., to shake; v. refl., to shake one's self, shake [shudder, quiver].

S

S, the nineteenth letter of the alphabet, is generally pron. as in Eng., but at the beginning of a word or syll., pron. like *z* in *zone*; when final, it is always sharp (= *ss*). For **ss** we generally write **sz** after a simple long vow., **ss** after short vow. or diphthong. In the German character **sz** is always used for **ss** when final, or before a cons., or after a long vow. or diphth. **sch** = Eng. *sh*; **w** after **sch** = Eng. *w* (not *v*, as usually). Before **p** and **t** the pronunciation of **s** *approaches* that of **sch**, at the beginning of words only, in general practice; although the grammars protest against this pronunciation.

Saft, subst. m., gen.-es, pl. **Säfte**, sap, juice.

saftig, adj., juicy.

Sage, subst. f., pl.-n, tale, myth, legend ; report.

sagen, v. a. w., to say, mention.

Sal, subst. m., gen.-(e)s, pl. **Säle**, hall, saloon, apartment.

Sált(h)üre, subst. f. comp., pl. -n, door of a hall or saloon [not = "hall-door," *i.e.*, street-door].

Salz, subst. n., gen.-es, pl.-e, salt.

sammeln, v. a. w., to gather, collect, assemble [conn. with **sam(m)t** ; see below].

Sam(me)t, subst. m., gen.-(e)s, pl.-e (rare), velvet [conn. with Eng. "samite" (Tennyson)].

sam(m)t, prep. gov. dat. only, together with, along with [**alle-sammt** = "all together ;" **ge-sammt** (adj.)= "collected ;" so also :]

säm(m)tlich, adj., collected, all ; adv. collectively, altogether, all.

sanft, adj., soft, gentle, quiet ; adv. softly, etc.

Sarg, subst. m., gen.-(e)s, pl. **Särge**, coffin, casket (for a corpse).

sasz, impf. ind. of **sitzen**, "to sit."

Satz, subst. m., gen.-es, pl. **Sätze**, leap, jump, bound ; [sentence (from **setzen**)].

Sau, subst. f., pl. **Säue** (of tame hogs), **Sauen** (wild) pig, hog ; sow (not necessarily confined to the female, as in Eng. See II., p. 62, l. 30, note).

sauer, adj., sour ; hard (of labour), K., p. 45, l. 15.

saugen, v. a., w. and str., **sog** or **saugte**, **gesogen** or **gesaugt**, to suck.

Schade(n), subst. m., gen.-n or -ns, dat. acc.-n, pl.-n or **Schäden** [compare decl. of **Friede(n)**, **Glaube(n)**, etc.].

schaden, v. n. (haben) w., **schad-ete**, **geschadet**, to harm, injure, do harm or injury to (dat. of obj.).

schádhaft, adj., damaged (not in good condition), the worse for wear.

schallen, v. n. (haben), **schallte** or [**scholl**], **geschallt** or (rarely) **geschollen**, to sound, resound, reecho.

schämen, v. a. refl., to be ashamed (acc. of pers. refl. pron., gen. of obj., or **über** with acc.). [**Schande**, subst. f., pl.-n, shame, disgrace ; hence :]

schändlich, adj., shameful, disgraceful ; adv. shamefully.

Schatz, subst. m., gen.-es, pl. **Schätze**, treasure.

schauen, v. a. and n. (haben), to look, gaze ; see, behold.

scheckig, adj., pied, mottled, spotted, piebald.

scheinen, v. n. (haben), **schien**, **geschienen**, to shine ; to seem, appear.

Schemel, subst. m., gen.-s, pl. ——, foot-stool.

schenken, v. a. w., to make a gift or present, give, present.

Scherbe, subst. f., pl.-n, sherd, potsherd ; splinter (fragment of broken crockery, glass, etc.).

Schere, subst. f., pl.-n, shears, scissors.

Schérenschleifer, subst. m. comp., gen.-s, pl.——, knife-grinder [prop. "scissors-grinder"].

schicken, v. a. w., to send [Syn. **senden**, "to send, despatch" (ambassadors, etc., of more important messages than **schicken**)] ; v. refl., to behave, conduct one's self ; v. refl. impers., **es schickt sich**, "it is proper, becoming," etc.

Schicksal, subst. n., gen.-(e)s, pl.-e, fate, lot, destiny. [Syn. **Geschick;** see above.]

schieben, v. a., **schob, geschoben,** to shove, push.

schiessen, v. n. (haben) and a., **schoss, geschossen,** to shoot.

Schiff, subst. n., gen.-(e)s, pl.-e, ship, sailing-vessel.

schlachten, v. a. w., **schlachtete, geschlachtet,** to slaughter, butcher.

Schlachten, subst. n., gen.-s, no pl. (inf. of prec.), butchery, slaughter; slaughtering.

Schlaf, subst. m., gen.-(e)s, pl. **Schläfe** (rare), sleep, slumber.

schlafen, v. n. (haben), **schlief, geschlafen, schläfst,** to sleep, slumber, be asleep.

schlafend, adj., no compar. (pres. part. of prec.), sleeping, asleep.

Schlag, subst. m., gen.-(e)s, pl. **Schläge,** blow, kick.

schlagen, v. a., **schlug, geschlagen, schlägst,** to strike, beat.

schlecht, adj., bad, evil (of moral character) [conn. with Eng. "slight"]; **schlecht** (= **schlicht) und recht,** plainly and honestly (K., p. 44, l. 5).

schleichen, v. n. (sein), **schlich, geschlichen,** to sneak, creep, crawl.

schleifen, v. a., **schliff, geschliffen,** to grind; polish; sharpen. [v. a. w., = "to raze to the ground," or "to drag along."]

Schleifen, subst. n., gen.-s, no pl. (inf. of prec.), sharpening, etc.

Schleifer, subst. m., gen.-s, pl. -e, grinder.

schleppen, v. a., to drag (along the ground); v. refl., **sich mit etwas schleppen,** to trouble

one's self by dragging a thing, II., p. 60, l. 3, and note.

schliessen, v. a. and refl., **schloss, geschlossen,** to lock, close, shut.

schlimm, adj., bad (of character, morally; or of circumstances).

Schloss, subst. n., gen.-es, pl. **Schlösser,** lock; castle. [Conn. with **schliessen.**]

Schlósshof, subst. m. comp., gen.-(e)s, pl.-höfe, court-yard of castle, castle-yard.

Schlüssel, subst. m., gen.-s, pl. ——, key [from **schliessen**].

schmal, adj., compar. **schmäler** or **schmaler,** scanty, narrow, confined.

Schmaus, subst. m., gen.-es, pl. **Schmäuse,** feast (hearty meal).

schmecken, v. a. w., to taste; v. n., to taste of, savour of (with **nach**).

schmeicheln, v. n. (haben) w., to flatter (dat. of pers.).

Schmerz, subst. m., gen.-es, pl.-en, or **Schmerzen,** m. gen.-s, pl.-n, pain. [Eng. "smart."]

schmücken, v. a. w., to deck, adorn, ornament, beautify.

Schmutz, subst. m., gen.-es, no pl., dirt, filth. [Eng. "smut."]

schmutzig, adj., dirty, soiled.

Schnabel, subst. m., gen.-s, pl. **Schnäbel,** beak, bill (of a bird).

Schnalle, subst. f., pl.-n, buckle.

schnalzen, v. n. (haben) w., to smack (the tongue), to click with the tongue (to a horse).

schnappen, v. n. (haben) w., to snap (gov. **nach**).

schnarchen, v. n. (haben) w., to snore.

Schnecke, subst. f., pl.-n, snail.

Schnee, subst. m., gen.-s, no pl., snow.

Schneeflocke, subst. f. comp., pl.-n, snow-flake.

schneeweiss, adj., no compar., snow-white, white as snow.

Schneeweisschen, subst. prop. n. dim., Snow-white [see **Sneewittchen**].

schneiden, v. a., schnitt, geschnitten, to cut.

schnell, adj., quick, fast; adv. quickly, fast.

Schnitt, subst. m., gen.-es, pl.-e, slice; cut (from **schneiden**).

schnuppern, v. n. (haben) w., to snuff, sniff, scent, go about smelling (of a dog, etc.).

schnüren, v. a. w., to lace (corsets, boots, etc.).

schnurren, v. n. (haben) w., to whirr, hum (noise made by rapid revolving motion, as of a spinning-wheel).

Schnürriemen, subst. m., gen.-s, pl.——, lace, lacing, lacing-strap or string (of corsets).

schon, adv., already, ever; as soon as; of very frequent occurrence; meaning best illustrated by examples: **schon heute**, "as early as to-day (no later);" **ich werde es schon tun**, "I shall be *sure* to do it;" often left untranslated.

schön, adj., fair, beautiful, pleasant, agreeable, fine; adv. beautifully, etc.

Schönheit, subst. f., pl.-en, beauty.

schöpfen, v. a. w., to draw (water, etc.).

Schornstein, subst. m. comp., gen.-(e)s, pl.-e, chimney.

Schrank, subst. m., gen.-(e)s, pl. **Schränke**, cupboard, chest, press (for clothes, etc.). [die **Schranke** = "the limit;" pl. **Schranken**, "the lists, barriers (at a tournament)."]

Schreck, subst. m., gen.-s, pl. -e (rare); or **Schrecken**, subst. m., gen.-s, pl.——, fright, fear, terror.

schreien, v. n. (haben), schrie, geschrie(e)n, to cry out, scream, shout.

Schubkarren, subst. m. comp., gen.-s, pl.——, wheelbarrow.

Schuck, low Germ. form of **foll**.

Schuh, subst. m., gen.-(e)s, pl. -e, shoe.

Schuld, subst. f., pl.-en, guilt, debt, fault; **es ist meine S.**, "it is my fault;" **schuld sein**, to be the cause of any thing (gov. **an** with dat.). [**schuld** is here used like a pred. adj., and may be spelt with a small letter or cap.]

schuldig, adj., guilty; owing, indebted (dat. of pers., acc. of thing); **ich bin ihm zehn Taler schuldig**, "I owe him ten dollars."

Schule, subst. f., pl.-n, school.

Schulter, subst. f., pl.-n, shoulder.

Schulze, subst. m., gen.-n, pl. -n, bailiff, magistrate, officer [corrupted from **Schuld-heiss**, "a person who collects or demands debts"].

Schürze, subst. f., pl.-n, apron; dim. -chen, n.

Schüssel, subst. f., pl.-n, dish; salver, tray.

schütten, v. a. w., schüttete, geschüttet, to shake out, empty out.

schütteln, v. a. w., to shake (dim. of prec.); v. refl., to shake one's self, shake, quake.

Schüttern, subst. n. (inf.), gen.-s, no pl., shaking, shock.

schwach, adj., compar. **schwächer**, weak.

schwank, adj., no compar. [unsteady, swaying to and fro], lank, lanky, K., p. 41, l. 14, note.

schwärmen, v. n. w., to swarm.

schwarz, adj., compar. **schwärzer**, black ; dark.

schwarzharig, adj. comp., black-haired.

Schwefel, subst. m., gen.-s, no pl., sulphur, brimstone.

schweigen, v. n. (haben), **schwieg, geschwiegen**, to be silent, keep silent.

Schwein, subst. n., gen.-(e)s, pl. -e, pig, hog (general word) ; dim. **-chen**, n.

schwer, adj., heavy ; adv. heavily.

Schwester, subst. f., pl.-n, sister ; dim. **-chen, -lein**, n.

schwingen, v. refl., **schwang, geschwungen**, to vault (into a saddle, on a horse, etc.; gov. auf with acc.).

schwirren, v. n. (haben) w., to whirr, flutter (as the wings of a bird).

schwören, v. n. (haben), **schwor** or **schwur** (subj. **schwüre**), **geschworen**, to swear, take an oath [fluchen = "to curse, utter imprecations;" **schwären** (schwor, geschworen)="fester"].

sechs(e), card. num., six ; ord. **sechste**, sixth.

Seele, subst. f., pl.-n, soul.

seelenfroh, adj., heartily glad [glad in soul].

Segel, subst. n., gen.-s, pl——, sail (of a ship).

sehen, v. a., **sah, geschen, sieh, siehst**, to see, behold.

sehr, adv., very, very much [Scotch "sair," Eng. "sore," as in "sore afraid"].

Seide, subst. f., no pl., silk.

Seil, subst. n., gen.-(e)s, pl.-e, rope, cord. .

sein, v. n., auxil. of tense (sein), impf. ind. **war**, part. gewesen, pres. ind. **bin, bist, ist, sind**, seid, sind ; pres. subj. sei, to be (used as copula in a sent. and as auxil. of perf. and plupf. with many neut. verbs, particularly of motion) [formerly spelt **seyn**, to dist. from foll.] ; used as aux. of the perf., plupf., and fut. perf. with neuter verbs (particularly of motion) ; v. n. impers., to belong to (gov. dat.), K., p. 43, l. 20 ; to feel (gov. dat. with **zu Mut** understood). For difference between **es ist, es sind**, "there is, there are," and **es gibt**, see under **geben**, above.

sein or **seiner**, gen. sing. third pers. pron. sing. m. (and n. when referring to animate objects ; see **es**), his, its (her, referring to fem. dim., as **Mädchen** ; hence :)

sein, -e, poss. adj., third pers. sing. m. (and n. of animate objects), his ; its (hers). [Properly only used when referring to the subj. of the sent., or of the principal sent. ; when referring to anything else, the poss. adj. of third pers. should be replaced by the gen. case of the demonstr. (**dessen, deren, dessen**, or **desselben**, etc.)].

seit [or **seitdém**], subord. conj., since (of time, not cause).

seit, prep. gov. dat., since ; **seit vielen Tagen**, for many days past.

Seite, subst. f., pl.-n, side.

Seitentasche, subst. f. comp., pl.-n, side-pocket, pouch.

Seitenweg, subst. f. comp., gen. -(e)s, pl.-e, side-path, side-road, by-way.

selber, selbst, pers. pron. of

emphasis, self [never used by itself as a refl. pron., but always in conj. with a subst. or other pron., as : **ich selber,** "I myself;" **ich sehe mich selbst,** "I see *myself* (emphatic)]; adv., even.
selten [adj., rare, scarce ;], adv., rarely, seldom, hardly ever.
séltsam, adj. (from prec.), rare ; singular, peculiar.
setzen, v. a. w. (caus. of **sitzen**), to set, place (in a sitting position).
seufzen, v. n. (haben) w., to sigh.
sich, refl. pron. third pers., all genders, sing. and pl., himself, herself, itself, themselves ; recipr. pron., each other.
sicher, adj., secure, safe.
sie, pers. pron., third sing. fem., gen. **ihrer** or **ihr,** dat. **ihr,** acc. **sie,** she, her, it (of inanimate obj.).
sie, pers. pron. third pl., all genders, gen. **ihrer** or **ihr,** dat. **ihnen,** acc. **sie,** they, them. [When written with a capital letter, it is used as pron. of address, instead of the second pers. sing. and pl., the verb agreeing with it in the third pers. pl.]
sieben(e), card. num., seven ; ord. **siebente,** seventh.
Silber, subst. n., gen.-s, no pl., silver.
silbern, adj., no compar., of silver, silver ; silvery.
singen, v. n. (haben), **sang, gesungen,** to sing.
sinken, v. n. (sein), **sank, gesunken,** to sink.
Sinn, subst. m., gen.-es, pl.-e [or **-en**], sense ; mind ; disposition ; **im Sinn haben,** to have in mind, to intend.

sinnen, v. n. (haben), **sann, gesonnen,** to reflect, think.
[**Sitte,** subst. f., pl.-n, custom ; manner ; pl. morals ; hence :]
síttsam, well-behaved, modest, mannerly.
sitzen, v. n. (haben), **sasz, gesessen,** to sit.
Sneewíttchen, subst. prop. dim. n., Snow-white. [Low Germ. dialectic form of **Schneeweisschen.**]
so, adv., so, thus ; such (before adj.) ; conj., so (frequently to be left untranslated) ; it is very common as introducing a princ. sent. when preceded by a dep. sent., as : **wenn du die Linsen ausgelesen hast, so sollst du mitgehen ;** or an imper., as : **bleib fromm . . . so wird dir . . . Gott beistehen,** A., p. 1, l. 4.
sog, impf. ind. of **saugen,** "to suck."
Sohn, subst. m., gen.-(e)s, pl. **Söhne,** son ; dim. **Söhn-**[**chen**], **-lein,** n.
sollen, v. n. (haben), aux. of mood, pres. ind. **soll, sollst, soll, sollen,** etc. ; pres. subj. **solle ;** impf. ind. and subj. **sollte ;** part. **gesollt ;** no imper., shall, must ; **ich soll es tun,** "I am to do it. [Indicates that the subj. of the verb is under the control of some other person ; of moral obligation rather than physical (see **müssen**). "Shall," when mere aux. of fut. tense in Eng., is to be rendered by **werden** (see **werden, wollen**). Shares the peculiarities of other aux. of mood, as : **er hätte es tun sollen,** "he ought to have done it" (though the form : **er sollte es getan haben** is also admis-

II

sible), see **dürfen. Er soll es getan haben,** "He *is said* to have done it."]

[**sóndern,** v. a. w., to separate ; dist. from :]

sóndern, coörd. adv. conj., but (used after a neg. when there is a correction of the whole or part of a previous statement ; hence "not only—but also" = **nicht nur—sondern auch ; aber** is always used after an affirmative proposition ; also after *a neg.* sent. if introducing, not a correction, but a limitation of, or an addition to, a previous statement ; as : **Er hat es noch nicht getan, aber er wird es tun,** "He has not yet done it, but he will do it"). [Conn. with **besonders ; sonderbar,** Eng. "asunder," hence the meaning.]

Sonne, subst. f., pl.-n, sun.

Sónnenstrahl, subst. m. comp., gen.-(e)s, pl.-en, sunbeam, ray of the sun.

[**Sónntag,** subst. m. comp., gen. -(e)s, pl.-e, Sunday.]

Sónntagskind, subst. n. comp., gen.-es, pl.-er, child born on Sunday, lucky child [accordingto the common belief to that effect].

sonst, conj., otherwise, else ; adv. formerly, generally, usually [conn. with **sondern**] ; **sonst niemand,** nobody else ; **sonst nichts,** nothing else.

Sorge, subst. f., pl.-n, care, anxiety.

sorgen, v. n. (haben), to feel care, be anxious ; take care of (gov. **für**).

[**spannen,** v. a. w., to span, stretch ; see **aufspannen.**]

sparen, v. a. w., to spare ; save, save up.

Spasz, subst. m., gen.-es, pl. **Späsze,** joke, jest ; fun.

speien, v. n. (haben), **spie, gespie(e)n,** to spit.

Speise, subst. f., pl.-n, food.

Spiegel, subst. m., gen.-s, pl. ——, looking-glass, mirror ; dim. **Spieglein,** n.

Spiel, subst. n., gen.-(e)s, pl.-e, play, game, sport ; **aufs S. setzen,** to set at stake (as in gambling).

spielen, v. n. (haben) w., to play, gambol, frolick.

Spielmann, subst. m. comp., gen. -(e)s, pl.-**leute,** minstrel (man who plays on an instrument).

Spindel, subst. f., pl.-n, spindle, on which the thread is wound in spinning flax, etc.

spinnen, v. a., **spann, gesponnen,** to spin.

spitz, adj., pointed, sharp.

[**Spitze,** subst. f., pl.-n, point, sharp point (in the pl. = "lace."]

Spott, subst. m., gen.-es, no pl., mockery, scorn ; **S. treiben,** to make fun of (gov. **mit**).

spotten, v. n. (haben) w., **spottete, gespottet,** to mock, jeer (gov. **über** with acc.).

Spotten, subst. n. (inf. of prec.), gen.-s, no pl., mocking, jeering, mockery.

sprechen, v. n. (haben), **sprach, gesprochen, sprich, sprichst,** to speak [more general expression than **reden** or **sagen** ;] to utter, pronounce (judgment, sentence, etc.).

sprengen, v. a w. (caus. of **springen**), to cause to spring or run ; to make (a horse, etc.) gallop (neut.), to gallop ; to burst open.

springen, v. n. (sein), **sprang, gesprungen,** to jump, leap ; to run; to burst (= **zerspringen,** see below).

Spruch, subst. m., gen.-(e)s, pl. **Sprüche,** speech, saying; prophesy, wish (D., p. 17, l. 1), magic spell [proverb]; dim. **Sprüchlein,** n. [Conn. with **sprechen.**]

spüren, v. a. w., to notice, feel.

Stadt, subst. f., pl. **Städte** (with long **ä**), city, town; dim. **Städtchen.**

Stall, subst. m., gen.-(e)s, pl. **Ställe,** stable, stall; sty. [Conn. with **stellen** and **stehen.**]

Stand, subst. m., gen.-es, pl. **Stände** (place where one stands), standing; position; rank; condition (of life) [conn. with **stehen**].

stand, impf. ind. of **stehen,** "to stand;" subj. **stände** or **stünde.**

stark, adj., comp. **stärker,** strong.

stärken, v. a. w. (caus.), to strengthen.

Staub, subst. m., gen. -es, no pl., dust; hence:

staubig [or **stäubig**], adj., dusty.

stechen, v. a., **stach, gestochen, stich, stichst,** to stick, prick.

stecken, v. n. (**haben** or **sein**), **stak** or **steckte, gestocken** or **gesteckt, stickst** or **steckst,** to stick fast, stick. [The weak forms of conjug. are in more general use; and **haben** is the more usual aux.]

stecken, v. a. w., to stick (a pin, etc., into a pers. or thing).

stehen, v. n. (**haben**) irreg., **stand** (subj. **stände** or **stünde**), **gestanden,** to stand; v. impers., to suit, become, be becoming to (dat. of pers.).

stehlen, v. a., **stahl** (subj. **stähle** or **stöhle**), **gestohlen, stiehl, stiehlst,** to steal.

steigen, v. n. (sein), **stieg, gestiegen,** to rise, ascend; **ans Land s.,** to go ashore.

Stein, subst. m., gen.-(e)s, pl.-e, stone.

steinern, adj., no compar., of stone, stone.

Steintrog, subst. m. comp., gen. -(e)s, pl.-e or **tröge,** stone-trough.

Stelle, subst. f., pl.-n (place where a thing is put), place; spot; position; from

stellen, v. a. w. (caus. of **stehen**), to set upright, put to stand, place, set.

Sterbelager, subst. n. comp., gen.-s, pl.——, death-bed.

sterben, v. n. (sein), **starb** (subj. **stürbe**), **gestorben, stirb, stirbst,** to die, expire.

[**steuern,** v. a. w., to steer; hence :]

Steuermann, subst. m. comp., gen.-(e)s, pl.-leute, steersman, helmsman, man at the wheel.

Stich, subst. m., gen.-(e)s, pl.-e, prick, stab (given with the sharp point of a weapon).

sticken, v. a. w., to embroider.

stief–, prefix, step–, as in :

Stiefkind, subst. n. comp., gen. -es, pl.-er, step-child.

Stiefmutter, subst. f. comp., pl. -mütter, step-mother.

Stiefschwester, subst. f. comp., pl.-n, step-sister.

Stieftochter, subst. f. comp., pl. -töchter, step-daughter.

still(e), adj., still, silent, quiet.

stillen, v. a. w., to quiet, silence, calm; to appease (one's appetite); to nurse (a child at the breast).

stillschweigend, adj., silent; adv., silently.

Stimme, subst. f., pl.-n, voice.

stolpern, v. n. (sein) w., to stumble.

Stolz, subst. m., gen.-es, no pl., pride; haughtiness, arrogance. [May be a justifiable pride, which Hochmut never is.]

stolz, adj., comp. -er [or stölzer], proud, haughty (of persons); magnificent, gorgeous (of things); adv. proudly.

stopfen, v. a w., to stop up; stuff; [darn (stockings, etc.)].

stoszen, v. a., stiess, gestoszen, to knock against (gov. an with acc.), push; to bump, jolt; mit dem Fusze s., to kick.

strafen, v. a. w., to punish.

Strahl, subst. m., gen.-(e)s, pl. -en, beam, ray.

Strasze, subst. f., pl.-n, street, road, highway [from Lat. stratum, "way laid down"].

sträuben, v. refl., to struggle, resist (gov. gegen).

Sträuben, subst. n., gen.-s, no pl. (inf. of prec.), struggle, struggling, resistance.

Strauch, subst. m., gen.-(e)s, pl. Sträuche, bush.

Strauss, subst. m., gen.-es, pl. Sträusse or Sträusser, bunch of flowers, nosegay, bouquet. [Also = "ostrich," with pl. -e or en; and "fight, combat" (poetic word), with pl. Sträusse.]

strecken, v. a. and refl. w., to stretch, extend.

Streich, subst. m., gen.-(e)s, pl. -e, stroke, blow; trick.

streicheln, v. a. w., to stroke, caress.

streichen, v. a., strich, gestrichen, to stroke, smooth, brush.

streifen, v. a. w., to [strip] brush by, touch lightly; graze; trail; verge upon (gov. an with acc.).

Strick, subst. m., gen.-(e)s, pl. -e, cord, rope.

stricken, v. a. w., to knit.

Strumpf, subst. m., gen.-(e)s. pl. Strümpfe, stocking.

Strumpfband, subst. n. comp., gen.-es, pl.-bänder, garter.

Stube, subst. f., pl.-n, room, apartment; dim. Stübchen, n. [hence "stoup," from the Dutch].

Stück, subst. n., gen.-(e)s, pl. -e, piece, bit, fragment; dim. -chen, n.

Stuhl, subst. m., gen.-(e)s, pl. S-tühle, chair [Eng. "stool"]; dim. Stühlchen, n.

Stunde, subst. f., pl.-n, hour (division or point of time); an hour's walk, league (measure of distance). [Uhr = "clock, timepiece." Conn. with stehen, "the point at which time stands." Occurs in Eng. as "stound" in Gay, etc.]

stürzen, v. a. and refl. w., to fall, tumble, fall headlong, precipitate, rush, plunge, sink, overturn.

suchen, v. a. w., to seek, search for (also gov. nach).

Suppe, subst. f., pl.-n, soup, broth.

süsz, adj., sweet.

T

T, the twentieth letter of the alphabet, is pron. as in Eng. The combination th, as pron. in Eng., is unknown in Germ. Until lately, h was frequently inserted after t to indicate that the preceding vow. was long, as in Muth; but this h is now dropped (as Mut). It was also found at the beginning of words,

without any reason, and is still
in general use in many words
(as thun, Thüre, etc.), but is
omitted in this ed.; words beg.
with tha—, thu—, etc., should
therefore be sought under ta,
tu, etc. (as tat, tun, etc., for
that, thun, etc.).
Tag, subst. m., gen.-(e)s, pl.-e,
day.
Tagesanbruch, subst. m. comp.,
gen.-(e)s, no pl., break of day,
day-break, dawn.
Tanz, subst. m., gen.-es, pl.
Tänze, dance.
tanzen, v. n. (haben) w., to
dance.
Tänzer, subst. m., gen.-s, pl.
—— [dancer], partner.
Tänzerin, subst. f., pl.-innen
[dancer], partner.
Tasche, subst. f., pl.-n, pocket,
pouch.
tat, impf. ind. of tun, to do.
Taube, subst. f., pl.——, dove,
pigeon; dim. **Täubchen**, n.
Táubenhaus, subst. n. comp.,
gen.-es, pl.-häuser, pigeon-
house, dovecot.
Taufe, subst. f., pl.-n, baptism,
christening.
taufen, v. a. w., to baptise,
christen.
taugen, v. n. (haben) w., to be
of use, be useful.
táumeln, v. n. (haben or sein)
w., to stumble, stagger, totter
[with haben when the *action*
only is indicated; with sein when
direction is specified or im-
plied].
Tausch, subst. m., gen.-es, pl.
-e (sometimes **Täusche**), exchange.
tauschen, v. n. (haben) and a.,
to exchange. [täuschen = "deceive."]
tausend, card. num., pl.-e, a

thousand (not generally used
with def. art.).
táusendmal, num. adv., a thousand times.
Teil, subst. m. and n., gen.
-(e)s, pl.-e, part, share, portion [m. in the sense of "al-
lotted share or portion"]; zu
T. werden, to fall to the share
of (dat. of pers.); T. nehmen,
to share in [take an interest in]
(gov. an with dat.)
Teller, subst. m., gen.-s, pl.——,
plate, platter; dim.-chen,
-lein, n.
Tha-, etc., for subst. beginning
thus, see under ta, etc.
Thron, subst. m., gen.-(e)s, pl.
-e, throne. [The h is retained
here on account of its Greek.
origin.]
tief, adj., deep.
Tiefe, subst. f., pl.-n, depth.
Tier, subst. n., gen.-(e)s, pl.
-e, animal, beast; dim.-chen,
-lein, n.
Tisch, subst. m., gen.-es, pl.-e,
table; dim.-lein, n. [art. of
furniture; **Tafel**, a table with
food on; also tablet (for writ-
ing)].
Tochter, subst. f., pl. **Töchter**,
daughter; dim. **Töchterlein**, n.
Tod, subst. m., gen.-es, no pl.,
death.
todt, see tot.
Tonne, subst. f., pl.-n, barrel,
puncheon.
Topf, subst. m., gen.-es, pl.
Töpfe, pot; dim. **Töpfchen**, n.
Tor, subst. m., gen.-en, pl.
-en, fool. [**Tor**, n., gen.
-es, pl.-e = "gate."]
tot, adj., no compar., dead, deceased [formerly spelt todt].
töten, v. a w., tötete, getötet,
to kill, slay [formerly spelt
tödten].

Tótenbett, subst. n. comp., gen.
-es, pl.-en, death-bed.

tótschiessen, v. a. sep., **schoss,
geschossen,** to shoot dead,
kill with a shot.

Trab, subst. m., gen.-es, pl.-e
(rare), trot.

traben, v. n. (**haben** or **sein**), to
trot. [With **haben** when *action*
only is indicated, with **sein,**
when *direction* is also expressed
or implied.]

tragen, v. a., **trug, getragen,
trägst,** to bear; carry; endure.

Träne, subst. f., pl.-n, tear.

trauen, to perform the ceremony
of marriage, unite in marriage
(said of the minister, etc., per-
forming the ceremony) [**trauen,**
n., = "trust"].

Trauer, subst. f., no. pl., mourning [sorrow; grief, sadness].

träufeln, v. n. (**haben** or **sein**),
to drop (of water, etc.), to drip,
come down in drops.

traurig, adj., sad, sorrowful (from
Trauer).

treffen, v. a., **traf, getroffen, triff,
triffst,** to hit, strike (a mark);
to meet (a person, gov. acc.).

treiben, v. a., **trieb, getrieben,**
to drive; **Spott t.,** to make fun
of (gov. **mit**).

trennen, v. a. w., to separate,
divide.

Treppe, subst. f., gen.-n, stair,
staircase, stairs.

treten, v. a. and n. (**haben**), **trat,
getreten, tritt, trittst, tritt,** to
tread, step; walk; [v. a. to
kick (= **mit dem Fusze t.**)].

treu, adj., faithful, true [**wahr**
is used of moral or logical truth,
as opposed to untruth or false-
hood].

Treue, subst. f., no pl., faithful-
ness, fidelity.

trinken, v. a., **trank, getrunken,**
to drink (of men) [**saufen** is
used of beasts; compare **essen,
fressen**].

Trinken, subst. n., gen.-s, no pl.
(inf. of prec.), drinking (the act
or habit).

trocknen, v. n. (**sein**) and a. w.,
trocknete, getrocknet, to dry,
wipe dry.

Trog, subst. m., gen.-(e)s, pl.
-e or **Tröge,** trough.

Tropfen, subst. m., gen.-s, pl.
——, drop.

trösten, v. a. w., **tröstete, getröstet,** to comfort, console; v.
refl., to console one's self.

trüb(e), adj., dim (of sight, etc.);
discoloured, muddy (of water);
sad, gloomy.

Trunk, subst. m., gen.-es, pl.
Trünke, act of drinking; drink,
draught (what is drunk) [also of
the habit of drinking; the form
Trank is also used, but only in
the sense of "draught," "thing
drunk"].

trunken, adj., drunken, drunk,
intoxicated.

Tuch, subst. n., gen.-(e)s, pl.
Tücher, cloth; dim. **Tüchlein,**
n.

tüchtig, adj., thorough, useful
[from **taugen,** Eng. "doughty"].

Tugend, subst. f., pl.-en, virtue
[from the same as prec.].

tun, v. a., **tat, getan,** to do;
to put (= **antun,** B., p. 34,
l. 9). [The impf. is the only
verbal form which retains the
clear trace of the old formation
of that tense by reduplication]
**Einem etwas zu Leide, zu
Gut(e) t.,** to do a pers. an injury, a benefit; **sich etwas zu
gut(e) tun,** to give one's self a
treat, have a treat; **einen Eid
tun,** to take an oath.

Tür(e), subst. f., pl.-en, door ;
dim.-lein, n.

Turm (or Turn), subst. m.,
gen.-(e)s, pl. Türme, tower,
turret.

Túrteltàube, subst. f. comp., pl.
-n, turtle-dove [the former component is imitative of the cooing
of the dove] ; dim.-täubchen,
n.

U

U, the twenty-first letter of the
alphabet, is pron. like Eng. *oo*,
when long as in *food*, when short
as in *good*. With Umlaut (ü Ue)
it pron. like the Fr. vow. *u*,
with lips rounded, and protrud-
ing even more than in forming ö.

übel, adj., compar. übler, superl.
übelst, evil, bad.

über, prep., gov. dat. and acc.,
over, above ; at, about, concerning (in the latter sense always
with acc.); at the end of, after
(of time with acc. only), as :
über ein Jahr, "at the end of
a year ;" heute über acht
Tage, "a week from to-day ;"
(of time) throughout (after its
case, as : den Tag über,
throughout the day). [In composition often insep.]

überáll, adv., everywhere.

überdénken, v. a. insep. irreg.,
-dachte, -dacht, to think over,
think about.

übergében, v. a. insep., -gab,
-geben, -gib, -gibst, to give
over, give up, surrender.

übergròsz, adj., no compar.,
over-great, excessive, overmas-
tering.

überlàut, adj. and adv., no
compar., over-loud, too loud, ex-
cessively loud.

überlégen, v. a. insep. w., to

consider (turn over in one's
mind).

Uebermùt, subst. m. comp., gen.
-(e)s, no pl., arrogance ; wan-
tonness.

übermütig, adj., arrogant ; over-
bearing.

übernáchten, v. n. (haben) insep.
w., -nachtete, -nachtet, to
pass the night.

übertréffen, v. a. insep., -traf,
-troffen, -triff, -triffst, to
excel.

übrig, adj., no comp., left over ;
remaining : die übrigen, the
rest. A., p. 3, l. 31.

um, prep., gov. acc. only, about,
round about, around (of place) ;
at, about (of time, as : um zehn
Uhr, "at ten o'clock ") ; for (of
purpose), for, concerning, about,
in behalf of. Is frequently used
with the supine (or inf. with zu)
to express purpose, the rest of
the phrase coming between um
and zu, as : er kam um mir
das Buch zu bringen, "he
came *in order to* bring me the
book ;" also with the subst.
Willen and a gen. (particularly
of pers. prons., which then have
a special form) between, as : um
meinet-, ihret-, etc., willen,
"for my, her, their, etc., sake ;"
um des Friedens willen,
"for the sake of peace ;" with
pron., um may also be omitted.
In composition is often insep.,
and sometimes indicates *change*.

úmbringen, v. a. sep. w. irreg.,
brachte, gebracht, to slay, kill
[= um das Leben bringen].

úmdrehen, v. a. and refl. sep.
w., to turn round ; turn.

úmgucken, v. refl. sep. w., to
look round.

úmhauen, v. a. sep., hieb, gehauen, to hew down, cut down.

umhér, adv., round about (rings umher).

umhérsehen, v. n. (haben), to look round, look about.

umhérspringen, v. n. (sein), sprang, gesprungen, to jump about, run about.

úmkehren, v. a. and refl. sep. w., to turn around.

úmsehen, v. refl. sep., sah, gesehen, sieh, siehst, to look around, look about one.

úmwenden, v. a. and refl. sep. w. irreg., wendete or wandte, gewendet or gewandt, to turn around.

umzíehen, v. a. insep., -zog, -zogen, to surround.

[úmziehen, v. refl. insep., to change one's clothes; v. n. (sein), to change one's residence, move.]

umzíngeln, v. a. insep. w., to surround.

un-, neg. prefix, = Eng. "un-."

únbelohnt, adj., no compar., unrewarded.

únbeschädigt, adj., no compar., unhurt, unharmed.

und, coörd. cop. conj., and.

úngedúldig, adj., impatient.

úngeschickt, adj., awkward, clumsy.

úngewiegt, adj., unrocked, without rocking or being rocked (part. of wiegen, "to rock," with neg. prefix).

Únglück, subst. n., gen.-(e)s, no pl., misfortune, ill-luck.

únglücklich, adj., unhappy, unfortunate, unlucky.

únkenntlich, adj., unrecognisable.

Únkraut, subst. n. coll., gen. -(e)s, pl. Unkräuter (rare), weed, weeds.

únmöglich, adj., impossible; adv., not possibly.

Únrecht, subst. n., gen.-(e)s, no pl., wrong, injustice; U. haben, to be wrong; mit U., wrongfully.

únrecht, adj., wrong, unjust.

Únschuld, subst. f., no pl., innocence.

únschuldig, adj., innocent, guiltless; guileless.

unser, gen. pl. first pers. pron., our, hence:

unser, -e, -, poss. adj., our (decl. like ein. When used without a subst., the forms unsrer, -e, -es, der, die, das unsrige or unsere are used).

unten, adv. of place, below, down below.

unter, prep., gov. dat. and acc., under, beneath, below (of place); among (of number).

úntergehen, v. n. (sein) sep., gieng, gegangen, to go down; sink, set (of the sun).

unterríchten, v. a. insep. w., -richtete, -richtet, to instruct, teach.

únterstellen, v. a. sep. w., to place under, set under.

únwahr, adj., untrue, false.

Unwahrheit, subst. f., pl.-en, untruth, falsehood.

Urteil, subst. n. gen.-(e)s, pl.-e, judgment; sentence (pronounced by a judge); verdict; opinion.

V

V, the twenty-second letter of the alphabet, is pron. like Eng. f in all Germ. words. [In foreign words pron. as in Eng.] It replaces Eng. f in many words, as Vater, "father," voll, "full," Vogel, "fowl," etc.

Vater, subst. m., gen.-s, pl. Väter, father.

väterlich, adj., fatherly, paternal.

ver-, insep. prefix (opposite of er-), signifies loss, "away from," etc. (comp. Eng. "for-" in "forget," "forgive," "forlorn "). Thus geben ="give," vergeben = "forgive" (properly "to give away, make a present of "); vergehen = "pass away."

verárbeiten, v. a. insep. w., verarbeitete, verarbeitet, to work up (material into some form), to work out, elaborate.

verbeíssen, v. a. insep., verbiss, verbissen [to bite down], repress, swallow (anger, pain, etc.).

verbérgen, v. a. insep., verbarg, verborgen, verbirg, verbirgst, to hide, conceal.

verbíeten, v. a. insep., verbot, verboten, to forbid (dat. of pers.).

verbórgen, adj. (part. of verbergen), hidden, concealed, secret.

verbreíten, v. a. insep. w., verbreitete, verbreitet, to spread abroad, spread ; v. refl., to extend, spread.

verbrénnen, v. n. (sein) insep. w. irreg., verbrannte, verbrannt, to be consumed with fire, be burnt, burn ; v. a., to consume with fire, burn.

verbúttet, adj. (part. of verbutten), stunted, dwarfed ; neglected. A., p. 9, l. 16.

Verdácht, subst. m., gen.-es, no pl., suspicion ; V. haben or hegen, to entertain suspicion ; in Verdacht haben, to suspect [from verdenken].

verdérben, v. n. insep., verdarb, verdorben, verdirb, verdirbst, to be spoiled or ruined, to spoil ; v. a. w., to spoil, ruin.

Verdárben, subst. n. (inf. of

prec.), ruin, ruination, perdition.

verdíenen, v. a. insep. w., to deserve, earn.

verdríesslich, adj., vexed, ill-humoured, cross [vexatious] ; adv., ill-humouredly, etc.

Verdríesslichkeit, subst. f., pl. -n [ill-temper, vexation] ; annoyance.

verflíessen, v. n. (sein) insep., verfloss, verflossen, to flow away, run away (of water, etc.) ; pass away, pass by (of time).

[vergében, v. a. insep., vergab, vergeben, vergib, vergibst, to forgive (dat. of pers.) ; adv. vergebens, in vain ; hence :]

vergéblich, adj., vain, in vain ; adv. vainly, in vain [= vergebens].

vergéhen, v. n. (sein) insep., vergieng, vergangen, to pass away, pass by, pass (of time) ; to perish.

vergéssen, v. a. insep., vergasz, vergessen, vergiss, vergissest, vergisst, to forget.

vergíften, v. a. insep. w., vergiftete, vergiftet, to poison.

vergnügt, adj., (part. of -en), pleased, happy.

vergönnen, v. a. insep. w., to grant [conn. with Gunst].

verkáufen, v. a. insep. w., to sell.

verkleíden, v. a. insep. w., verkleidete, verkleidet, to dress up (in strange garments), disguise ; v. refl., to disguise one's self.

verlángen, v. a. insep. w., to demand, require ; ask for ; desire (gov. nach).

verlássen, v. a. insep., verliess, verlassen, verlässest, verlässt, to forsake, desert, leave (in the sense of forsaking) ; v.

refl., to depend upon (gov. **auf** with acc.).

verlíeren, v. a. insep., **verlor, verloren**, to lose.

verlóren, adj. (part. of prec.), lost (Eng. "forlorn").

[**vermählen**, v. a. and refl. insep. w., to unite in marriage, marry; hence:]

Vermählung, subst. f., pl.-**en**, marriage, wedding.

verráten, v. a. insep., **verriet, verraten**, to betray.

verrostet, adj. (part. of -**en**), rusted, rusty.

versámmeln, v. a. and refl. insep. w., to gather together, assemble, collect [conn. with **sammt** and **zusammen**].

verscheíden, v. n. (sein) insep., **verschied, verschieden**, to expire [lit. "depart," from **scheiden**, "to part;" **verschieden**, adj., = "different," and in pl. "several"].

verschlíessen, v. a. insep., **verschloss, verschlossen**, to lock up, lock.

verschlíngen, v. a. insep., **verschlang, verschlungen**, to swallow, devour.

verschlúcken, v. a. insep. w., to swallow, devour.

verschmähen, v. a. insep. w., to despise, scorn; reject with scorn.

verschweígen, v. a. insep., **verschwieg, verschwiegen**, to keep silent about, keep secret, conceal (dat. of pers.) [**verschwiegen**, adj., = "silent, taciturn"].

verschwínden, v. n. (sein) insep., **verschwand, verschwunden**, to disappear, vanish.

verséhen, v. a. insep., **versah, versehen, versieh, versiehst**, to make a mistake about a thing, overlook (D., p. 18, l. 21); to attend to, manage (S., p. 51, l. 9, and note); v. refl., to make a mistake, to blunder; to expect (gen. of object).

versénken, v. a. insep. w., to lower down, lower, let down.

versínken, v. n. (sein) insep., **versank, versunken**, to sink down, sink.

verspótten, v. a. insep. w., **verspottete, verspottet**, to mock at, jeer at, mock, deride.

verspréchen, v. a. insep., **versprach, versprochen, versprich, versprichst**, to promise.

Verstánd, subst. m., gen.-**es**, no pl., understanding, intellect (from **verstehen**); hence:

verständig, adj., reasonable; intelligent.

verstécken, v. a. insep. w., to hide, conceal (from a pers. who is searching the obj.).

verstéhen, v. a. insep., **verstand** (subj. -**stünde** or **stände**), **verstanden**, to understand, comprehend.

verstéllen, v. refl. insep. w., to disguise one's self, dissemble.

verstórben, adj. (part. of **versterben**), deceased.

versúchen, v. a. and n. (haben) insep. w., to try; attempt.

vertáuschen, v. a. insep. w., to exchange, give in exchange (gov. **für** or **gegen**).

verüben, v. a. insep. w., to practise, perpetrate.

verúrteilen, v. a. insep. w., to condemn, sentence (to death, punishment, etc.).

verwándeln, v. a. and refl. insep. w., to change, alter.

verwándt, adj., no compar., related, connected; subst. der,

die, -e, pl.-n, ein, -er, relation, connection. [Grimm has incorrectly pl. **seine Verwandte und Bekannte.**]

verwésen, v. n. (sein) insep. w., to undergo corruption, decay.

verwúnden, v. a. insep. w., **verwundete, verwundet,** to wound.

verwúndern, v. refl. insep. w., to wonder, to be astonished or surprised.

Verwúnderung, subst. f., no pl., astonishment, surprise. [**Bewunderung** = "admiration."]

verwünschen, v. a. insep. w., to curse; lay under a magic spell, bewitch [in the latter sense, the partic. form **verwunschen** also occurs, especially as adj.].

verzéhren, v. a. insep. w., to consume, devour.

viel, -e, -, or, when used without a subst., **-er, -e, -es,** pl.-e, adj. of quant., much, many; adv. (or indecl. subst. n.) of quant., much. [Decl. in sing. and pl. when referring to number; not decl. when referring to quant.]

vielleícht, adv., perhaps, perchance [lit. "very easily"].

vier[e], card. num., four; ord. **vierte,** fourth.

Víertel, subst. n., gen.-s, pl. ——, quarter.

Víerteljàhr, subst. n. comp., gen.-(e)s, pl.-e, quarter of a year, quarter.

Víertelstùnde, subst. f. comp., pl.-n, quarter of an hour.

Vogel, subst. m., gen.-s, pl. **Vögel,** bird (Eng. "fowl"); dim. **Vög(e)lein,** n.

voll, adj., full [gov. gen. and acc. and sometimes occurs, even as pred., in the extended form **voller**].

vom, contr. for **von dem.**

von, prep., gov. dat. only; of (after verbs, and sometimes after subst., replacing the gen. of a subst. not used in that case); from (place); by (with *personal agent* after pass. verbs. as : **ich werde von meinen Eltern geliebt,** "I am loved by my parents").

vor, prep., gov. dat. and acc., before (of time, with dat. only, and place with dat. or acc.); in front of (place); for, on account of (cause, dat. only).

vorbeí, adv., past (of place); past, gone (of time).

vorbeígehen, v. n. (sein) sep., **gieng, gegangen,** go past, to pass by.

vorbeikommen, v. n. (sein) sep., **kam, gekommen, kömmst** or **kommst,** to come past, pass by.

vorbeíspringen, v. n. (sein) sep., **sprang, gesprungen,** to run past.

vorbeítraben, v. n. (sein) sep. w., to trot past.

vórfallen, v. n. (sein) sep. impers., to occur, take place.

vórgehen, v. n. (sein) sep., **gieng, gegangen,** [to go before (dat. of pers.)]; impers., to go on, take place, pass.

Vórhang, subst. m., gen.-(e)s, pl.-hänge, curtain; **die V. vorziehen,** to draw or close the curtains.

vorhér, adv., before.

vorhín, adv., before.

vórig, adj., no compar., preceding, before.

vórkommen, v. n. (sein) sep. impers., **kam, gekommen,** no imper., **kömmst** or **kommst,** to happen, occur; seem, appear.

vorn(e) or **-en,** adv. of place, in

front, at the front or head (of a procession, etc.).

Vórrat, subst. m. comp., gen. -(e)s, pl. - räte, provision, stock.

Vórschein, subst. m., appearance, hardly ever used except with **kommen** and **bringen** in the phrases **zum V. kommen**, to make one's appearance, appear, come forth; and **zum V. bringen**, to bring to light, show.

Vórteil, subst. m., gen.-(e)s, pl. -e, advantage, profit ["first share," from vor and Teil].

vórteilhaft, adj., advantageous, profitable.

vorüber, adv., past, gone.

vorübergehen, v. n. (sein) sep., gieng, gegangen, to pass by (gov. **an** with dat.); pass away.

Vórwurf, subst. m., gen.-(e)s, pl.-würfe, reproach [from vórwerfen, "a thing thrown up to you"].

vórziehen, v. a. sep., zog, gezogen, to draw before, to draw, close (curtains, etc.). [; to prefer.]

W

W, the twenty-third letter of the alphabet, is pron. like Eng. *v*, except after sch and z, when it is pron. like Eng. *w*.

Wa(a)re, see **Ware**.

wachen, v. n. (haben) w., to wake, be awake.

wachsen, v. n. (sein), wuchs, gewachsen, wächsest, to grow, increase.

Wächter, subst. m., gen.-s, pl. ——, watcher, watchman, guard.

wahr, adj., true, truthful.

währen, v. n. (haben) w., to last, endure.

während, prep., gov. gen. only, during, throughout [also found with dat.] ; subord. conj., while, whilst [pres. part. of prec.].

Wahrheit, subst. f., pl.-en, truth.

Wáhrzeichen, subst. n., gen. -s, pl.—— [sign, omen ;], signal, proof (S., p. 49, l. 7).

wägen, v. a., wog, gewogen, to ascertain the weight of, weigh [intrans. form of wiegen, see below].

Wald, subst. m., gen.-es, pl. **Wälder**, wood, forest.

Wáldhaus, subst. n. comp., gen. -es, pl.-häuser, house in the forest or woods ; dim.-häuschen, cot or hut in the woods.

wälzen, v. a. w., to roll.

Wand, subst. f., pl. **Wände**, wall (of a room, partition-wall); [Mauer = "surrounding wall (of house, garden, town," etc.). Wall = "fortified walls of a town," "ramparts."]

wann, interrog. adv. of time, when [see wenn, als].

Wanne, subst. f., pl.-n, flat-pan, tin, bath-tin.

war, impf. ind. of sein.

Ware, subst. f., pl.-n, ware, wares, goods (for sale).

warten, v. n. (haben) w., wartete, gewartet, to wait, tarry.

warúm (for worum), interrog. adv., why, what for.

was, comp. rel. pron. n. (of wer), gen. wessen, dat. wanting, acc. was, what, that which [not used when the antecedent is expressed, except when that antecedent is a n. adj. or pron., when it always replaces welches. Was is not used (either as rel. or interrog.) in dat. or acc. gov. by a prep., being replaced by **wo-** (before vow. **wor-**) before the prep., as **wo-für,** for what, what for, for which; **worin,** in what or which, wherein. The dat. is wanting, and is replaced by **wo** with prep., as just said, being seldom required as indir. obj. (**welcher** replaces it in this case if necessary).]

was, interrog. pron. n. (see prec.), what?

was, interrog. adv., how? (=**wie?**) [why? (= **warum ?**).]

was, indef. num., for **etwas,** something, anything.

waschen, v. a., **wusch, ge-waschen, wäschest,** to wash.

was für ein, -e, -, pl. **was für,** interrog. adj. pref., what kind or sort of [**ein** is omitted in sing., also before nouns of quantity, material, etc.].

Wasser, subst. n., gen.-s, pl. —— (rare), water.

weben, v. a., w. and str., **wob** or **webte, gewoben** or **gewebt,** to weave.

wecken, v. a. w., to awaken, wake up, arouse.

wedeln, v. n. (**haben**) w., to wag (the tail; gov. **mit**).

Weg, subst. m., gen.-(e)s, pl.-e, way, road.

weg, adv., away.

wegen, prep., gov. gen., on account of [often follows its case, esp. with pers. pron., which then have the term. -t, and form one word with it, as **meinet-wegen,** etc.; sometimes also with dat.].

wégnehmen, v. a. sep., **nahm, genommen, nimm, nimmst,** to take away.

wégschieben, v. a. sep., **schob, geschoben,** to push away.

wégspringen, v. n. (**sein**) sep., **sprang, gesprungen,** to jump or run away.

Weib, subst. n., gen.-(e)s, pl. **-er,** woman, wife (less respectful than **Frau**).

weich, adj., soft; gentle; tender.

Weide, subst. f., willow [; also = "pasture"].

weigern, v. a. w., to refuse; v. refl., to refuse, object.

weil, subord. conj., because [sometimes, but rarely, = "while"].

Weile, subst. f., pl.-n (rare), while (space of) time; dim. **-chen,** n. [**lange Weile** or **Langweile,** = "tedium, ennui."]

Wein, subst. m., gen.-(e)s, pl. **-e,** wine.

weinen, v. n. (**haben**) w., to weep, shed tears.

Weinfass, subst. n. comp., gen. **-es,** pl.-**fässer,** wine-vat, butt or barrel of wine.

weise, adj., wise.

Weise, subst. f., pl.-n, manner, mode, way; [also = "tune, melody." Used with gen. sing. f. of adj. to form adv. of manner, as **glücklicherweise** (or gl. **Weise**) fortunately ("in fortunate wise").]

weisen, v. a., **wies, gewiesen,** to show, point.

weiss, pres. ind. first sing. of **wissen,** "to know."

weiss, adj., no comp., white. [**Einem etwas w. machen,** "to practise an imposition on a pers."]

weissgedeckt, compound adj. (part. of **decken**), covered with white, with a white covering.

weit, adj., wide; far, distant; adv., widely; far off; comp. **weiter,** further, furthermore.

weítergèhen, v. n. (sein) sep.,
gieng, gegangen, to go further, go on, proceed.

weítertreíben, v. a. sep., **trieb,
getrieben,** to drive further,
drive on.

weíterzìehen, v. n. (sein) sep.,
zog, gezogen, to go further,
go on one's way.

welcher, -e, -es, pl.-e, rel. pron.,
who (of pers.), which, that (of
things). [Interchangeable with
der as rel. pron., exc. after pers.
pron. See **wer.**]

welcher, -e, -es, pl.-e, interrog.
pron. and adj., which (of
two).

welcher, -e, -es, pl.-e, or
welch' (undecl.), demonstr.
pron. num., what! [used with or
without indef. art. after it ; in
the former case not decl.].

welcher, -e, -es, pl.-e, or undecl., indef. num., some ; pl.
several, a few.

Welt, subst. f., pl.-en, world
[orig. **Werlt,** Eng. "world"].

wenden, v. a. and refl. w. and
irreg., **wendete** or **wandte,
gewendet** or **gewandt,** to turn.

Wendeltreppe, subst. f. comp.,
pl.-n, winding stair-case [first
component from **wenden**].

wenig (or -er, -e, -es, pl.-e),
adj., little (of quantity), pl.
few [decl. when referring to
number, not decl. when relating
to quantity ; compare **viel**].

wenn, subord. conj., if (of condition ; **ob** = "whether") ; when
(of time) used with pres., perf.,
fut., and fut. perf., also with
impf. for *habitual* or *repeated*
action ; **als** with impf. and
plupf. ; **wann** is interrog.

wer, pers. interrog. pron., gen.
wessen, dat. **wem,** acc. **wen,**
n. **was,** no pl., who? (Stands

for both genders, and refers to
pers. only.)

wer, pers. comp. rel. pron., (he)
who, (she) who, (they) who
(= derjenige welcher ; never
has an antecedent, as it includes
both rel. and antec. See **was**);
**wer nur, wer immer, wer
auch** = "whoever, whoso-
ever."

werden, v. n. (sein), **ward** or
wurde (pl. **wurden,** etc., not
**warden), geworden, werde,
wirst, wird,** to become, get,
grow ; aux. v. of tense (forms
fut. and fut. perf., gov. inf.)
shall, will ; aux. v. of voice
(forms passive, gov. past part.),
to be ; to turn into (with **zu**), as
zu Stein w. ; v. impers., **zu
Teil** w., to fall to the lot of
(dat. of pers.) ; **zu Mute** w., see
Mut. [See **wollen** for examples of difference between
werden, sollen, and **wollen.**]

werfen, v. a., **warf** (subj. **würfe),
geworfen, wirf, wirfst,** to
throw, cast.

wert, adj., worth (gov. acc.) ;
[worthy, valuable.]

wetzen, v. a. w., to whet, sharpen.

Wetzstein, subst. m. comp.,
whetstone.

wickeln, v. a. w., to wrap, roll
(up) ; see **auseinanderw.**

wider, prep., gov. acc. only,
against, in opposition [**gegen**
also = "toward ;" as prefix
= Eng. "with-" in "with-
stand," etc., and is always insep.].

widerstéhen, v. n. (haben),
widerstand (subj. -**stünde),
widerstanden,** to withstand,
resist, oppose (dat. of pers.).

wie, interrog. adv., how? subord.
conj. of comparison, as (compar.
of equality), than (compar. of in-

equality) [see **als**] ; when (of
time, = **als**); as soon as.
wieder, adv., again [dist. from
wider, prep., "against"].
wiederbringen, v. a. sep. irreg.,
brachte, gebracht, to bring
back, return.
wiedergeben, v. a. sep., **gab,
gegeben, gib, gibst**, to give
back, return.
wiedersehen, v. a. sep., **sah,
gesehen, sieh, siehst**, to see
again [; **auf W.**, "to meet
again " (Fr. *au revoir*).]
Wiege, subst. f., pl.-n, cradle.
wiegen, v. a. w., to rock, cradle.
[**wiegen**, v. n., **wog, gewogen,
wieg, wiegst**, to have weight,
weight (acc. of weight). [**wäg-
en** is the trans. form ; see
above.]
Wiese, subst. f., pl.-n, meadow.
wild, adj., wild ; savage.
Wild, subst. n., gen.-es, no pl.,
game (wild animals).
Wildnis, subst. f., pl.-isse,
wilderness.
will, pres. ind. of **wollen**, "will."
Wille(n), subst. m., gen.-ns or
-n (rare), pl.——, will, desire,
volition ; **um** governing **W.** has
gen. between prep. and **W.**
with peculiar forms of pers.
pron., as : **um ihretwillen**, for
her sake, etc. ; compare **wegen**,
and see **um** [the prep. may also
be omitted].
[**willigen**, v. n. (haben) w., to
consent ; gov. **in** with acc.; gen.
in comp. with **ein** (see **einwilligen**).]
Wind, subst. m., gen.-es, pl.-e,
wind.
Winter, subst. m., gen.-s, pl.
——, winter.
winzig, adj., small, tiny.
wir, pers. pron. first pl., gen.
unser, dat. acc. **uns**, we, us.

Wirbel, subst. m., gen.-s, pl.
—— [whirl, rapid rotation ; (of
the water) eddy ;], crown of the
head.
wirken, v. a. w., to work, take
effect.
Wirt, subst. m., gen.-es, pl.-e,
host, landlord.
Wirtshaus, subst. n. comp., gen.
-es, pl.-häuser, tavern, inn.
wissen, v. a. irreg., **wusste, ge-
wusst**, imper. **wisse**, pres. ind.
weiss, weisst, weiss, pl.
wissen, etc., to know, know
of, have knowledge (of things,
not of pers. Comp. **kennen**).
wo, adv. of place, interrog. and
rel., where ; (sometimes of
time) when ; [used before prep.
instead of **was** (interrog. and
rel.), and **welcher** (referring to
inanimate obj.; see **was**).]
Woche, subst. f., pl.-n, week.
wohl, adv., well ; as particle in
very common use ; in questions
expresses doubt, as : **wird er
w. kommen ?** "*do you think* he
will come ?" in statements, ex-
pects assent, as : **er wird w.
kommen**, "*no doubt* he will
come ;" **ja wohl**, yes *indeed ;*
Sie haben es w. vergessen,
"*I suppose* you have forgotten
it."
wohl, adj., well (of health).
wohlan ! interj. (of encouragement), very well ! well, then !
courage !
wohlgehen, v. n. (sein) sep. impers., **gieng, gegangen**, to go
well with, fare well with (dat. of
pers.).
wohltun, v. n. (haben) sep. irreg.,
tat, getan, to do well to, benefit (dat. of pers.).
wohnen, v. n. (haben) w., to
dwell, live, reside (**leben** = "to
be alive ").

Wolf, subst. m., gen.-(e)s, pl. **Wölfe,** wolf.

wollen, v. a., aux. of mood, impf. **wollte** (ind. and subj.), part. **gewollt,** pres. ind. **will, willst, will,** pl. **wollen,** etc. (subj. **wolle**), to be willing, will ; to be on the point of doing, etc., about to do, a thing. [Indicates exertion of the *will* of the subj. ; when Eng. "will" is mere aux. of fut. tense, it must be trans. by **werden,** as : **ich WERDE ertrinken, und niemand WIRD mich retten** = "I *shall* be drowned, and nobody *will* save me" (mere statement of future fact) ; but : **ich WILL ertrinken, und niemand SOLL mich retten** = "I *will* be drowned, and nobody *shall* save me" (determination to commit suicide by drowning).]

worán, adv., whereto, etc., to what or which, etc. (wo replacing rel. or interrog. pron. ; so in foll.)

worin, adv., wherein, to or into what or which.

Wort, subst. n., gen.-es, pl.-e (connected words, as in a sent.), **Wörter** (detached words, as in a dictionary), word.

wozu, whereto, wherefore, to or for what or which (see **woran**).

wund, adj., wounded, lacerated, sore.

Wunde, subst. f., pl.-n, wound.

Wunder, subst. n., gen.-s, pl.——, wonder (wonderful thing), miracle ["astonishment" = **Verwunderung**].

wúnderbar, adj., wondrous, wonderful, strange, miraculous [dist. from -lich].

Wundergabe, subst. f. comp., pl.-n, wondrous, miraculous or magic gift.

wúnderlich, adj., queer, odd, strange [dist. from -bar, above].

wundern, v. refl. w., to wonder, be astonished or surprised.

wúnderschön, adj., wondrously or exceedingly beautiful.

wúndstechen, v. a. sep., **stach, gestochen, stich, stichst,** to wound by pricking, to lacerate, make sore.

Wunsch, subst. m., gen.-es, pl. **Wünsche,** wish, desire.

wünschen, v. a. w., to wish, desire.

Wurst, subst. f., pl. **Würste,** sausage.

wurde or **ward,** impf. ind. of **werden.**

Wurzel, subst. f., pl.-n, root.

wusste, impf. ind. of **wissen,** "to know."

X

X, the twenty-fourth letter of the alphabet, is pron. as in Eng. (= **ks**) ; is never found at the beginning of Germ. words, and only occurs in a very few words, as **Hexe, Axt,** etc.

Y

Y, the twenty-fifth letter of the alphabet, never occurs in Germ. words in modern orthography, though it was formerly used to dist. the verb **sein,** "to be," from the poss. adj. **sein,** "his."

Z

Z, the twenty-sixth and last letter, is of much more frequent occurrence in Germ. than in Eng.

It is the dental aspirate, and as such replaces the Eng. *th* in the dental series of mutes. Where it occurs in Germ. words, the corresponding Eng. words will generally have *t*, as **zu,** "to ;" **zahm,** "tame ;" **Zange,** "tongs ;" **Zunge,** "tongue," etc.

zahm, adj., comp. **-er** or (rarely) **zähmer,** tame.

Zange, subst. f., pl. **-n,** pair of tongs, tongs.

zart, adj., comp. **-er** or **zärter,** tender, gentle.

[**Zauber,** subst. m., gen. **-s,** pl. —— (rare), magic ; hence :]

Záuberspruch, subst. m. comp., gen. **-(e)s,** pl. **-sprüche,** magic spell, charm.

Zehe, subst. f., pl. **-n,** toe.

zehn(e), card. num., ten ; ord. **-te,** tenth.

zeigen, v. a. w., to show, point out [dist. from **zeihen** and **ziehen**].

Zeit, subst. f., pl. **-n,** time [Eng. "tide"] ; **Einem die Z. bieten** (to give a pers. the time of day), bid him good-day ; **Zeitlang,** which is often written as one word, is really only **Z.** with the adj. **lang** added ; thus **eine Zeit lang** or **Zeitlang,** "for some time."

zer-, insep. pref., indicating destruction, as **reissen** = "tear," **zerreissen** = "tear to pieces ;" **springen,** "spring," **zer-springen,** "spring to pieces, burst," etc.

zerbréchen, v. n. (sein) and a. insep., **zerbrach, zerbrochen, zerbrich, zerbrichst,** to break to pieces.

zehren, v, a. w., to consume, devour.

zerreíssen, v. a. insep., **zerriss,**

zerrissen, to tear to pieces, tear up ; v. n., to be torn, tear.

zerspríngen, v. n. (sein) insep., to fly to pieces, burst.

ziehen, v. a., **zog, gezogen,** to pull, draw ; v. n. (sein), to move, march, go.

Ziehen, subst. n., gen. **-s,** no pl. (inf. of prec.), drawing, pulling ; draught.

zierlich, adj., neat, graceful, pretty.

[**Zins,** subst. m., gen. **-es,** pl. **-en,** tax, toll (interest) ; hence ;]

Zínshahn, subst. m. comp., gen. **-(e)s,** pl. **-hähne,** cock due as rent, toll-cock, rent-cock, or simply cock. [See K., p. 41, l. 17, note.]

zittern, v. n. (haben), to tremble, shiver, quiver.

Zorn, subst. m., gen. **-(e)s,** no pl., anger, rage.

zornig, adj., angry, enraged.

zu, prep., gov. dat. only, to, toward (of motion to a pers. or place ; with proper names of towns, however, **zu** = "at," and "to" is rendered by **nach** —see **nach**) ; **zu** also = at, of the place of entrance or exit, as : **zum Fenster hereinkommen,** "to enter at the window ;" at (rest in a place, with prop. names of towns, etc., also with **Haus,** as **zu Hause,** "at home") ; at (of time, used only with **Zeit,** "time," **Stunde,** "hour," and in the phrase **zu Abend,** "by evening") ; to, for (of purpose). [Eng. "to" before pers. is to be rendered by the dat. without prep., if it is merely the equivalent of the indir. obj.; thus : give the book to me, to. this man" (= "give me, this man, the book"), **geben Sie mir, diesem Manne, das Buch;**

12

but "come to me" = kommen Sie zu mir. As prefix, zu often = "on, onward," as zugehen, "to go on ;" it sometimes follows a noun, with nach before it, as : nach dem Hause zu, "toward the house ;" zu is also used as particle before the inf. when gov. by another verb or to express purpose, which is then called the supine, and expresses purpose, with or without um ; see um. It is also used as though it were a pred. adj., meaning "shut," "closed," as : das Fenster ist zu (supply geschlossen), "the window is closed."]

zúdecken, v. a. sep. w., to cover, cover up.

zuérst, adv. of time, at first, at the beginning, before all, first (before any one else).

zufríeden, adj., contented, satisfied.

zufríedensprèchen, v. a. sep., sprach, gesprochen, sprich, sprichst, to satisfy.

zúgehen, v. n. (sein), sep., gieng, gegangen, to go up to, approach (gov. auf with acc.).

Zügel, subst. m., gen.-s, pl. ——, rein ; reins ; bridle.

zúkehren, v. a. sep. w., to turn toward, turn to.

zúlassen, v. a. sep., liess, gelassen, lässest, lässt, to leave closed, keep closed (B., p. 38, l. 28) [; to allow, permit].

zum, contr. for zu dem.

zumál, adv., especially as.

zünden, v. a. w., zündete, gezündet, to kindle, inflame, light (a fire).

Zunge, subst. f., pl.-n, tongue.

zur, contr. for zu der.

zurück, adv., back, backward, back again.

zurückbleiben, v. n. (sein) sep., blieb, geblieben, to remain behind, stay behind, be left behind.

zurückbringen, v. a. sep. irreg., brachte, gebracht, to bring back.

zurückhalten, v. a. sep., hielt, gehalten, hältst, hält, to hold back, restrain.

zurückkehren, v. n. (sein) to turn back, return.

zurückziehen, v. a., to draw back, pull back ; withdraw ; v. refl., to withdraw, retire.

zusámmen, adv., together [conn. with sammt, sammeln].

zusámmenhalten, v. a. sep., hielt, gehalten, hältst, hält, to hold together, keep together.

zusámmenkommen, v. n. (sein) separate, kam, gekommen, kömmst or kommst, to come together, meet.

zusámmenleben, v. n. (haben) sep. w., to live together.

zusammensuchen, v. a. sep. w., to gather together, collect.

zusámmentun [v. a., to put together] ; v. refl. sep., tat, getan, to close.

zúschliessen, v. a. sep., schloss, geschlossen, to lock, close.

zúsehen, v. n. (haben) sep., sah, gesehen, sieh, siehst, to look on (dat. of obj.).

zúsprechen, v. n. (haben) sep., sprach, gesprochen, sprich, sprichst, to speak to, address ; to speak (kindly) to, speak words of comfort, comfort, console (dat. of pers.).

zútragen, v. refl. imp. sep., trug, getragen, trägst, to happen, come to pass [v. a., to carry to].

zútun, v. a. sep., **tat, getan,** to close ; v. refl., to close.

zuvór, adv., before, in anticipation.

zuvórkommen, v. n. (sein) sep., **kam, gekommen, kömmst** or **kommst,** to get ahead of, anticipate.

zúwerfen, v. a. sep., **warf, geworfen, wirf, wirfst,** to throw toward (dat. of pers.).

zwängen, v. a. w., to force, squeeze [caus. of **zwingen**].

zwar, adv., in truth, to be sure, indeed [old Germ., **zu ware** = "in truth"].

zwei(e), card. num., two ; ord. **zweite,** second.

zweimal, num. adv., twice.

Zwerg, subst. m., gen.-es, pl.-e, dwarf ; dim.-lein, n.

Zwergenhaus, subst. n. comp., gen.-es, pl.-häuser, dwarf's house.

Zwilling, subst. m., gen.-(e)s, pl.-e, twin (from **zwei**).

zwölf(e), card. num., twelve ; ord. -te, twelfth.

GRAMMATICAL APPENDIX.

I.—ELEMENTS OF THE CONSTRUCTION OF SENTENCES.

§ 1. Every sentence contains three essential parts, viz.: the *subject*, of which something is said, the *predicate*, that which is said of it, and thirdly, the *word making the assertion*, which may be contained in the same word as the predicate, but is not necessarily so. Thus, in the sentence: "he sings," "he" is the subj., "sings" contains both the assertion and the predicate, *i.e.*, not only says something of the subj., but also states what that something is, being equivalent to "is singing;" in the sent., "he has sung," "has" is the *assertion*, "sung" is what is asserted, or the predicate.

[NOTE.—The word making the assertion is also called the *copula*.]

§ 2. In compound tenses, the auxiliary verb of tense (**haben, sein,** or **werden**) contains the assertion; hence:

N.B.—*That part of the verb which contains the assertion will, for brevity's sake, be spoken of in the following remarks as* THE VERB. It is this member of the sentence, the position of which is most absolutely fixed in a German sentence, particularly in principal sentences.

§ 3. Sentences are of two kinds (as regards their rank and construction), viz. : Principal (or Independent) and Subordinate (or Dependent); and the position of the Verb varies in these two kinds of sentences very materially.

A.—PRINCIPAL SENTENCES.

§ 4. A Principal Sentence is one which does not depend on any other sentence.

PLACE OF THE VERB IN PRINCIPAL SENTENCES.

§ 5. Principal Sentences in German always have the Verb (*i.e.*, that part containing the Assertion) in the *Second place ;* or in other words, the verb is the *Second Idea* (not necessarily the second *word*) in the Principal Sentence.

(*a*) The normal sequence of words in the sentence is : Subject, Verb (containing the assertion), Predicate. Other words than the subject, however, frequently begin the sentence.

(*b*) In Eng. the subject almost invariably precedes the Verb, and the Verb is therefore, when some other member of the sentence precedes the subject, in the *third* place, as : *To-morrow I shall go.*

(*c*) In Germ., on the other hand, when any member of the sent. other than the subj. begins the sent. (which is more frequently the case than not), the Verb still retains its place as the *Second Idea* or Member, the subj. being in such cases thrown *after* the Verb, as : **Morgen werde ich gehen** (" To-morrow *shall I* go ").

N.B.—This is the one fixed rule of German construction which is departed from in very few cases, even in poetry ; all such cases, real or apparent, will be found explained or noticed in the notes.

PLACE OF THE SUBJECT IN PRINCIPAL SENTENCES.

§ 6. The Subject (with its enlargements), when not the first member of the sent., usually follows immediately after the Verb.

PLACE OF THE PREDICATE IN PRINCIPAL SENTENCES.

§ 7. The Predicate may be included in the Verb, which is the case in simple tenses (*e.g.*, "he *sings*") ; or it may consist of a part. or inf., in compound tenses (*e.g.*, "he has sung ") ; or it may be an adj. (as : "he is *good*") ; or a separable particle. In any of these forms, its proper place in a principal sent. is *last ;* it may, however, when it is desired to emphasize it, come at the beginning of the sentence, in which case (as stated above) the subj. is thrown after the Verb. Hence the following further rules :

(*a*) In compound tenses, the participle and infinitive come at the *end* of the sent. (*i.e.*, after all the enlargements of either Verb, Subject, or Predicate), as :

He will sing a beautiful song this evening.
Er wird heute Abend ein schönes Lied singen.

She has seen very wonderful things on her voyage.
Sie hat auf ihrer Reise sehr wunderbare Dinge gesehen ; or, Auf ihrer Reise hat sie, etc.

The song of this bird is very beautiful.
Der Gesang dieses Vogels ist sehr schön.

[NOTE.—In this last sent., "dieses **Vogels** " is merely an enlargement of the subj., not a separate member of the sent. ; see below.]

(*b*) Where the infin. and part. are both present, the latter always precedes the former, contrary to the Eng. practice, which places the infin. first, as :

He will *have had* many opportunities.
Er wird viele Gelegenheiten gehabt haben.

(*c*) A pred. adj. precedes both part. and inf., as :
He will have been good.
Er wird gut gewesen sein.

(*d*) In compound verbs the separable particle comes *last* in simple tenses, but precedes (and is written in one word with) the part. or inf. (if both are present, it precedes the part.) ; as :

He goes out every day.
Er geht jeden Tag aus.
He has gone out to-day.
Er ist heute ausgegangen.

(*e*) Conjunctions are not counted as members of the sent., or as ideas ; as:

John is here, *but* Henry is not here,
Johann ist hier, aber Heinrich ist nicht hier.

Where, however, the subject of the two sentences thus connected is the same, it is regarded as occupying its place (though not expressed) before the Verb, which then immediately follows the conjunction, as :

Yesterday he came to me, *and* invited me to the ball.
Gestern kam er zu mir, und lud mich zu dem Balle ein.

[NOTE.—Several instances occur in these Tales in which the conj. does throw the subj. after the Verb, to which attention is called in the notes at the proper place.]

INTERROGATIVE AND IMPERATIVE SENTENCES.

§ 8. In Interrogative Sentences the word that asks the question begins the sent. ; hence :

If there is no other interrogative word (pron., adj., or adv.) the Verb will stand first in an interrogative sent. ; otherwise it will come second, as :

Has he been here to-day ?
Ist er heute hier gewesen ?

but :

Who has been here to-day ?
Wer ist heute hier gewesen ?

The position of the other parts of the sent. is the same as in assertive sentences.

§ 9. In Imperative Sentences, in the Second Person, the subj. is seldom expressed, and the Verb is always first ; in the Third Person, the Verb *may* precede the subj., but does not necessarily do so.

VARIATIONS OF THESE RULES.

§ 10. As above remarked, both the Predicate and the Subject may vary their position in the sent., from considerations connected with the importance one desires to attach to them, or to some other member of the sent. ; but that of the Verb as the *second idea* of a principal assertive sentence is seldom departed from, and *never* for mere reasons of emphasis. The real deviations from the rule in this respect are commented on in the notes where they occur ; the following are some of the *apparent* deviations :

(*a*) When a principal sent. is preceded by a dependent sent., the Verb is the first word in the latter, as :

Because I love my son, I punish him.
Weil ich meinen Sohn liebe, bestrafe ich ihn.

If I had money, I should also have friends.
Wenn ich Geld hätte, würde ich auch Freunde haben.

EXPLANATION.—In this case, the whole complex clause (" Because—him ; " " If—friends ") is regarded as one, in which the subordinate sent. forms the first idea, the Verb of the principal sent. thus forming the *second idea* of the clause taken as a whole.

[NOTE.—In these and similar cases the particle **so** frequently introduces the second, or principal, clause, immediately followed by the Verb.]

(*b*) In quotations, the parenthetic expressions, "said he," "thought I," etc., have the subj. after the Verb (as generally in Eng. and always in French), the preceding part of the quotation forming the first idea (as though it were the object of the Verb), the Verb again coming second, as :

"I think," said I, "that he will come."
"Ich glaube," sagte ich, " dass er kommen wird."

B.—DEPENDENT SENTENCES.

§ 11. Dependent or Subordinate Sentences are such as depend upon another sent., and may be introduced by a rel. pron. or adv., or a subord. conj. They differ materially in construction from Principal Sentences, chiefly in the position of the Verb.

§ 12. The Verb in Dependent Sentences comes *last*; the Predicate immediately precedes it, with its various parts in the same *relative* order as in a Principal Sentence; *i.e.*, participles precede infinitives, and a pred. adj. or separable particle precedes both, as :

He admitted that the concert had been very fine.
Er gab zu, dass das Concert sehr schön gewesen sei.

He said that he would go out to-morrow.
Er sagte, dass er morgen ausgehen werde.

§ 13. The Subject, in a Dependent Sentence, comes as early as possible in the sent. ; *i.e.*, if not itself the word connecting the sent. with the sent. on which it depends, immediately after such connecting word, as :

The man, who was here yesterday, came again to-day.
Der Mann, welcher gestern hier war, kam heute wieder.

The man, whom I saw yesterday, came again to-day.
Der Mann, den ich gestern sah, kam heute wieder.

[NOTE.—In these two sentences the rel. clauses are mere enlargements of the subj. (**Mann**) of the principal sent. ; hence the Verb **kam** is *second*, according to rule.]

§ 14. The position of the Verb is, however, not by any means so rigidly fixed in Dependent as in Principal Sentences. Thus in compound tenses the Verb (auxil. of tense) is frequently found preceding both inf. and part. For instances, see notes.

§ 15. The auxil. verbs of mood (**dürfen, sollen,** etc.), and a few others similarly used (**lassen, sehen, hören,** etc.) even require the auxil. of tense to precede the inf.

and part. in the compound tenses in dep. sentences, as :

He said that he had been obliged to do it.
Er sagte, dass er es habe tun müssen.

§ 16. The sep. particle in compound verbs is not separated from the simple tenses of the verb in a dep. sent., but precedes it, and is written in one word with it, as :

He says that you are going out.
Er sagt, dass Sie ausgehen.

SPECIAL CONSTRUCTIONS.

§ 17. In conditional sentences the conjunction "if" (**wenn** or **ob**) is often dispensed with, the Verb being then placed at the beginning of the sent., as :

Had I only done this before, I should now be happy.
Hätte ich dies nur früher getan, (so) würde ich jetzt glücklich sein.

[NOTE 1.—This construction is very much more frequent in German than in English. It seems to take its form from that of the interrog. sent., with which a conditional sent. has something in common.]

NOTE 2.—In this construction the principal sent. (the *apodosis*) is usually introduced by the particle **so** (Comp. § 10, Note).]

§ 18. The conj. **dass**, like the Eng. conj. "that," is frequently omitted when stating a fact; in this case the sent. assumes the construction of a principal sent., the Verb, however, being in the *subj.* mood (usually pres. or perf.) to show its subordinate character, as :

He said he had done it.
Er sagte, er habe es getan (for: dass er es getan habe).

Other Members of the Sentence.

§ 19. As the other members of a sent. (which are enlargements of one or other of the three essential members) have the same relative position in all sentences, whether principal or dependent, they may be treated of in this place.

(*a*) Nouns or pronouns gov. by prepositions precede simple objects not gov. by prepositions, whether nouns or pronouns, direct or indirect objects, as :

He has written a letter to me.
Er hat einen Brief an mich geschrieben.

(*b*) Pronouns, unless as under (*a*), precede nouns, as :

He has written me a letter.
Er hat mir einen Brief geschrieben.

He has given it to my sister.
Er hat es meiner Schwester gegeben.

(*c*) Of several pronouns in different cases, the dat. comes before the gen., the acc. before both, as :

He has given it to me.
Er hat es mir gegeben.

(*d*) With nouns, the person precedes the thing, except as under (*a*), as :

He has given my sister a book.
Er hat meiner Schwester ein Buch gegeben.

(*e*) Time before place, as :

He has been here frequently this week.
Er ist diese Woche oft hier gewesen,

(*f*) Other adverbs (as, for instance, the neg. **nicht**) precede the member of the sent. which they modify.

II.—DECLENSION OF ADJECTIVES.

§ 1. Adjectives used as predicates are not declined.

§ 2. Adjectives used as attributes are declined in one of the three following ways :

(*a*) When preceded by the *definite article*, or any determinative word declined like it, they take the termination —**e** in the nom. sing. of all genders, and in the acc. sing. fem. and neut. ; otherwise, —**en** throughout.

(*b*) When preceded by the *indefinite article*, or any determinative word declined like it, they take the terminations of **dieser** in the nom. and acc. sing. of all genders ; otherwise, —**en** throughout.

(*c*) When preceded by *no determinative word*, they take the termination of **dieser** throughout.

REMARKS.—1. The strong termination —**es** is frequently omitted in the nom. and acc. neut.

2. The strong termination —**es** of the gen. sing. masc. and neut. is often replaced by —**en** before nouns having —**es** in the gen.

3. Adjectives used as substantives still continue subject to these rules, as : **der Kranke**, "the patient ;" but **ein Kranker**, "a patient," etc.

4. Adjectives in the compar. and superl. degrees are subject to the same rules, their declensional inflexion following the inflexion of comparison, as : A better man, **Ein besserer Mann.**

[Stock's "Wortfolge" (Geo. Bell & Sons, London, 1s. 6d.) is highly recommended as an Exercise-Book in construction.]

Der Taucher.

„Wer wagt es, Rittersmann oder Knapp,
Zu tauchen in diesen Schlund?
Einen goldnen Becher werf' ich hinab,
Verschlungen schon hat ihn der schwarze Mund.
5 Wer mir den Becher kann wieder zeigen,
Er mag ihn behalten, er ist sein eigen."

Der König spricht es und wirft von der Höh'
Der Klippe, die schroff und steil
Hinaushängt in die unendliche See,
10 Den Becher in der Charybde Geheul.
„Wer ist der Beherzte, ich frage wieder,
Zu tauchen in diese Tiefe nieder?"

Und die Ritter, die Knappen um ihn her,
Vernehmen's und schweigen still,
15 Sehen hinab in das wilde Meer,
Und keiner den Becher gewinnen will.
Und der König zum drittenmal wieder fraget:
„Ist keiner, der sich hinunterwaget?"

Doch alles noch stumm bleibt wie zuvor;
20 Und ein Edelknecht, sanft und keck,
Tritt aus der Knappen zagendem Chor,
Und den Gürtel wirft er, den Mantel weg,
Und alle die Männer umher und Frauen
Auf den herrlichen Jüngling verwundert schauen.

25 Und wie er tritt an des Felsen Hang
Und blickt in den Schlund hinab,
Die Wasser, die sie hinunterschlang,
Die Charybde jetzt brüllend wiedergab,
Und wie mit des fernen Donners Getose
30 Entstürzen sie schäumend dem finstern Schoße.

Und es wallet und siedet und brauset und zischt,
Wie wenn Wasser mit Feuer sich mengt,
Bis zum Himmel spritzet der dampfende Gischt,
Und Flut auf Flut sich ohn' Ende drängt,
35 Und will sich nimmer erschöpfen und leeren,
Als wollte das Meer noch ein Meer gebären.

Doch endlich, da legt sich die wilde Gewalt,
Und schwarz aus dem weißen Schaum
Klafft hinunter ein gähnender Spalt,
40 Grundlos, als gieng's in den Höllenraum,
Und reißend sieht man die brandenden Wogen
Hinab in den strudelnden Trichter gezogen.

Jetzt schnell, eh die Brandung wiederkehrt,
Der Jüngling sich Gott befiehlt,
45 Und — ein Schrei des Entsetzens wird rings gehört,
Und schon hat ihn der Wirbel hinweggespült,
Und geheimnißvoll über den kühnen Schwimmer
Schließt sich der Rachen; er zeigt sich nimmer.

Und stille wird's über dem Wasserschlund,
50 In der Tiefe nur brauset es hohl,
Und bebend hört man von Mund zu Mund:
„Hochherziger Jüngling, fahre wohl!"
Und hohler und hohler hört man's heulen,
Und es harrt noch mit bangem, mit schrecklichem Weilen,

55 Und wärfst du die Krone selber hinein
Und sprächst: Wer mir bringet die Kron',
Er soll sie tragen und König sein!
Mich gelüstete nicht nach dem theuren Lohn.
Was die heulende Tiefe da unten verhehle;
60 Das erzählt keine lebende glückliche Seele

Wohl manches Fahrzeug, vom Strudel gefaßt,
Schoß gäh in die Tiefe hinab;
Doch zerschmettert nur rangen sich Kiel und Mast
Hervor aus dem alles verschlingenden Grab. —
65 Und heller und heller, wie Sturmes Sausen,
Hört man's näher und immer näher brausen.

Und es wallet und siedet und brauset und zischt,
Wie wenn Wasser mit Feuer sich mengt,
Bis zum Himmel spritzet der dampfende Gischt,
70 Und Well' auf Well' sich ohn' Ende drängt,
Und wie mit des fernen Donners Getose
Entstürzt es brüllend dem finstern Schoße.

Und sieh! aus dem finstern flutenden Schoß
Da hebet sich's schwanenweiß,
75 Und ein Arm und ein glänzender Nacken wird bloß,
Und es rudert mit Kraft und mit emsigem Fleiß,
Und er ist's, und hoch in seiner Linken
Schwingt er den Becher mit freudigem Winken.

Und atmete lang und atmete tief,
80 Und begrüßte das himmlische Licht.
Mit Frohlocken es Einer dem Andern rief:
„Er lebt! er ist da! es behielt ihn nicht!
Aus dem Grab, aus der strudelnden Wasserhöhle
Hat der Brave gerettet die lebende Seele!"

85 Und er kommt; es umringt ihn die jubelnde Schar;
   Zu des Königs Füßen er sinkt,
   Den Becher reicht er ihm knieend dar,
   Und der König der lieblichen Tochter winkt,
   Die füllt ihn mit funkelndem Wein bis zum Rande;
90 Und der Jüngling sich also zum König wandte:

   „Lang lebe der König! Es freue sich,
   Wer da atmet im rosigten Licht!
   Da unten aber ist's fürchterlich,
   Und der Mensch versuche die Götter nicht,
95 Und begehre nimmer und nimmer zu schauen
   Was sie gnädig bedecken mit Nacht und Grauen."

   „Es riß mich hinunter blitzesschnell,
   Da stürzt' mir aus felsigtem Schacht
   Wildflutend entgegen ein reißender Quell;
100 Mich packte des Doppelstroms wütende Macht,
   Und wie einen Kreisel mit schwindelndem Drehen,
   Trieb mich's um, ich konnte nicht wiederstehen."

   „Da zeigte mir Gott, zu dem ich rief,
   In der höchsten schrecklichen Not,
105 Aus der Tiefe ragend ein Felsenriff,
   Das erfaßt' ich behend und entrann dem Tod.
   Und da hieng auch der Becher an spitzen Korallen,
   Sonst wär' er ins Bodenlose gefallen."

   „Denn unter mir lag's noch bergetief
110 In purpurner Finsterniß da,
   Und ob's hier dem Ohre gleich ewig schlief,
   Das Auge mit Schaudern hinuntersah,
   Wie's von Salamandern und Molchen und Drachen
   Sich regt' in dem furchtbaren Höllenrachen."

115 „Schwarz wimmelten da, in grausem Gemisch,
Zu scheußlichen Klumpen geballt,
Der stachlichte Roche, der Klippenfisch,
Des Hammers gräuliche Ungestalt,
Und dräuend wies mir die grimmigen Zähne
120 Der entsetzliche Hai, des Meeres Hyäne.“

„Und da hieng ich, und war mir's mit Grausen bewußt,
Von der menschlichen Hilfe so weit,
Unter Larven die einzige fühlende Brust,
Allein in der gräßlichen Einsamkeit,
125 Tief unter dem Schall der menschlichen Rede
Bei den Ungeheuern der traurigen Oede.“

„Und schaudernd dacht' ich's, da kroch's heran,
Regte hundert Gelenke zugleich,
Will schnappen nach mir; in des Schreckens Wahn
130 Laß' ich los der Koralle umklammerten Zweig;
Gleich faßt mich der Strudel mit rasendem Toben,
Doch es war mir zum Heil, er riß mich nach oben.“

Der König darob sich verwundert schier
Und spricht: „Der Becher ist dein,
135 Und diesen Ring noch bestimm' ich dir,
Geschmückt mit dem köstlichsten Edelgestein,
Versuchst du's noch einmal und bringst mir Kunde,
Was du sahst auf des Meeres tiefunterstem Grunde.“

Das hörte die Tochter mit weichem Gefühl,
140 Und mit schmeichelndem Munde sie fleht:
„Laßt, Vater, genug sein das grausame Spiel!
Er hat euch bestanden, was keiner besteht,
Und könnt ihr des Herzens Gelüsten nicht zähmen,
So mögen die Ritter den Knappen beschämen.“

145　Drauf der König greift nach dem Becher schnell,
　　　In den Strudel ihn schleudert hinein:
　　　„Und schaffst du den Becher mir wieder zur Stell',
　　　So sollst du der trefflichste Ritter mir sein,
　　　Und sollst sie als Ehgemahl heut' noch umarmen,
150　Die jetzt für dich bittet mit zartem Erbarmen."

　　　Da ergreift's ihm die Seele mit Himmelsgewalt,
　　　Und es blitzt aus den Augen ihm kühn,
　　　Und er siehet erröten die schöne Gestalt,
　　　Und sieht sie erbleichen und sinken hin;
155　Da treibt's ihn, den köstlichen Preis zu erwerben,
　　　Und stürzt hinunter auf Leben und Sterben.

　　　Wohl hört man die Brandung, wohl kehrt sie zurück,
　　　Sie verkündigt der donnernde Schall;
　　　Da bückt sich's hinunter mit liebendem Blick,
160　Es kommen, es kommen die Wasser all,
　　　Sie rauschen herauf, sie rauschen nieder,
　　　Den Jüngling bringt keines wieder.

NOTES

SCHILLER'S TAUCHER.

THIS beautiful Ballad, one of the finest in ballad literature, was composed by Schiller in 1797. It is interesting as the first fruit of the author's close friendship with his fellow-poet and rival, the great Goethe, who indeed seems to have furnished him with the story on which the poem was founded. In this story, a certain Nicolas Pescecola (Fish), a professional diver of Messina, was induced by King Frederick, of Naples and Sicily, about the year 1500 A.D., to explore, for the reward of a golden vessel thrown into the whirlpool by the king, the hidden depths of the terrible Charybdis ; and having returned alive from his first plunge, was tempted, by the offer of a large sum in gold, to take a second plunge, from which he never returned. This professional diver, actuated as he was only by a greed of filthy lucre, is ennobled by the poet into the heroic youth of the ballad, whose motives are the noble ones of honour and fame ; and whose second and fatal plunge is incited by the still higher motive of love. The versification is iambic, *i.e.*, consists of feet composed of a short or unaccented syllable followed by a long or accented one (◡ ◢) ; but these iambi are freely replaced by anapæsts, or feet consisting of two short syllables followed by one long (◡ ◡ ◢).

As an illustration, the scansion of the first stanza is given below :

Wĕr wāgt | ĕs Rīt | tĕrsmănn ō | dĕr Knäpp,
Zŭ taū | chĕn ĭn dīe | sĕn Schlūnd?
Eïnĕn gōl | dĕnĕn Bĕch | ĕr wĕrf' | Ĭch hĭnäb ;
Vĕrschlūng | ĕn schŏn hāt | Ihn dĕr schwär | zĕ Mūnd.
Wĕr mĭr | dĕn Bĕch | ĕr kănn wīe | dĕr zĕī | gĕn,
Er māg | Ihn bĕhäl | tĕn ĕr īst | seīn ĕī | gĕn.

It will be observed that the last two lines in the stanza have a half foot (one syllable) more than the other four ; also that, while the first, third, and fourth lines consist of four feet, the second has only three.

The pupil will observe that in this Ballad, as in all poetry, the strict rules of construction are frequently departed from. Thus the inf. and part. repeatedly occur before other members of the sent., instead of being placed last (see ll. 2 and 4) ; and in subord. sentences, the verb is not always last (see l. 5). It is comparatively seldom, however, that the fundamental rule, requiring the verb containing the copula (see App.) to be the second idea in the princ. sent., is departed from.

The rhymes (as in Scott's poetry) are often very imperfect. Thus we have such rhymes as steil, Geheul; Getose, Schoosze; rief, Felsenriff; kühn, hin.

---

l. 2. zu tauchen. The inf. would be last in prose.

l. 4. The part. is here first, for emphasis, and the verb third, not second.—Mund, 'gorge.'

l. 5. Wer, here rel. pron. ; the antec., which is properly contained in this word, is repeated in the next line (er).—kann would be last in prose, as being in a dep. sent.

l. 6. er ist, etc., 'it shall be ;' pres. for fut.; er here, of course, refers to Becher.

l. 10. der Charybde Geheul, 'the howling of Charybdis,' *i.e.*, 'the howling Charybdis.'

l. 11. Wer—Beherzte, 'who is brave enough,' 'who has the courage.'

l. 12. Zu tauchen; this sup. depends on der Beherzte in the

previous line.—**nieder**, as sep. pref., would precede the sup. **zu tauchen** in prose.

l. 13. **die Ritter, die Knappen**; 'the knights and squires;' omission of the conj.

l. 14. **Vernehmen's**, 'hear it (his words);' = **vernehmen es**; a frequent elision.

l. 15. The first foot in this line (**sehen**) is a trochee, *i.e.*, a long followed by a short syll. (– ⌣), instead of an iambus.

l. 16. **will**; the sent. is princ., and would take the verb after the subj. (**Keiner**) in prose; so also in the next sent.

l. 18. **der—waget**, 'who will venture down,' or 'is (bold enough) to venture down;' the indic. for subj. (**wage**) for the sake of the rhyme.

l. 20. **sanft und keck**, 'gentle, yet bold.'

l. 21. **der Knappen—Chor**, 'the trembling train of squires,' *i.e.*, the train of trembling squires; compare note to l. 10.

l. 22. Here again the conj. 'and' is omitted; compare l. 13.

l. 24. **verwundert**, 'wondering,' 'in wonder.'

l. 25. **Hang**, 'the brink,' the overhanging ledge.

l. 27. **die Wasser**, 'the waters' (pl.).

l. 28. **wiedergab**; again the verb last in a princ. sent., instead of being at the beginning of the sent., as should be the case with the subord. sent. (**wie er**, etc.) preceding, as it does.

l. 29, 30. 'And as with the distant thunder's rumbling

       From its gloomy lap they come foaming and tumbling.' [1]

es refers, indefinitely, to the whirlpool.

l. 31. 'And it bubbles and seethes and roars and hisses.'

l. 34. 'And flood upon flood hurries on, never ending' (Lytton).

l. 35. 'And never will be exhausted or emptied.'

l. 36. **Als**, 'as though;' **ob** or **wenn** is omitted; hence the verb immediately follows.

l. 37. **da**, redundant.—**legt sich**, 'is calmed,' 'subsides.'

l. 39 has only three feet, like the preceding line.

l. 40. **als gieng's**, 'as though it reached down,' compare l. 36, note; **es** is indef. and impers., and cannot refer to **Spalt**, which is masc. Compare also l. 14, note.

l. 41. **reissend**, 'raging;' refers to **Wogen**.

---

[1] Lord Lytton's Translation.

l. 47. der Rachen, 'the jaws' of the 'yawning cleft' (gähnender Spalt), l. 39.—er—nimmer, 'he is seen no more,' lit. 'shows him-self ;' nimmer = nicht mehr.

l. 49. stille wird's, 'all grows silent,' 'silence reigns.'

l. 50. brauset es hohl, 'there's a hollow roar.'

l. 51, 52. 'And (this cry) is heard quivering from mouth to mouth.' Supply : 'these words,' or 'this cry,' as obj. of hört.

l. 53. 'And more and more hollow 'tis heard to howl ;' es referring to the whirlpool ; see l. 30, note.

l. 54. 'And still they wait in anxious and dread suspense ;' es here refers to the spectators.

l. 55. Und wärfst du, 'and e'en though thou shouldst cast ;' omission of wenn auch ; hence verb first.   Lines 55–64 are supposed to be spoken by one of the spectators.—selber, 'itself ;' refers to Krone.

l. 56. Wer; see l. 5, note.

l. 58. Mich gelüstete nicht, 'I would not covet,' subj. mood, with conditional force ; impers. verb (see Gloss.).

l. 59. verhehle, 'may conceal' (subj. mood).

l. 60. 'No happy, living soul (creature) will (ever) tell,' i.e., no creature will be so fortunate as to live to tell ; erzählt, pres. for fut.

l. 61. Wohl manches Fahrzeug, 'full many a bark.'

l. 63, 64. 'But keel and mast alone, shattered to pieces, wrenched themselves from the all-devouring grave.' zerschmettert refers to Kiel und Mast, which words are also modified by nur ; alles is obj. of the part. verschlingenden.

l. 66. 'They hear the roar come nearer and ever nearer.'

l. 71, 72. Observe the variation in these two lines from the closing couplet of the 6th stanza.

l. 73, 74, 'And lo! from the dark and swirling gulf a snow-white object is raised,' lit. 'from the darkly swirling gulf it (something) is raised white as a swan,' i.e., as swan's-down.   It is better to substitute snowy, or snow-white, in translating, as being a phrase more familiar to the English reader ; es here and in l. 76, below, indicates the yet indistinct object.

l. 75. wird blosz, 'are bared,' i.e., become visible ; sing. verb with two subjects, though both precede the verb.   See p. 19, l. 11, note.

l. 76. 'And it swims with vigor and unflagging energy.'

l. 78. **Winken,** 'beckoning,' 'greeting.'

l. 79. 'And he drew a long breath, and drew a deep breath;' the pron. omitted, as is frequently the case.

l. 81. **Mit Frohlocken,** 'jubilantly,' 'with delight.'

l. 82. **Es behielt ihn nicht,** 'it retained him not,' *i.e.*, he is free from its grasp. **Es** here again refers to the mysterious depths of the whirlpool.

l. 84. **der Brave,** 'the brave youth;' **brav** generally means 'excellent,' 'good,' rather than 'brave' (*i.e.*, courageous); but may be best transl. 'brave' in this passage.—**die lebende Seele,** 'his soul alive.'

l. 85. **es umringt; es** is here redundant, representing the real subj. **Schar.**

l. 88. **winkt,** 'beckons,' not 'winks.' See Gloss.

l. 90. **also,** 'thus,' 'with these words.'

l. 91. **Es freue,** etc., 'let him rejoice, whoever,' etc.; the redundant **es** representing **wer,** which is subj. of both sentences.

l. 94. 'And let not man tempt,' etc.; **versuche** is imper.

l. 96–99. 'I was hurled downward like the lightning's flash (quickly as lightning); when (**da,** lit. then) from a rocky shaft there rushed toward me with wild flood a furious stream.'

l. 100. **Doppelstrom,** the double force of the descending flood and of the torrent that poured out from the rocks at the side; transl. simply 'eddy,' or 'double eddy.'

l. 104. **höchsten,** 'utmost,' 'most urgent.'

l. 108. **ins Bodenlose,** 'into the abyss,' lit. 'the bottomless (deep).'

l. 109. **bergetief,** 'mountains deep.'

l. 110. **purpurner;** purple is the colour of the shadows as seen by divers beneath the sea, rather than black.

l. 111. 'And though here all was for ever silent,' lit. 'slept to the ear;' either because the creatures were voiceless, or because the poet supposed (though wrongly) that sounds could not be heard in the water. The former explanation seems preferable.

l. 112. 'yet the eye looked down with shuddering;' supply **doch;** in prose the constr. would be: **so sah (doch) das Auge mit Schaudern hinunter.**

l. 113, 114. '(and saw) how it swarmed with,' etc., lit. 'was astir, alive.'

l. 115, 116. 'Darkly there swarmed in horrid medley, coiled up in disgusting masses.'

l. 117. **Der stachlichte Roche,** 'the prickly ray,' either the thornback, which has a row of spines along its back, or the sting-ray, which has a sharp spine for self-defence in its tail.—der **Klippenfisch,** 'the chætodon,' a small fish of ugly shape, though brilliant colours ; not = 'lub-fish,' as given in the dictionaries, which means 'dried codfish,' and is the Eng. equivalent for **Klippfisch.** The **Klippenfisch** is so called by the poet from its frequenting submarine rock-clefts.

l. 118. 'The hideous, misshapen hammer-headed shark,' lit. the hideous monstrosity of the, etc.; the same figure as in l. 10 (see note).

l. 120. **des Meeres Hyäne ;** so called on account of its voracity.

l. 121. **und war's,** etc., 'and was horribly aware of it,' lit. 'was conscious of it to myself with horror.' The **es** after **war** is gov. by the partic. adj. **bewusst,** being the older form of the gen., instead of the later **sein ; mir** is refl. and ethical dat. See note to p. 7, l. 2.

l. 123. 'Amid spectres (monsters) the only sentient breast,' *i.e.*, the only creature endowed with sense and feeling. **Larven ;** see Gloss.

l. 127. 'And with a shudder (shuddering) I thought of it, then a something crawled up (to me).' The latter **es** refers to some dimly discerned monster of the deep, such as the octopus or devil-fish.

l. 129. **in des Schrekens Wahn,** 'in a frenzy of terror.'

l. 130. **der Koralle—Zweig,** 'the branch of coral to which I had clung.'

l. 132. **Doch—Heil,** 'yet 'twas for my weal,' *i.e.*, it was the saving of me.

l. 133. 'The King at this is sheer amazed.'

l. 138. **auf—Grunde,** 'in the undermost depths of the sea.'

l. 140. **mit—Munde,** 'with coaxing lips,' lit. 'with flattering mouth.'

l. 141. 'Let this be enough, father, of your cruel sport.'

l. 142. **euch,** ethical dat.

l. 143. **was—besteht,** 'what no one (else) will stand.'

l. 144. 'Then let the knights put the squire to shame ;' mögen is here used with the force of the imper.

l. 147. 'And if thou bring me back the goblet ;' omission of wenn. **schaffen** in this sense is weak ; it is strong only in the sense of 'creating ;' **zur Stelle schaffen,** 'to bring (to the place where the speaker is).'

l. 148. **der trefflichste Ritter mir,** 'the foremost (lit. most excellent) of my knights.'

l. 149. **Ehgemahl** may be parsed as nom. or acc.; in the latter case it is neut., referring to **sie.**

l. 151, 152. 'Then his soul is seized (as though) with heavenly force, and a keen flash darts from his eyes.'

l. 155. **Da treibt's ihn,** 'then is he impelled.'

l. 157. 'Full well they hear the breakers, in sooth they return.'

l. 158. **Sie** is, of course, acc., obj. of **verkündigt.**

l. 159. 'Then there's one who bends down,' etc.; **es** here refers to the princess.

l. 160. 'They come, they come, the waters all;' **es** representing the subj. (**Wasser**) before the verb.

l. 162. 'Not one (of them) brings back the youth.' This verse is short by a foot, thus indicating the suddenness of the catastrophe.

GLOSSARY

TO

SCHILLER'S TAUCHER.

B

ballen, v. a. w., to roll, roll up.
beben, v. n. (haben) w., to tremble, quiver.
Becher, subst. m., gen.-s, pl.
——, goblet, beaker, cup.
bedecken, v. a. w., to cover, veil.
begehren, v. a. w., to desire, wish for [sometimes gov. gen.].
begrüszen, v. a. w., to greet, salute.
beherzt, partic. adj., courageous, brave; **der Beherzte** (l. 11), partic. subst., the brave man. See note.
bergetief, compd. adj., mountains-deep.
bestimmen, v. a. w., to determine, appoint; set aside, promise (l. 135).
bewusst, partic. adj., conscious, aware; gov. (refl.) dat. of pers., and gen. of thing. See note to l. 121.
Blitz, subst. m., gen.-es, pl.-e, lightning, flash.
blitzen, v. n. (haben) w., to flash.

blitzesschnell [compd. adj., quick as lightning, quick as a flash;], adv., like lightning, like a flash.
bodenlos, compd. adj., bottomless; **das Bodenlose,** subst. n., the abyss.
brav, adj., excellent, good; **der Brave,** subst. m., the fine, brave man, fellow (l. 84). [Like Fr. **brave** it generally means "good" or "excellent" rather than "brave," for which latter the adj. **tapfer** is used.]
brandend, partic. adj., surging, heaving, billowing.
Brandung, subst. f., pl.-en, surge, surf, breakers.
brausen, v. n. (haben) w., to roar, rush.
brüllen, v. n. (haben) w., to roar, bellow.

C

Charybde, subst. f. prop., Charybdis (from the Greek), a whirlpool in the Straits of Messina, between Sicily and Italy.

Chor, subst. m., gen.-(e)s, pl.
Chöre [chorus]; train, troop,
crowd, circle (l. 21). [das
Chor, n., = the choir (of a
church).]

D

dampfen, v. n. (haben) w., to
steam ; pres. part. and adj.
-d, steaming.
darób, adv., thereat, at it.
dárreichen, v. a. sep. w., to hand
over, present, offer.
Donner, subst. m., gen.-s, pl.
——, thunders.
donnern, v. n. (haben) w., to
thunder ; pres. part. and adj.
-d, thundering.
Doppelstrom, subst. m. comp.,
gen.-(e)s, pl.-ströme, whirlpool, eddy (lit. "double
stream ").
Drachen, subst. m., gen.-s, pl.
——, dragon.
drängen, v. a. w., to force, press,
urge, push ; refl. (recipr.), to
crowd or press one upon the
other. [Trans. form of **dring-
en**.]
dräuen, v. a. w., to threaten,
menace.
drauf, contr. for **darauf**.
[**drehen**, v. a. and refl., to turn,
twist, twirl.]
Drehen, subst. n. (inf. of prec.),
gen.-s, no pl., turning, twist-
ing, twirling.

E

Édelknecht, subst. m. comp.,
gen.-(e)s, pl.-e, page, squire.
Édelgestein, subst. n. comp.
coll., gen.-(e)s, no pl., precious
stones, jewels (coll. form of
Edelstein).

Éhgemahl, subst. m. and n.
comp., spouse, consort ; husband
(m. or n.) or wife (n. only).
See note on l. 149.
Éinsamkeit, subst. f., pl.-en,
loneliness, solitude.
entgégenstürzen, v. n. (sein
w., to rush against or toward
(dat. of person).
entrínnen, v. n. (sein), **entrann**,
entronnen, to escape from (gov.
dat.).
Entsétzen, subst. n., gen.-s, no
pl., horror, terror.
entstürzen, v. n. (sein) w., to
rush, gush forth from (gov. dat.).
erfássen, v. a. w., to seize, grasp,
take hold of.
erröten, v. n. (sein) w., **errötete**,
errötet, to blush (turn red).
erschöpfen, v. a., to exhaust ;
refl., to exhaust one's self, be
exhausted.
éwig [adj. (no compar.), eternal,
everlasting ;], adv., forever,
eternally.

F

Fáhrzeug, subst. n. comp., gen.
-(e)s, pl.-e, vessel, ship (properly a conveyance of any sort).
Fels(en), subst. m., gen.-en,
-ens, dat. acc.——, -en, pl.
-en, rock [; compare decl. of
Buchstabe, etc.].
Félsenriff, subst. n. comp., gen.
-(e)s, pl.-e, rocky crag, point
or ledge of rock ; reef.
félsig(t), adj., rocky. [Schiller
frequently has these forms in
-igt, icht, with an added -t ;
comp. **rosigt**, **stachlicht**, below.]
Fínsterniss, subst. f., pl.-e,
darkness, gloom, obscurity.
flehen, v. a. w., to beg, entreat,
pray.

Fleiss, subst. m., gen.-es, no
pl., industry, assiduity, vigour.
Flut, subst. f., pl.-en, flood,
stream ; water.
fluten, v. n. (haben) w., -ete,
geflutet, to wave, heave ; pres.
part. and adj. -d, heaving, billowing (l. 73).
Frohlócken, subst. n. (inf. of
corresponding v.), gen.-s, no
pl., rejoicing, gladness, delight.
fúnkeln, v. n. (haben) w., to
sparkle, flash ; pres. part. and
adj. -d, sparkling, flashing.
fúrchtbar, fúrchterlich, adj.,
terrible, frightful, awful, dreadful ; adv., terribly, etc.

G

gäh (or jäh) [adj., headlong ; precipitous ; steep ;], adv., headlong, precipitously.
gähnen, v. n. (haben) w., to
yawn, gape ; pres. part. and adj.
-d, yawning, gaping.
geballt (past part. of ballen),
adj., rolled up, heaped up.
Gefúhl, subst. n., gen.-(e s, pl.
-e, feeling, sentiment.
geheímnissvoll [comp. adj.,
mysterious, inscrutable ;], adv.,
mysteriously, inscrutably.
Geheúl, subst. n. freq., gen.-(e)s,
no pl., howling, howl.
Gelénk, subst. n., gen.-(e)s, pl.-e,
limb, joint.
Gemísch, subst. n. coll., gen.
-es, pl.-e, mixture, medley,
confusion.
Gestált, subst. f., pl.-en, shape,
form, figure.
Getóse [or Getöse], subst. n.
freq., gen.-s, no pl., uproar,
roar, noise, din, tumult.
gewinnen, v. a. insep., gewann,
gewonnen, to win, gain.

Gischt, subst. m., gen.-es, no
pl., spray, vapour.
gnädig, adj., gracious, merciful ;
adv., mercifully.
grässlich, adj., horrible, horrid,
dreadful, awful.
Grauen, subst. n. (inf.), gen.-s,
no pl., horror, dread.
gräulich, adj., horrid, horrible,
hideous.
graus, adj., dreadful, fearful,
horrible, horrid.
grausam, adj., cruel.
Grausen, subst. n. (inf.), gen.-s,
no pl., horror, dread, awe.
grimmig, adj., fierce, cruel.
gründlos, adj., no compar., bottomless.
Gürtel, subst. m., gen.-s, pl.
——, girdle, belt, zone.

H

Hai, subst. m., gen.-(e)s, pl.-e,
shark.
Hammer, subst. m., gen.-s, pl.
Hämmer [hammer ;], hammer-
headed shark.
Hang, subst. m., gen.-(e)s, no
pl., overhanging edge or margin,
brow (of a precipice).
harren, v. n. (haben) w., to wait,
tarry, linger.
Heil, subst. n., gen.-(e)s, no pl.,
salvation, rescue, saving ; weal,
good. [Conn. with Eng. "hail"
and "heal." See heilen in
former Gloss.]
heránkriechen, v. n. (sein) sep.,
kroch, gekrochen, to creep up,
crawl up (toward the speaker).
hervórringen, v. a. refl. sep.,
rang, gerungen, to wrench
one's self loose, free one's self
with a wrench.
heulen, v. n. (haben) w., to howl ;
pres. part. and adj. -d, howling.

heut(e), adv. of time, to-day, this day.
Hilfe [or Hülfe], subst. f., no pl., help, assistance, aid, succour.
Himmelsgewält, subst. comp. f., pl.-en, power from heaven, heavenly power.
himmlisch, adj., heavenly, celestial.
hinábblicken, v. n. (haben) sep. w., to look down, glance down.
hinábschiessen, v. n. (sein) sep., schoss, geschossen, to shoot down, dart down.
hinábsehen, v. n. (haben) sep., sah, gesehen, sieh, siehst, to look downward.
hinábwerfen, v. a. sep., warf, geworfen, wirf, wirfst, to throw down, cast down.
hinábziehen, v. a. sep., zog, gezogen, to draw down, pull down.
hináushangen, v. n. (haben) sep., hieng, gehangen, hängst, to hang (out) over.
hineínschleudern, v. a. sep. w., to hurl in, fling in.
hineínwerfen, v. a. sep., warf, geworfen, wirf, wirfst, to throw in, cast in.
hínsinken, v. n. (sein) sep., sank, gesunken, to sink down, fall down.
hinúnter, adv., down, downward (away from the speaker).
hinúnterklaffen, v. n. (haben) sep. w., to gape or yawn downwards; to open yawning downwards.
hinúnterreissen, v. a. sep., riss, gerissen, to tear down, pull down, hurl down.
hinúnterschlingen, v. a. sep., schlang, geschlungen, to swallow down, gulp down.
hinúntersehen, v. n. (haben) sep., sah, gesehen, sieh, siehst, to look down, gaze down.
hinúnterwagen, v. a. refl. sep. w., to venture down.
hinwég, adv., away, off (stronger form of weg).
hinwégspülen, v. a. sep. w., to wash away.
hóchherzig, adj. comp., magnanimous, noble (lit. "highhearted").
Höhe, subst. f., pl.-n, height, elevation; summit, top.
Höllenraum, subst. m. comp., gen.-(e)s, pl.-räume, space or realm of hell.
Höllenrachen, subst. m. comp., gen.-s, no pl., jaws of hell, mouth of hell.
Hyäne, subst. f., pl.-n, hyena.

J

jubeln, v. n. (haben) w., to shout (for joy), be jubilant; pres. part. and adj. -d, joyful, jubilant; adv. joyfully, gladly, with shouts of joy.

K

keck, adj., bold, fearless, undaunted, courageous.
klaffen, v. n. (haben) w., to open up, gape, yawn.
[klammern, v. a. refl. w., to cling to (gov. an with acc.).]
Klippe, subst. f., pl.-n, cliff, precipice, rock.
Klíppenfisch, subst. m. comp., gen.-es, pl.-e, chætŏdon (a fish of ugly shape. See l. 117, note).
Knapp(e), subst. n., gen.-en, pl. -en, page, squire (the attendant of a nobleman or knight).

Korálle, subst. f., pl.-n, coral.
Kreisel, subst. m., gen.-s, pl.
——, top (for spinning).
kühn, adj., bold, keen ; daring,
courageous, undaunted ; adv.
boldly, etc.
Kunde, subst. f., no pl., knowledge ; information, news.
[Kunde, m., = "customer."]

L

Larve, subst. f., pl.-n [mask ;],
spectre, monster.
leeren, v. a. w., to empty, exhaust ; v. refl., to empty one's
self, exhaust one's self.

M

Macht, subst. f., pl. Mächte,
might, power. [Syns. Kraft,
Gewalt ; see under Kraft in
former Gloss.]
mengen, v. a. and refl. w., to
mix, mingle.
Molch, subst. m., pl.-e [sala-
mander,], reptile.

N

Nacken, subst. m., pl.——, nape,
neck. [See the syn. Hals in
former Gloss.]
niedertauchen, v. n. (sein) sep.
w., to plunge down, dive down.

O

Oede, subst. f., no pl., desolation,
solitude.

P

Preis, subst. m., gen.-es, pl.-e,
prize [price ; praise ; in this sig-
nification has no pl.].

púrpurn, adj., no compar., purple.
See note to l. 110.

R

Rachen, subst. m., pl.——, jaws,
gorge.
ragen, v. n. (haben) w., to rise,
project ; pres. part. and adj.,
-d, projecting.
rasen, v. n. (haben) w., to rage,
be furious, rave ; pres. part. and
adj., -d, raging, furious.
Rede, subst. f., pl.-n, speech,
language. [Syn. Sprache,
which means language, or the
faculty of speech ; R. = also
"a speech," or set form of
words.]
reissen, v. a., riss, gerissen, to
tear, pull ; pres. part. and adj.,
-d, raging.
[Riff, subst. n., gen.-(e)s, pl.-e,
reef, crag (projecting point of
rock).]
ringen, v. n. (haben) and refl.,
rang, gerungen [to wrestle],
wrest, wrench (one's self free).
See note to l. 63.
Ritter, subst. m., gen.-s, pl.——,
knight, cavalier.
Rittersmann, subst. m. comp.,
gen.-(e)s, pl.-leute, knight,
cavalier.
Roche, subst. m., gen.-n, pl.-n,
ray (a flat fish of ugly shape,
allied to the family of skates).
See note to l. 117.
rósig(t), adj., rosy, ruddy. Comp.
felsig(t), above.
rúdern, v. n. (haben) w., to row.
See note to l. 76.

S

Salamander, subst. m., gen.-s,
pl.——, salamander (a kind of
lizard, not a marine animal,

though specified by the poet as
such).
Sausen, subst. n. (inf.), gen.-s,
no pl., rushing, whistling, howling ; blast.
Schacht, subst. m., gen.-(e)s,
pl.-e, and **Schächte,** shaft (of
a mine), cleft, gorge, chasm.
schaffen, v. a. w., to procure ;
see note to l. 148. [The strong
verb (**schaffen, schuf, ge-
schaffen**) = "to create." The
weak verb also = "to have to
do with a person," as : **was
habe ich mit dir zu s.,** "what
have I to do with thee?" and
dialectically (South German)
"to work."]
Schall, subst. m., gen.-(e)s, pl.
Schälle, sound, noise, tone.
Schar, subst. f., pl.-en, crowd,
multitude, host.
schaudern, v. n. (haben) w., to
shudder.
Schaudern, subst. n. (inf. of
prec.), gen.-s, no pl., shuddering, horror.
schauen, v. a. w., to behold, see.
[More explicit than its syn.
sehen.]
schäumen, v. n. (haben) w., to
foam ; pres. part. and adj., -d,
foaming.
scheusslich, adj., horrid, loath-
some, disgusting.
schier, adv., almost [as adj.
= Eng. "sheer"].
schleudern, v. a. w., to hurl,
fling.
schlingen, v. a., **schlang, geschlungen,** to swallow [to en-
twine].
Schlund, subst. m., gen.-(e)s,
pl. **Schlünde,** mouth, jaws,
gorge, abyss.
Schosz, subst. m., gen.-es, pl.
Schösze, lap, bosom ; depth,
abyss.

schrecklich, adj., terrible, dreadful.
Schrei, subst. m., gen.-(e)s, pl.
-e, cry, scream, shout.
schroff, adj., steep, precipitous.
schwanenweiss, adj., no compar., white as a swan (as swan's-
down).
Schwimmer, subst. m., gen.-s,
pl.——, swimmer.
schwindlich(t), adj., giddy,
dizzy (see **felsig(t),** above).
schwingen, v. a., **schwang, geschwungen,** to swing, wave.
See, subst. f., pl.-n, sea, ocean.
[Syn. **Meer.** Der **See,** m.,
= "the lake."]
sieden, v. n. (haben) w., **siedete,
gesiedet,** to seethe, boil. [The
str. v. (**sott, gesotten**) is trans. ;
comp. the Eng. adj. "sod-
den."]
Spalt, subst. m., pl.-e [also-e, f.,
pl.-n], slit, cleft, rift, fissure,
gap, chasm.
spritzen [or **sprützen**], v. a. and
n. (haben), to spurt, gush.
spülen, v. a. w., to wash out,
rinse.
stachlich(t), adj., prickly.
steil, adj., steep, precipitous,
sheer.
Sterben, subst. (inf.) n., gen.-s,
no pl., dying, death.
stillschweigen, v. n. (haben),
schwieg, geschwiegen, to be
silent [inf. used as subst. n.,
silence].
Strudel, subst. m., gen.-s, pl.
——, whirlpool, eddy, vortex.
strudeln, v. n. (haben) w., to
eddy, bubble, boil ; pres. part.
and adj., -d, eddying, boiling.
stumm, adj., dumb, mute, silent.
[**Sturm,** subst. m., gen.-(e)s, pl.
Stürme, storm, tempest.]
Sturmessausen, subst. comp. n.,
gen.-s, no pl., whistling or roar-

ing of a storm, tempestuous
roar.

T

tauchen, v. a. w., to dive, plunge.
Taucher, subst. m., gen.-s, pl.
——, diver.
teuer, adj., compar. teurer, superl.
teuerst, dear, precious (of commercial as well as moral value).
tiefúnterst, comp. superl. adj.,
bottom-most, very deepest or
lowest.
Toben, subst. n. (inf.), rage, fury,
violence.
Trichter, subst. m., gen.-s, pl.
——, funnel, gorge.
trefflich, adj., excellent, eminent,
choice.

U

umármen, v. a. insep. w., to embrace.
umklámmern, v. a. insep. w.,
to cling to, embrace ; past part.
and adj., -t, see note to l. 130.
umríngen, v. a. insep. w., to surround [not conn. with the strong
v. ringen, "to wring," but der.
from Ring].
úmtreiben, v. a. sep., trieb, getrieben, to drive around, cause
to move in a circle.
unéndlich, adj., no compar., endless, never-ending.
Úngeheuer, subst. n., gen.-s, pl.
——, monster.
Úngestalt, subst. f., pl.-en,
monstrosity, monstrous shape.

V

verhéhlen, v. a. insep. w., to
hide, conceal (dat. of pers. from

whom the thing is hidden).
[The old strong part. verhohlen
appears in the adv. unverhohlen, "without concealment."]
verkündigen, v. a. insep. w., to
announce, proclaim.
vernéhmen, v. a. insep., vernahm, vernommen, vernimm, vernimmst, to perceive,
hear.
verwúndert, adj. and adv., astonished, surprised ; in astonishment or surprise.

W

wagen, v. a. w., to dare, venture.
Wahn, subst. m., gen.-(e)s, no
pl., illusion ; frenzy, madness.
wallen, v. n. (haben [and sein])
w. [to walk, make a pilgrimage ;], to wave, heave. [In the
former sense it takes haben
when *action* only is expressed,
sein when *direction* also is
meant.]
Wásserhóhle, subst. f. comp.,
pl.-n, watery grave or abyss
(lit. "water-cavern").
Wásserschlund, subst. m. comp.,
gen.-(e)s, pl.-schlünde, watery
gorge or abyss.
wégwerfen, v. a. sep., warf,
geworfen, wirf, wirfst, to
throw away, cast away, fling
away.
[weilen, v. n. (haben) w., to
wait, tarry.]
Weilen, subst. n., inf. of prec.,
gen.-s, no pl., waiting, tarrying,
expectation.
Welle, subst. f., pl.-n, wave,
billow.
wíederkehren, v. n. (sein) sep.
w., to return, come back.

wíldflutend, partic. comp. adj., with wild flood, raging.

wímmeln, v. n. (haben) w., to teem, swarm.

[**winken,** v. n. (haben) w., to beckon, signal (see note to l. 78).]

Winken, subst. n., inf. of prec., gen.-s, no pl., beckoning, waving, signal.

Wírbel, subst. m., gen.-s, pl. ——, whirlpool, eddy.

Woge, subst. f., pl.-n, wave, billow (less common than **Welle).**

wüten, v. n. (haben) w., wütete, gewütet, to rage, be furious or wild ; pres. part. and adj. -d, raging, furious.

Z

zagen, v. n. (haben) w., to tremble, be timid or afraid ; pres. part. and adj. -d, timid, afraid, fearful ; adv., timidly, etc.

zähmen, v. a. w., to tame, subdue, repress.

zerschméttern, v. a. w., to dash to pieces, break, destroy utterly ; past part. and adj. -t, dashed to pieces.

zischen, v. n. (haben) w., to hiss (imitative word).

zugleích, adv. of time, at the same time.

Zweig, subst. m., gen.-(e)s, pl. -e, twig, branch, bough.

www.ingramcontent.com/pod-product-compliance
Lightning Source LLC
Chambersburg PA
CBHW030128030726
47498CB00007B/2604